D1496609

Also By Winfield Strock

Voices Amongst the Aether

Adventures Above the Aether

Aether Legion

Ghost Court

Poisoned Passions

The Veneer Series
   The Veneer Clause
   The Perfect Telescope
   Zealot's Folly
   Cupid's Avatar

TO JESSICA
DIVE IN

Red Sounding

By

Winfield H. Strock III

Bookateer Publishing
www.bookateerpublishing.com

ISBN: 978-1-5030-5339-7

Edited by Holly Yurchison
Cover art by James Christopher Hill
Published by Ryan Twomey-Allaire

Dedication

As a Cold War submariner, I dedicate this book to those on both sides of the Iron Curtain who made nuclear war too unpalatable to contemplate.

As a fellow outsider, I dedicate this book to those who sit atop the razor's edge between their uniqueness and a desire to be accepted.

As a man of faith, I dedicate this book to those who live a life of love, resolving to abandon judgmental ways.

"If you can't fight for me or for your own survival, fight for the men, women, and children of the world who never saw this coming."

Contents

1.	A Familiar Stranger	1
2.	Better a Filthy Survivor Than a Tidy Corpse	5
3.	Nobody's Counsellor or Confessor	11
4.	The Cause of Death Seems Simple Enough	19
5.	As Sure as a Bullet	25
6.	All in the Name of Order	31
7.	No Place to Hide	35
8.	Never Easy	39
9.	Spell it Out	47
10.	The Right Girl for You	55
11.	Spinning Out of Control	59
12.	Nemnogo Vydra	67
13.	Black Wharf	73
14.	An Angel All the Same	77
15.	Ethical Ambiguity	83
16.	The Red Fleet's Wrath	87
17.	It's Like Borscht	93
18.	A Reward for a Hero or a Bullet for a Freak	97
19.	Cursed Ship	103
20.	Haunted	107
21.	Zhora's Ghost	113
22.	An Awkward Proposal	119
23.	Nika's Choice	123
24.	Rasputitsa	129
25.	One Final Goodbye	133
26.	Teg Vy Yemu	139
27.	Vladlena	145
28.	Nightmares in the Stars	149
29.	We're Already Dead Men	153
30.	This is Not a Drill	159
31.	Kill Me, Please	165
32.	Warmongers	169
33.	I'm Old, But I'm Not Dead	173
34.	Mrs. Koryavin	179
35.	The Wolf and the Rat	185
36.	Love and War	191
37.	When Two Liars Agree	194

38. Your Love Will Die   201
39. Back From the Dead   207
40. Flushing a Stalker   213
41. Chef's Surprise   219
42. A Midwatch Revelation   223
43. Deterrence   231
44. An Angel's Fury   237
45. We've Got a Madman Aboard   239
46. You've Got the Wrong Guy   243
47. Duty   249
48. Angel in the Dark   253
49. It's Only Murder   259
50. A Game of Chess   265
51. Hunger and Hate   269
52. They Come in Your Sleep   273
53. Impossible Girl   277
54. I Make Do!   285
55. Soviet Resolve   287
56. No More Fear   291
57. Disarray   295
58. Riot at the Mausoleum   301
59. Love's Desperation   307
60. In for a Penny, in for a Pound   311
61. Doctor Anatoli's Secret   317
62. Evil with a Capital 'E'   321
63. Anarchy   327
64. Zhora is the Key   331
65. Claustrophobia   337
66. Last Glimpse of Sunlight   341
67. Acting Captain   347
68. Assault on the Command Center   353
69. Restitution   357
70. Water of Life   361
71. New Pantheon   365
72. Doomed Ship, Damned Crew   371
73. The Monster Inside   375
74. Shared Blood Shared Crimes   381

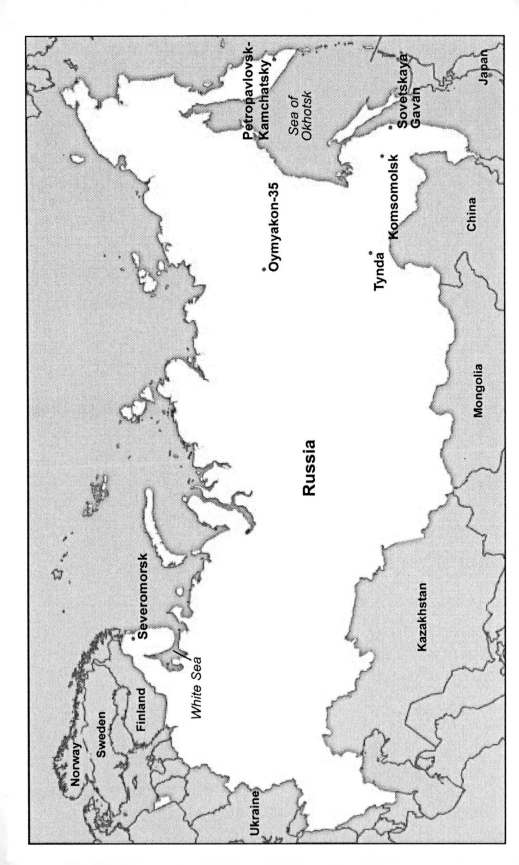

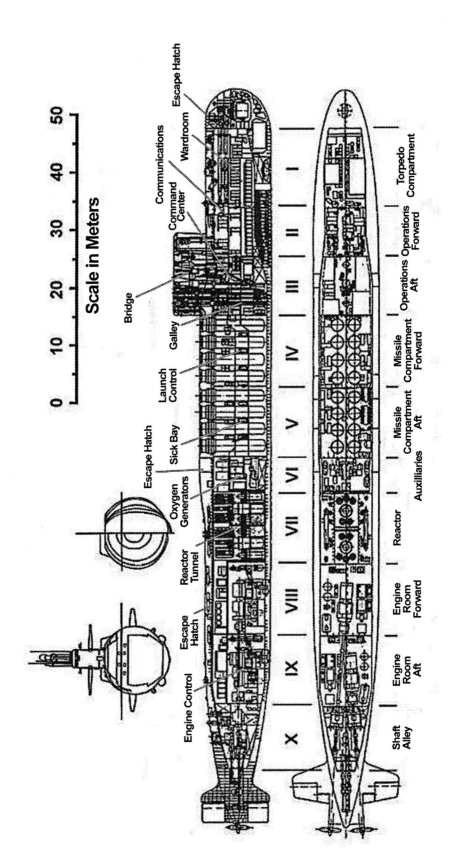

Scale in Meters

0 10 20 30 40 50

Escape Hatch
Wardroom
Communications
Command Center
Bridge
Galley
Launch Control
Sick Bay
Escape Hatch
Oxygen Generators
Reactor Tunnel
Escape Hatch
Engine Control

I II III IV V VI VII VIII IX X

Torpedo Compartment
Operations Forward
Operations Aft
Missile Compartment Forward
Missile Compartment Aft
Auxilliaries
Reactor
Engine Room Forward
Engine Room Aft
Shaft Alley

A Familiar Stranger

ONE

Outside Oymyakon-35, a gulag in the Yakutskaya A.S.S.R.
November, 1, 1982

Frigid air stung Private Porshenko's lungs as he trudged into the dim forest through groin-deep snow. The steel butt of his AK-47, like an antenna for the cold, transmitted a dull ache through his snow-camouflaged parka.

"Be quiet and quick," the major ordered. "Keep each other within sight as you spread out and don't get lost."

The Major's name meant nothing to Porshenko. It hadn't mattered with the other three he'd served this year. Two majors transferred away quickly. They'd served their brief penance and gone back to civilization. The third had justified his exile by committing further crimes against Oymyakon-35 inmates and staff. Private Porshenko bid farewell to that last major through the iron sights of his rifle. He'd been on the firing squad.

Lost in the Siberian wilderness, Oymyakon-35's warden had dubbed it 'a logging town on lockdown.' The witty phrase painted the frozen, squalid prison with broad strokes. The gulag relied on its remoteness more than the meager fence with its rusted barbed wire. Animals and frostbite took down the bold and deterred the sane . . . until now.

"Why bother searching? He'll die overnight." He had wondered.

"This convict has friends in all the wrong places," the Major insisted. "He'll have transportation out there, somewhere. And if he escapes, our court martial won't end as cozy as a gulag."

Sharp and brave, clean and honorable, this major impressed Porshenko, but worried him more. *What dark deed sees a soldier of his caliber among the forgotten?*

The soft snow-scape swallowed distant sounds until the small noises he made felt deafening. His footfalls sounded like a shovel digging through loose sand, his breath huffed like a train at the station. He looked left, then right; only two men in the world knew his whereabouts.

A wolf's howl chilled his blood below freezing. He forced himself to take the next step away from his safe, warm barracks, further into the spruce and snow maze. The wind sighed to nothing, then shifted.

A scream, gunfire, and shouts sent him shuddering. He threw up his rifle and aimed as he searched. He scanned right, and then left . . . lost, alone. Another choppy assault rifle's report sent him racing, stumbling and groaning through the snow.

Beneath evergreen boughs, through shallower snow, he ran faster until he found a comrade, fallen at the tree line's edge. A beast hunkered over the man and tore into his throat. Violently it shook free bits of parka, scarf, and uniform. Blood splashed out onto the snow, dark, almost black in contrast. Porshenko stood breathless and watched. The beast bore a human form. Dressed in tatters, the demon hardly wore enough to stave an autumn night's chill, yet remained focused on its feast, impervious to the cold. Grey flesh shone strangely in the moonlight, as though hewn from polished stone, translucent, with black veins beneath. The creature stopped and tilted its head. Ears, long and pointed like devils of old, twitched. Private Porshenko raised his rifle, his grip quivering. Slowly the creature turned to face him.

"Come, boy, come and see your comrade."

Porshenko shuddered and blinked. A man, not a

monster, rose to his feet. Reddish blond hair blended into a deep red beard. His broad brow shaded his large eyes from the night's meager light. Porshenko's head ached when he fought to recall what he'd seen only a heartbeat ago. The size and shape remained the same, yet details had shifted in the dim light.

This man, with his thick arms, wide shoulders and squat frame, resembled his father. Only the colors were wrong, pale smooth skin and the hair.

"Your weapon," the stranger's whisper sounded as though spoken from within his frostbitten ear, "you have no need of it."

Porshenko stole a glance behind the stranger and met his Major's lifeless gaze. Yashkin had been his name. It slammed into his head like a tombstone.

Images flickered in the corners of Porshenko's mind, bloody fangs, a blood soaked demon's face. Pain knifed through his skull. He shook it off and realized he'd dropped his rifle.

The stranger smiled. "Come with me. I have questions." He held out his hand.

"Who are you?" Porshenko whispered.

The stranger recoiled, his features tightened, tensed. Warily, he allowed a smile. "Answer my questions and I shall share my name." He pulled the Private close in an iron embrace. "Hold tight."

Porshenko clutched the threadbare tunic. His stomach fell with the first leap. The stranger leapt in great gliding strides through the woods. His stomach lurched. Often they landed high in the trees where the stranger's grip and kick tore at the tough bark. The wind of their speed numbed the soldier's cheeks and crept through his layered uniform. Vertigo swept through him and his mind reeled. Sights, sounds, and consciousness all bobbed like a buoy in a storm.

It all stopped as suddenly as it started. They stood amidst dark timbers, blackened by fire, white with snow, cracked and crumbling from dozens of seasons, dozens of

3

thaws, a house burned decades ago.

"I once built this home," the stranger said. He motioned to the dilapidated remains. He looked again to the Private. "Why do so many soldiers search for one prisoner?"

"He endangers the State," Porshenko answered through chattering teeth. "He threatens us all with his lies and treachery."

"And if they do not find him?"

"More men will come with search lights, dogs, and helicopters too."

"More and more, you press in upon my quiet life."

"Who are you?"

"I am Sevastyan. I am part of the wilderness that culls your herd. These woods were mine before your father was born."

Sevastyan approached and grasped the soldier by his shoulders. "Forgive me, I'd no intentions of killing your comrades, but they left me no choice."

Porshenko's heart sank and his shivers vanished. The man's features melted away, revealing the monster he'd forgotten until now. Closer than before, he looked into yellow irises aglow with the moonbeams, cracked and bleeding in spots. They revealed the demon's fear.

"What are you?" he asked in a whisper. It took tremendous effort to say even that. He felt a scream boiling inside, yet he felt paralyzed by those yellow ember eyes.

Sevastyan features softened as the monster pitied him. "Surely you know, just as you know that now I have my answers, you will die and I must run."

Better a Filthy Survivor Than a Tidy Corpse

Leninskiy Komsomolsk Shipyard, in the Soviet Far East
November, 1, 1982

The klaxon sounded twice before the intercom blared.

"Fire in Auxiliaries Compartment, Level Two."

Lieutenant Mikhail Koryavin jumped from his bunk and scrambled to pull his boots on as he hopped into the passageway. *Not tonight, not while I'm on duty.* He buckled his belt as he raced through Operations Compartment Aft, past the zampolit's office, the fan room, ducking through the watertight door. He stopped to slam it shut before he resumed his sprint between the missile tubes.

Stinging odors, burning rubber and ozone, assailed his nostrils. At the door from Missile Compartment Aft to the Auxiliaries Compartment, two crewmen stood and watched the flames atop Oxygen Generator One. Insulation melted from a conduit, sparks crackled and jumped from the exposed copper.

"Shut power for this equipment!" Mikhail ordered, slapping one sailor on the shoulder. The man leapt into action, darting through the knee-high flames. The second sailor turned to Mikhail and shrugged.

"The shipyard is responsible for manning the fire brigade."

Mikhail's heart sunk and his blood boiled. "If we don't act, we die."

The sailor threw his hands up. "The firefighting system is torn apart, like everything else. What will we do except wait for hoses from the pier?"

Mikhail shut his eyes and envisioned all the ship's systems. No water, a spreading fire, and no time to wait for assistance; something had to extinguish the flames. The air thickened and new odors crept in. The hull's insulation if set ablaze would transform this compartment into an oven.

Mikhail clutched the sailor by his shoulders. "Go pressurize the waste tank, open the valves and leave them open."

The sailor's eyes widened. "But Lieutenant-

"Now, do it."

The young man nodded and ran. Mikhail tore off his undershirt and fashioned a mask. He picked his way through the fiery room. He dove for the ladder leading to the upper level and nearly fell back into the flames. The steel ladder rails had singed his hands. He peeled strips of his shirt and used them to hold the ladder as he ascended. A distant hiss reverberated in the pipes and gave him hope. The orange glow intensified below; the fire began to spread. He snatched a pipe wrench from a nearby tool bin and struggled to undo the end cap placed by the shipyard. With the hull valve gone from the waste tank, safety demanded the backup valve be capped off. Now he prayed for the strength to overcome their effort. His vision dimmed and his ears rang.

Not yet, not now.

He threw the blanking flange aside and clambered for the valve. In the thickening smoke and blossoming heat, he strained to stand and tugged the valve open. A high-pitched squeal grew to a throaty roar as human waste geysered into the ceiling. The crew's filth struck the hull above, plumed out, and rained all around Mikhail. Coughing, choking, exhausted, Mikhail crumpled to the deck and shut his eyes. He allowed a smile as consciousness faded.

"Disgusting!" Zampolit Dimitriev screamed. "Shit, and piss all over the machinery!"

Mikhail stood at attention in the captain's stateroom. He felt his hair touch the wood paneled ceiling, heard the buzz of the fluorescent light glaring centimeters above his brow. Less than arm's length before him sat Captain Borodin and his zampolit, Dimitriev.

Dimitriev's bloodshot eyes and bloated figure, his fish and vodka breath, all spoke of a man who'd be dead in an alley somewhere if not for his family's devotion to the Party. He'd wheezed between rants in their meeting. Mikhail imagined Dimitriev's family got him commissioned as a political officer to keep him busy and out of trouble. Assignment to a submarine in the Soviet Far East kept him out of sight. He'd been a bad fit for submarine life from the start. His poor health and discomfort, crammed in with so much grimy machinery and bodies, kept him up on deck most days.

"The shipyard fire brigade will need shots for the filth you subjected them to,"

Despite a hot shower and fresh uniform, the stench still oozed from Mikhail's pores. Captain Borodin drew in a deep breath that caught in his throat and he winced. Mikhail clamped his jaw tighter, stifling a chuckle.

He'd awoken on the pier, surrounded by the shipyard's medical staff. Only at his insistence did the doctor allow him to return to the ship. The fire brigade had plucked him from the fetid, smoking submarine.

"If not for my actions, the compartment would've been gutted," Mikhail said flatly.

"Conjecture!" Dimitriev stood and wagged a finger at him. "You don't know that."

Though responsible for the crew's ideological integrity, the zampolit had taken particular interest in the ship's schedule and the avalanche of technical difficulties which pushed the launch date beyond the horizon. Rumor had it, Dimitriev stood on the verge of prison or praise. A glowing report from K-389's maiden voyage might tip the scales in his favor.

The captain clasped a hand over the fuming political officer's forearm and stood. "And you don't know anything about submarines, Comrade Zampolit."

Captain Borodin looked old; too old to shepherd a crew of inexperienced and exhausted sailors out on an unseaworthy submarine. Thick iron-grey brows shaded watery blue eyes. Broken blood vessels kept his complexion rosy for all the wrong reasons. Frostbitten winds and the pressure of command had marred the man's face. Years at the periscope had warped his spine into a permanent slouch. His uniform bore the stains and wrinkles of a man with no time for politics or sleep.

"The man attended to his ship as best he knew how," Captain Borodin explained, his gravel voice sounding tired, annoyed. "We'll recover from the filth with some elbow grease."

"Accountability!" Dimitriev began, "Junior Lieutenant Koryavin, Savior of the Fleet, must spearhead the cleanup effort."

Captain Borodin shook head. "As division officer, his men will bear the brunt of his decision, but I believe they'll be pleased to have equipment to clean rather than rubble. You too, I thought, would be equally pleased with Comrade Koryavin's efforts to keep us on schedule."

"But the-

Dimitriev stopped the moment he met the Borodin's gaze. A counterfeit grin hung beneath a warning glare.

Dimitriev looked to Mikhail and offered a shallow nod. He apologized through clenched teeth. "Thank you, comrade, for your zeal. May it yield less odorous successes in the future."

He excused himself, squeezed past Mikhail, and shut the door as he left.

"He's just jealous," Captain Borodin said with a sneer.

Mikhail frowned. "Captain?"

The captain chortled until a cough cut him short. "You spread shit with more efficiency than any Politburo member."

"I only wanted to save the ship," Mikhail offered.

Captain Borodin shook his head. "No, no, you did a good thing."

His brow furrowed. "What concerns me more, your haste to sacrifice yourself."

The captain opened his door and led Mikhail out. Shorter, the aging sea captain didn't need to duck beneath the dangling cables and makeshift lighting strung among the pipes above. The staccato of impact wrenches and metal grinders' whine; all these spoke to the harried pace to complete the ship's overhaul. Captain Borodin watched as Mikhail took in the filthy, din-filled chaos.

"This is not truly a ship," the captain said. "And we're not yet on a critical mission. Why throw your life away for this steel hulk so easily?"

"Is it not my duty, Captain?"

A coughing chuckle erupted. "A hundred days beneath the waves lies ahead. And a month or two after we recover from that, we'll dive into it all over again. This ship will claim your youth soon enough. Chase women and capture love while you've energy."

Mikhail swallowed hard. Metal dust, adrift in the ship's wheezing ventilation ducts, itched in his lungs and dried his throat. The copper brazing's pungent aroma stung his nostrils.

The captain's charge brought back agonizing memories. Past romantic failures burned hotter than any welding torch across the cracked vessel that was his heart. He felt the pressure of his captain's stare.

"This ship and the sea are my love, Comrade Captain," Mikhail answered.

Captain Borodin's iron gaze probed Mikhail. Like the ship's sonar, he seemed to silently examine him.

"Aye, some find more solace in a mistress whose vices

and virtues stand out more clearly. Keep your wits and ration your courage, Lieutenant, and you may survive the bride you've chosen."

Nobody's Counsellor or Confessor

"As your ship's doctor, I prescribe a night of drunken debauchery," Anatoli said with a gurgling chuckle.

Rosy cheeks adorned the doctor's sallow features. Mikhail had considered it ironic that the ship's physician seemed in the poorest health among the crew. But though he appeared only a wrinkled drape of skin on a knobby-boned skeleton, his constitution always withstood the harshest treatment, especially when drinking.

Mikhail pulled his shipmate closer. "I know Anatoli, you've said this three times tonight."

The doctor snickered. "So get drunk already."

Mikhail surveyed the smoky bar, *Uspokoysa,* and shook his head. Half the K-389's officers stood along a wall, leaning over the high tables or sitting in the stools. Their objective, a row of women dressed and painted to negotiate their evening; a sailor's wages for a night of passion.

A bench made of thick wood ran the length of that wall. The women here guarded their purses more closely than their modesty or pride. They winked and nodded, laughed and gasped with practiced skill at all the proper cues.

Posters plastered the concrete walls, a collage of propaganda, health reminders and factory slogans. In a few small niches, minute pieces of crude art hid the blistered paint: a tugboat, the shipyard landscape, a faceless portrait.

From a bar whose lacquered surface faded away years

ago, shipyard workers eyed their naval comrades, not a cheerful face among them. The bartender and his staff refereed peace between the two crowds while serving vodka, black bread, and fish. *Uspokoysa* stood, besieged by lonesome young sailors anxious to squeeze a lifetime of revelry into every evening ashore.

"I think we've enough drunken sailors for one establishment," Mikhail cautioned. "I only came to Sick Bay to play another game of chess." He eyed the women once more and ran his fingers through his hair nervously. "My heart belongs to the K-389."

Anatoli followed Mikhail's gaze and snorted. "Not to worry, after you saved the ship with a fountain of turds and toilet paper, I gave you enough immunizations to protect you against anything these tramps carry."

Mikhail studied the women. Uniquely unappealing to most, the dregs of Komsomolsk's gutter, one caught his eye. Scrawny even by gulag standards, she met his gaze with dark green eyes unwavering and unashamed. She raised her shot glass to salute him without a false smile or a forced twinkle in her eye.

A hammer-blow drove between his shoulder blades and Mikhail's glass crashed on the floor.

"Go on, latrine commissar," a raspy voice commanded. Mikhail winced and looked over his shoulder.

Lieutenant Boreyev's goading grin completed the thick-headed missile officer's taunting efforts. "She's thin as a fishing pole, but just as flexible. If I couldn't break her, you're in no danger."

Mikhail drew in a deep breath, exhaled through clenched teeth, and forced a smile. "I've no intention of breaking the lady. I'd rather behave like a gentleman and see where that leads."

"She's no lady," Boreyev snickered. "And gentlemen don't shower themselves in shit."

Mikhail stood slowly. He turned and stepped toe to toe with Boreyev. He glared down at the stocky lieutenant. "Better a filthy survivor than a tidy corpse."

"You're drunk, Lieutenant Boreyev," Anatoli observed. "Go and bother someone else."

Boreyev stepped back, frowned and examined Mikhail from beneath his broad Neanderthal brow. He raised his clenched fists and took a boxer's stance.

"Are you looking for a fight?" he asked with a crooked grin.

"I'm not," Mikhail explained. He brought his fists up and rose to the balls of his feet. "But I'll not back down from one, ever."

A tense tide of quiet swept through the room.

"Damn your foolish pride," Anatoli cursed in a low voice. "Take your frustrations out some other way, or I'll have you both taken back to the ship in irons."

"We're going to have fun at sea, I can see that already." Boreyev said with a sharp laugh. He stared back, wild-eyed from between his thick fists.

Mikhail's smile remained hidden.

Boreyev dropped his hands, shook off his fighting posture and slapped Mikhail's upper arm. Mikhail moved not a millimeter, his grim mask held fast. The stout missile officer shrugged, snickered, and melted back into the crowd.

A hand gripped Mikhail's shoulder from behind and he whirled about, ready to fight. His jaw dropped as his fierce gaze met that of an equally fierce woman. Something seeped in from the hard edges of her eyes and showed in her faltering thin frown. Like him, she appeared ready for any fight; weary, wary, and too stubborn to back down.

"Would you rather spend tonight in a hospital bed, or mine?" Her stern-set features softened and she smirked. "I can provide the irons too, if you like."

Boreyev had joined Anatoli. With no seat to go back to, and everyone watching, Mikhail offered an arm to the slim woman.

"Lieutenant Mikhail Koryavin at your service."

"Nika, simply Nika," the woman replied. "Unless you prefer another name, I've had several."

He ushered her to the bar and ordered a bottle of vodka and two glasses. He leaned against the thick wood. "You'll not find I'm not nearly as rambunctious as my shipmates, hardly any fun at all, really."

Nika set the glasses atop the bottle and nodded toward the stairs. "As long as you're paying, I'll be fine. I could use a break from rowdy sailors."

Atop the stairs he followed her down a drafty, littered hallway. Nika looked to him while she unlocked the door. "You can pay, can't you?"

He nodded.

Inside the apartment, more concrete greeted him, devoid of posters to hide its peeled skin of paint. Spacious but sparse, the room's original purpose, like the establishment below, had been to support industry. A thin mattress atop a collapsible bed served as bedroom. And hotplate on a table was her kitchen. Along the opposite wall he examined four factory windows with only whitewash to offer privacy or shield against the bitter winds.

"What's your flavor, sailor?" Nika asked as bent down, unzipped and peeled off her plastic boots.

At his silence she looked back at him. "Oh, did you like the boots?"

"They're nice," he whispered nervously.

"Ah, I'll put them back on then." She sat on the edge of her bed. Rusty bedsprings squealed at her waifish frame. "Anything else you'd like me to wear?"

"All of it," he murmured.

Nika's eyes widened. "What is this? Are you here to arrest me? The bartender told me he took care of all that."

"No," Mikhail said.

"What's wrong with you?" she wondered with a scowl. "You were full of fire downstairs, but now . . .

As her voice trailed off a snide crooked smile emerged. "I'm not exactly your type, am I?"

"What?" Mikhail asked in a shocked whisper.

Nika sprang up from the bed, raced to him and put a finger to his lips. "Shush, there's no cause for alarm. As long as I can get a finder's fee, I'll fetch you a handsome young man to keep you warm. I know a few in town."

Mikhail grabbed her by the wrists and pushed her backwards until he threw her onto the bed. "Don't you dare say that," he growled. "I'm no *pidor* and I'm no policeman either."

"Alright, don't pick a fight with me," she said as she kicked his legs. "I only wanted to figure you out so we can move this along. I've got a long night ahead of me and I'd just as soon get the pleasantries over if I'm to make any money."

Mikhail lunged at her and pushed her onto her back. He grabbed her skirt, yanked off, and threw it across the room. He grasped the waistband of her leggings and peeled them off. Nika squirmed backwards on her elbows until she lay diagonally across the bed in only a sweater and a leather jacket.

Mikhail unbuttoned his tunic and pants, letting each drop as he shed them. He crawled onto the bed over top of Nika, examining her as he crept up her body to meet her astonished gaze. Like any Soviet monument, she bore her bleak life with a harsh, angular beauty. Her soft looking skin was cool to the touch and firm, like a statue worn smooth by brutal seasons. She brought her hands up to his lips.

"No kissing," she whispered with a pouting frown.

She rubbed her hands together and grinned.

"What're you doing?" Mikhail muttered.

"Getting ready to do . . . this." She reached down and grabbed him. All his muscles drew taut. From the shadowy corners of his mind, unwelcome demons leapt. The unexpected touch unlocked memories of his stepfather. The way he'd groped and grabbed, whispering kind words, loving words all the while. He'd been so friendly but he'd been such a traitor. He plunged Mikhail into the cold, dark waters of betrayal, shame, and drowning, impotent fury.

"You sick bastard," she yelled. "I don't do *that*!"

Mikhail examined her, panicked. In his shock-induced

stupor, he'd puked, all over her. He scrambled to his feet as Nika shoved him away.

"Nika," he began, his voice trembling still from the wake of fear and hurt a decade old. "Nika, I don't know what happened. I'm so sorry."

"What was that?" she screamed.

"Shut up and let me think," Mikhail spat back. "If you hadn't been so damned pushy . . . I tried to tell you . . .

Nika stood and marched into the bathroom. The pipes groaned and thumped as she turned on the faucet, cussing under her breath all the while. She emerged with a bucket, a sponge, and disinfectant.

"I'll buy you a new mattress and new sheets," he promised.

"Where?" She shook her head and peeled away the soaked bedding. "There's none in Komsomolsk to buy, *comrade.*" Her final word stung Mikhail with its tone. "This isn't some naval academy dorm. I had to steal these from a hospital."

She turned from her work and glared. "The least you can do is clean up after yourself."

As the layers of sheets came off, Mikhail heard the mattress crinkle; a layer of yellowed plastic protected the mattress. Nika shrugged as she noticed his surprise.

"This isn't the first time someone's messed up my bed. Those guys ask in advance and pay extra though."

Once they'd finished, Mikhail stood and stumbled to a nearby chair. He abandoned the glass and upended the bottle. The burning liquid washed away the thin film of vomit that coated his lips, mouth, and throat. He shuddered at the tiny chunks of dinner he re-swallowed and shivered at the return of his childhood curse. From across the two continents the monster's sick interludes still haunted Mikhail. He wanted to crush something, kill someone, to burn something down, anything that might tear the tie between past and future. Only Nika's silent stare made him realize, he sat shaking with a stranglehold on the empty bottle.

"And I thought I was fucked up," Nika observed.

Mikhail ran his fingers through his hair. "I don't even know where to begin, how to . . ."

Nika dropped her sponge and bucket, shuffled closer and took his hand in hers. It embarrassed him to realize how much it trembled.

"I think I understand," Nika whispered.

Mikhail's lungs seized up. He looked into her eyes and felt fragile, like newspaper in the fireplace.

"I was a shivering mess my first few times as a teen." Her gaze lowered and lost focus. Her eyes darkened.

"I'm no *pidor*," Mikhail insisted. "I like women."

A harsh laugh escaped Nika. She looked up at him and laughed again. "You've a funny way of showing it."

"I would love to bed you," Mikhail continued, his voice sounding like a plea. "It's just . . . hard." He let out a nervous laugh. "I mean, difficult."

Nika turned from him and walked to where her leggings lay. As she bent to retrieve them, Mikhail admired her long legs and firm bottom. Were she not a continent away from Moscow, she might've been a ballerina.

After a long silence between them, Mikhail marched to the table, poured himself a tall glass of vodka and gulped it down. The liquor slid down his gullet and stung every millimeter. He let out a great sigh. Eyes closed, inhaling the odors of a filthy apartment, old garbage, mildewed shower curtains, and the musky undercurrent of sex, he turned to face Nika.

"I don't suppose you play chess?"

She flinched, eyes wide, and blinked.

"You're still paying, right?" she asked with a half-smile. It faded as she explained. "I've got people to pay. I don't pay, I sleep in the street."

Mikhail grinned and shook his head. "What else have I to spend my money on except a quiet night with someone who understands me more than anyone else?"

"Calm down, sailor, I'm nobody's counsellor or confessor."

The Cause of Death Seems Simple Enough

Mikhail raced through the shipyard. He dodged crate-laden forklifts and ducked cranes as they swung tons of steel. Ice patches had sent him tumbling twice already and he vaulted more. Lungs on fire, fingers frozen numb, he fought not to fall down the ship's brow as he raced across. The sentries on deck saluted with raised AK-47's. Mikhail's stomach fluttered as he slid down the ladder into the Command Center.

"Looks like you found a woman worth your time," Boreyev observed, "and your money."

"Yes," he answered between gasps.

"Be glad I'd had my fill of her nights ago, then." The broad-shouldered, squat man slapped Mikhail's shoulder as he passed. "Otherwise she'd been in no shape for even a soft-spoken gentleman like you."

"Yes," Mikhail replied. "Very kind of you."

Boreyev shook his head, followed behind Mikhail and entered the wardroom of K-389. A dozen wooden chairs surrounded a long table, all adorned with cobalt blue velvet. The wood-panelled walls arced in over the table and completed the appearance of a stately conference room squeezed into a barracks dorm. A tea set sat on a smaller table at one end and the captain's chair sat at the opposite end.

Doctor Anatoli sat in his chair, his head hung just above a steaming cup of tea. The man's pallor looked sickly, even for the jaundiced doctor. Others gathered around the blue felt table leaned into their tea and groaned as the wardroom door closed with a slight click. The small quiet room seemed set for a funeral, with all the mourners gathered.

Captain Borodin entered. As one, the officers stood to attention and waited for their commander's nod before they sat again.

"What happened last night?" Borodin asked. A somber expression settled into his features.

Each officer looked to their comrades for an answer.

"What happened to Seaman Yanukovich?" he asked.

With a finger leveled at Boreyev, Captain Borodin continued. "Lieutenant Boreyev, he was in your division, was he not?"

Boreyev stiffened. "He *is*, Comrade Captain."

Borodin shook his head. "*Was*, he died last night in his bunk. His chief discovered him after he failed to muster this morning." With a frown he added, "Have you not seen to your men yet this morning?"

"No Comrade Captain, like many of us, I was a little late returning aboard last night."

The captain stood and studied the plaques on the wall, commemorations to K-389's accomplishment over its decade-long life. "It's been my philosophy that the rigors of in-port repairs make a sailor yearn for the sea. The shipyard is different. We watch as strangers work on our systems. Many sit by and wait for the fire brigade to save their home."

He turned to examine his officers and winced at what he saw. "Doctor, I need you to examine the body. Lieutenant Koryavin, I want you to conduct an investigation. I must know why and how this happened."

Mikhail's throat dried instantly. The room rippled with heat as he felt himself flush. "I'll do my best, though I'm hardly qualified."

"You are an officer of the Red Fleet," Borodin growled. He paused, cooled, and took a deep breath. "We solve our problems or we invite another stranger to our home. The police, I'm not worried about. We'll work with them. They're undermanned and happy to have our help. But those NKVD bastards love a witch hunt. Those State lackeys are always looking to promote themselves closer to Moscow."

A hushed meeting followed. The ship's business pushed on. Officers armed with reports and graphs bemoaned their meager progress and the lack of resources to see the work through. Once the meeting ended and everyone filed out, Captain Borodin motioned for Mikhail to remain and shut the door.

"Our professionalism slips, one drunken night at a time," Borodin said.

"So it seems, Comrade Captain." Mikhail felt Borodin's gaze weigh heavy on him. "I must admit, I too arrived late this morning."

The captain's iron stare softened, a tired smile emerged, and he wagged a gnarled finger at Mikhail.

"That, that is why I've appointed you as investigating officer. You're young, idealistic enough, to value honor and justice . . . even if it means convicting yourself."

"The cause of death seems simple enough," Anatoli explained. "This boy was beaten to death."

Doctor Anatoli and Mikhail stood within Sick Bay, an elongated closet bordered by a medicine cabinet, book shelves, and an 'examination table' that normally doubled as a desk and occasionally Anatoli's bunk when he found himself too tipsy to find his stateroom. A heap of medical records sat in the corner, tossed there to make room for a haphazard autopsy. The corpse of Seaman Yanukovich lay before them on the table, in a black plastic body bag.

"But the sentry found him in his bunk," Mikhail countered. "And he didn't look nearly as bad as what you've indicated."

"The bruising took some time to rise to the surface,"

the doctor replied. "Not a single bone broken, he'd been pummeled in a way that left no outward marks."

Anatoli looked up from his work, over his spectacles. An expectant pause blossomed.

"What is it Doctor?"

"You do not know what that likely implies?" he asked in a whisper.

"Something sinister based on the look you're giving me."

Anatoli reached past Mikhail and shut the door to his office. "Sometimes men take matters into their own hands. A bar of soap in a pillow case has been used to punish thieves in the past. They swing the pillowcase with such speed, the pain is sharp. Such punishments take a couple of men to pin their subject down with a sheet while others hammer him repeatedly."

"I've heard of this, but never known anyone to die from a blanket party."

Anatoli leaned over and unzipped the body bag. Inside Seaman Yanukovich lay naked, covered in narrow bruises each from four to eight centimeters in length.

"These 'trials' typically end with a severe beating about the torso, but," the doctor began.

With a small, bright flashlight, the doctor illuminated the boy's temple. A large bruise blossomed across this depressed section of skull. Deep purple, with yellowing outlines, it seemed diffused and larger than the rest.

He continued, "It appears someone got over zealous."

"I don't know who did it, but everyone knows why." Boreyev's smug response trickled a chill down Mikhail's spine.

The two sat in the wardroom while the crew assisted the shipyard in getting K-389 back on schedule. The grating peal of metal grinders and the impact wrenches' rat-tat-tat set Mikhail's teeth on edge.

"And what," Mikhail asked slowly, "was that, Lieutenant Boreyev?"

"Yanukovich was," he shrugged, his features soured, "you know, a *pidor*."

Mikhail felt his stomach tighten. "Pardon me, a what?"

Boreyev's face reddened as he scowled. "You know, a *pederast*, a lover of boys and men."

"A homosexual?" Mikhail asked. He ran his fingers through his hair. "Seaman Yanukovich, a sailor in the Red Fleet?"

"It happens more than you realize," Boreyev insisted. He grinned. "I had my doubts about you until you met Nika."

Mikhail straightened in his chair and cleared his throat. "I pour my heart into my work and my duty, not women."

"Poor substitutes," Boreyev continued. "As much as I adore my Motherland, I've never had patriotism take my breath away the way a good woman or a very bad woman has."

Mikhail tapped his pencil on the pad before him. "Back to the murder of our crewmate, Seaman Yanukovich."

"No one intended to kill him," Boreyev said with a shrug. "But no one will mourn his passing either."

"How can you be so smug about it, so nonchalant?"

Boreyev threw his hand up. "Look, I don't even know what happened. Maybe he got in over his head in Black Wharf."

"And what do you know about it, the area they call Black Wharf?

Boreyev's gaze narrowed, his brow creased. "I only know as much they told everyone when they arrived in Komsomolsk, it's where perversions abound . . . and sailors die. We've all been warned not to go but deviants will go where their tastes are satisfied."

"Yet you've no desire to see justice done?"

"Fate judged him harsher than any of us dared."

Mikhail thought of his stepfather, of all the dark moments alone with him. Mikhail had prayed for deliverance. He'd thought on murder many times, especially afterward, in those strange moments where his abuser offered condolences and kind words. Through pain, shame, and tears, he'd prayed for an accident to claim his stepfather's life. He'd even held the instrument in his hands. On that farm death lurked in every task, every labor. He'd lacked the courage, not to kill him, but to explain his motive and survive the life he imagined. He'd have been labeled a *pidor* for having allowed it for so long and a murderer for ending it with patricide. He swallowed hard, focused on his duty, and leveled his glare at the stocky lieutenant across from him.

"Will your crewmates feel any more comfortable knowing they might set sail with a murderer?"

Boreyev withdrew a cigarette, lit it, and took a long drag. He stared back at Mikhail and exhaled a great smoky sigh. "I don't like what you're implying. And I especially don't like who you're implying is involved."

Mikhail grabbed the wardroom phone, pressed the buzzer, and waited.

"Duty officer; this is Lieutenant Koryavin. Have all Missile Division personnel arrested and confined to the Torpedo Room."

Boreyev frowned. "The Torpedo Room; why not their quarters?"

Mikhail unclenched his jaw. "I'll need to examine their pillow cases and shower kits."

As Sure as a Bullet

Northern Fleet Headquarters in Severomorsk, Murmansk;
November, 1982

Lieutenant Zhora Ivankov examined the scale model of his submarine and caressed it as he walked along its length. Project 685 represented the latest in Soviet technology. While his fellow officers drank and mingled with the headquarters brass and party officials in attendance, Zhora kept his focus on the nuclear powered sword of the sea. So beautiful, so deadly, he almost hoped for war, to feel its power.

"You approve of the design?"

Zhora stiffened at his father's sardonic question. Without looking up from the cutaway view of the submarine's interior, he answered flatly.

"Yes, Admiral Ivankov."

"Good, Lieutenant Ivankov," his father replied. "I wouldn't want to disappoint you."

Something in that last part held a sharp edge. Zhora looked up and asked, "What is this about, Comrade Admiral?"

"Will you stop by my office tonight?" he asked with a tone that removed any doubt; this was no request.

"Yes, Comrade Admiral."

Hours later, Lieutenant Ivankov marched into Admiral Ivankov's enormous office. The long walk through the building's cavernous halls reminded him of the power his father wielded, the power he expected to wield himself one day. Before the revolution this estate housed royalty, friends of the Tsar. Zhora snickered to himself. *Seems things haven't really changed all that much.*

When he entered his father's office, Zhora examined a map of the Northern Fleet's sphere of influence and responsibilities. From Angola to Communism's jewel of the Caribbean, Cuba; and from submarines under the Arctic ice to scientific vessels near Antarctica; the Northern Fleet's power impressed friend and foe alike.

To his left, he spied charts of the Atlantic Ocean's depths, the playground of submarines. These framed the battleground of the secret war between two superpowers. To his right, a fully stocked bar and a fireplace bookended a small ornate table. On it sat an oversized chess set.

The Admiral stood and marched to the bar where he poured himself a drink. He motioned for Zhora to join him. He set a second glass out, hesitated, and then poured his son's drink. Before Zhora could make a toast, his father upended his glass and emptied it. He poured another.

"To Project 685," Zhora blurted.

His father glared, nodded, and drained his glass.

"Sorry I'm late," Zhora said. "I didn't want to tell my captain about our meeting, so I didn't slip out of his post brief meeting until moments ago."

The Admiral motioned to the chessboard and he took his seat behind the white pieces. Before Zhora sat his father made his first move.

"Hardly worth hiding your parentage from him," his father began. "He won't be your commanding officer anymore."

"What?"

The Admiral motioned to the opposite chair. "Your move."

"I'm not in any mood to play chess."

"That's your mother talking." He stared at the empty seat. "Sit and play."

Zhora grabbed the stuffed leather chair as he fought his father's command. "You're transferring me?"

"Your mother always said you were clever," the Admiral admitted with a chuckle. "Let's see how clever." He folded his arms, leaned back, and dropped his gaze to the board between them.

Zhora sat and examined the board. His father's first move, aggressive and traditional, offered no clues to his motives. His face bore the mask of an old warrior. It always had. Small shining eyes refused to meet his son's gaze yet still betrayed his feelings. Zhora returned his father's opening move in kind with its proven counter.

Move and countermove, I'll shove the pieces around but I won't play his game.

The game progressed several hushed turns while Zhora turned the riddle over in his mind. The Arctic winds rattled the window panes. Logs in the fireplace hissed and popped as the heat crept into the sap.

"I graduated top in my class," Zhora offered. "I've been singled out as an expert sonar officer and tactician. I've worked as hard as you asked. I've earned my place aboard the greatest ship. Whatever strings you pulled in my favor, I didn't need them."

The Admiral grinned and reinforced his wall of pawns. "Your professional accolades aren't in question."

A chill rippled across Zhora's arm as he took his turn quickly. "You would undermine my career over how I conduct my private life?"

Eyes fixed on the board, his father frowned. He shook his head and advanced his knight. "For an Ivankov, or any ambitious man, nothing is private."

A fever washed over Zhora. He moved his bishop out to threaten the exposed knight. The chiseled marble piece struck the board with a sharp report. "How can *you* judge me?"

The Admiral's eyes widened. His nostrils flared and cheeks flushed. Zhora felt the room grow colder.

"*I* am not a perverse monster." his father countered.

27

"What!?"

"I fought hard to earn this admiralship. I clawed my way through competitors. In the wake of my success I left enemies eager to torpedo my career. I didn't raise a *pidor*, but that's what you've become. Your perversions will destroy all I've built."

Zhora's skin grew clammy in the cold room as sweat seeped from every pore. His head felt hot and fragile, like the sizzling logs in the fire.

"A man doesn't rise to this office without spies. I expected you to make some trouble, a young man, on his own for the first time. But this? As much as I love you, it still turns my stomach."

Zhora clenched his teeth and focused on the chessboard. He'd managed to lose pieces and position in the last few moves. He hadn't meant to play but he still fumed at his impending defeat.

"Men, Zhora," his father hissed, his features twisted with disgust. "You prey upon men."

Dry, hard laughter erupted from Zhora. "I don't 'prey' on anyone, Father. I've loved and been loved more in these past years than you have your adult life."

His father slid his queen into position. "Check."

Zhora shoved the board off the table at his father. The pieces flew and tumbled.

"Can we stop playing games? Can't you let me handle my life?"

"We can fix this, salvage your soul, and save both our careers." His father sounded desperate for the first time.

"What?"

"You don't think I'll suffer for your sickness? You don't think my enemies aren't aching to humiliate me? Your perversions will kill me as sure as a bullet."

For the first time, his father met his gaze. Fear's shadow extinguished the gleam in the admiral's eyes. He couldn't remain an iron tyrant forever. Zhora's career wasn't merely a father's wishful legacy but the aging man's retirement plan. Without a successor, the Ivankov family's enemies would swarm over the old man in his final years. They'd strip him of his prestige and the protections it afforded.

His father bent down and picked up the pieces. "It's not too late to fix this. I realize my absence allowed too much of your mother's influence. But I can help you get you back on the proper path."

"I know what people will think if they discover my . . . interests," Zhora muttered. "I keep my liaisons quiet. Those I date are in greater danger, with lives less secure than mine. We understand the dangers of publicly sharing our relationship."

"You understand less than you think," his father chided.

Zhora joined his father in restoring the chessboard. "You would put so much importance on who I spend my evenings with?"

"What you do," his father sputtered. "Who you see is wrong, very wrong."

"More wrong than adultery?" Zhora blurted. He held his breath and waited for the thunder roar and lightning.

His father's face lost all its color as he glared at Zhora. He only dropped his gaze when he walked away and sat back at his desk. "I've got a lot of work to do and you need to start packing."

"That's it?" Zhora ventured.

The admiral's pen stopped. "Yes. You'll be transferred as far from Moscow as I can send you. Once you get to Pacific Fleet HQ, you'll have your pick of the ships out there; I'll arrange that much."

"I've called you an adulterer to your face, you've labeled me a monster, and we're just going to say our goodbyes on that?"

His father stood and blinked twice before he answered. "No goodbyes Lieutenant. Dismissed."

Zhora took a deep breath, came to attention, and offered a crisp salute. "I will do my best to honor the Ivankov family."

The admiral returned the salute. "Defy the laws of nature again and you'll no longer *be* an Ivankov."

All in the Name of Order

Leninskiy Komsomolsk Shipyard, in the Soviet Far East,
November, 1982

In the wardroom, Mikhail examined his notes.
Last night's sentries noticed nothing extraordinary.
Yanukovich's division, to a man, told one of two stories.
Half comprised the section on duty and had been too busy
or too tired to see anything. The rest had been drunk in
the local bars like most of the crew, including Mikhail. The
doctor's notes offered no definitive time of death to place
the murder on board, but Anatoli swore the man hadn't
been fit to crawl into the bunk he'd died in.

A knock shook Mikhail from his frustrations. A
monolithic man of forty-nine stepped in, offered a salute
and stood at attention.

"Michman Anton Gorelov, reporting as ordered."

"Please, Comrade Michman, have a seat," Mikhail
offered.

His crooked, flattened nose and scar-etched knuckles
spoke of a hard life. Shining black hair and thick eyebrows
reminded Mikhail of Stalin.

"Comrade Michman, you're the highest ranking enlisted
man aboard K-389, right?" Mikhail pointed across the
wardroom table with his pencil.

"Yes, Comrade Lieutenant." He relaxed in his chair and
ran his hand across the blue felt tablecloth.

"So you've dealt with *pidors* before?"

"Odd, you saying that word," Gorelov answered with a sneer.

Mikhail's chest tightened. "Please, answer the question."

Gorelov's casual expression faded and his gaze hardened. "I've seen plenty fuck-ups in the Fleet."

"Have you ever known them to warrant a blanket party?"

"Been dealt one myself." The old seadog grinned. His two front teeth, silver-capped, reflected the wardroom's light. The rest formed a crooked fence of old tobacco-stained enamel. He withdrew a cigarette pack from his shirt pocket and offered Mikhail one before lighting his own.

"You, a senior enlisted man, a victim of such abuse?"

"Just a petty officer then. Yes. Didn't kill me," he answered with a broad grin. "Helped get my shit strait as a better sailor."

"You hardly look like a man who sat still for a beating."

The man's grin widened and his dark eyes gleamed. "Sent a few to sick bay."

"Have you ever been part of administering one?"

Gorelov leaned forward, rested on his elbows, and he drew in deeply from his cigarette.

"You're not going to find enough proof. Release the men. Shouldn't arrested them in the first place."

"Are you threatening me?"

Gorelov sat up and grabbed the table's edge. The previous gleam in his eyes faded.

"Order comes from everyone marching to the same music," Gorelov explained. "Leaders gotta lead with a strong, fair hand. Somebody went too far. That's how people get hurt . . . more than they should."

"But why threaten me?"

Gorelov shook his head. "Not a threat, a warning. Pick your battles. Choose your enemies." He pursed his lips and his gaze wandered off as he sought a clearer answer. "You can't catch your man. Too many others in on it."

"You suggest that I ignore this sailor's death?"

"No," Gorelov replied with an apologetic tone. "It's done.

We've gotta learn from it."

He wrung his gnarled hands until his fingers found wide scar white with age. He rubbed it repeatedly.

"I wish I'd been in on it," he said and met Mikhail's gaze before continued. The michman's eyes looked like keyholes into a past of pain, given and received, all in the name of order.

"You wish you'd beat him?"

"He wouldn't be dead," Gorelov answered. "They tried to set the boy straight. Everybody's got secret quirks. But you got to keep 'em secret. He'd have learned that with me. The next day we'd be back to work, together, as crewmates. We'd understand each other."

Mikhail stared at Gorelov, battered but not beaten, brutish but not cruel.

"Look," Gorelov began. "You got your job. I got mine. I'm doing mine right now, protecting a good officer from himself."

"You're protecting me?"

"Start a witch hunt and *someone* burns at the stake."

"Twenty men under arrest and no suspect?" Captain Borodin asked.

Mikhail stood at attention across the long wardroom table. He felt his fellow officers' stares like sunlight through a magnifying lens. A glance at Boreyev magnified the anxious heat building up under Mikhail's uniform. In the brutal winter of Komsomolsk, standing on the frozen steel deck, he still felt like he could manage a sweat.

"The doctor's cause of death offers no clues," he answered flatly. "Neither have there been any evidence pointing toward a culprit. This man's death could've happened hours prior to his return to the ship. The sentries reported nothing amiss topside or below decks. Unless we're prepared to invite investigators onto our ship, we'll have to chalk this up to a night on the town gone wrong."

Captain Borodin stared at Mikhail. The silence thickened and settled.

"Lieutenant Boreyev," the captain began. "This was a man under your command, are you satisfied with Lieutenant Koryavin's investigation?"

Boreyev took a look sip of his tea before answering. "Seaman Yanukovich was known to have eccentric and dangerous tastes he entertained ashore." He snuck a glance at Mikhail before looking at their captain. "I suspect these led to a tragic mystery we'll never know the truth behind."

No Place to Hide

SEVEN

The Soviet Railroad Station at Tynda, in the Soviet Far East November, 1982

"This can wait until daylight," Sergeant Vasin insisted. "It'll be ten degrees warmer by then."

He adjusted his grip on the rifle strapped over his shoulder.

Iosif shook his head. "No, if I delay a minute, my next job will be much colder, a prison labor camp. Logging inland you'll be lucky to only freeze your fingers and toes off."

Car by car, train by train, the two marched their lengths and inspected them. The squat yard worker, Iosif, used a hooked steel pole to test each connection's tightness to the next car. Even for a midnight arrival, he followed his protocol with animated and energetic fervor. He rapped against the sides before either climbing up or sliding a door open to verify their contents. Barely tall enough to reach the ladder, his pole helped hoist him up. Vasin felt himself sweat just watching this barrel of a man work.

"You really think people would step out on a night like this to steal turnips and coal?"

They marched beside a new arrival, a dozen cars of coal. The steel arteries of industry shined silver in the lamppost lights. Vasin stole a glance at the wind-worn shack they'd been in when the train arrived and tried to imagine himself warmer by looking at it.

"Especially coal," Iosif shot back. He punctuated his decree, jabbing at the icy night air with his gloved fist. "Industries need piles of it, but many families scrounge for it, teenaged boys sneak into the rail yard, like a squad of Spetsnaz commandoes. Does the railroad congratulate me for keeping tons of potatoes safe? No, they castrate me over a handful of coal."

"Calm down, Iosif. Let's get this over while I can still feel my feet."

A rumbling tumble of steel and stone caught the Sergeant's ear. Something stirred in a coal car behind them. Both whirled about, the bold Iosif racing to chase the mystery down. A whimpering yelp halted Sergeant Vasin. He brought his rifle up. The freezing metal against his cheek felt like a cool salve against the heat of his fear. Though like an injured dog, the noise held a throatier note, larger, more terrified than hurt. Whatever cried out, it quit as fast as it broke the silence.

Iosif scrambled up the coal car's ladder. "Damn pilfering *tsygan*, I've got you now."

"Wait," Sergeant Vasin shouted. He aimed skyward and fired into the night. The staccato blast of his AK-47 tore through the snow-insulated quiet night. "Let's get some help out here. Something's not right."

"*Bozhe moi*," Iosif murmured from atop the ladder.

As Sergeant Vasin inched closer, rifle ready, he marveled at Iosif's stillness and absence of emotion in his voice. "What is it, Iosif, what do you see?"

"Dead," he replied in a stupor. "It's the Pushkin brothers; they've been a thorn in my side for a year now; always outsmarting me, always one step ahead."

"How'd they die?"

"Horribly," Iosif replied, "like slaughtered animals."

"Come down, then, there's nothing you can do."

"No, I'll at least pull their bodies out for a decent burial." Iosif climbed into the car.

The stout man's mumbling and stumbling halted suddenly.

"Iosif, do you see anything from up there; someone running from the train perhaps?"

The wind howled and the station's sign back at the cozy shack creaked. Vasin's attention remained locked on the rail car.

"Iosif?"

From the car's other side, footsteps trod closer. Vasin checked his rifle before sidestepping to the break between coal cars.

"Iosif, are you alright?"

A chill ran through Vasin's skin, deep and without shivers. The night cold felt warm in comparison to the ice that settled on his soul.

"Whoever you are, stand still." Vasin slowed his pace and crept closer. He knelt and peered to the other side. Nothing.

The absence of an answer hung over Vasin's heart like an anvil. He swallowed hard and doubled back. A blur startled him. A hand, cold and firm as iron, clasped his throat. Claws ripped the AK-47 from his hands. In a few bounding leaps, the monster had carried him, like a mouse snatched up by an owl, to the rail yard's end. In the dim remnant of distant lamppost-light Vasin looked into his enemy's eyes.

A strong brow of pale smooth skin shaded dark eyes while long locks of red hair poured down onto a tattered tunic. The man's smile showed the whitest teeth, and his jawline reminded Vasin of an uncle he'd loved as a child. Uncle Bogdan lived on the edge of a small town in Amur as his ancestors had forever. He'd taken Vasin fishing whenever his parents' arguments made staying in their cramped home intolerable.

"You are a clever one," the stranger offered with a menacing smile. "Your gunfire warned others, called them to your aid. For that I must move again."

Holding Vasin by the throat, the stranger turned him toward a retreating train. "Where does that one go?"

"The shipyard at Komsomolsk-on-Amur."

"So many people, so many machines," the stranger growled. His grimace waned and a thoughtful smile emerged. "Perhaps I shall hide better among the herd this next time."

Shouts from the rail yard rang out, shouts for Sergeant Vasin. As he craned his neck to see his comrades, the stranger pulled him closer. The odor of death, old enough to sour yet new enough to sink deep into Vasin's nostrils, this awoke the Sergeant to his captor's true face. A tear escaped along with a terrified whine before iron fingers closed tight on his life and ended it with a crack.

Never Easy

EIGHT

Leninskiy Komsomolsk Shipyard, in the Soviet Far East
November, 1982

Five days aboard trains, Zhora yearned for fresh air and room to stretch out. His final stop at Komsomolsk-on-Amur nearly made him climb back in the densely packed railcar. A squat town of concrete and wood, it looked like a scab on the shipyard, an industrial behemoth teeming with activity.

Dressed in drab patchwork clothes, its citizens lumbered through their daily tasks. Few ventured a glance at the navy truck he rode in through town. If not for the shipyard, they'd still be bargemen, fishermen, and lumberjacks. The State had pulled them up from a pre-industrial life fifty years ago and left them to manage the rest.

The town's odors of river mud and garbage gave way to the sting of smoldering steel and burning diesel as the shipyard's gates loomed near. Bright blue-white stars sparkled from the hissing welders' torches. Grinders whined and spat amber sparks. Rivet guns rattled and puffed. Amidst the workers, he found K-389 in dry dock. Like a prehistoric beast lured into a pit, it sat idle and suffered the labors of men.

They fought time and melded new steel to old. A decade of patrols in the Pacific left scars and rusted age spots. Two nuclear reactors, sixteen missiles, and over a hundred men, all relied on this aging hull to hold back the pressures of the deep and withstand the crashing waves.

Zhora shook his head and muttered a prayer while he marched across the brow. A young sailor eyed him as he approached. Bright emerald eyes examined him. Handsome with his strong jawline and high cheekbones, he almost made Zhora forget himself. Admiral Ivankov's final words grounded him and he focused again on the mask he must wear.

"Lieutenant Ivankov, reporting for duty as ordered."

"Cheer up Comrade Lieutenant. We're in port all year 'round. Vodka and women are only a stone's throw away."

"Sailors belong at sea, don't you agree?" Zhora wondered sharply.

"Sounds like something an admiral might say, not a common sailor, Comrade Lieutenant."

"Enough; are all sailors aboard K-389 so glib?"

"Huh?"

Zhora leaned in until he smelled last night's vodka on the sentry's breath. "Do you all care so little about the security of the Soviet Union, that you would gladly ignore your duty to defend it?"

The sentry snapped to attention. "No Comrade Lieutenant, I'm . . . only . . ."

"Never mind," Zhora snapped. "If we're done here, I'll proceed below and report to Captain Borodin."

The sentry stepped aside and saluted. "Welcome aboard K-389, Lieutenant Ivankov."

Zhora picked his way across the deck, over and around air hoses, stray tools, and debris, until he reached the open doorway into the ship. Shipyard cables and hoses squeezed against him as he descended the ladder leading down to the Command Center. The ship smelled of welding rods and brazed copper, burning and pungent. Work topside and in every corner of every room between the Command Center and the Wardroom rapped upon the steel above and below like hail. He marched through the mayhem and entered the Wardroom.

The veneer paneled quiet inside enveloped Zhora like a felt blanket. Captain Borodin sat slumped at the table poring over thin papers of pink, green and yellow, carbon copies with black waxy sheets between them.

"Have a seat, Lieutenant Ivankov," Captain Borodin offered. "I'm sure your train ride from Europe and across Asia has left you exhausted."

Zhora nodded but remained on his feet. "I've also spent too much time in chair to accept one just yet."

"Top of your class, an expert in sonar systems and an outstanding tactical officer," the captain said. "Why your talents are wasted aboard a ballistic missile submarine defies logic. I would ask what sins landed you aboard K-389, but the answer might ruin my own hopes for a quiet retirement."

"Captain," Zhora replied, stunned. "I hope to serve K-389 well and I don't want anything in my past to endanger either of our careers."

"Good. As construction nears completion, in the coming months, the rest of your division will report in. You'll serve as sonar division officer and tactical officer."

Zhora beamed. "Yes Comrade Captain."

"And Lieutenant," the captain said as Zhora began to leave.

"Yes sir?"

"These men mean well, even if they don't seem so."

A frown briefly creased Zhora's brow. "Aye, aye, Comrade Captain."

From the Wardroom, Zhora marched aft. Outside the Crew's Mess, he stopped and examined the Ship's Galley. Great square gaps in the flooring and counters; the ovens hadn't been installed. He ducked through a watertight door, into Missile Compartment Forward. Huge missile tubes bookended the passageway. They stretched from above the pressure hull and into the bilges below.

Though empty now, this forest of steel would soon rival nations in destructive power. Simultaneously thrilled and disappointed, Zhora dismissed the kind of world such an assault left the victor to inherit. Mutual assured destruction smashed the bottom out of conquest's cup.

From Missile Compartment Aft he entered the Auxiliaries Compartment. A stinking mélange of burnt equipment and insulation mixed with human waste sank into his lungs and stuck. He hastened his pace and held his breath until he entered the Reactor Tunnel. Its lead shielded passage protected the crew from radiation. Thick pipes sang with steam. They jutted up from the deck below and elbowed aft.

He followed those pipes through Engine Room Forward, where electricians and their equipment modified and distributed the ship's power.

In the Engine Room Aft Zhora looked out over steam turbines. A scarecrow in grimy coveralls caught his attention. The man's angular pale face and thick flaxen hair bore as much grease as the uniform he wore. He towered over two crewmen, speaking as much with his hands as with his voice.

Zhora crept closer, remaining out of the man's sight. "You there, where do I find Lieutenant Koryavin?"

"I am he . . ." The man spun about, his mouth agape. "Zhora, Zhora Ivankov?"

"I am called Lieutenant Ivankov by filthy petty officers who forget their place!" Zhora's scowl dissolved and the two burst into laughter. "I would embrace you, but my uniform, I have *some* pride in it."

Mikhail's glee dimmed. He eyed the others present before he spoke. "Tonight, come drink with me, we'll catch up. A lot has changed since the academy."

"What-

"Tonight, we'll reminisce." Mikhail shook his head and gestured to the desalination plant in pieces. "But now I've work to do."

Then, he grinned and the dingy surroundings melted away, the pungent odors of welding shrank from Zhora's senses in the wake of that smile. He'd forgotten how it warmed his heart, like the sun's rays on a frost-dusted day.

Mikhail's eyes shifted again to his crewmates before he spoke. "I'll explain more tonight."

"Misha, it's so good to have a friend out here," Zhora whispered as the two strolled down the streets of Komsomolsk.

Even without Murmansk's White Sea wind, Komsomolsk's cold crept deeper through his jacket and felt colder than anything he'd ever known. But seeing his old academy roommate, Mikhail, finding a friend so far from home warmed him enough to melt winter's sting.

"I know, I know," Mikhail admitted. "I still can't believe you've been sent to an old turtle like K-389. I thought you would be on a new attack submarine, running circles around those Americans."

"When your father and admiral labels you a monster," Zhora began, "opportunities dry up."

Mikhail turned to face him, mouth agape. "What, why?"

But before Zhora offered an answer, it crept into his friend's features. Indignation faded into pity, concern transformed into disappointment. Mikhail had changed in the years apart. He'd lost the passionate fervor Zhora remembered, his inquisitive attitude that once challenged the rightness of everything and clung to the traditions of no one. For the first time in their evening stroll, the icy cobblestone streets chilled his feet.

Mikhail fashioned a smile and tugged at Zhora's sleeve. "Come, let's have a drink and catch up on old times. Afterward, I've got a friend I'd like you to meet."

Two hours drinking at *Uspokoysa*, Zhora had learned

all he cared to about Mikhail's career, but nothing about the man within the uniform.

"I'm boring you now," Mikhail said, frowning.

"It's not that," Zhora answered as he clutched Mikhail's forearm.

Mikhail stiffened then smiled. "Come, then, I've got someone I'd like to introduce you to."

With a bottle in one hand and three glasscs in the other, Mikhail maneuvered through the crowd to a set of stairs. Zhora examined the smoky room. Two dozen men cajoled and bribed for the attention of the same half dozen women. Zhora shook his head and shuffled upstairs.

"I work so much and relax so little," Mikhail said from atop the stairs. "Since I've met my new friend, I've spent a month's pay in half that time."

Zhora watched Mikhail at the end of a hallway, bottle cradled in one arm, glasses teetering and tinkling atop it as he worked the lock on a door. Mikhail looked back and snickered nervously.

"It's worth it. The nights I spend up here keep me sane."

The apartment inside offered no clues to Mikhail's elation. Peeled-paint walls looked more like winter tank camouflage, with splotches of bright white, faded white and concrete grey. Compared to the barroom's warmth of tightly packed bodies, this apartment seemed only a degree warmer than the alley outside. His attention focused on one welcome sight, a chess set.

"Do you still play?" Mikhail asked. He set down his burden and poured vodka in each glass.

"It's been awhile," Zhora answered. "So you might stand a chance now," he added with a chuckle. He felt his smile dissolve and a shadow hover over his heart.

"Misha, what's happened to you? You seem so guarded, locked up."

"You always cut to the chase," Mikhail answered, a hint of hurt in his voice. His soft brown eyes dimmed, his propped up smile fell. "The world happened. The weight of the world around me, like the tide, pushed me back, drove me to the bottom, and left me gasping on the shore."

"Sorry I'm late," a woman's voice startled Zhora as she burst into the room. "Oh, hello, I didn't realize we'd have company tonight."

Emaciated, pale, this whore needed no introduction as such; her makeup stood out like a neon advertisement. Her vinyl pants and matching jacket, with their rows of unnecessary zippers almost made him laugh out loud. After a long silence, she put a hand on her hip and offered a wry smile.

"Get a good look, anything more'll cost you."

Mikhail stepped between the two and laughed. "Nika, this is my old academy roommate, Zhora Ivankov. Zhora, this is my counsellor, Nika."

"Counsellor?"

"Shut up," Nika said with a chuckle, gently slapping Mikhail's cheek. She turned to Zhora. "He just says that to piss me off. You're an old roommate? We're new roommates."

Zhora watched her glide across the room and empty a small paper bag she'd concealed in her jacket. Orange juice concentrate, canned meat, and a roll of crackers tumbled onto a thin mattress. The room seemed to hum and vertigo set in.

"You've domesticated a whore?" Zhora wondered aloud.

Nika's eyes widened and she brought her hands to her face, gasping to complete her mock shock. "Oh no, he's called me whore!" She grimaced, then smirked. "I'm more hurt that you'd think me so easily tamed."

"Zov, please," Mikhail countered, his brow furrowed, eyes piercing.

"That, that's the first time you've called me Zov, when you chastise me for pointing out the obvious and absurd." Zhora crossed his arms and inhaled deeply. "What happened to my Misha? What happened to the farm boy I helped through the academy? What happened to the man I loved?"

Nika pursed her lips and slid towards the door. "I'm

going to go find some cigarettes that won't burn like diesel fumes in my lungs."

As she shut the door, Mikhail turned to answer. "There's a lot about me you've misunderstood."

Zhora reeled. "That's quite an understatement."

"Nika's helped me figure it out."

"Really? You've gotten yourself sorted out by a whore with a heart of gold? Shall I help you arrange for the marriage or is there any point since you've already skipped to the honeymoon?"

Mikhail poured them each a glass, thrust one in Zhora's hand before upending his own, draining it. "You never make things easy, do you?"

"Just this once, I will," Zhora said, seething. He stormed out the door.

He raced down the stairs and shoved his way through the drunken herd. Into Komsomolsk's streets he ran until a pile of clutter in the dark tripped him. In the darkness, lit only by the stars, he cursed that ice-cold air. The rush into the cold had brought tears to his eyes.

Spell it Out

NINE

Ten huddles of men muttered and smoked at the dry dock's edge. Bundled and stomping against the cold, they looked like a murder of crows pecking about for a morning morsel. Zhora eyed them as he followed his fellow officers across K-389's brow up to the dry dock.

"Crew of K-389," Michman Gorelov bellowed. "Assemble and come to attention!"

As the men rushed to comply, Zhora looked to Gorelov and then to the lieutenant beside him on the brow, Mikhail. It hurt to see him so close yet feel him so far away.

So passionate about his work, yet so unsure of himself anywhere else.

They'd spent the last several hours on a plan to accelerate the overhaul. In their hours together rebuilding the ship, Zhora hoped to repair their relationship. Like a crowbar, he planned to work around the edges of Mikhail's sealed heart.

Mikhail met his gaze and whispered. "We need to talk more." He sounded urgent, apologetic.

"Yes," Zhora answered. He managed a thin smile. "If we can manage to whip this crew and this old ship into shape, there's hope for us yet."

Gorelov marched to the brow's pier-side end, where Captain Borodin stood, waiting. With a crisp salute, the Michman reported. "Comrade Captain, K-389 assembled and ready for inspection."

Borodin pursed his lips, took in a deep breath, and returned Gorelov's salute. The captain led his officers off the brow and as they approached the formation, each officer marched to his division. The captain, the zampolit, and the doctor stood opposite the crew.

"Today we move forward, more focused than before," Captain Borodin began. "Yesterday I approved a plan proposed by energetic and promising officers, Lieutenants Koryavin and Ivankov. As I trust them in this, I trust you to give them your best effort."

He looked to the two and motioned for them to step forward.

Zhora and Mikhail took their place before the captain, saluted, then turned to their crew.

"As of today, the crew will fall under a curfew," Zhora announced. A murmur rippled through the ranks. "Shore patrols will round up any stragglers."

"As established milestones are met, the restrictions will lift," Mikhail added, pointing to a graph on his clipboard. "But as deadlines slip, greater restrictions will apply."

"Officers will observe the curfew too," Zhora explained. Most officers stiffened at this. With a glance back to Zampolit Dimitriev, Zhora continued. "There are no class differences here, after all, are we not Soviets?"

With a strained, squinting smile, Dimitriev nodded.

"In a week's time," Mikhail told them, "we'll evaluate our progress and reap the rewards of our labors or redouble our efforts."

The captain dismissed the crew. And while most either returned to the ship or huddled with their friends to enjoy a cigarette, Gorelov joined the two lieutenants.

"Hope your plan shapes up fast or things'll get worse," he said.

"Michman Gorelov," Zhora began with a smile. "I hope you're part of the solution, rather than an obstacle to it."

"I've set the first week's goal low enough to enhance our chances of success," Mikhail interjected. "A small victory might be what this crew needs first to believe in themselves."

Gorelov flashed his silver-toothed smile. "Smart." He turned to Zhora as he lit a cigarette. "I'm not bucking for captain. Worry about your back-stabbing wardroom. I just want to enjoy ports and endure deployments."

"We're standing on top of each other now," Boreyev sniped. "We've got half a crew in a tenth of the submarine."

Mikhail motioned for Boreyev to follow him. They picked their way through knots of sailors, some working others muttering among themselves. Through the watertight doors just wide enough for each man to fit through single file, Mikhail led them to Level One of Missile Compartment Aft. Between the tubes, where freshly loaded onions draped their sharp earthy aroma over the odors of diesel and fresh paint they stopped. Mikhail drew in a deep breath and waited for his crewmate's complaint.

"Mikhail, I know you and your academy friend think you're smart, but-

Mikhail threw his hands up in frustration. "This only ends two ways, bad or worse. We either find a way to work together or we fail and get orders to auxiliary ships. Captain Borodin will be relieved in disgrace."

Boreyev clutched Mikhail by his collar and drove him into the bulkhead.

"Share some of the captain's favor," Boreyev whispered. "You and your friend soak up all the gravy while the rest of us starve. Starving makes us desperate, dangerous."

"Work with me in this and we'll both see promotions soon enough," Mikhail promised. "Zhora and I came up with this plan, but there's bound to be room for improvement, room for more recognition than just us. Share in the dream and share in the rewards. You'll not be forgotten in the daily reports."

"Competition," Boreyev answered. "Let us divide into

two teams working in parallel, make a sport of the effort."

Mikhail studied the man while he considered his proposal.

"Give me Michman Gorelov and we'll choose our team to compete against you and Zhora."

"We must make this work." Mikhail grasped Boreyev's meaty hands and pulled them free. He straightened his coveralls and glared. "We'll have this fight again on an icebreaker in the Arctic if we fail."

Two weeks into the new plan, amended by Boreyev's desires, Zhora and Mikhail examined their strategy for the coming shift. With the new shift in teams, the stocky Missile Officer and his Michman mentor managed to stay ahead of Mikhail and Zhora's team.

"You haven't batted an eye at the team selection?" Zhora asked as he went over the daily reports with Mikhail.

"I left it to Boreyev. It seemed a small price to pay for his cooperation."

"Only *true* Soviets on his team."

Zhora's emphasis on 'true' concerned Mikhail. Halfway down the rosters he discerned a pattern. No Jews or gypsies marred Boreyev's team. Every derelict Russian, every man of questionable character, everyone who might've earned a blanket party in Lieutenant Boreyev's division missed the cut in his choice of teammates.

"We're left with dead weight and outcasts," Zhora said. "They'll only help cement what all of Boreyev's kind already think of the rest of us."

"Us?"

Zhora tilted his head and winced. "If he knew about us, we'd be on that team too."

"We're leading that team, Zov. What are you getting at?"

Zhora glared.

"He doesn't know anything about us," Mikhail said.

"You're an admiral's son. I'm as Russian as they come."

"Take a walk with me." Zhora grabbed him by the upper arm and escorted him forward. "We'll grab our coats and inspect the hull."

Fifteen minutes and not a word later, they descended the scaffold stairs to the dry dock's basin. From here K-389 loomed above them, her torpedo tubes open, like nostrils of a great cylindrical beast. Wooden blocks bigger than both men, put together, bore the ship's keel and looked tiny as slippers on an elephant. The ship looked ready to topple over. The shipyard cacophony rang in the basin's depths. Zhora marched underneath the ship until his head nearly touched the hull.

"Who are you anymore?" he asked, bewildered. "How can you forget so much of what we were to each other?"

"What? Wait, let me explain," Mikhail implored. An avalanche of memories tumbled through his mind. Frantically, he fought to make quick sense of them, to find the hidden meaning within.

"I loved you!" Zhora screamed. "And you loved me."

"It's not that simple."

"Explain that to me," Zhora insisted. "Spell it out."

The shipyard's whistle blew one long, melancholy note; time for shift change.

"When we met in the academy, I'd never known the love of anyone except my mother. Even she kept herself at arm's length. But what she refused to see, what I couldn't convince her of, was my stepfather's constant abuse. His twisted idea of love left me with no steady frame of reference. I never sought the affections of women because every romantic moment dredged up nightmares too horrible to stomach."

A dozen feet away, from the ballast tank access, three men slid out. They wobbled off, as though drunk or still half asleep from a nap. Oblivious, they stumbled to the basin's steps leading home.

"But I'm not like that," Zhora insisted. "I'm no molester of children. I loved you from the moment I met you. I thought we shared at least that."

Mikhail ducked his head and moved further beneath the ship. He examined the seal of a valve that supplied water to the torpedo tubes. In the center, a titanium ball valve sat tightly in place. He stared at the shining orb as he explained.

"We were roommates, friends. Your help and friendship got me through the academy."

"That's all?" Zhora spat back.

"No, let me finish." Mikhail moved further down the keel, his hand running along the ship's skin above them.

"Our friendship was deeper than any I'd ever known. I imagined you my older brother. You encouraged me. You taught me to embrace who I am and dismiss what others might think."

Mikhail stopped. His gaze dropped to concrete floor between them.

"I love you as much as a man, a real man, can. But when we celebrated our graduation, when we got so drunk the whole night swam in vodka, you kissed me, and I you. That's when the nightmare took hold again. That's why I threw up on you right after you kissed me."

"So, I'm not a real man?"

"That's not what I meant. I know what I mean but I can't find the words to say it." Mikhail shook his head, eyes closed. "I pour my heart into that ship and I hope to earn the respect of every crewmember aboard. We're working so well together, let's focus on that."

"And we'll just forget that I love you?"

"Damn it Zov, will you let go of that?" Mikhail reached out grabbed Zhora by the shoulders. "I care about you, but not like *that*. It never was *that* for me."

"I and your horrific stepfather are the same, monsters?" Zhora muttered through gritted teeth.

"Those are your words, not mine," Mikhail replied.

"*Yebena mat*! If I'd known you'd treat me this way, I'd not have begged for orders to this miserable ship. You were my final hope for a safe, sane life."

Mikhail pulled his friend closer. "Listen, you don't understand the kind of danger you're in. Let me tell you about the death of Seaman Yanukovich."

The Right Girl for You

Zhora glared at his shipmates in *Uspokoysa,* all members of Lieutenant Boreyev's team. The others dared not venture so far from the ship with curfew so early. Only Anatoli's presence lifted his spirits. The jaundiced scarecrow of a doctor sidled up beside him at the bar, offered a broad smile, and clapped Zhora on the shoulder.

"Doctor's orders, that's what I'll tell them when we arrive after your curfew," he said in a hoarse voice. After a series of rib rattling coughs, the man produced a cigarette. He lit it, and a few deep drags settled his breathing. "Hard work needs equally hard play to balance the toxins."

Zhora had been ready to scream. Mikhail's single-mindedness, Boreyev's bigotry, and the news of Seaman Yanukovich; he felt his world implode with every hour. Hope shrank like the sun's rays on the hull of a sinking submarine. Without the doctor's aid, he'd have gone mad within K-389 or been arrested as he marched across the ship's brow.

Knuckle down and see this through, or defect. Both options loomed like twin anvils atop bamboo reeds, waiting for him to test either.

A boney hand slapped him between the shoulder blades. "There you go, lad," the doctor offered with a phlegmy chortle. "Mikhail seemed refreshed whenever he spent time with her, maybe you should try a dose of the same medicine."

Zhora followed the doctor's eyes over his shoulder and up. Nika stood with Boreyev. The troll of a man grinned, patted her cheek, and handed her a fistful of rubles. She returned his kindness with a wincing smile and marched to the bar. After she threw back a shot of vodka, she turned to meet Zhora's gaze. She snickered and inched closer, weaving around the shipyard workers between them. As she approached, Anatoli slipped past her, deeper into the bar, closer to the wall where painted ladies winked and waited.

"Well if it isn't Mikhail's bitchy friend." Nika watched for his reaction, dropped her snide smile and apologized.

"Look, I didn't realize you were coming over or that you'd be so pissed about . . . whatever."

She withdrew a cigarette and lighter from her black vinyl jacket, lit it, and took a few quick puffs, all in one fluid motion. Through the billowing smoke she squinted. "To be fair, it was my apartment."

"Why come over here, why talk to me, why offer any apologies?" Zhora asked, flush with anger.

"Listen, I know I'm only a whore," she began flatly, "but I like Mikhail, sort of. He's pretty fucked in the head, but maybe that's why I get along with him. Besides, for what he pays for, I get a break from mattress wrestling and a couple of laughs."

She took a long drag from her cigarette and blew the smoke right into Zhora's face.

"So," she said with a wink, "I figure you need to blow off some steam so you and Misha can be friends again."

"What? No!" Zhora recoiled.

She tossed her head back and laughed a thick throaty laugh. "Relax pretty boy, I've got just the right *girl* for you." The gleeful glean in her eyes faded. "It'll cost you a little, a finder's fee, if you're interested."

He took her by the arm and briskly escorted her to the bar's corner. "What are you implying?"

"I got confused with Mikhail, I've got to admit," she began. "But you're easy to spot. I know some folks you might like. I could set up a date."

"How, how can you say this?"

Zhora became keenly aware of all the K-389 sailors in the room. Eyes probed him from every corner. He felt them peering between the cracks in his façade, glaring at the true *him* he hid to survive. They'd pounce on him the way they had Seaman Yanukovich any second.

"How can it be so obvious?" he whispered.

"You don't look at me like a fresh steak or an unopened bottle of vodka," she replied with a thin smile. "It's not obvious to your crewmates because they're not accustomed to being ogled by men the way I am."

Sweat evaporated in waves as the room cooled and the pressing gazes shrank back into his paranoid imagination. Unexamined pieces of the puzzle lay before his mind's eye, ready to snap together.

"You mentioned your nights with Misha, a break from mattress wrestling; you two aren't . . .

Nika snickered and shook her head. "No. I thought you two were closer, I thought you knew about his problem."

"So, he doesn't want me," Zhora muttered, "and he doesn't want you either? What does he want?"

"Look," Nika said in a curt tone. "I earn or I freeze, do you want to meet one of my friends or not?"

Zhora shook his head. "I've not got time enough for anything now, but I'd like to meet with you again sometime, to help me understand Mikhail."

Zhora strolled over to Anatoli, who leaned against one of the high tables and spoke in soft tones to one lady. Before Zhora picked up any of their conversation, the woman slapped Anatoli across the cheek and stormed off.

"Come on Doctor, it looks like we'll make curfew after all since we've missed our chance at love."

Anatoli snickered and slid down the table's edge until Zhora caught him. His words poured out like oil.

"The ladies of the Black Sea ports are broader minded. They understand the extra effort it takes to stimulate an advanced mind like mine."

"I don't know what you're talking about," Zhora replied with a groan as he helped the Doctor to his feet, "but if it made a whore blush, you'd better keep it to yourself."

Spinning Out of Control

Two weeks into the revised plan, Boreyev's team earned all the extra time in town. In those weeks Zhora stared daggers into Mikhail as they planned each shift's new priorities. Mikhail tried to focus on the ship's success to get through the tensest moments. Everyone else seemed pleased, everyone except the two men responsible for the turnaround in productivity. Amidst the chatter of hammers and the hum of drills, the ship's intercom blared.

"All officers, report to the Wardroom immediately."

Mikhail slipped in behind Zhora and found they were the last to arrive. The zampolit eyed them, his ruddy fat cheeks arched in a smile that left his eyes narrow slits.

"Chaos!" Dimitriev sneered. "Your little plan to circumvent the system has backfired. The shipyard's buckling under the unexpected strains you're subjecting their equipment to."

Captain Borodin's thick brows wrinkled as he shut his eyes and shook his head. "That's not how I wanted to start this meeting, Comrade Zampolit."

"But they've tried to tamper with an established system," Dimitriev urged. "They've got to be educated on the error of such wild thinking."

The captain motioned to Boreyev. "Tell us, Lieutenant, what happened tonight."

Boreyev stood at attention and spoke as though struggling to withhold his anger. "The shipyard reports that both welding sets assigned to this dry dock are down for repair and will be for some time, a week or two. The shift manager also reports several other tools have fallen apart from misuse and will be unavailable until replacement parts arrive. Also, we've run out of ship-board yellow, to paint the interiors."

Captain Borodin's shoulders sagged. "Are we ruined so quickly?"

"Proven success!" Dimitriev said. "This shipyard has been building ships for decades," he explained. "They've followed a strict plan for those decades and nothing like this ever happened before."

Zhora leaned in and tapped on the blue felt table. "Captain, may I have an hour to investigate this? Something's not making sense."

Mikhail trotted behind Zhora. They jogged through the shipyard with Zhora changing course seemingly at random.

"What're we looking for?" Mikhail asked.

"How should I know what *you're* looking for?" Zhora answered. He glared back over his shoulder. "I hardly know you."

"Come on, now, we've got a lot riding on a good idea. What're we looking for?"

"When I see it," he growled, "I'll be sure to let you know."

Following in his crewmate's wake, he plowed through throngs of workers newly arrived for the second shift. Mikhail caught a flash of something as they passed the linoleum shop. And then he slowed to take in an odd sight.

"Hey, Zhora." His friend continued to stomp through the shipyard.

"Lieutenant Ivankov!" Mikhail shouted louder. "Come look at this, will you?"

Fists knotted and reddening, Zhora stopped and turned. He marched back. Mikhail pointed to someone they knew with something not his.

"Why's Petty Officer Shulga carrying a paint bucket marked 'K-252'?"

Zhora stared, angry and impatient at first, but as he studied the bucket of yellow paint his grimace showed signs of sinister satisfaction. He turned to Mikhail. "Go and collect the shipyard superintendent. Tell him whatever you must to get him down to the ship. I'll meet you in the Wardroom with more information."

"Bribes, you're holding out for bribes?" Captain Borodin asked.

Mikhail had lured the superintendent, Savva Chendev, down with promises of caviar from the captain's stores. An overture to improve relations, he'd called it.

Despite the charges Borodin leveled against Chendev, the man kept his head high and spoke with a noble, authoritative tone.

"Families will starve without your crew's generosity," Chendev insisted. "Our wages buy next to nothing and even if they did, food shortages make a trip to the grocer's a gamble at best. Military food shipments never fail, never fall below quota. We must barter for goods to survive. As long as your crew limits its focus to a few compartments, our bargaining power drops to nothing."

"Outrage!" Dimitriev shouted. "My men have paid you in stores from our own pantry?"

Mikhail watched Captain Borodin scowl at Dimitriev. "You're holding onto the wrong piece of the puzzle Comrade, Zampolit," the captain warned. "And they're not *your* men."

The captain examined Chendev. Mikhail saw a man whose narrow chest puffed with pride. His small raven's eyes gleamed with greed.

"It's how this shipyard has operated for more than my twenty two years working here." Chendev explained. He held his head higher and drew in a deep breath. "Change invites chaos."

Outside the Wardroom, footfalls tromped hard and fast until the door flew open. Wild-eyed, Zhora burst in and searched the room for his captain. Zhora's words tumbled out, like a duffle bag full of grenades.

"The bastards have reallocated our equipment," he shouted between gasps. "One welding machine assigned is in pieces"

Captain Borodin blinked his eyes wider. Others around the table displayed their shock with gasps, gaping mouths and scowls. Zhora continued.

"It's been scavenged over years to keep other welding equipment running."

"We had to put our equipment where it would do the most good," Chendev quipped.

Zhora whirled around and leapt upon the man. A flash of steel shot from the folds of his friend's jacket and pressed into Chendev's flabby throat. Zhora held a linoleum knife. Its sickle edge gleamed. He pressed the blade into the man's flesh near his jugular.

"I should tear your throat open and paint this ship with your blood," Zhora bellowed.

Mikhail inched closer to his friend and reached out for the knife. Zhora glared back.

"Please, Zov," Mikhail began softly. "Please don't do this, don't ruin what we've accomplished so far."

Chendev's lips trembled as he pleaded. "Please, I'm only looking out for my people."

"There are other ways," Mikhail offered as he looked at both men. "The superintendent is right about one thing, the stores in Komsomolsk lack much and military food stores *are* given high priority."

He looked to Captain Borodin. "There are ways we might find to keep your men working and their families from starving."

The captain nodded. "When our galley is restored, we will open it to all working aboard K-389. I'm sure no one will object if your men take a portion of these meals home."

Dimtriev's jaw dropped. But before he spoke, the captain offered his own justification.

"Future soldiers and sailors of the Soviet Union live in those homes. While we ready ourselves to defend against enemies abroad, we can defeat starvation at home."

Zhora pulled away from Chendev and turned to Captain Borodin. Mikhail plucked the weapon from his friend's hand and examined it. A glistening droplet of crimson clung to the blade's tip.

Captain Borodin stood and looked at his men. "Leave, everyone except the superintendent."

Silence reverberated in those first moments before the officers filed out. Dimitriev remained in his seat until the captain's glare convinced him otherwise. He sidestepped past Zhora and Mikhail, giving each an admonishing stare before he exited.

"Lieutenant Koryavin," the captain growled. "Escort Lieutenant Ivankov to the torpedo room and have him kept under guard."

In the torpedo room, minutes crept by without a word between its only inhabitants. Gutted months ago and neglected for higher priority systems, the room bore decapitated gauge boards. Tangles of pipe and wire hung like winter branches and withered vines over the vacancies created. Mikhail occupied himself in the expanding silence by assessing the room's readiness. An hour passed before Mikhail broke.

"What happened?" he asked.

"My world's spinning out of control," Zhora snapped. "I couldn't let one more thing slip, not at the hands of a thief; especially a pompous thief."

"I think you're blowing this all out of proportion."

Zhora threw his hands up. "My father disowned me, my

best hope for love can't stand the thought, you've handed the ship's recovery plan to a man who's all but confessed to Yanukovich's murder."

Zhora smiled with his face yet glared with his eyes as he continued. "I'd say, up until that sniveling toad threatened to end our repairs, I've held up rather nicely."

"You're still a naval officer, still my best friend, still smarter than that brute, Boreyev."

"Listen to yourself, Misha," Zhora countered. "You've sacrificed every shred of dignity to a submarine that'll forget you before you set foot ashore."

"What're you talking about?"

"Boreyev wins the captain's heart with each success. Never mind that we masterminded the process, or that you gave Boreyev everything he wanted just to buy his support." Zhora shook his head. "And don't even get me started on us, or Nika. What's love without intimacy? What's a man without love?"

"Tell me, you're so clever," Mikhail whispered angrily.

"You're a corpse waiting to happen, a martyr aching for a cause."

Mikhail leaned back upon the bulkhead behind him and slid to sit upon the deck just inside the torpedo room. He stared blankly at the torpedo tube doors ahead. More open-ended pipes rose from between the tubes like a cathedral organ. "I suppose you're right."

Zhora turned to face his friend and shook him by the shoulder. "Wake up! I'm not telling you this to help you justify your pitiful life. I'd hoped to wake up the brave farm boy I once knew. Don't let the world walk you to your grave. Do something! Fight back! Take charge!"

"This isn't what I expected to find," Captain Borodin interjected from the watertight door. "Is this how you handle prisoners I put under your command?" His voice lacked the grave undertone of before, though his displeasure rang true enough. He motioned for the two to accompany him. "Let's settle this in my stateroom."

Mikhail ushered Zhora through the passageways,

up a series of ladders, to the stateroom just outside the communications hub and the Command Center. As he entered, a hushed silence enveloped him.

"You threatened a man's life," Captain Borodin began. He stared into Zhora's eyes as though searching for answers. "I had to bargain for yours as a result."

"He admitted to a crime and-

"He did," the captain said as he cut Zhora off. "But did you need to kill him?"

Zhora shook his head. "I only meant to scare him into giving us what we deserve."

"I saw murder in your eyes."

"Outrage," Zhora argued, "nothing more."

Captain Borodin drove his fist down onto his desk. "And you deserve more outrage than your Captain? *I'll* have to answer for any slip in the schedule! Do you deserve more outrage than the zampolit who depends on a distrusting crew to keep his position secure?"

"No Comrade Captain."

"You didn't see *me* with a knife in my hand," Borodin said as he stood and stepped closer to Zhora, until they stood six centimeters apart. "If I could slay the bastards responsible *and* replace them with eager and competent workers . . ." His voice trailed off and he found himself staring at his own clenched fist.

"A crew must act as one," he explained. "The officers must be of one mind. So long as we do, we carry the power and respect of our entire wardroom with us into the torpedo room, the engine room, anywhere we go alone to take charge of men too scared or too ill-equipped to carry on. Don't let them see you lose control or they'll crumble when there's nothing left to hold onto except your leadership."

Zhora swallowed hard and stiffened. "Yes Comrade Captain." His stolid gaze wavered.

"Something more troubles you, Lieutenant?"

With a nod, Zhora's words avalanched. "Boreyev, Lieutenant Boreyev, he's been given an unfair advantage in this competition he's devised. We stand no chance and

65

he's excluded all the . . ."

"Sloths?"

"And more, Captain, it's hard to detail what he's done," Zhora continued. "No Jews, gypsies, or other *undesirables*."

Captain Borodin looked at Mikhail. "Is this true?"

Mikhail nodded.

"How, how is this possible?"

Mikhail looked to the floor between them before he answered. "Lieutenant Boreyev needed convincing about our plan. He fought to return to the old ways until we worked out a competitive option at his request. I gave him complete control in team selection, hoping he'd be better for the ship if he were part of the winning team."

The captain shook his head. "A noble thought, but you've cheated half the crew out of any chance for a night on the town."

"I wasn't thinking of the crew," Mikhail countered flatly. "The ship must come first."

"Don't ever say that again." Captain Borodin's grim gaze chilled Mikhail. His stomach solidified.

"Ships are built, deployed, and eventually rust. But these men, you must tend to like the miracles they are. They are links in an ever-expanding chain, chains linked side by side to hold up the world. We all must remember who we stand beside as we tempt the deep and descend into darkness. This ship won't save you, won't love you, or mourn your passing."

He clasped Mikhail by the shoulders. "It's time you loved more than steel and a uniform." With a sideways glance at Zhora he spoke. "And you need to restrain your enthusiasm for justice. We've got to make this system work or be swallowed by the anarchy."

"Captain," Zhora ventured, "what's to become of us?"

"We'll keep this outburst to ourselves in the wardroom. You'll honor my advice. Disgrace my wardroom again and there's no room for further mercy. You've been warned."

Nemnogo Vydra

TWELVE

Zhora looked to his watch, nearly midnight. He drew in a deep breath of icy air and let out a sigh. Relieved by the alley's aromas, mildew, melting snow mixed with coal, diesel and urine. He favored this stench tonight over the shipyard and submarine. He looked up and admired the night sky. Bookended by drab apartments of Komsomolsk, the crisp air lent crystal clarity to the sea of stars. So clean and bright, aloft in a velvet tapestry, their beauty held him motionless.

Captain Borodin had relaxed the curfew for a few days. He'd said the crew deserved it. In reality, half the crew needed it to carry on. With no hope of outperforming Boreyev's handpicked team, Zhora and Mikhail expected nothing. But true to his word, the captain valued his crew too much to keep them bottled up forever. The crew's built up tensions, shackled to their work with no relief in sight, brought his mind back to his actions earlier, with the prostitute, Ivan.

Exhausted and ashamed, relieved and invigorated, Zhora tried to sort his conflicted heart. The young man he'd spent the evening with hadn't disappointed, but he hadn't been anything more than a diversion, a hired therapist for frustrations impossible to diminish any other way. Of course there was another way, but a companion, an equal in a meaningful relationship, that door slammed shut as fast as he'd tried to open it with Mikhail.

A snicker escaped as he wondered if his father ever fought to shed the same shame. To pay for a lustful substitute for true intimacy, had his father heart enough to feel the difference? Funnier still, the father who felt no shame from his shallow adulteries felt shame enough and more for the son whose relationships he labeled perverse.

A glint of light caught his eye and he stopped. A phone booth beckoned. Had it materialized in this desperate moment or had he not seen it these past few weeks until he needed to see it? One person remained who might love him enough to rescue him. One person warmed his heart and tugged at his soul when he thought of her. It surprised him to look down and see the receiver in his hand as he stood in the booth, unaware of how he got there.

It took an hour to make the connection and five minutes of ringing before she answered.

"Hello?"

"Hello, Mother."

"*Nemnogo Vydra*, what's the matter?"

Little Otter, her pet name for him since his childhood days, it spiraled back time and buckled his knees. Not since his adolescence had he heard her kindness. Tears welled up and stung as the cold siphoned their heat.

"Oh, Mama, I've been through so much," his own trembling voice startled him. "Father sent me away and I've no one out here, no one to trust, to turn to, to love."

"I know, I know," she offered. "He told me about it after you left."

"It's so hard and I'm so alone. It seems like everyone's turning their back on me."

"Have you tried to meet a girl out there? I hear Eastern girls are very good to their husbands."

"What?" The phone slipped from his fingers and clattered against the glass. He scrambled to pick it back up. "Mother, you know my interests lie elsewhere."

She cleared her throat and leveled her tone. "Teenagers go through confusing phases as they grow up. You've indulged it long enough. Set your mind right and accept your responsibilities as a man."

His heart sank and his blood boiled. A dark door in the corner of his mind burst open and he remembered the day when he stopped being her little otter. She'd discovered his secret and shut her heart to him. She didn't despise him as his father had, but she shelved her love and withheld her affections.

"I held you too much as a child," she said, her voice thick with guilt and pity. "I loved you too much and it stunted your development into manhood."

"No, you don't know what you're talking about," he screamed. "My heart's path, fate laid out before we knew each other, before I took my first breath."

She snorted. "You can't know that. Why would you say that?"

"Because I know that I've known my differentness since my first memories."

"I can't support this fantasy of yours. I'm sorry you're going through a tough time, but it had to happen sooner or later. You stubbornly held onto this crutch of yours long enough. It's time to bear the burden of manhood. It's time to take a wife, give me grandchildren, and take your career more seriously."

Zhora fell to the booth's floor, his breathing fast and shallow. His mother's voice cried out, small and tinny. The scratched glass pressed around him and the air thickened until drawing it in felt like a tug of war. Blackness tightened his vision, a noose of emptiness.

"Rough night last night, Zov?" Mikhail's friendly tone scraped across Zhora's heart like fingernails across an itching scab.

"Very," he answered curtly. "Let's focus on our plan for the missile compartments."

Mikhail winced before he answered. "It should be pretty

simple, they're nearly identical."

"Will you take this seriously?" he spat back, his neck afire and fists clenched. "I've no intention of being blamed for an oversight in this project. It's my last remaining chance to leave this place in anything other than a coffin or irons."

"Calm down, Zov." Mikhail clasped him by the shoulder. "The superintendent's been cooperative, Captain Borodin evened out the teams, and the shipyard workers seem happy to eat with the crew. They built the galley and mess hall in record time."

"And I've eaten every dinner since then in the Engine Room."

"You did put a knife to the man's throat. The captain had to do something."

"And now you dine with him every evening," Zhora observed. "Have you made your peace with this extortionist's schemes?"

Mikhail stood still and stared into Zhora's eyes. Pain, sorrow and compassion, like storm clouds on a blustering day each darkened his gaze briefly. What remained hurt Zhora to behold, knowing what they'd never become.

With an emerging smile, Mikhail spoke. "I'll join you for dinner tonight, if you'll have me."

More salt in a fresh wound, yet . . . "Sure, Misha, we'll have a grand feast amid the turbines and compressors."

Half a day later, the two sat atop the port propeller shaft with a towel for a tablecloth between them. A broken loaf of black bread, a bottle of vodka, and a tin filled with fish chowder sat on the cloth.

"I'm not sure if you'll save me from myself or drive me mad," Zhora said with a half-smile.

Mikhail's broad grin threw Zhora's heart into a fog again. But when his old friend's features turned frightened and his pallor faded, Zhora turned to see what caught the man's attention.

Captain Borodin stood staring through them, his coat glistening with melted snow, his features gaunt.

"Petty Officer Shulga has been slaughtered. I need you, Lieutenant Ivankov to join Doctor Anatoli. You two will work with the police." Sunken eyes widened. "Find the madman responsible."

Black Wharf

THIRTEEN

On the long ride in the police car from the shipyard gate to the morgue, Zhora dreaded this first step in the murder investigation.

Under the flickering florescent bulbs, Petty Officer Shulga's corpse seemed to twitch. Shadows played across pale blotchy skin. His body lay on a concrete examination table. Zhora's attention drifted up to the man's throat. It'd been ripped apart with a chunk the size and shape of a small lemon missing. But as barbaric the wound appeared, the surrounding skin bore no sign of blood.

"This is how you found him?" Anatoli asked the medical examiner, startling a shudder from Zhora.

"Aside from cutting away his clothes, yes," the city's medical examiner explained. The doctor's apologies and excuses had begun the moment Anatoli introduced himself. Though normally a hospital physician, he'd been recruited often by the police to examine any suspicious corpses they stumbled upon.

"I'll want to look at those clothes," Zhora interjected. "Hopefully no crucial clues have been obliterated."

"No, no," the doctor whimpered as he fidgeted and shuffled out. "I carefully bagged up the boy's uniform. It's in a locker. I'll go and get it."

Anatoli bent over the body and ran his gloved hand along the skin from Shulga's knee to his ribs, occasionally applying pressure. He stood, rubbed his chin and frowned.

Zhora's stomach clenched while he watched. The same fingers the doctor had touched the corpse with now stroked his chin and played with his lower lip.

"What is it?" Zhora whispered.

The medical examiner entered the room holding up the bag like a prize fish. "Here you are."

"Was there a large pool of blood at the scene of the crime?" Anatoli asked.

"No, minimal blood was spattered, signs of a struggle, but hardly any pooled around the body. Why?"

"This man's been exsanguinated," Anatoli reached down and pressed at the flesh around Shulga's torn throat. "It's unnatural, the absence of blood."

"A gaping wound like that makes it very easy to bleed out."

"But no blood near the wound," Anatoli explained. "And none pooled in parts of his body beneath the level of the wound. Eventually, the outpour ceases as the body's blood pressure drops. I'd guess he'd been hung upside down to lose as much blood as he has. But even that wouldn't have so completely emptied him. It's as though he were siphoned dry."

"But who would do that and why?" Zhora asked.

"Your friend went to the old docks, Black Wharf," the medical examiner explained with a shrug. "Maybe he got in the middle of something or saw something he shouldn't."

"Justice stands on firmer ground than 'maybe'," Zhora said as he stared at his crewmate's corpse. "Drugs," he blurted in a daze, "has his body been tested for drugs?"

"Samples have been sent to the hospital, but there's no telling how long before any results come back."

"Begin your autopsy, Doctor Anatoli," Zhora ordered. "I'll examine the scene of the crime."

"Find what you're looking for before it gets dark," the

policeman insisted as he scanned their surroundings nervously.

"You fear these people?" Zhora asked. "You're their only hope for order and peace."

"They don't want either."

Zhora's nostrils flared and his palms sweated. Fear of those unseemly unseens didn't phase him, it was the neighborhood. On the night of Petty Officer Shulga's murder, Zhora had been only a block away.

"What all goes on along Black Wharf?" he asked.

"Thugs, drugs, and worse, all along the old docks."

"Worse?" Zhora asked. "And you allow it?"

"I obey my superiors," the policeman spat back. "I patrol where I'm told and I respond to the dispatches." He dropped his gaze and stared where Shulga's body once lay. "This place is extra dangerous for anybody in a uniform."

The concrete street gave way to a planked boardwalk beneath a wooden wharf. Nearly black, the timbers gave a little, almost like thin carpet, as Zhora walked around searching for clues. The Amur's wavelets lapped against pylons beneath his feet and echoed off the wharf's underside above. From the corner of his eye a glint of light caught his attention. The setting sun's rays played along the water's surface and the reflected light danced among the rafters above him. But what he spied came from a crevice between the wharf's supports and a building old as the port itself. A pair of eyes stared into the river's glittering surface, unmoving, unflinching.

Zhora crept closer and discovered a face wrapped around those mesmerized eyes. Wrinkled and gaunt, mouth agape and eyes vacant, the man looked to be about forty yet his dark brown hair and style of clothes suggested a man half that age.

"You there," Zhora whispered. "Did you see my man murdered last night?"

"I screamed," the man murmured. "It's all I could do."

Zhora leaned closer. The stranger withdrew deeper into his crevice.

"Tell me more."

With a blank-faced, mouth agape, he answered. "Eyes big as the moon, I drowned in them."

"The murderer?"

He nodded slowly and cringed. "Looked hideous, like a sewer rat."

"Who, what?"

A smile dawned. Empty eyes warmed. "Then he looked like my cousin, except for the red hair."

"Which was it man? Think!"

The vagrant met Zhora's gaze and frowned as though uncertain of his own testimony. "He was a sewer rat until I screamed, then he was my cousin."

The policeman stepped into the crevice and tugged at the gibbering codger. "Come on old man, we'll see if a night in jail will help you make more sense."

The man chuckled. "Yes, that's it. Lock me up where my cousin can't get me." He clambered for the officer's hands and pulled himself to his feet. "I'll be safe there."

As he pulled the filthy madman from his hole, the policeman looked over his shoulder to Zhora.

"He's fried his mind long before last night. I wouldn't put much faith in his testimony."

"It sounds like I should question his cousin," Zhora offered.

The policeman examined his prisoner at arm's length. The man cringed and threw up his arms. The policeman grabbed the man by the chin and brought him out into the light.

"Boris? Boris Koplikov? Is that you?"

The man smiled and nodded.

The policeman's jaw sagged and his eyes widened. "I went to school with this man. We're the same age."

"What happened?" Zhora asked.

"Drugs," the policeman answered shaking his head. "It must've started after the cousin you want to question died. He drowned two years ago."

An Angel All the Same

FOURTEEN

Mikhail stood at the apartment's window. The unsleeping, tireless shipyard stood out. The eye-searing blue-white of a welder's torch and the shower of embers from a grinder's wheel gave the appearance of a festive event. Mikhail knew better. He examined the streets below. A fractured web of streetlights offered sparse oases among a desert of black. In those dark streets a murderer lurked.

"It's your move," Nika said, a little more forcefully this time.

Mikhail returned to the table, examined the board between them, and made his move.

Nika laughed and took the piece he'd just put in jeopardy. "I'm winning. You should make up your mind to play the game or chase your friend."

Mikhail moved again and cut her chuckling short. "Only the end determines the winner."

Nika's pouting frown blossomed. She paused to pour herself another drink. "You really love Zhora, even though you say you don't."

"He's the closest friend I've ever had."

"That's nice." Nika offered a brief grin before she focused on their game.

Mikhail sat across from her and poured himself a glassful of vodka. He looked through the clear liquor, through the smudged cup at the chessboard. As he lifted the glass higher he found himself looking at Nika. Peering over the edge he examined her while she studied the board. Her intense concentration nearly made him laugh. Pursed lips, creased brow, and piercing gaze, showed that she took her chess seriously. He gulped down half his glass, took a breath, then finished it and smiled.

"You're the closest girlfriend I've ever had."

She shot him a glare and scooted her chair back from the table. "Don't say that. Don't say that and mean it."

"What?"

"First of all, you're paying me. Secondly, I'm simply not girlfriend material. Thirdly, this is usually when the paying stops and the fighting begins."

"This has happened before?"

"Every once in a while, some clod gets it in his head that because we've shared a bed and I've laughed at their jokes, we'd be perfect together. Then I open their eyes. They cry or scream, sometimes take a swing at me. After that, we part ways, both of us pretty pissed."

A smile grew across Mikhail's face. "So if I stop paying you-

"Don't even joke about that."

"But you're not really doing your job, are you?" He felt the chilly room grow warm. "As I see it, I should only pay half what everybody else does."

"What? We tried that once, remember? If you're going to try and back out of what you owe me-

Mikhail stood and darted around the table. Nika jumped up from her chair and took it in her hands, holding it out to fend him off.

"I'm only half a man until I break down whatever barrier stands between me and intimacy. We've had several nights together since that first one. I'm ready to try again."

Nika raised the chair higher between them. "Sex I can do, dating's whole different animal." As she set her weapon down she wondered aloud. "What makes you think you'll not throw up this time?"

"Just relax and let me try."

"You're cleaning it up all by yourself this time if you get

sick again."

Mikhail nodded as he inched closer.

"That look in your eyes," she ventured, "I'm not sure I like it."

He reached out and touched her cheek. Once closer, he nudged under her chin to put her lips on a collision course with his. She put a hand up between them.

"No kissing," she insisted in a whisper. "I've already told you, no kissing."

"But why?"

"Don't push me another millimeter. You won't like what you get."

Mikhail backed away half a step. "Okay." He took her by the hand and led her to the bed. She reached up to unbutton her shirt but he grabbed her hand.

"Let me do everything, I think that'll make this go better than last time."

With that, he took her in his arms and laid her down on the bed. Slowly he unbuttoned her blouse and continued to undress her. With each step he paused to touch her soft pale skin and fought to accept the gentle purpose in his efforts over the nightmare pounding at the cellar door of his mind.

Mikhail drew in a deep breath, held it, and let it out slowly.

"That turned out . . . alright," Nika said.

"Wow, that's the best you can come up with? It must've been pretty bad."

"Okay, so not much happened. That's an improvement from the puking." Nika rolled over onto her side and propped her head up. She traced her fingernail through his chest hairs and smiled. "I thought you liked my honesty."

"Okay, if we're being honest, why won't you consider taking our relationship further?"

"Further than merchant and customer?" She offered a quizzical grimace. "I'm not sure where 'further' leads."

Mikhail glared at her.

"Girlfriends want husbands and wives want babies," she explained. "I'm not geared for marriage, too many bad relationships."

Mikhail turned on his side to face her. "I want a woman that understands me enough to be patient and can work with me through moments like this."

"Stop paying me and see how much patience I have."

Anger simmered in Mikhail's forehead and the pressure pushed words out too fast. "You're a whore, I get it. You get money, I get attention. You cater to my needs because that's what puts food on the table and keeps you from the streets. I get it."

"Good." Her stern features hit him like gust from the wintry city streets.

Mikhail pulled himself up and left the bed. "Shut up. Shut up and listen, really listen." He paced across the apartment. Turning, he explained. "I paid to come up here, I always have. But I didn't pay to have someone offer understanding when I lost control. I didn't pay for you to share your pain. You did that on your own."

Nika got up from the bed and marched into the bathroom. After a few minutes, the toilet flushed and she marched back out, her heels thumping every step to where her clothes lay. As she dressed, she replied.

"I'll keep that in mind for the future: don't sympathize with whimpering men, they'll cling to you like a starving orphan."

"Damn it, I want to slap that attitude right out of your mouth."

Nika stiffened and clenched her fists. "Here we go. This is what I've been waiting for."

Mikhail marched to the corner, beside the bed, and dressed himself. From the edge of his vision, he watched her stand, stunned as he got ready and headed for the door. Her posture stiffened and she crossed her arms.

"This is what I've been talking about," she said. "It never fails."

"You push me away, what else can I do?"

And then it hit him. He spun around and glared at her, incredulous at what he'd discovered. "This is what you've wanted all along. This is your method to keep the pain away."

"Pissing people off, driving them away? How's that helpful to me? My business is making people happy."

Mikhail stepped closer. "We're more alike than you realize. I can't take hold of a woman without my nightmares jumping out at me. You can't hear someone profess their love without remembering how hurtful love's been. We're both broken halves, two different sides of the same tormented coin."

He slid his hand around the back of her neck and drew her near. His breathing felt strained, like his lungs were a guitar and his breaths strummed across the strings. He reached up and took her chin between his fingers. She pulled back, eyes aglow with indignant anger. Her nostrils flared and she struggled to break free, not enough to escape, not violent enough to erupt into a melee, but just enough to let him know she wrestled with doubt and fear.

Mikhail's heart swelled as he spoke from it, like a gushing fountain. "You beauty goes deeper than this. You've shown me a way out of a dark and lonely life. You've shared your tragedy and helped me face mine." He winced and smiled. "Despite your past my heart sees an angel all the same."

He let go and she stumbled backward. Mikhail threw his coat over one arm walked out.

Ethical Ambiguity

"It makes so little sense," Anatoli muttered and sighed.

Zhora poured over their notes in the cramped Sick Bay. A mad witness saw his dead cousin, or a sewer rat, gnawing on Petty Officer Shulga's throat. The body had been bled dry with uncanny efficiency. The undigested pills in Shulga's stomach indicated he'd only recently purchased narcotics stolen from the local hospital or pharmacy. The few denizens of Black Wharf they questioned kept tightlipped about everything.

"Find the bastards yet?" Michman Gorelov stuck his head through the open doorway.

"There are so few clues to go on," Anatoli explained. "We're doing the best we can."

"We need to send those shits a message," Gorelov said.

"And what would that be?" Zhora asked.

"Don't fuck with us."

Zhora approached Gorelov until their faces stood millimeters apart. "And you'd make sure nothing like that ever crossed their minds again?"

"I heard you were smart," Gorelov answered with a crooked grin. He rubbed his thumb across his knuckles.

"And I heard you might share something in common with our quarry," Zhora countered.

Gorelov frowned and jerked back. "What?"

"Murder, Yanukovich's murder to be precise."

"Wait," the Michman said as he backed up, "that was

different."

"Seems like some parts of the crew act just like those scoundrels in town, they keep secrets to protect their own."

"Yanukovich's case is closed. Shulga's needs your full attention. The crew wants justice."

Zhora straightened his tunic and stood at attention. "Michman, Gorelov, I order you to inform the crew that the section of town known as Black Wharf is off limits until my investigation comes to a close. Furthermore, the men are to go into town in groups of two or more, never alone."

"Aye, Comrade Lieutenant." With that, he marched off.

"Well handled, if you're looking to make an enemy of the Michman," Anatoli warned.

"That man's barbaric justice hurts innocent and guilty alike," Zhora shot back.

"It's kept navies running since men first braved the seas. Men like that have kept an iron grip on the crew and allowed ship's officers to concern themselves with tactics and strategy."

"I should ignore what his iron grip meant to Yanukovich?"

"Why concern yourself with a death that happened before you reported aboard? We've a perfectly nasty mystery with Petty Officer Shulga's case."

"Mikhail told me a little about it," Zhora muttered. "I can't believe he let that incident pass without a more thorough investigation."

Anatoli looked up from his notebook. The doctor's watery bloodshot eyes shocked Zhora with their venom. "Don't doubt Lieutenant Koryavin's commitment. I think he realized what he was up against and declined to unnecessarily unhinge the command for no gain. No murderer would've been found." Anatoli returned to his notes and shook his head. "The navy's ways are not always the kindest."

Zhora examined the doctor and wondered aloud. "Everyone calls you by your first name, even the captain. Why is that?"

Anatoli kept his focus on the page and chuckled. "I'm

a doctor, not a proper officer. Familiarity lends comfort to those I treat. They trust old Doctor Anatoli."

The man's eyes lost their twinkle in that moment and his voice struck an odd note.

Anatoli tapped his pencil at his notes. "Some of Shulga's nails were bent back, as though he scraped them across a hard surface. Under one nail I found some strange material. I should get it under the microscope."

Zhora leaned over the Sick Bay examination table and stared down at the doctor. "Can we not trust each other?"

"We all have secrets," Anatoli admitted without looking up from his scribblings. "We guard them because they threaten our lives. They hang over us like an executioner's axe." He sat up, put his hands into his lower back and stretched backward with a sigh. Grabbing his head by the chin and back of his head, he twisted it left and right until a soft pop elicited a satisfied groan. "Wouldn't you agree, Zhora Ivankov?"

The way Anatoli used his name, like he'd snuck into his heart and took a peek, made Zhora nervous. Hairs tickled against the back of his collar.

"You know my father?"

Anatoli shook his head. "I only know Admiral Alexi Ivankov by reputation. I see a man before me, superior in wit but lacking the ethical ambiguity of a successful flag officer."

"I nearly sliced a man's throat in the wardroom," Zhora interjected, "that's hardly ethical."

"Those are the actions of a passionate officer, eager to see the task through, not a man willing to ship his son to the farthest reaches of civilization to have his talents wasted on an old missile boat."

Zhora smiled and nodded. "Well done, doctor, well done. Does everyone aboard K-389 wonder why I'm so far from home?"

"Only those who know your name and can put a puzzle together, a puzzle with only two pieces."

"Ah, but the puzzle still remains incomplete," Zhora

added. "Are there any speculations about why I'm here?"

"Some believe we're destined for a special mission, precious to the admiralty. Others believe you dishonored your family somehow."

"A very bourgeois term, dishonored, don't you think?"

The doctor laughed until his coughing cut it short. "Dimitriev would certainly agree."

"And so we're back where we began," he mused. *Or are we?*

Anatoli shrugged. "I suppose so. I suppose we'll just carry on keeping our secrets to ourselves."

Clever, Doctor. You've managed to bring up your hypotheses and gauge my reaction. You know more about me now than when our conversation began. Your kind old doctor's guise caught me off guard, a mistake I'll try not to make ever again.

The doctor shot Zhora a sideways glance and offered a thin knowing smile.

"I think I'll go back to the docks tonight," Zhora said. "I'll see if tongues loosen in the moonlight."

Anatoli sprang from his chair, only to wince and stumbled against the bulkhead. He rubbed his lower back. "Don't go. It'll be too dangerous. If the murderer doesn't get you, cutthroats and thugs will."

"I'll follow my own advice, Doctor," Zhora replied. He placed a hand on Anatoli's shoulder and urged the sallow scarecrow to sit. "I'll recruit someone to join me."

The Red Fleet's Wrath

SIXTEEN

Zhora looked to his left, through the bathroom door, at Ivan. The man lay on the bed, fingers interlocked behind his neck, only a swath of sheets across his waist. Handsome for a street urchin, Ivan would have to do for now. If Anatoli knew what he'd meant by recruiting help for his investigation . . .

What would he do?

He realized how little he knew the doctor. He turned again and watched brownish water slog from the faucet.

"It's always like this?" Zhora asked. "The water, I mean."

"Yeah, you just have to be patient, sweetheart. Don't get your panties in a bunch."

Zhora examined himself in the mirror. Stress and confinement within the submarine had taken its toll. Pasty, his skin looked dull in the bare-bulb light. Large eyes looked like shadowed caverns with dark circles beneath them.

"What do you know about the sailor murdered near here?"

"I didn't do it."

"I haven't accused you, Ivan," Zhora said through his teeth. "I'm trying to bring this madman to justice."

"Well if I didn't do it, and you're not accusing me, why are we talking about it?"

Now grey, the water chugged and sputtered. Zhora sighed.

"As I've said," Zhora began before he took in a deep breath, "I'm trying to track this killer down before more die."

"I stay away from trouble," Ivan explained. "I don't know any more than you. You're the first sailor I've seen in months."

The faucet spat and hissed. Clear water flowed and looked magical in contrast with what had come before. Zhora shoved a dingy cup under the trickling stream. A knock at the door startled him.

"I'm busy," Ivan answered in a sing-song voice. "You'll have to come back later."

Zhora upended the cup and drank. Grit slid down his throat. Grit shifted between his toes. A gritty film covered everything in the tiny apartment. He hated that he'd come to such a place, that he'd sunk to such desperation.

With the new year, 1983, perhaps a new start waited around the next corner. Maybe the doors shut by his father in the West might open in the East. No more skulking around. So far from the Kremlin, a chance encounter might provide the relationship he'd hoped for with Misha.

The apartment door shattered inward. Two figures rushed in. Ivan shrieked. Muffled voices roared and growled. The two men leapt on Ivan and hammered him with short clubs.

Zhora shook off the shock and lunged at the nearest man. Thick chested, with powerful arms, his foe shrugged him off and cursed.

"You killed one of our crew," a familiar voice bellowed behind him. "Feel the Red Fleet's wrath!"

A club crashed across Zhora's head. The room dimmed and tipped over. Warm water trickled down his neck. No, not water, blood. The floor bucked and swayed. He struggled to stand. His eyes fell in out of focus on a man standing before him.

"*Bozhe moi*! It's Lieutenant Ivankov," the masked man exclaimed.

"Get out of here," the thick man shouted.

Ivan whimpered somewhere behind and beneath Zhora.

"I knew something was wrong about you," the barrel chested man said.

As Zhora's jumbled head settled, the stranger's stance and stature came together.

"Boreyev!"

The man grabbed Zhora's wrist and slung him into the dresser. Zhora slid to the floor. He rolled over and stared into Ivan's bloody, bludgeoned face.

"I didn't want to kill anyone," Boreyev whined. "But too much has happened."

The club came down with a deep, wet thump, right into Ivan's temple.

"I'm doing the navy a favor by killing a perverted monster like you."

Zhora watched the club swing down in a blur. He threw his hand up and stopped it. The club made a loud crack and his arm went numb. Then he realized the club hadn't cracked.

Floodgates of adrenaline coursed through him. He sprang to his feet, vaguely aware his right arm wriggled like a rubber bicycle tire. He drove his left fist into Boreyev's masked face and heard the pig's nose as it caved in with a satisfying crunch.

The club found his ribs, left then right, then all over again. Each blow drove him back until he crashed through glass, through the window.

He tumbled for hours it seemed. He counted the broken bones and numbered the slivers of falling glass as he somersaulted to the street below. He stared at the cobblestones as they raced to meet him. A pain-tsunami washed over him and submerged him in shock. The world's lights and sounds were filtered by it, muffled under the agony.

Nothing. He felt nothing except a burning pain in his neck. The river, he smelled the river. A breeze dragged across his face like icy sheer drapes. He was moving, sliding along the Amur River's litter-cluttered shore. He vaguely realized his feet as they rumbled and bumped along behind him over rocks and garbage. He floated along the Amur, but not in it, beside it. The sharp pain in his neck and shoulder became more distinct. An iron vice pierced his skin and tugged at his flesh. He was being dragged. High grass parted around him and folded back across his path. His captor pulled him deeper into the marsh. Not more than ten meters, just far enough for the grass to envelope him. The vice dropped him and his head thumped to the damp cold ground.

Zhora awoke, certain only minute or two had passed. The moon hovered close, looked larger than normal. A faint red aura surrounded it. He blinked, squinted and realized he stared into a man's face. Deep red hair, coarse and braided at the ends framed a face pale and bright as the full moon. Eyes ink black stared into his. They shone with the brilliance of intensity and burned with hunger.

"So beautiful," Zhora managed.

"It is a trick. You will see my true face soon enough. You are dying," the man said. "I plucked you from your death to give it more meaning. It will sustain me another few days."

"Who are you?"

"Who I am hasn't mattered in centuries. I am part of nature's brutal balance."

"A murderer? No, more than that?" Zhora recalled Shulga's corpse, exsanguinated, clean and clear of any blood. "A vampire?"

The man's eyes strained at the word as though it dragged across his soul like a serrated blade. All pretense of humanity fell from his gaze as he reached for Zhora and opened his mouth, exposing two elongated fangs. The beauty faded. A grey-skinned devil with black veins and filthy strands of matted red hair drew near. The creature's breath stank like a butcher's garbage bin, full of ripened blood and flesh.

"Wait," Zhora exclaimed with a painful cough. "I can offer you something."

"Only your blood."

"The police, the military, my comrades," Zhora spat out in a panic, "they'll all be looking for me. We've assembled some evidence and a witness. You need me to keep you hidden in the city. They'll hunt you down, day and night."

The creature uttered a low growl. "Is no place safe? Has humanity overrun the world?"

"Help me get to a hospital," Zhora pleaded. "Save me and I promise I'll save you."

"My keen senses do not err, you will die soon. Your promise means less than your blood."

Again the creature opened its mouth and drew near.

"Wait! Make me a vampire and I'll guarantee you a safe home forever," Zhora's breath caught in his throat as he realized what he'd said.

Agony struck where his neck and shoulder met. Along his veins and arteries the pain leapt out like chain lighting. Muscles barely alive imploded with pain. His stomach clenched and his lungs emptied. His fractured vision dimmed until the world's curtain descended with a heavy velvet silence.

It's Like Borscht

At the dry dock's end, across the thick gate that held back the Amur River's ink-black waters, seven sailors aimed their AK-47's toward the heavens. One final thunderous salvo and Lieutenant Zhora Ivankov's memorial concluded. Mikhail leaned against the guardrail and watched a black wreath with Zhora's photo float downstream toward the sea.

Bloodied clothes were all they found of Zhora. Some were found at the wharf's edge, others downstream along the riverbank. After a week, Captain Borodin concluded he'd been murdered, his body dumped into the icy river. Even if he'd survived his attacker, no one stood a chance against the churning current and hypothermia.

Rumors of the male prostitute found dead and a number of Zhora's personal effects in the victim's apartment had an odd effect on the memorial. Many of the crew kept quiet and avoided Mikhail. Their discomfort mushroomed into a dark thunderhead over the day's events.

At the service's conclusion most meandered back to the ship. A few came to offer their condolences or share a fond memory. Mikhail hardly heard any of them.

"It is a shame to lose so clever and dedicated an officer," someone offered, their voice just loud enough to overcome the wind.

Mikhail turned to see Boreyev and his heart skipped a beat. Bloodshot eyes held a vacant stare. Both eyes were blackened and a thick bandage covered his nose.

"You say you got that in a fight with some locals over Shulga's murder?"

"Yeah. I mentioned how we and the police should march down there and clear the whole place out. We should've rounded everybody up for questioning." His words fell out of his mouth like marbles in a jar tipped over. He stared into the water and beyond.

Zhora's death had shaken the stout missile officer more than Mikhail imagined possible. *Was it Zhora's death, the mystery behind it, or the loss of two sailors so close together? The two had been rivals, not friends.*

"I keep expecting him to jump out and surprise us, to tell us it'd been a big joke," Boreyev said with a halfhearted chuckle.

Mikhail chuckled. "Zhora wasn't a practical joker. He was always too intense for that."

"We should share a drink, to commiserate over our loss."

"That's alright, Boreyev," he answered with a practiced smile, "I'm not in the drinking mood. Thanks for the offer though."

"You'll be seeing Nika then?"

Mikhail drew in a deep breath and let it out slowly. "Look, what's going on? What're you after?"

"Nothing," Boreyev said with a shrug. "I'm just asking." He tilted his head to one side and squinted. "I thought I'd pay her a visit, but it's hardly worth going if you'll have her tied up all night."

Before he knew it, Mikhail had Boreyev by the throat, bent backwards over the guardrail. "I don't know what fucking head-game you're playing, but I just lost the only true friend I've ever had. All I can think of is that I wish that were your wreath in the river instead of his."

Boreyev grimaced. "If I fancied boys, maybe you'd have gotten your wish."

He twisted free. He brought his fists up, ready to fight.

"How close were you two, Mikhail? Did you share a

bunk? Did you share more? Do you fuck Nika or do each other's nails? If that's all you do, take the night off and give a real man a chance to blow off some steam."

Mikhail raised his fists and crept around Boreyev in a wide arc. As he did, both realized another crewmate stood nearby, Seaman Kipchak. Both men relaxed their stance. Boreyev held his chin high and marched back to the ship.

"I remember when Lieutenant Ivankov first reported aboard," Kipchak said. He walked to the guardrail and stared at the vanishing wreath.

"He gave me a hard time for being glib," the man said. "I didn't know what glib meant."

"Are you on our repair team?" Mikhail asked.

Kipchak scowled and looked down at his shuffling feet. "I was, until the captain reorganized the teams."

"Is something wrong?"

"No, comrade, I just . . . It's different, that's all."

"Was there something else?"

He looked back to the ship and then at Mikhail. "I'm not sure. But I agree. I wish it were that bastard's funeral today."

Mikhail stiffened and frowned. "Seaman Kipchak, that bastard is a lieutenant in the Soviet navy."

Kipchak turned to face him. "So are you, Comrade Lieutenant, and so was . . . Lieutenant Ivankov."

"You heard our . . . conversation?"

"I did," Kipchak admitted quietly. He looked to the floor between them and back up. "Whatever Lieutenant Ivankov was outside the ship, he treated me like a human being and not like some dog or subhuman. If he was that way, I never felt like we had anything but mutual respect for each other."

"But could you condone such behavior? Could you work side by side with such a man?"

"I have and probably still do."

Kipchak thought a moment. "It's like borscht."

"Huh?"

"Borscht makes me want to puke. I don't want to see it,

smell it, or especially, eat it. I know plenty of crewmates who love it. So long as they don't make me eat it I'm not going to hate them for it. Also, I look away while they eat."

"It's not the same thing."

"For me it is. I just try to keep things simple. We've all got something in our closet, something we're not ready to share with the world, right?"

Mikhail stared into the younger man's eyes, searched for some hidden meaning, and found none. He'd simply said what Mikhail needed to hear.

"That's the most sense you've made yet, Kipchak."

"Glad I helped clear things up," he replied with a wry smile.

A Reward for a Hero or a Bullet for a Freak

EIGHTEEN

Zampolit Dimitriev hummed while he examined his papers across the wardroom table from Mikhail. Through tiny wire-rimmed glasses the political officer scanned each forward and backward.

"Acquaintances, hmm? You knew Lieutenant Ivankov before?"

"We roomed together at the academy."

Dimitriev peered over his files and narrowed his gaze. "I, ah, see." He scribbled in a small notebook. "And you worked extensively together aboard K-389, in close proximity?"

"We did. It's a submarine after all. Close is how it all fits on the inside."

The zampolit stopped writing and glared. He drew in a deep breath and let it out slowly. With a thin smile he continued.

"Indeed. And whose idea was it to circumvent the standard shipyard procedure for overhaul?"

Mikhail shrugged. "We came up with it together. We went over the resources and realized the crew competed against itself. Chendev's workers extracted larger bribes as a result."

Dimitriev shook his head with his eyes closed. "Defying standard procedure, breaking out from protocols, those are the mark of an egotistical elitist."

"The only problem came from Chendev. He should be in irons."

Dimitriev sat back and scowled. "You're treading on thin ice, Comrade Lieutenant."

He set his papers down one by one into piles. With each new pile he neatly aligned with the others. By the time he finished, an arc of yellow and white enveloped his seat at the table. He scanned them from left to right with a grin that grew wider as he progressed. Once finished, he gave the papers an approving nod and looked up at Mikhail.

"Sacrifice. Our nation asks much of us, even in death. In order to fuel our struggle against invaders, we make heroes of many fallen comrades to inspire others to greater sacrifice. Many heroes of The Great Patriotic War shone brighter due to the talents of the Military Council."

"They lied?"

Dimitriev leaned forward and slammed his fists on the table. Papers floated from their piles and drifted to the floor. "Don't take that tone with me Lieutenant," he hissed. "I afford the Captain leeway in deference to his rank."

"I apologize, Comrade Zampolit. I forget your rank sometimes." Mikhail cleared his throat and adjusted his tunic, waiting for Dimitriev's nod. As the fat-faced man accepted his apology, Mikhail reworded his question. "The zampolits crafted an idyllic hero from common men to bolster morale?"

Dimitriev nodded and offered an approving smile. "Imagery. Photographs taken in the studio depict their subjects in a more flattering light. We provided enhancing contrasts and spoke to popular themes."

"And what theme will Lieutenant Ivankov's death speak to?"

"Petty Officer Shulga was lured to a den of deviants, enticed to buy souvenirs for his family back home. They robbed and murdered him in the struggle. Lieutenant Ivankov, incensed by the injustice done, spearheaded an investigation that lead to a fight to the death between him and the fiend."

"I see," Mikhail began. "But we don't know that the murderer's dead. In fact, I'm certain of the opposite."

Dimitriev shut his eyes and shook his head. "Irrelevant. Let the local police worry about that."

"And the part where he ran off by himself?"

The zampolit's eyelids fluttered and his patient plastic smile widened. "You were with him, his partner in this investigation. While you interrogated a local bar patron, Lieutenant Ivankov saw the man responsible escape out the back and ran after him. You followed, but lagged behind the lithe lieutenant, an avid marathon runner."

"And the male prostitute the police found murdered?"

Dimitriev's lips whitened before he offered a calm reply. "Lieutenant Ivankov's effects were stolen from his abandoned uniform *after* his death. The prostitute's death was an unrelated squabble over the treasures found."

Mikhail looked down at his trembling hands and back to Dimitriev. The zampolit looked back, peaceful and friendly as ever. An expectant arch in his eyebrow prodded Mikhail to speak.

"And what if I'm uncomfortable with the history you've crafted?"

The friendly smile faltered and his gaze grew cold. "I have another version if this one doesn't suit you."

The zampolit stood and walked to the tea set. He explained an alternative while he poured and seasoned his cup.

"Lieutenants Ivankov and Koryavin *were* the murders we sought. They drugged Petty Officer Shulga and dragged him to a den of deviants where they sexually abused him before they slaughtered him. With their bloodlust boiling, they turned to those male prostitutes for another night of psychotic debauchery which got out of hand. The guinea pig for the night resisted and Ivankov died with his victim in the struggle. Koryavin's cleverness kept us in the dark until a crucial piece of evidence linked him to the crimes."

He waived his hand dismissively. "I've not yet determined what that crucial piece of evidence is, but it'll come to me before you're shot for your detestable crimes."

Mikhail's lungs ached and reminded him to breathe. He

stared at Dimitriev, watched him sip his tea and return to his seat. He met Mikhail's gaze and allowed a thin smile.

"Surprised? You thought, because Captain Borodin spoke gruffly to me, and I offered no firm rebuttal, I was a weak and powerless man?" He set his cup down and leaned across the table. As he did, his pleasant features transformed. Mikhail stared at a demon centimeters from his face.

"Life and death, and worse," Dimitriev whispered. "I have tools at my disposal to defend the State against the parasites of vice within and the predators of capitalism without."

He slid back into his chair, picked up his cup and drew in a deep breath, eyes closed. When he opened them, the serene smile and calm demeanor of a cat settling in for a nap emerged.

"You are a junior lieutenant, no? Surely a hero, who helped track down a murderer, and masterminded the ship's rapid overhaul, deserves a promotion."

Dimitriev took a long drink, smacked his lips, and sighed. "Choose. Another star for a hero or a bullet for a twisted freak, which will it be?"

A young face, bruised and pale peered in from under the corner of Mikhail's conscience and gave him a hollow-eyed scolding stare.

"Comrade Dimitriev, before we go any further, I must tell you about Seaman Yanukovich's death."

"Junior Lieutenant Koryavin, step forward and come to attention." Dimitriev's nasal voice pierced the shipyard din. A week had passed since that long afternoon in the ship's wardroom with the zampolit, this devious scribe of State approved truth. As he marched before the crew and came to attention, he considered the alternative and held his breath rather than scream.

"Junior Lieutenant Mikhail Iosivich, Koryavin, for your decisive efforts in the swift overhaul of K-389 and your bravery during the pursuit and execution of the murderer of the old docks, I am proud to award you the Order of Nakhimov, second class."

Dimitriev marched from his place beside Captain Borodin to Mikhail. After a crisp salute from Mikhail and a returned salute from the zampolit, he pinned the red and silver star on his jacket lapel.

"Wise. You have proven yourself doubly wise for shielding these men from the details of these two tragic deaths," Dimitriev murmured through smiling clenched teeth. "I hope it won't take nearly so much coaxing next time."

He stepped back and saluted until Mikhail returned his salute. Once Dimitriev stepped back in rank, Captain Borodin marched out from his peers and halted between Mikhail and his crew.

"While we mourn the loss of Lieutenant Ivankov, a hero and martyr, I want to recognize the brilliance of his comrade, instrumental in the quickest turnaround in shipyard history. But first I must scold him for being out of uniform."

The captain scowled at Mikhail. In the silence, the shipyard cacophony rose and fell with the wind. Borodin looked to the crew and back to Mikhail.

"As of this morning, he is no longer a junior, but a full lieutenant in the Red Fleet."

Captain Borodin walked over to Mikhail and grabbed his hand, clasped it in both of his and shook it. His cheerful grin and weary eyes gave Mikhail a peek into the weight of the man's responsibilities and the ease with which he bore them. Then, without warning, the Borodin snapped to attention. Mikhail came to attention and they exchanged salutes. After a nod to Gorelov, the captain stepped closer.

"Whatever Dimitriev said," Borodin began, "whatever you two discussed, keep it to yourself unto the grave."

"K-389, come to attention!" Gorelov bellowed behind

Mikhail. As one heels clicked together, gloved hands slapped tight to their sides. "Dismissed."

Captain Borodin looked over his shoulders before he continued. "By the time you're an old captain like me, you'll need a coffin the size of this submarine for all the secrets you'll keep."

Cursed Ship

NINETEEN

With sunrise still an hour away and breakfast a mere memory, Mikhail watched a formation of sailors march closer, new crewmates for the K-389's first deployment after years of overhaul. Captain Borodin mentioned the navigator, a senior lieutenant, should be leading a group of twenty-six. He counted thirty and the man leading them bore triple gold epaulets and two stars, a captain, third rank.

"Stand by to render a captain's honors," Mikhail bellowed to the sentry.

The phalanx of sailors came to a halt just across the ship's brow and their senior officer marched across with a stack of records tucked under one arm. Tall for a submariner, his drooping eyelids and deliberate gait spoke of a slow and steady man, neither quick to temper or wit.

The sentry rang the ship's bell and plainly announced over the intercom, "Captain, third rank, reporting."

Mikhail saluted the senior officer. "Welcome aboard K-389, Comrade Captain."

The man eyed him and the sentries before returning the salute. "Captain Vladislov Konev, reporting as ordered with a supplement to the crew of twenty-nine."

"We weren't expecting a man of your rank," Mikhail said apologetically. "Some arrangements will need to be made for your quarters."

"I am to be second in command," he explained, "at least

for now. My quarters should be unoccupied."

"Yes Comrade Captain, they are. I'll see to it they're made ready."

"Have they been previously occupied? I understood that I'm the first executive officer aboard K-389 since its induction into the shipyard. Surely my quarters haven't been commandeered for some other person or purpose."

"No Comrade Captain, I don't know what state they're in and only want to ensure-

Captain Konev waved him off. "Enough. See to it my men are taken care of. I'll go below and find Captain Borodin."

Before Mikhail managed a reply the loping Konev marched to the hatch and descended. Flushed and fuming, he took a few deep breaths of late February air before he crossed the brow and addressed those men waiting.

"Captain Konev has gone to meet with the Captain. I'll see to it the rest of you are situated and settled in."

A lieutenant in the first rank looked to a michman beside him. "Michman Ovechkin, please take care of our enlisted men. We've come a long way to get muddled up now."

"Muddled?" Mikhail asked.

"Sorry Lieutenant, we've been through a tough trip with Captain Konev. He hijacked us along the way and has kept us jumping at our shadows ever since." The man extended a hand and shook Mikhail's.

"Senior Lieutenant Pudovkin, ship's navigator reporting."

"The ship seems so much larger out of the water," Pudovkin observed. "It's uglier too."

Mikhail grinned and shrugged as he continued his dry dock basin tour with Pudovkin, the new navigator. Bright enough for advanced training, he'd made Senior Lieutenant while serving aboard a destroyer in the Black Sea Fleet.

Beneath his wavy blonde hair, a deep tan spoke of many days on deck.

"We searched for American submarines in the Mediterranean with no luck." Pudovkin shook his head. "Our captain reported otherwise. Supposedly we tracked the American to Egypt and later off the coast of Libya. Those were good ports, though we weren't allowed to wander far in Egypt."

"You've already seen so much," Mikhail mused. "You'll see the inside of that," he jerked a thumb at the hull above them, "more than you'll ever care to. You'll have every millimeter memorized by the time we return to Avacha Bay."

"This is my reward for good marks in school?" Pudovkin asked. "I wanted sailor's life *on* the sea, not *under* it. I wish I'd partied like my classmates."

"You've been to sea on submarines before?" Pudovkin asked.

"No," Mikhail answered. "But I've heard enough of Michman Gorelov's stories."

Above the echoing machinery and hissing welding torches, distant cries rang out. Two or three men shouted and screamed. One voice grew nearer, louder. Mikhail tried to pinpoint its origin and found himself looking up.

A blur fell across his field of vision. A wet crash scared him back with a startled gasp. A shipyard worker had fallen meters from where they stood. His body lay contorted and crushed in a tangled mess of blood-soaked coveralls and protruding bone. The man's brain spilled out like a grocery bag of cauliflower and tomato paste, thrown to the concrete.

Angry shouts from atop the dry dock failed to catch Mikhail's attention. A crude tattoo of a skull and crossed axes identified the man as a welder he'd worked with to repair leaks in the fire suppression system. Though folded in half by a shattered forearm, the image remained unmistakable.

"Who is that up there, shouting?" Pudovkin asked. "He

105

seems angry at this man for dying."

Mikhail's blood chilled and he shivered. "That'll be the shipyard superintendent, Savva Chendev. He's become more motivated lately, to the point of madness. Some say our ship is cursed and he's in a hurry to see it leave."

Haunted

TWENTY

In his office, Shipyard Superintendent, Savva Chendev slammed his phone down.

Tamar had better be ready for a rough night after the trouble she put me through. She'll be on her knees begging for her husband's job before she finishes fixing dinner.

Savva snickered. *She'll be on her knees alright.*

As he left the shipyard, he looked over his shoulder. He offered a dismissive wave to the gate guards as he began his walk home. He walked faster than the night before. His heartbeat rattled in his narrow chest loud enough to compete with the shipyard's distant din. As he left the safety of the well-lit perimeter fence, his pace picked up and his eyes darted from shadow to shadow.

Then his recurring nightmare resurfaced and he hastened his pace. He diverged from his usual route home, ducked into an alley, then doubled back. Searching every shadow, racing for every sanctuary of light along the five-minute walk home, he breathed easier at the sight of his front door. Like a loved one waiting at the train station, the big wooden door warmed his heart and urged him on.

He ran the final ten meters and collapsed against the door's cold surface. When he'd caught his breath he fumbled to unlock it. A tide of fear rose as he struggled for the one key to save him from the terror that haunted his walk home two nights already this week.

The lock turned; he stumbled in, and he fell to the floor.

"Welcome home." The ghost's kind words trickled down his spine and he shivered.

"What do you want?" Chendev moaned. "Why haunt me so?"

From atop the stairs, Chendev watched Zhora's apparition descend. The man who'd put a knife to his throat a month ago, the man who'd searched in the forbidden part of town for a murderer and found himself the next victim, Zhora Ivankov's lips wore a grin yet conviction smoldered in his eyes as he approached.

"Two words," the revenant said, "justice and freedom."

"Justice for who? Freedom for who?"

"Justice for all," Zhora answered, looming overhead. "Freedom for all."

He looked the same and yet different. Every best feature stood out and Savva detected no flaw in his appearance. Chendev had been to the theater once, when he was married. The actors, even the men, wore makeup that accentuated their features. This ghost appeared more alive yet less real.

"Justice for all?" he asked. "Even me?"

Zhora crouched beside him and patted him on the cheek. The ghost's hand felt like a statue's, cold, smooth, and firm.

"For you justice demands a criminal pay for his crime."

A whimper escaped as he crawled away. "I'm no criminal. I do what must be done to keep our community alive."

Zhora glided closer until his face hovered centimeters from his own. A mime's caricature of pity warped his features.

"That may have been true once, but as you grew in power, greed took control."

"How can you accuse me of things you know nothing of?"

Zhora's throaty chuckle made his skin crawl with goose bumps. "We've had this conversation before."

"No, I'd remember that."

"The same power I hold over that memory opens your

past to me like filthy magazine. I fed on your memories as much as I've tasted your blood."

Chendev backed up until he pressed into the door. The penetrating cold felt different against the back of his head, no longer a soothing cool salve. Its chill only magnified the shiver of fear.

"Freedom," he began, afraid to hear the ghost's answer, "Freedom even for me?"

The ghost's smile broadened beyond possibility, stretching to reveal teeth long, thin, and sharp, like rows of scalpels.

"Don't worry," the phantom assured him. "Your freedom shall be from my hauntings and mine shall be to visit justice on others. Push your men to do their job. Don't be cruel but realistic. Hold you men accountable as I call you to account for your greed now. Once K-389 departs, I shall find other haunts to occupy."

Zhora's body coursed with the man's blood. His mind reeled within the experience. It felt so hot in his throat and stomach. The warmth rippled out in waves through his own veins. And as he drank in life's liquid he also grew drunk on the man's dreams. Thoughts, experiences, memories and fantasies, all these flooded Zhora's mind as he consumed the man's life.

"Tamar, why won't you come over?" Savva Chendev pleaded. "I know Gregor won't be home for the next twelve hours."

He pressed the phone tighter to his ear.

"I don't want to do this anymore," Tamar replied. Her resolve sounded only a hair firmer than the last time he'd convinced her.

"You are all that stands between that oaf of yours and a demotion to cleaning out the dry dock basin," Chendev threatened. Gregor's incompetence, though overstated, had

made him the last choice for welding shop foreman but Tamar's talents changed the Chendev's mind more than once.

A toddler screamed in the background. Chendev guessed Semyon by the desperation in the wailing. Chendev often wondered who his father might be.

"You've always been Gregor's greatest asset, his wisest move. Come see me tonight."

Tamar shouted to quiet Semyon before she offered a nervous reply. "I won't. I think Gregor suspects."

"You give the man too much credit."

"Still, if he finds out, I'll be dead before anyone else knows what's happened."

"And if I were to find a way to free you from that fear?"

"How?" she snapped back. "Would you move in and watch over me like a damned guardian angel?"

"No," he said in a low tone. "I'd move you in with me after his funeral."

"You would murder my children's father?"

"The shipyard is a dangerous place. Any number of things might kill him tonight."

"I'll call the police!"

"And report an accident?" he asked calmly. But her nerve, her spiteful nature after all he'd done for their family, rose like a boiling tide inside.

"Would you report a conversation we never had?" he bellowed.

Indignant fury foamed over. "What might an illiterate housewife have to say against me?" he growled.

Zhora fought to stop, struggled with the urge to continue, to revel in the experience until it came to an ultimate end. Only Savva's repugnant and machinations helped him stop. Such a greedy man, he doled out scraps to his neighbors and even less to the average family in Komsomolsk. That he took men's wives for his own pleasure sickened Zhora but that he reveled in the secret sabotage of each home set his anger afire. *Yet this man must live. His power over the shipyard has begun to make an impact in the schedule. We*

110

must get out of here before we're discovered or Sevastyan loses control.

The thought of his mentor helped stay his growing addiction and racing hunger. Sevastyan's simple-minded approach had boxed in the older vampire. His belief in being part of nature's death process kept him from really exploring the full benefit of his abilities. Though Zhora may have laid it on a bit thick, Chendev's belief in a ghost haunting him until he righted certain wrongs carried their plan further faster. It didn't hurt that Zhora also enjoyed horrifying the pompous bastard.

Zhora worked to contort those final memories in the man's mind, to cloak those moments in the fog of a dream. He withdrew his narrow fangs and cleaned up the few droplets standing in the crook of the man's collarbone.

Petty Officer Shulga's torn corpse came to mind. Sevastyan's bestial, brutal feedings left little chance for a long career as a vampire in a populated town. Gently, he carried the man up to bed and set him down. He peeled off shoes and jacket before dragging the thick blanket over him. Zhora walked over to the bathroom. He turned on the water and examined his hands and face, eager to get cleaned up before he left. He looked up to the mirror over the sink and gasped.

What he saw struck him like a hangman's noose. His handsome features had begun to deteriorate, to transform. Beneath skin turned whitish blue, his blood vessels darkened. Facial features once handsome and chiseled from marble, now looked gaunt and sagged like a veil of old leather over his skull. He struck the mirror and shattered it, unsure of how his wave of rage transformed into action so quickly. That he despised his failing visage didn't surprise him as much as his own reaction, seen as if witnessing someone else's angry outburst.

He slipped out of the house and leapt from rooftop to rooftop. He heard heartbeats in the streets below with greater clarity than he felt his own feet as he ran. Only the blood of another revived a connection to his own body.

111

Otherwise it felt like vehicle he piloted from within an insulated cockpit.

Sevastyan crouched on the building's corner like a gargoyle and watched each pedestrian as they passed into and out of sight.

"Too many people," he complained. "Your advice, to siphon without killing, leaves me weak and hungry."

"They'll not bat an eye at people tired and sick," Zhora countered. "By covering our tracks with nightmares instead of corpses we prolong our survival."

Sevastyan turned to Zhora and glared. "I am a proud predator, not a slithering parasite."

"If we don't change our tactic, we can't survive. Would you like to become extinct, like other predators set in their ways?"

"You think yourself so smart. When we feed on so many and leave so much larger a footprint, haven't we exchanged one risk for another? If I remain this weak and draw the attention of so many victims still alive, the-"

"Don't try to figure it out," Zhora snapped. "You've been apart from humanity so long, you hardly understand them." He softened his tone. "They'll be afraid to mention their nightmares. That's what keeps so many people from ever sharing the truth, fear of being an outcast, fear of being labeled different. They'll all think they're the only ones with disturbing nightmares."

"How can you be so sure?" Sevastyan stood and closed until the two stood a hand's width apart.

Zhora smiled and shrugged. "I'm not. But I know that we'll be out of here before they catch on to what we're doing."

"You play a game with our lives."

"Don't be so paranoid. I'm securing our future aboard a nuclear submarine. We'll have a home hidden from the world with access to every coast of every ocean. One big gamble and we secure our future for decades to come."

Zhora's Ghost

TWENTY-ONE

Konev observed the crew as they stood in formation. He watched and waited, for what no one knew. They'd been called out and mustered on the pier for an hour. The new executive officer hadn't finished unpacking before he crept from level to level, compartment to compartment, inspecting ship and crew. He had grilled the men on their duties and questioned every equipment discrepancy. Rumor spread that he'd not slept since his arrival. The next morning he called for all hands out on the pier in formation. Konev startled the crew when he finally spoke.

"The crew's quarters aren't fit for animals, your uniforms *are*, and discipline has fallen apart."

Mikhail drew in half a breath and stole a glance at Captain Borodin.

"Don't look to Captain Borodin," Konev bellowed. Mikhail thought the man spoke directly to him until he watched the executive officer march up to another in ranks. He leaned back and looked down his long narrow nose at the crew.

"He may love you like a father. I don't. I love our nation and despise our enemy. I seek only to protect ourselves and allies from the infectious disease of avarice and ego. America props up dictatorships in Iraq and Panama while they support terrorists in Afghanistan."

Konev paced back to where Borodin, Dimitriev, and Doctor Anatoli stood. He stopped at the zampolit and clapped a hand on the man's narrow shoulder.

"I've heard enough from Comrade Zampolit Dimitriev to know where my duty lies. You *will* find a patriotic fire in your heart or you *will not* serve aboard K-389. Morale *will* improve. Positive attitudes *will* drive positive results."

Silence, save the riveter's rhythm, was the crew's first reply. Michman Gorelov raised his fist above the ranks. "A cheer for Captain Konev. Ura!"

"Ura!" the crew cried in unison.

"A cheer for Captain Borodin. Ura!"

"Ura!" they cheered louder.

"And a cheer for Captain Dimitriev. Ura!"

The brief silence brought a chuckle to the back of Mikhail's throat. And then-

"Ura!"

The zampolit's grin at the cheer brought Mikhail's laughter tumbling out. The new navigator, Lieutenant Pudovkin, jabbed him in the ribs.

"First, you'll clean up the ship," Konev continued, "and then you'll clean up yourselves. Michman Gorelov, set the men to their task while I train the officers on the future of K-389."

"I will relieve Captain Borodin after K-389's initial patrol following the overhaul," Captain Konev explained in a low tone. He looked down his nose at the officers gathered around the wardroom table. His lingering gaze worried Mikhail.

Konev stiffened and craned his neck to search the room. "Where's my missile officer?"

"I, ah, think the lieutenant's overseeing some critical t-t-targeting exercises," answered Lieutenant Dovzhenko, the new Communications Officer. Thin with jet hair and piercing deep green eyes, he could've been Nika's brother except for the hesitant way he spoke.

Nika crept into the center of Mikhail's thoughts where

he examined her beautiful flaws, sharp tongue and sure wit.

"You, daydreamer," Konev snapped, "go and invite Boreyev to my meeting."

Mikhail bolted upright and nodded. "Yes Comrade Captain."

Outside the Wardroom the intercom played music, *Smuglianka*. Knots of men sang along while they cleared shipyard debris and swept up the dust and metal shavings. Through Operations Compartments Forward and Aft, Mikhail saw sailors making joy in their toil. Some muttered and cursed, but most knew better and poured their hearts into the music while they poured sweat into their work. Into Missile Compartment Forward he passed two men wrestling. A glare from him and a word from their audience ended the horseplay. They apologized and picked a broom and a mop. Mikhail offered a nod and a grin before resuming his trek.

An armored room along the compartment's starboard side contained Launch Control, nerve center for Armageddon. Mikhail knocked on the door and slipped his identity card through a waist-high slot. He eyed the peephole and waited. He heard the bolt slide aside and the door opened. A young petty officer nodded curtly and ushered him in.

"Where's Lieutenant Boreyev?" Mikhail inquired as he slipped in and slid the door shut behind him.

The petty officer looked over his shoulder to the three petty officers poring through papers and entering data into a computer console.

Mikhail cleared his throat and spoke loud enough for all to hear. "He wasn't in formation this morning and now Captain Konev's noticed his absence in the wardroom. What's wrong with him?"

The missile chief picked his way through the close quarters, around the men at work on the targeting computer and stopped millimeters from Mikhail.

"He's not well," he whispered. "He's got a touch of

something. We let him catch some rest in the back." The pudgy man looked to have been a champion wrestler once. A dozen years cramped in a submarine had avalanched his bulk to his belt-line. Genuine concern in the man's eyes halted Mikhail's casual observation.

"Take me to him."

"He said he slept aboard last night," the chief explained as he ushered Mikhail through the tiny labyrinth. "He's cool to the touch, says he's had horrible nightmares, and can't find the energy to even get up on his feet."

They stood over Boreyev. The man's face lacked any color save the shadowy crescent under each eye. His placid expression and ghostly pallor reminded Mikhail of Seaman Yanukovich's corpse in that body bag. He leaned over the man and pressed the back of his hand against the sleeping officer's cheek.

"Leave me alone!" Boreyev moaned as he shrank back on his elbows.

"Boreyev, Captain Konev's holding a meeting in the wardroom," Mikhail explained. "What's happened to you?"

The man shook his head and shut his eyes. "I don't know. I was out last night . . . and then I was here."

"Come on now," Mikhail said as he offered his hand. "Let's get you into the wardroom before we all earn Konev's wrath."

As he lead Boreyev to the wardroom, Mikhail kept looking back to ensure the man followed and remained conscious. Lieutenant Boreyev's eyes darted from crevice to crack, always searching the shadows.

"Do you believe in ghosts?" Boreyev asked.

The man's demeanor disturbed Mikhail. Shaky, timid, and polite, Mikhail never imagined the brawling bully in such a state.

"I believe in science," Mikhail replied. "But that only means that I don't believe ghosts until I see evidence otherwise."

"I'm sorry for what I said at Ivankov's memorial."

Those words burned in Mikhail's heart as he heard

them. He spun about and grabbed Boreyev by the throat. Ready for the more powerful man to fight back, it shocked him to feel the man's muscles slacken as he surrendered.

"I've been a bastard, I know. But I'm going to change."

"Don't get all weepy just because you're going to be late to this meeting," Mikhail growled through his grimace.

"No, you don't understand. I've seen things in my dreams, haunting things. Zhora's spirit convicted me last night."

"Have you told anyone else this?"

"No."

"If you value your career, which I don't, you'll keep such dreams to yourself. Snap out of it man. It's not like you lost a friend. It's not like you killed him."

Boreyev's knees buckled and he slid down the bulkhead to the deck. "No, you're right. I shouldn't let it get to me so."

"Tell me the story you want told. Konev will ask me what you were doing and why."

Topside, Mikhail watched the sun set. He only had a few minutes before another of Konev's tabletop exercises. They'd discussed every ship system, the strategic mission, and navigation. The wardroom walls fit like a second skin after so many hours. The chair's cushion hugged his butt like a scuba wet suit. The next subject brought a lump in his throat, tactics, Zhora's specialty. Cold air and crisp silence soothed him like a salve.

"Strange couple of evenings," a voice behind him said.

He turned to see the sentry, Seaman Kipchak.

"What's strange?"

"Lieutenant Ivankov's been dead a month and last night I saw his ghost."

"You're joking," Mikhail said with a nervous laugh.

"No."

"But I heard the duty officer found you asleep at your station last night."

Kipchak dropped his gaze to the black steel deck between them. "Yes."

"Perhaps it was a dream."

"I'm not the only one," Kipchak said soberly. "The night baker saw him near the galley."

"Did he say anything? What did he do?"

Kipchak smiled and his eyes glistened. "He said, 'I'm fine, don't worry about me.'"

Though skeptical, Kipchak's words comforted Mikhail, calmed him. He looked to the thin gold ribbon of sunlight trapped between the horizon and the overcast sky.

Kipchak's snickering brought Mikhail's drifting mind back to reality. He looked to the young sailor and noticed him blushing.

"Lieutenant Ivankov also said I was adorable."

Laughter between the two men drowned out the metal grinders nearby.

An Awkward Proposal

TWENTY-TWO

"Bridge Officer, all compartments report no leaks."

Mikhail looked to Captain Borodin before he picked up the microphone. "Understood, Control Officer, ensure the crew remains alert."

Under the captain's tutelage, he served as Bridge Officer for the ship's first test. Gushing torrents from the Amur River poured into the dry dock. Two years of work, and months supervised by Mikhail and Zhora, all of it immersed in the churning waters, a baptism before their first voyage. From K-389's bridge atop the shark fin sail, Mikhail looked to the white stripe from the basin's bottom to the tip of the guardrail. The depth markings within the concrete indicated six meters of murky waters beneath them. It had barely begun lapping against the keel.

"What's the hold up on those pumps?" he wondered aloud.

"There's a flu going around the shipyard," Captain Borodin said. "They're shorthanded."

He looked to the captain. The older officer offered a wincing grin.

"It'll be a long, tedious day."

A faint hiss from the deck caught Mikhail's attention. He focused his binoculars on two brassy disks, from one a halo of mist sputtered. Keeping his gaze on it, he grabbed the microphone again.

"Control Officer, check ballast vent, Tank One. The

starboard valve hasn't properly seated."

"Understood, machinery crews will investigate."

Mikhail leaned over the edge of the bridge and craned his neck to examine the ship. Three sailors huddled over the mid-ship's hatch smoking. They hovered over the opening like campers around a fire.

"Deck Sentry," Mikhail began, hoping his stern tone came across the radio, "spread your men out across the ship and inspect for leaks, especially the ballast vents. I want this ship to be our home, not a tomb."

"Yes, Comrade Bridge Officer. Sorry, Comrade Bridge Officer."

The men scrambled to each ballast tank vent location and reported all starboard vents exhibited the same minute leak.

Mikhail considered all the ship's systems and how they interacted. Dozens of diagrams ran through his mind, the captain watching and waiting all the while.

"Control Officer, check the starboard list controls, I think a fuse has blown. All starboard vents are in neutral."

Shortly after the Control Officer's reply the hiss from the forward vents changed pitch then vanished. The Sentry soon reported all vents shut. Mikhail looked to Captain Borodin, who fought to remain aloof yet his tight-lipped smile revealed his pride.

Moment by moment, hour by dragging hour the waters rose and the cycle of crisis returned. By sunset the ship floated in the dry dock, an enormous aquarium with one giant fish. A creaking squealing crane hoisted the ship's brow up from its resting place beside the dock and set it down between ship and shore. Within an hour, Captain Borodin took the microphone in his hands and addressed the crew.

"K-389 is officially a ship again. He's been tested as have we and both have come through better for it. Celebrate tonight but don't overdo it. We have but a few days to fix what problems arose today and to top off our supplies. I'm invoking a curfew each night. Tonight everyone will be aboard by midnight. Each night afterward curfew will be an hour earlier."

"Your ship didn't sink? I thought that's what submarines did," Nika quipped.

"Submarines don't sink, they submerge," Mikhail replied. "Anchors and enemies sink."

They lay together in bed, a plate of crackers and caviar from the ship's stores between them. Still struggling with intimacy, Mikhail considered tonight a small victory. So much more remained to conquer but the barrier no longer seemed impregnable. While he prepared himself another cracker his eyes drifted to Nika's slender figure. She rubbed her hand across her bare hip. Though still mischievous and snarky, Nika's edges had softened over the weeks.

He rolled off the squeaky bed's edge and shuffled over to his pile of clothes. From his coat he pulled a thick envelope, turned and brought it to her.

"What's this?" she asked. With a nod from him, she opened it. As she did he explained.

"You'll need that to get into officer housing near Petropavlovsk."

She sat up and pulled herself to the bed's edge and read. When her jaw dropped Mikhail continued.

"If you'd rather stay here, burn it all. But if not, we're married in the eyes of the State and you're eligible for an apartment . . . we're eligible for an apartment at the submarine base."

"What?" She stood and threw her hands up. "Why would you do that? And why would you think I'd agree to it? I'm not getting married. I'm not pushing out babies. I'm not doing your filthy laundry or any of that."

"When you were no one to me, I shared my darkest secret," Mikhail said.

"I haven't," she interjected.

"You didn't shy away, you stuck with me and helped me find a way out. You're the only one I can talk to." He watched her face tighten as she drew in a deep breath.

"So you think my life's so bad that I'll jump on a train with you?" she asked in a low growl. "You think I'd be desperate enough to become your wife?"

He returned to pluck at his clothes, putting on his underwear and pants before he replied with a sheepish grin.

"Actually, I'm going to sea. You'll have to ride the train yourself. I need you. I thought you'd be eager to leave this life behind. I thought we were good for each other. I know about your past-

"You really don't," she countered.

Mikhail studied her. Defiance burned in eyes shaded by pain. So thin and pale, she still looked strong and full of fight.

He finished dressing before he walked over to her and took her in his gloved hands. Piercing dark green eyes glared back. She shivered in his leather-gloved grip and fought to stifle it. He pulled her close, leaned in and kissed her. She stiffened in his arms. Her lips tightened across her teeth as she resisted without fully withdrawing. Just as quickly, he let go and marched to the door.

"If you're not interested, burn the envelope," he said flatly. "If you are, I'll see you in Petropavlovsk."

Tears trickled down Nika's cheeks. "Why'd you do that? I told you, no kissing."

He opened the door, took one step out before looking back. "I'm leaving soon, never to return. I didn't want to leave any regrets."

Nika's Choice

TWENTY-THREE

Nika stared at the folder she'd pulled from the envelope. Papers declaring her Nika Koryavin shook in her hands. Mikhail and the official's signatures sat above a conspicuously empty line for hers. Insurance papers, travel documents, all bore signatures that bookended, hovered over, or sat beside an empty place for Mrs. Koryavin to sign.

Under her bed another suitor beckoned. The small metal bottle contained a handful of honeymoons with no husband to answer to. Mikhail's sweet nature and generosity were bait for a trap she'd seen too many times. She served men who loathed their wives, beat them, and, cheated on them, all with no more remorse than a master who must whip his unruly dog.

"I'm nobody's dog," she said to no one.

But you're somebody's slave, a voice whispered from the shadows of her mind. She felt the bottle struggling to roll out from under the bed and jump into her hand. She heard it serenade her. She reached between her legs and helped her quiet friend out of his hiding place. The aluminum film tube rattled lazily as she brought it up to examine it.

Is this your ideal husband?

"I need this to make everything else make sense. Without it I'll come unglued."

You're alone, talking to yourself about marrying a bottle of pills. Does that sound like you've got a handle on things?

"Shut up. People want too much. People hurt too much."

You helped Mikhail and he's grateful. He wants to help you.

"He wants to help himself get more of me than I'm willing to give. He's pushing me."

Stop arguing then and take your pills. What's stopping you?

Nika rolled the bottle back and forth in the palm of her hand. From the corner of her eye the papers and ticket beckoned.

You see an opportunity to escape, to elevate yourself out of the muck you call life.

"I'm happy here."

Come on, you can't be serious. You prefer exchanging your body for room, board, and the occasional high from those pills? You could ride out of here and into the life of a naval officer's wife.

"What if it doesn't work? What'll I do then? How will I cope if I can't find these pills? What will I become without them? He might throw me out on the street. I'd be worse off with no helping hand like this in sight."

You don't even have to love him for it to work. You'll give your body to strangers easy enough, why not one man for the rest of your life?

"He wants more." Nika paused. Something hung over her, a dangerous thought that she feared to utter, feared to give any more energy than it already possessed. "I want more."

She stood and hurled the bottle. It rattled as it rolled from the corner where it landed. She tore her gaze from the wobbling vial and shivered.

A knock frightened a shudder from her. She looked to the door. The knock came again, but not from the door, behind her. She turned on her toes slowly, and stared, her mouth agape. Zhora stood outside her window, her third story window, and knocked.

His skin seemed lit by a soft spotlight, every exposed millimeter looked perfect. Part of her mind warned her of the scene's incongruity. Yet she crept toward the window and unlocked it. A frigid gust rattled the panes and she fought to open one window and offer a hand to Zhora as he tiptoed in.

"I wondered when you and your imaginary friend might take a break and let me in," Zhora mused.

"Shut up," she countered. "I thought you were dead."

He snickered and nodded. "Don't count me out yet. I'm still kicking and I've got a laundry list of people I owe for all their help." He lowered his head and leveled his gaze on her. "Which brings me to my visit; I hope you're schedule's open. We've got a lot to discuss."

She retreated. "No, you died. You're dead."

"I didn't," he answered in a whisper, "I really didn't. But you might." His grin grew, like an ivory zipper of teeth encompassed by blood red lips.

"Don't make me scream," she warned. Normally she'd threaten to hurt a man herself but something about him made want to scream, really, really scream.

Zhora crept closer and felt the heat radiating from the whore. Her panting breaths and pounding heart urged him closer despite trying to take this meeting slow.

"Don't scream," he said softly. "I only wanted to get some answers from you before I left Komsomolsk."

Nika grabbed a wooden chair and held it up between them. "Why threaten to kill me then?"

He put up his hands and shrugged. "Sorry, it's become a habit lately. I've been on a quest for answers before I return to the ship. I'm content with letting them think me dead until I've finished my business."

"What business?"

"I've got an opportunity to learn why and to what extent the world around me is the way it is. I'm curious enough to unlock all the mysteries I can before K-389 leaves Komsomolsk."

Nika held the chair higher. "What do you want from me?"

Zhora turned and walked to the other chair in the room

and sat. From it he examined the chess set he'd seen his first night in the squalid apartment.

"You and Misha, how're you two doing?"

"Fine."

Her pulse and breathing, both ran wild for a moment. Zhora snatched the white rook from the chessboard and threw it at her. "A lie."

"And how would you know?"

"Lucky guess actually, thank you for confirming it."

Nika set her chair down, turned it backwards, and straddled it as she sat. She rested her forearms across the chair's back. "So, we're not fine. He's told me he's leaving and he's invited me to come along as his wife."

"Sounds like your prince charming has arrived. What's wrong? There's something you're not telling me."

"I'm not sure I want to go."

Zhora plucked the white knight from the chessboard and threw it at her. "You would throw away what I've sought my whole life? You would cast aside the one man I thought might make my soul complete?"

"Calm down," Nika insisted. "I'm just not certain I'm prepared to have a man controlling my life. It might not work out and where will I be then?" She blinked and shook her head. "And why am I confessing this to you?"

"My mother married a man who grew bored with her before I was born. She loved me and I her. We consoled each other about his absence. You have maybe that to look forward to, certainly better than your future here."

"Do you know how many young sailors have proposed over the years?"

Zhora looked her up and down. "I imagine those will come to a halt soon."

"Shut up!"

Zhora stood and Nika quickly came to her feet, chair in hand. He reached into his coat pocket and threw a fistful of money on the table.

"What's this?" she asked.

"I want to taste what my Misha tasted. I want to know

what attracts him so."

"Sweetheart, if you haven't figured that out yet, well, I guess that'd make you a *pidor*."

The room rippled and shrank as he focused on Nika. As though pulled on a cable, she grew close fast without a step. He nearly lost his breath until he realized, it hadn't been her that moved but him. He took her in his arms and looked into her eyes, their faces centimeters apart. Her body felt fiery against his cold skin and her pulse thrummed like the hypnotic drums of an ancient time. They seduced and infuriated him. In that moment when time ballooned and he closed the gap between them in half a breath, she began to gasp.

"What are you doing?" she whispered, breathless.

"I want to taste the love between you," he whispered back. Before she asked another annoying question, he sank his teeth into her shoulder.

Blood, hot and thick, gushed into his mouth and he drank thirstily. Nika groaned and clawed at his shoulders. After his first deep drink, she lost her will and he reined in his hunger. He sifted through her thoughts, brushed aside everything else until found those coveted moments. Each conversation, each intimate touch, all these he fondled and felt. To see Mikhail from within Nika's eyes, to feel his caresses from within her skin, he dove deeper to feel those moments more completely. In this playground he giggled and cried.

He tumbled through her memories, through dozens and dozens of men through the years. His own flesh responded to her infused blood and grew warm. As he rolled through the years and the men, one face leapt up from beyond time to frighten her, to scold her, to take control of her.

"Don't, papa, don't," Nika muttered.

He'd barely noticed her grow limp in his arms. Only

when the theater of her mind flickered and dimmed did he withdraw his fangs. Her head rolled back, eyes wide, and she let out a long gurgling sigh.

"No, not yet," he pleaded. "I want more moments like this."

Her fiery limbs cooled and her body collapsed in his arms.

Zhora fell to the floor, buried his face in her shoulder and wept.

Rasputitsa

Aboard the K-389

From the bridge, Mikhail, Captain Borodin, and the pilot eyed the mouth of the Amur River. Carmel waters churned and rippled as they drained into the Amur Liman, a brackish channel between Asia and Sakhalin Island. Spring's first green sprouts peeked out along the riverbank. A curtain of light rain greyed the swampy surroundings. Mud-murkied runoff poured into the Amur as the land shed its winter coat. These sights brought Mikhail soggier memories. The *rasputitsa* season had always plunged his farmland hometown into a world buried in mud. Thawing ground eagerly drank melting snow. Oxen, cars, everything sank into a waist-deep quagmire for months. And what the earth didn't consume the sky scooped up and dumped in sheets daily.

In school he'd been taught to be thankful for the icy winters and the rasputitsa that followed. Harsh seasons and Russian endurance had combined to push back powerful invaders. Russia tempered her people not with iron and fire but mud and ice.

Within the channel ahead, between mainland Asia and the island of Sakhalin, the Amur's waters dominated the brackish waterway. A few kilometers north, the Sea of Okhotsk beckoned the submarine to her deep waters.

"The easy part is over and I'm glad to be leaving," the

pilot said with a chuckle.

Mikhail offered a quizzical glance at the bearded old river rat. His face, what the thick beard of blond and grey failed to cover, bore the cracked leathery sheen of a weatherworn sailor long accustomed to and in love with his river. The man withdrew a pipe from his bridge coat and examined it. While he hunted in his pockets he explained.

"That Konev, nervous as a zampolit in the Kremlin."

Captain Borodin withdrew a cigar and lighter from the folds of his coat, laughing as he ignited the stogie. With a wink and a nod he leaned over and lit the pilot's pipe.

"He's the future," Borodin said and shook his head.

The pilot took a deep puff and nodded. He glanced at Mikhail before returning his gaze to Borodin. "Thank God we'll be dead before Konev's kind are in charge."

In their days-long journey he'd regaled them of every ship he'd escorted through the Amur's twisting and treacherous paths. He'd stood in this very spot on K-389's bridge ten years ago when it'd been newly commissioned. He and his partner had commanded K-389's every turn and engine order for the seven hundred kilometer long trek at nine kilometers per hour. Three and a half days they'd slogged through river and swamp with nary a solid navigational aid in sight.

Captain Borodin looked up to grey overcast sky. "Yes, thank God."

Konev shattered the peace through the bridge intercom.

"Bridge Officer, this is Captain Konev. It's time we move out to sea. Our pilot, is he ready? I've already sent men on deck to receive the tug."

Mikhail picked up the microphone but before he managed to respond, Captain Borodin took it.

"*Spasibo tovarishch* Konev, we'll send him down soon enough."

The pilot sneered. "He'll be thrashing mad."

"True," Mikhail chuckled. "But he'll not show the captain his anger."

Borodin nodded and grew pensive. In a whisper he

thought aloud. "But he'll take it out on the crew."

He brought the microphone up again. "Captain Konev, I'm sending the pilot down directly. See to it he's seen off with a proper thanks from a grateful crew."

"Aye, aye, Comrade Captain," Konev answered.

Captain Borodin saluted the pilot and Mikhail followed.

"Thank you for your service," Borodin began. "With your help our nation remains safe and secure."

The pilot returned their salute and dropped it quickly. Before he descended the ladder into the ship's Command Center, he hugged the captain and kissed his cheek.

"Beware Okhotsk's ice floes," he warned. "The thaw's come but rogue ice still claims a victim now and then for another month yet."

He turned to Mikhail and patted him on the shoulder. "You've a fine career ahead of you if you learn from both the good officers," he jerked a thumb at Borodin, "and the bad," he looked down the dim ladder-well below.

Before Mikhail managed a witty response, the man descended the ladder, humming an old Cossack tune as he dropped out of sight.

"The rest should be simple enough," Captain Borodin said with a nod. "I leave K-389 in your hands, Lieutenant Koryavin."

Mikhail saluted the captain before he too disappeared below. Looking over the edge of the bridge and aft, he watched Konev and a squad of sailors rein in the tug as it sidled up beside them. The lanky executive officer straightened his back and stretched his shoulders. When the pilot emerged from the mid-ships hatch, Konev pulled a can of caviar from under his arm. He saluted and presented it to the pilot. With a curt salute and quick thanks, the old river-master departed.

One Final Goodbye

Komsomolsk

Savva Chendev entered his house and waited. The hall clock thumped in time with the pulse pounding in his throat. Bells outside, a fire truck rumbled by, headed into the heart of town. Silence hung over his head like an overripe apple waiting to be plucked, devoured, and savored.

"You thought I was gone, didn't you?"

The phantom sounded sad, dejected that it'd been cast aside with such glee.

"Why are you still here?" the superintendent wondered, his voice quivering. "The submarine's gone and you should've left with it."

"Unfinished business," it said. "And my travel plans must be carefully made. I can't just hop aboard the K-389. The timing's not yet right."

The superintendent reached into his coat and unbuttoned it. He stepped through the foyer and listened, trying to pinpoint the lurker. The man's voice had echoed off the high staircase and plaster walls.

"What business then have you with me?" he asked. "You guaranteed you'd leave me."

"And so I shall. Tonight we say our goodbyes."

The voice rattled from the tile-floored room deeper into the home.

The kitchen!

He tiptoed closer and reached deeper into his jacket.

"Let me give you something," Chendev said, "a peace offering before you go."

A hand clamped down on his shoulder, each finger like an articulated iron bar. From behind his ear the intruder whispered.

"Let's have it then."

Chendev turned slowly. His foe let go and they stood arm's length apart.

"I've figured you out, Zhora Ivankov." He slipped the Makarov pistol out from the folds of his coat. "You're a fraud, a spoiled, angry, brat and a fraud."

Zhora looked down at the gleaming gun barrel, mesmerized.

"You're no ghost." Chendev brought the gun higher until he peered through its sights into the young naval officer's shining black eyes. "You drugged me and whispered horrific things in my ears. Your mutterings and narcotics muddled my memories. Tonight I'll stop you before you get the chance."

A throaty chuckle rose in Zhora's throat. "You're right about only two things. First, it ends now, but not as you planned it."

Chendev shuffled back a step and glanced to the shadows. He tightened his grip on the pistol and brought a second hand to hold it steady. Between the shivering iron sights he watched Zhora stretch out his hands and smile. The teeth seemed strangely narrow and long.

"And the second thing, what's that?"

"I'm no ghost."

Chendev's hands stopped shaking and he grinned. "I knew it!" He took half a breath and fired three shots into Zhora's face. The man fell to the floor with a yelp.

Ears ringing and nostrils stinging with burned gunpowder, Chendev fought to rein in his panicked panting. He kicked the body. It lay face down. He'd expected more blood.

"Maybe now you'll become a ghost and haunt me forever," Savva Chendev said to the corpse at his feet. He looked to the kitchen. He'd need to get this cleaned up before Tamar arrived.

A hand grasped his ankle and jerked him off his feet. He fell to the floor, tail bone first, then his head. The room rolled and spun. A dark spot loomed overhead with a shining flash of light beside it. His eyes fell into focus and the dark spot halted his heart. Zhora's face hovered over his. Three deep holes torn into his otherwise handsome features oozed black blood. This close, Zhora stank of rotten meat and mildewed clothing. What caught the light and his attention loomed closer; the linoleum knife.

Icy rain fell on the two vampires while they watched the blaze from atop the shipyard superintendent's home. The downpour drummed against Zhora's skin. The cold wet sheets should've sent him for cover, shivering himself sore. He felt nothing.

"You visit your ship and burn the whore's house," Sevastyan observed. "Why?"

Bells from the fire station rang across the town while crowds gather to watch. Zhora looked to his mentor and stifled a laugh.

Mentor, hardly.

The creature's beauty had faded as predicted. Even as the demonic monster, Zhora appreciated the beauty of a perfect predator, like the sharks of the sea. But the intellect or absence of it, cast Sevastyan in an uglier light.

"I told you I needed some things from the ship," he explained, "a fresh uniform and some papers."

"Tell me again why we let your ship leave without us? Help me believe you haven't betrayed our agreement."

"All those other memories you've absorbed, all those lives funneled through your mind, why haven't you gotten smarter?"

Sevastyan charged him in a blur, grabbed him by the arms with crushing iron hands. "Answer me!"

Lightning flashed across the sky, illuminating the curtain of rain all around them. Thunder rolled and echoed from the foothills across the Amur.

"Calm down, please," Zhora said. He smiled and looked to the roof they stood on. "You wouldn't want to wake Chendev sleeping below us."

Sevastyan snarled and threw him down. He turned again to watch the fire brigade engage the conflagration.

"They head for the submarine base near Petropavlovsk, a short journey," Zhora explained as he stood. "If we overtook them then, the whole Pacific Fleet would search for us in a tiny corner of the world. By waiting until they deploy on a standard patrol, we'll have months to put distance between us and any pursuit. We'll have oceans to hide in."

Sevastyan's gargoyle grimace coaxed a smile from Zhora. *He knows I'm right.*

"Besides, the ship's currently unarmed. They'll load weapons and stores. We'll arrive at the last minute to avoid any questions about why I hide from the sunlight."

Sevastyan turned from the flames and glared at Zhora. "But why the fire, why?"

"I killed the whore," Zhora admitted. "I hadn't meant to but I did. I set the place on fire to hide her body. They'd have seen how she died if I hadn't burned the building."

"And the man in the home below us, this superintendent, you wasted his blood."

Nausea sent a shudder through Zhora. "I've tasted his blood and it turned my stomach to know how he treated his own people, people who believed him their savior."

"But no fire?"

"You see what I see, yet you perceive so little," Zhora replied. Sevastyan's furious glare warned him and he relented.

"The whore I drained of blood. The police might connect

that with other such murders and consider Shulga's murder not closed or isolated to Black Wharf. That'd be bad for us."

Zhora recalled his efforts below and snickered. "That was justice for everyone. But I killed him with that same linoleum knife I'd threatened him with. The police will view that an entirely different matter. I can't be a suspect since I'm already 'dead'."

"You are reckless," Sevastyan growled. "Thousands of people in this city and you go among them without regard to the dangers. You go where people will recognize you."

"You've been a vampire for how long, a century, two? Have you not learned how to muddy their memories while you drink them in?" he asked. Sevastyan's wrinkled brow provided his answer.

"Those who saw me, those who knew me, they only remember seeing a ghost. Some aren't even sure they saw that much. They think me a dream." He snickered. "Boreyev thought me a nightmare."

"You play with them. You drain them like a parasite." Sevastyan dropped his gaze to the rooftop between them. "I have hunted alongside the wolf. I tracked and fed on criminals and in the lean times hunted stag and other simple prey." He looked up again. In his yellow irises Zhora saw something that chilled him more than the late winter rain: disdain.

"You are a monster."

Laughter rose in Zhora's throat until he shuddered from it. Sevastyan stepped back from him as he fell to his knees in uncontrolled laughter.

"Have you looked in a mirror?" he asked between gasps. "Have you any idea how ridiculous you sound?"

Zhora stood and turned his back on his undead companion. "In this modern world full of people and technology, there will be only two kinds of vampires, clever and dead. Go back to the woods if you dare. If I seem a monster it's because the betrayal of mankind still stings, it's still fresh in my mind. If I seem playful with my food, it's only because they toyed with me, tortured me enough to make me a spiteful revenant. If I seem reckless it's only because I gamble for big stakes knowing if I don't win I don't want to last another night in this carcass."

Teg Vy Yemu

Aboard the K-389

Concrete grey clouds pressed the sunset into a golden ribbon atop Russia's eastern shores. To the north, waves and ice danced together in the fading day's cool blue light. Further east Mikhail spied nothing but darkening seas. Nine hundred kilometers east-south-east until they'd reach the tip of the Kamchatka peninsula, then another three hundred to reach Avacha Bay and the submarine base nestled within. Until then K-389's arsenal included only ten AK-47's, two dozen Makarov pistols and six torpedoes.

"It's so much more peaceful up here."

Lieutenant Pudovkin's observation startled Mikhail. The navigator flashed a smile that gleamed in the dimming light. A tuft of his blond hair stuck out from his ushanka. He had the black fur side flaps pulled down tight over his ears.

"Peaceful, cold, and soon it'll be pitch black," Mikhail observed. He held up a thermos. "The cooks made delicious fish soup. It's still warm."

Pudovkin produced his own thermos. "I brought tea to keep me warm and wide awake through the night."

With a cursory salute, Mikhail descended the ladder-well. It still smelled of welding rods, ground steel, and fresh paint. As he abandoned the cool blue natural light of the twilight sky the stark white of fluorescent lights greeted him in the Command Center.

Communications from all parts of the ship whispered in one corner of a room cramped with pipes, cable conduits, and monitors. The Control Officer, Lieutenant Dovzhenko, gnawed at is fingernails while he flitted from station to station. Occasionally he'd lean over the Radar Operator and Sonar Coordinator's stations to take in new data about the world beyond and beneath K-389.

Panels beeped and buzzed. Hydraulic lines groaned and whined. Pneumatic systems huffed and hissed. Below decks, without the sea and sky to hold his attention, Mikhail felt the ship pitch and roll with the waves as the ship cut its way to the Pacific.

In the opposite corner sat the Ballast Officer, Michman Gorelov. With him were the helmsman, and two petty officers, the duty electrician and mechanic. The three sailors listened to their michman's stories of wild ports and adventurous voyages.

"Control Officer," the Radar Operator shouted, "something's on my radar."

"What, w-w-what it is?" Dovzhenko demanded in a panic. He stumbled through the room to see.

The frantic Control Officer and the panicked Radar Operator exchanged glances and stared at the radar screen. Mikhail peered over them and watched one signal as it grew in strength rapidly.

He reached behind him and threw the alarm switch. The klaxon blared throughout the ship. He grabbed the intercom microphone. "All hands to quarters. Battle dive, battle dive, radar threat on the horizon."

As one, all in the Command Center leapt to action. Gorelov dispatched the electrician and mechanic. He turned to his panel and prepared to dive the ship. The helmsman sat up straighter and scanned his instruments before he spoke.

"Control Officer, Helm standing by."

Lieutenant Dovzhenko stared, blank-faced at the helmsman.

A harried buzz rose in tempo and volume from the intercom. The radar screen lit up with two more signals searching the sea for K-389. The Radar Operator pointed at them, stunned.

"Control Officer," Gorelov shouted above the growing chaos, "the bridge hatch shut, all outer hatches shut. Ship's ready to dive."

"But, P-P-Pudovkin," Dovzhenko whimpered.

Mikhail stepped down from the Periscope Station and placed a hand on Dovzhenko's shoulder. The young lieutenant nearly jumped and spun to meet his gaze.

"He's already inside," Mikhail said softly. "He shut the bridge hatch. We should dive and change course."

"What would you recommend?"

No time to debate, for indecision. Mikhail reclaimed his place on the Periscope station and looked to Gorelov. The senior michman looked like a guard dog eager to pounce.

"Ballast officer, dive the ship," Mikhail commanded.

From every crewman in the room, from every monitor too, information and reports poured in. Mikhail's mind gradually rose above the waves of data as it came to him. The radar contacts had been a helicopter followed by two distant destroyers: all elements of a Soviet task force. They searched while K-389 evaded. This exercise offered training, but also accolades or embarrassment at Pacific Fleet Headquarters in Vladivostok.

The sonar operator pointed to dark green screen awash with bright green lines, like a heart monitor hooked to a humming bird.

"Sonar buoys," he hissed.

Then the crew heard them, little canisters dropped from the helicopter, sank into the sea and called out for K-389. They searched with their shrill cry for the steel and titanium hull big as a football field.

"Ahead full, both engines," Mikhail bellowed. "Helm, turn hard starboard and dive to three hundred meters."

The ship lurched to port and the deck pitched downward. Mikhail looked to the sonar operator, known to everyone as Ayatollah. A Georgian, new to K-389, the small man looked old for his age. Despite a bald head, the rest of his hair and beard were thick and coarse. With these features he gained his moniker for his resemblance to the Ayatollah Khomeini of Iran.

"Comrade Lieutenant, we cannot detect much at full speed," Ayatollah warned. "Do we want to blind ourselves?"

"Right," he conceded. "We'll continue on this course enough to put some distance between us if . . ." he looked up as if to see his hunters, "if they don't track us the entire time."

"We race from the helicopter but the destroyers we picked up on the horizon," Ayatollah began. "Do you want them to hear us from fifty kilometers away?"

"The destroyers," Mikhail whispered while he pieced together a plan. "Helm, all stop." He grabbed the intercom and selected the Torpedo Room.

"Have exercise torpedoes ready. Open all doors when ship's speed drops below eight kph."

To the Tactical Coordinator he spoke next. "Plot a spread across the lead destroyer's path."

Mikhail stepped down from the dais and stood beside the helmsman. He crouched beside him and whispered. "Things will get hectic. But once we fire the last torpedo, we're going to run like hell."

"Torpedo doors opening," Ayatollah reported.

Mikhail looked to the gauges, seven kph and dropping.

"The helicopters, they're leaving," Ayatollah exclaimed.

"Hold those torpedoes!" Mikhail shouted.

The Command Center grew silent save for the sonar buoys' persistent cry. In the hushed room Mikhail watched the crew collectively hold its breath.

Ayatollah put his hands to his headset and pressed them tighter against his ears. His frown worried Mikhail. He seemed puzzled.

"What is it?"

"Splashes above, very close, very big; not sonar buoys."

Thunder rumbled above, across the hull's length.

The ship shook and a single overhead light winked out. Ayatollah's expression darkened.

"Depth charge rockets from the destroyers. They're training rounds, only a tenth as powerful as the real thing."

From the sonar panel a voice emerged. Faint, eerie and echoing, it came from the destroyers, an underwater message from their crew.

"*Teg Vy yemu.*"

Gorelov hung his head while he pulled out a cigarette.

"What did they say?" the helmsman asked. "I could barely hear it."

The Michman straightened himself, lit his cigarette and sneered. "Tag, you're it."

Vladlena

The Port City of Sovetskaya Gavan, in the Soviet Far East

Zhora entered the cargo ship, *Amurya*'s, bridge. By the light of the ship's instruments the captain took on a ghostly glow. His thick black beard, black leather cap and tattered bridge-coat painted the portrait of a pirate. His rough features and grim expression spoke of a tough man hard to bargain with. To the ears of a vampire, his snare drum heartbeat told another story.

"We understand each other then?" Zhora asked the man. "I cannot accompany my cousin. I'm putting her life and my parents' eternal rest in your hands."

"Aye. You can trust me to deliver both safely and quickly."

With a nod, Zhora handed the man a satchel of money, all the cash he'd stolen from *Uspokoysa* before he torched it. "My uncle will hand you a similar bundle in Petropavlovsk."

"I'll have my men get your cousin and cargo stowed straight away."

Zhora grabbed the man's wrist and glared. The sailor looked to him, angry at first, then wide-eyed as he tested his captor's grasp.

"Mistreat the girl or cargo and you will wish you'd never seen either."

As he left the ship's bridge he looked out to the harbor. Cranes stood dark and looming, like great metal monsters.

The crews of only the most dedicated, or crooked, ships worked this late. For the right price black market items moved through these ports. For the right price a pair of caskets and a young woman might make it to Petropavlovsk without incident.

Crewmen muttered and grumbled as they nudged past him. Their scent triggered a familiar hunger, like when he smelled his mother's cooking. His stomach yearned and his mouth watered. He shook it off and watched them pick up their latest cargo.

Two modest caskets, each laden with weights for now, these the men hoisted and carried across the gangplank. Each would serve as their claustrophobic haven during the journey's daylight hours. All that remained to load aboard was Vladlena.

She'd been Nika's neighbor and coworker. A novice whore and a practiced drug addict, Zhora pulled her from the burning building. In a moment of hunger he drank her blood. In that intimate moment of shared consciousness he saw an ally. Alone, afraid, and eager to belong to someone, he offered her everything she'd ever wanted and more. He strolled down the gangplank to meet her.

Zhora took Vladlena's face in his hands. "You've done well so far. We traveled from Komsomolsk to Sovetskaya Gavan unmolested."

Vladlena clasped his hands and met his gaze with large compassionate eyes. "You saved my life."

"And you shall save us all." He offered his sweetest smile. "So, you remember your story?"

She nodded excitedly. "I am taking my aunt and uncle to our family plot in Petropavlovsk." She answered with the eagerness of a proud student in a spelling bee. "The bodies are not to be embalmed and must be buried within the week per our family custom."

"That should keep them from prying and possibly get us where we're going faster. You have the pistol and the knife well hidden but easily accessible like I taught you?"

She patted her jacket and nodded.

"We only trust this boatman as far as our money will allow," he began. With a wince he continued. "You'll stay with the caskets during the day and slip out at sunset, alright? We're grumpy risers and I wouldn't want you accidentally become breakfast."

"Will I have a casket one day?" she asked.

"Certainly," he answered with a wide grin.

"Who will watch over the three of us then?"

He patted her on the cheek. "We'll burn that bridge when we come to it."

"Cross."

"Pardon?"

Vladlena looked nervous, afraid she'd spoken out of turn. "You meant 'cross that bridge' didn't you?"

"You're right, of course," Zhora answered with a chuckle.

Zhora stood beside Sevastyan atop the ship's bridge. With Sovetskaya Gavan out of sight, only a dim glimmer remained on the horizon behind them. A sky black with storm clouds obscured the stars and moon above, casting the two in the dimmest light. Only a meager series of lights on the cargo ship's deck illuminated them.

"The nights grow shorter," Sevastyan mused. "Soon summer will make little time for hunting."

Zhora examined his companion as he looked up at the rumple-clouded sky, pensive and despondent.

"Soon? We've months yet."

"You still mark time as the living do."

"How much of your prior life do you remember?"

A smile emerged, exposing Sevastyan's fanged teeth. The creature's grin sat ill-fitting on his filthy mottled blue-grey skin. Yellow eyes showed hunger more than glee.

"I remember sensations," he answered, "the sun on my face, sweat across my brow as I worked the railroad. Mosquitoes biting, lips kissing, a mother singing, these I remember in patches like an old quilt."

Zhora crouched at the roof's edge and listened to the heartbeat below. It thrummed slowly, like a steam engine on a slowing locomotive. Nearly asleep and half drunk, the man fought to stay on course and cursed to himself.

"You trust Vladlena?" Sevastyan wondered.

"With my life."

"How? Why? She's nothing, she's no one."

Zhora stood and stepped within a hand's width of Sevastyan. "She idolizes me. I've offered her a fantasy of hers, a chance to turn the tables, power to prey on the world that's preyed upon her for so long. She'll do anything to see that dream realized."

Below, footfalls, the smell of freshly brewed tea and pipe smoke, all draw near and pass into the bridge. Two men spoke of course and speed, weather conditions and when the captain wanted to be woken. The graveyard shift had arrived.

"Let's get started," Zhora whispered. "I'm starving."

Nightmares in the Stars

TWENTY-EIGHT

Aboard the K-389, in the Sea of Okhotsk

"Ballast Officer, prepare to ascend to twenty meters." Mikhail opened the periscope's hydraulic valve. The cylinder hissed with rising pressure and the metal whined as it slid through the bearing overhead.

"Helm, come to course zero eight zero."

As the crew followed his commands, the ship lurched to port just enough for Mikhail to feel it. The ship angled upward just enough slide Mikhail's teacup across the nearby counter. He cursed under his breath and stowed it in its proper holder beside the Periscope Station's ashtray.

The 'scope emerged from the well between Mikhail's feet. He crouched to grasp its handles, unfolded them and rose until it came to a halt with a hushed thump. He leaned into the eyepiece and blinked. Darkness. Thirty meters beneath the waves and an hour past sunset and it still bothered him. No sunlight, not for another week.

"Tactical Coordinator, extinguish the lights."

The room vanished from his peripheral vision. As his eyes adjusted, constellations of indicators, from the tactical panel to his right to the ballast station on his left, dotted the darkness. Within the periscope lens even its onyx view revealed an emerging slate hue.

"Twenty five meters, Bridge Officer," the Ballast Officer bellowed.

The speaker nearby clicked. In the background he heard a chaotic electronic chorus.

"Four radar contacts, Bridge Officer."

The young man detailed specific signals he heard across the aether and described the ships likely to accompany each tone. Within Mikhail's head the fleet came together as a whole image, a cruiser, two destroyers, and a frigate. By class and model they took shape along the horizon of his mind's eye. Their voyage to Petropavlovsk served an additional purpose. A Pacific Fleet squadron honed their submarine tactics on K-389. Their relentless mock attacks and rain of sonar buoys, and persistent pinging had put the crew on edge in the first few days into the Sea of Okhotsk.

Ayatollah confirmed his sonar contacts matched each radar contact.

"One salvo and our score would be even," Ayatollah said.

"It would be nice to return the favor," Mikhail conceded. "But we've orders to cease our games at night. Those poor souls need a break from harassing us."

"Aye," the sonar-man said. "But wouldn't it be fun to see them scatter?"

"Twenty meters, Bridge Officer," the Ballast Officer reported.

As he spoke, a murky film slithered across Mikhail's periscope view and the utter blackness gave way to the blue-black of night. Stars winked high in a clear evening sky.

An ideal night for astronomy, he heard his stepfather say. A shudder rippled down his spine. The farmer fancied himself an amateur astronomer and had enticed Mikhail to join him for a fall night of stargazing. On the roof the man new to Mikhail's home had staged his homemade telescope, a thermos of hot tea and a pair of kitchen chairs. Excited for the opportunity, delighted his new stepfather seemed to be more than the harsh taskmaster he'd been in the field, Mikhail raced to peek through the glittering eyepiece. But the monster had other plans too, other means of warding off the autumn chill.

A hand on Mikhail's shoulder made him jump.

"Sorry to startle you Lieutenant Koryavin," Lieutenant Pudovkin apologized with a chuckle. "I'm here a little early, I know, but I'm your relief tonight."

After Mikhail caught his breath, he began the Bridge Officer litany. He explained the ship's operational status, sonar and radar contacts, and the captain's standing orders.

Pudovkin's grasped the periscope. "I relieve you as Bridge Officer."

Before Mikhail left the periscope station, Pudovkin reached out with one hand while he kept his eye pressed against the periscope and pulled him closer.

"I left a present on your bunk," he whispered. The man's bright smile managed to shine in the meager light.

"What?"

"I'd rather not say." His grin widened.

"Look," Mikhail began, whispering back through gritted teeth. "I don't like surprises. What is it?"

"Calm down, Mikhail. It's not a bomb and it's not my mother's underwear. I thought I'd loan you something. I thought it'd cheer you up after a rough day. It's not the kind of thing one talks about on the Periscope Station."

"Oh, okay, thanks."

Mikhail left the Command Center and descended to second deck. Ahead his crewmates ate, laughed, and chatted. Behind, his quarters beckoned. He must know what Pudovkin had done.

He thought of the academy. There'd been a classmate who hoped to ease Mikhail's tension with pornography. He couldn't have been more wrong about the outcome. The magazine enticed him. He hadn't seen a woman naked since his second and last date in school. But before long, nightmares rose up and he vomited all over himself, his bedding, and ruined the magazine. Angry and ashamed, Mikhail hid the evidence until lights-out and snuck out to clean his hidden sheets and uniform.

151

Nika can help me get over all that. If she's brave enough to trust me, if she loves me as much as I love her.

In the cramped quarters he stood between two rows of bunks, each curtained off from the shoulder width space between them. Dank socks and a hard day's sweat, these he smelled from the bunk to his left, Boreyev's bunk. Opposite was his bunk. Gingerly, he pulled back the curtain, as if whatever Pudovkin left might strike. The red light overhead reflected in a rectangular shiny object. He reached in and placed a hand on it. He turned on the small white light within his bunk.

Cassette tapes, their cases devoid of any information, three of them lay atop a small player with headphones bound with their chord nearby. Pudovkin had spoken of his visits to ports in the Mediterranean. He spoke of forbidden cultures in Egypt and Libya. Mikhail looked over his shoulder before he inserted a tape, donned the headphones and pressed the play button.

A jumble of noises crushed his eardrums and pierced his brain. He fought to find the volume knob and lessen the pain. Gradually he understood the rhythm, felt his heart thrum with the beat. Unintelligible words sounded exuberant, rebellious, and drunk with the power. He turned the case over, and in his hand and a scrap of paper fell out. He read it: "Van Halen".

We're Already Dead Men

TWENTY-NINE

Aboard the cargo ship, Amurya, in the Sea of Okhotsk

Within the small cargo ship, *Amurya*, Vladlena retreated into the hold. Apart from rough wooden crates and pallets laden with steel drums, two coffins sat. With little light they still managed to gleam along their lacquered seams. Away from the sea-spray, out of the heat-peeling winds, the room still felt cold. Rusted ship's ribs groaned as it pitched and rolled. The waves thundered and thrashed against its steel skin.

The ship's captain and two crewmen burst in through the door she'd jammed shut. With pale gaunt features and deep shadows beneath their eyes, the three looked exhausted. With only two bare light bulbs dangling above them, the men looked like horrors from a movie. The first mate's eyes darted to every shadow. The captain kept his calm and approached her with his hands held out to her. The third man clutched the first mate's shirt sleeve and kept watch behind them.

"Open them," the Captain insisted. "Open those caskets little Miss or we will."

"Please, don't."

"You brought a curse upon us," the first mate screamed. He shot his captain a nervous glance before he stepped closer. "We should throw those coffins overboard . . . and you with them."

The captain reached out and gently touched his first mate's arm. When the two locked eyes the first mate relaxed his posture and unclenched his fists.

"Something's happening to me and my crew," he explained, "and I'll know the cause. One quick peek and we're out of your hair, that's all I ask."

"Please don't open those coffins," she begged. "You'll never see another sunrise if you do."

"You're in no position to threaten, girl."

She dropped to her knees and clasped her hands together as she pleaded.

"Let me tell you my story," she asked. "If you listen and believe, you'll have less trouble on your hands and no desire to disturb my family."

The captain loomed over her while the first mate snuck up on the first oblong box. He hovered over it and looked to his crewmates.

"Tell me," the captain answered.

Vladlena stood and dusted off her pants. She began to stroll around the cargo hold. She examined it, touched the walls, and gained a new sense of calm in her features and tension in her posture lessened.

"I was an orphan," she began, "When my father died in the mines my mother left to get a new husband. She walked out to fetch water and never returned. Some say she hopped on a train for Tbilisi."

The three men glared at her.

"There's more," she added. "I roamed from home to home, always causing one kind of trouble or another, always kicked out to find a new home. I ended up in Komsomolsk. Starving and desperate, I took work where I found it. I became a whore."

The silent sailor in the back, who'd kept his eyes darting to the shadows, looked her in the eye.

"No one loves a whore. No one pities a whore. I've never been given anything that I didn't have to earn. I've been a throw-away person my whole life."

The first mate threw up his hands. "How long is this

story? At what point will it ever point to these two boxes and explain why we should leave them alone?"

She held up a finger to her lips. "I'm getting to that."

"One night I saw an angel. He was so handsome, I couldn't stop looking. He visited the whorehouse and offered one woman salvation. She rejected him."

The first mate scowled. "I've heard this before. You're one of those religious types seeing signs in everything."

"Or it's the drugs," the third man muttered.

The captain leaned closer. His features pinched up, as though he strained to hear her story clearer. She continued.

"He set fire to the building. He saved me from the flames. He didn't judge me for my past. Instead he offered me all that other girl rejected, and more."

"Wait," the captain said. "What?"

"Immortality," she whispered.

"How?" the first mate asked. "Where is he? What happened to him?"

Vladlena put forth her sweetest smile and held her most demure posture. "He's in that casket."

"Aww, he died before he made good his promise?" the first mate asked with mock grief.

"No, idiot," the captain said, "he's not dead."

He peered at the two dark oblong boxes. "Is he Vladlena?"

"I'm tired of this mystery," the first mate growled. He leaned on the casket.

"Don't," the captain shouted.

He shoved the lid off. It clattered to the deck. He stared inside. His mouth gaped open. Eyes wide, he wavered with the ship's pitch and roll, his feet never moving, as if held fast by an anchor.

"*Bozhe moi*," the first mate exclaimed. Breathless, speechless, he stared into the open casket at Zhora. He stumbled back.

Everyone looked down at the serene features of a monster's face. Zhora's skin resembled translucent whitish grey wax. A faint pinkish hue suffused the waxy flesh and blackened conduits of rotted blood stood out just beneath the surface.

"I'm going to go and get a . . . a . . ." the quiet sailor mumbled while he retreated to the exit.

"Shut it before he wakes," Vladlena suggested, "and you might live."

The captain looked to the retreating sailor. "We must take these on deck and throw them in the sea. Get another couple of hands down here."

The man nodded and ran out.

The captain turned to Vladlena. "She'll need to be dealt with too."

Vladlena stepped back, deeper into the dank cargo hold, and pulled Zhora's Makarov pistol from her coat. She held it with both hands to keep it from shaking.

"You don't listen," she said with a nervous giggle. "We could've got to Petropavlovsk without all this. You'll make me shoot you. Sure you're ill. Anyone who's lost that much blood would be."

"I wouldn't believe what you're suggesting if it weren't for the nightmares and the sickness we all share." He took his first step closer to Vladlena.

She stepped back until the bulkhead halted her retreat.

"You brought monsters aboard my ship," the captain said. "I'd heard the stories and always dismissed them. But the nightmares have convinced me, everyone's nightmares."

The first mate scurried to the coffin's lid and gingerly replaced it.

The room's door creaked and everyone's attention shifted to it. The handle wiggled and squeaked, then nothing.

The captain ran to it and tried to open the door. Though unlocked, the handle only opened a few centimeters before strained tension pulled it shut. He motioned for the first officer to peer through the crack as he tugged it open again.

"Someone's tied a rope to the knob outside and the other end's tied to the door across the passageway."

"Vasili," the captain whispered.

"Vasili, open this door," he shouted.

"No," the man whimpered.

The captain yanked on the door and pulled on it. "Vasili, if we act fast enough, the nightmares will stop. We can cast these monsters into the sea."

"But . . ." Vasili began, "what about my mother?"

"What about her? She's home in Sovetskaya Gavan, waiting for us to return."

"She's dying, cancer." He sniffled. "There's no other way to save her."

"No," the first mate screamed. "No, no, no!" with each word he tugged and clawed to part the door from its frame to no avail.

"When I'm made immortal, I can pass my gift on to my mother. It's the only way."

The captain turned to Vladlena. She brought her pistol to up again.

"I'm surprised too," she said with a shrug.

"It's not what you two think," the captain said to the whimpering man outside the hold. "It's not immortality. It's eternal damnation."

"What do you know?" she asked in a scream. The pistol shook in her hand as she erupted. "I've been damned my whole life. It's time someone else suffers. It's time for something to go my way. I'm tired of being tossed from bed to bed, slapped and spat on just to keep alive."

She stomped closer and closer in her tirade. The captain closed too, step for step, until he lunged for the pistol. He grabbed it, shoved its aim from his gut. He wrested it free and whipped the gun back across the girl's face. She fell to the floor.

The captain stood over her, pistol jammed into her soft, rosy cheek.

The coffin lid slid aside.

"Spilling Vladlena's blood cannot save you," Zhora said.

He rose from the coffin effortlessly until he stood on its edge. He stepped down and held a hand out to the horrified first mate. "It will only bring my wrath."

"We're already dead men," the captain replied.

Zhora offered a thin smile. "*How* you die, that's what's

at stake. Cooperate and you'll slip into a gentle slumber. If you make trouble, well, we've time enough to torture you until you're too hoarse to scream."

This is Not a Drill

THIRTY

Aboard the K-389

Against Mikhail's closed eyes the dawning sun glowed red. Birds chirped and the wind buffeted against the flimsy farmhouse roof.

The klaxon awoke him. His sun had been the red lights of his quarters. The birds had been the first sonar buoys dropped from the helicopter above. The wind had simply been the ventilation in his bunk.

"All hands to quarters," the intercom commanded. "Battlestations."

He rolled out of his bunk and watched his roommates peer out from their curtains.

"Hurry now," he chided, "we might win this one."

"It's an entire squadron of ship hunting us in shifts," Dovzhenko whimpered.

"That squadron needs to practice hunting submarines every bit as much as we need to learn how to operate ours," Mikhail said. "Now come on before Konev chews your ass again."

Mikhail dressed and marched out before he heard Dovzhenko's feet hit the deck.

Grumbling weary men trudged to their stations. Konev weaved his way through the narrow passage, between the men. With a fresh shave and neatly combed hair, he stood out among his comrades. Too tall for many parts of the ship, he kept his neck angled to one side.

"Come on, men," he said with forced enthusiasm. "Show those bastards what you're made of." With that, the Executive Officer raced up the ladder to the Command Center.

"He's the bastard for being so chipper," Seaman Kipchak muttered.

"I heard that," Mikhail snapped. "Don't make this exercise any harder than it has to be. Don't heap a court martial on our list of firsts for this crew."

"Sorry, Comrade Lieutenant, it's just . . . "

Mikhail halted and held the man's gaze. "I know it's rough. We've had it easy compared to a regular fleet boat. Now's the time we earn our place among the fleet."

"All hands to quarters, battle stations, this is *not* a drill," the intercom blared.

Mikhail's stomach turned to lead and he found himself staring, blank-faced at Kipchak. The boy's stunned expression matched his own. Without another thought or word, they raced to their stations.

In the Command Center Mikhail took his position at the chart table. Lit from underneath, the chart displayed the sea's terrain beneath the submarine. From here, Mikhail compiled data from others in the room and built the scenario around them as information funneled in.

Captain Borodin entered the Command Center with long quiet strides and took his place beside Pudovkin.

"Report, Bridge Officer. What do we have?"

"An unidentified submerged contact, Comrade Captain." Pudovkin's nervous report garnered a long quiet look from Borodin. He took the lieutenant by the shoulders.

"This is what we've trained for. Treat it as you would any exercise."

Pudovkin nodded. "I thought I might gain a tactical advantage in tomorrow's exercises by getting ahead of our projected track.

"Show me."

The two men stepped off the periscope station and over

to the chart table where Mikhail stood. Pudovkin pointed to a rectangle on the chart. K-389's plotted position was two nautical miles north of the box.

"You've violated our operation instructions," Captain Borodin stated in a level tone.

Pudovkin winced. "I interpreted our exercise instructions loosely, to gain an advantage." He awaited the captain's reprisal.

"It's done, Lieutenant, and we've discovered something dangerous as a result."

"Yes Comrade Captain. It seems they've positioned themselves on the opposite side of our forces above and dropped beneath the thermal layer to further avoid detection. What they hadn't counted on, was for me to gradually move out of our maneuvering envelope."

"Pass the word, quietly," the captain whispered, "the ship is to remain silent. Also let them know an enemy lurks in the sea, an American submarine."

Pudovkin crossed the Command Center and spoke with Michman Gorelov. The man's broad brow furrowed and his eyes shined a warrior's gleam. He gathered the duty electrician and duty mechanic. After a brief huddle each man scurried in an opposite direction, eyes wide.

"Captain," Mikhail ventured from across the chart table, "the submarine's position relative to ours almost suggests they know where our submarine is, or at least where it's supposed to be."

Borodin met Mikhail's gaze. The tired, grandfatherly countenance he'd grown to love as a father had vanished. He looked like he'd lost a loved one. Shocked and mournful, he cast his eyes down to the thin paper. Spokes, bearings of their sonar contacts, spread out. Four terminated in notations all had seen for several days. The fifth nexus on the page held only the words, 'unknown submarine'.

"If so, our enemy knows our codes and our nation's defense may already be undone."

Konev and Dimitriev entered the Command Center. Konev scanned the room before looking to Borodin.

"Americans?" he asked.

Borodin nodded.

"The fleet. Get the fleet above to chase them off," Dimitriev insisted.

Borodin and Konev glared at the zampolit. The man frowned and crossed his arms. He turned from the two and strolled to the Ballast Officer, Gorelov. The Michman winced when Dimitriev settled into one of his standard motivational speeches to him and the helmsman.

Captain Borodin brought Konev to the tactical chart and apprised his second in command of their situation. Konev angled his head back and looked down his long nose at Pudovkin's brazen interpretation of his orders and nodded to Mikhail at the mention of his theory.

From there the two captains marched to the sonar station. Turning from his large green display, still wearing huge padded headphones, Ayatollah explained the conditions of their surveillance.

"We are both beneath the thermal layer. The American shows no indication he's tracking us."

"How did we gain them and they don't detect us?"

"Comrade, Captain, you don't have faith in us?" Ayatollah asked with a smirk.

"It's not you. K-389 is an old ship."

"Judging from the noises we're picking up, they're just as old," Ayatollah answered. "Sturgeon class submarine."

He nodded toward a redheaded young sailor examining his sonar screen, squeezing his headphones in tighter. "That boy," Ayatollah continued with chuckle.

"Vetrov, he's new. He's still investigating whale farts and rain squalls." His smile vanished. "You noticed something, didn't you boy?"

Vetrov offered a wincing smile and nodded.

"Good man," the captain said with a nod. He slapped Ayatollah on the shoulder. "Good work. I'm sure your training helped."

"He's a sharp young pup." Ayatollah looked back to Vetrov and winked.

162

"They are within Soviet waters," Konev said through clenched teeth. "Contact the fleet to run them off."

Borodin put his arm around Konev and walked him past Mikhail, to the Command Center's aft starboard corner. He looked up into Konev's eyes. Mikhail's heart jumped when his captain spoke.

"And what if Lieutenant Koryavin's theory is true? Have they broken our code? Do they know the Pacific Fleet's orders?"

Mikhail wondered if the men knew how the panel behind them reflected their conversation and made it possible for him to hear.

"Notify headquarters and let the Americans continue to think us unaware?" Konev whispered.

Borodin shrugged. "We might do well to monitor them, gather data, and let the Admiralty in Vladivostok deal with the intelligence we gain."

Konev snickered and nodded. "And I thought you too long in the tooth for political plays."

"It's not politics," Borodin countered with a growl.

"Of course not."

Captain Borodin brought his fist down on a locker. The room fell silent except for the machines. The sonar equipment echoed the sounds of the ocean. Hydraulic piping hissed as the helmsman moved the rudder and stern planes.

"We'll continue our daily maneuvers," the captain said. "But brief the men, we're not going to battle stations during the day, we'll go at night."

"Captain?"

"With codes possibly compromised and dangerous games across the globe, I'm not worried about making admiral. I'm concerned about our nation's secrets. We'll have our battle-stations team focused on tracking these weasels at night."

Kill Me, Please

THIRTY-ONE

Aboard the cargo ship, Amurya

The *Amurya* pitched until only the clouds and rain filled the pilothouse window. When it crested the wave, a weightless lurch knotted in Zhora's stomach for a heartbeat, before careening down into the sea's trough where the hull thundered and shuddered. The storm-clouded sky vanished and room darkened in the chasm between waves.

"We will die," Vasili moaned. With grey teeth he bit at nicotine-stained fingernails. His bloodshot eyes widened and darted with every screech and squeal of the cargo ship's riveted seams.

"There's no other way," Zhora insisted. At the ship's wheel he felt every wave tug then shove the rudder. "We cannot pull into any port, your crewmates made sure of that. And where we're destined, they'd gun this rusted hull to pieces before we put ashore."

"You have nothing to worry about, you're immortal."

Zhora laughed. "A moment in the sun will kill me as surely as a bullet to your brain." He paused. Lightning tore across the sky and revealed sheets of rain and waves at war with each other. For a moment, atop the wave, Zhora looked out on kilometers of churning ocean, ranks of waves crashing and clashing.

Darker depths pulled his thoughts deeper. A heart already stone cold felt a bitter chill.

"I don't relish immortality trapped in a sunken ship, a life of starving madness. That would be as real a hell as I might ever imagine."

Vasili swallowed hard, withdrew and lit a fresh cigarette, and put a hand on the wheel. "What must I do?"

A fanged grin emerged and Zhora clapped the man's shoulder. "There's a brave fellow." He pointed to the compass and the sea ahead. "Steer the course I've outlined in the log. Don't let anything deter you. If other ships signal you, ignore them."

"Vladlena will check on you periodically. Don't let her distract you. I know she's a darling little woman and a former whore. I feel your blood grow warm at the mention of her name and I hear your pulse pound. Stay on course, follow your instructions, and the two of you will have millennia to enjoy each other." He chuckled. "And your mother, when we save her, she can nag the two of you every night."

"Mother wouldn't," Vasili began. But when Zhora chuckled and slapped him on the back, he laughed along with him and nodded.

Zhora descended into the *Amurya's* belly. Ahead he heard the ship's crew moan and whimper. He turned into the captain's quarters and grinned. Zhora's stomach trembled at the sight of the man tied to his bunk. Hunger rose like the waves outside. Shadowy emotions darkened his heart and clashed with his desire. *Wouldn't I have mourned this man's fate not long ago?* Anger swelled up and crushed his doubts. *No, never.*

"Kill me," the captain begged in a whisper. The man's pallor spoke of blood loss and his sunken eye sockets of torture and a sleepless week.

"You could've seen your family," Zhora hissed. "If only you'd dismissed your weakness for the illness we hoped you would. You insisted on making us enemies."

"Kill me, please."

"I'll grant your wish when I've set foot on Kamchatsky soil. Until then, you and your stubborn crew will feed me

166

and my friend. I warned you yet you defied me. I offered you peace and you brought my wrath upon yourself. Mercy is a ship that's sailed long ago for both of us, my friend."

In the cargo hold, Zhora stood still and watched Vladlena. She slept on a mattress beside the hold's door, curled around a bundle of pillows taken from the crew's quarters. Within arm's reach the Makarov pistol sat. No Nika, she was a fragile waif with no sense of herself in the world. Like the sea's flotsam, she floated along with life's tides and storms. Always eager to please and hungry for attention, she made a loyal if unheroic assistant.

"I miss my Siberian forests," Sevastyan whispered when he entered.

"Go back then" Zhora countered. "I can handle this alone."

"How can you be so confident and lost at the same time?"

Zhora turned from his task to face the woodsman. "There are two kinds of people, those who act and those who are acted upon. I'd rather be in a mess of my own making than reacting to the stupidity of my peers."

"In the memories we shared, when I first fed on you," Sevastyan said, "you weren't so hateful. I saw a sad young man, uncertain of so much."

"The world judged me harshly because of who I loved," he answered. Within his numb senses, a warm ache throbbed in his throat. Heavier it became and his shoulders slouched under the burden. "My options shrank until I'd nowhere to turn."

The ship ratcheted up the next wave. The engines moaned. Meager light from the night's storm laden-sky seeped in. Lightening flashed.

Zhora choked down the pain and straightened himself. "Now, thanks to you, I'm free."

"Free?"

The crest's foam hissed against the hull.

"I'm free to find love and free to exact justice upon those who judge me harshly."

The bow pitched downward and the ship rumbled into the darkness again.

Warmongers

Aboard the K-389

"War, you would provoke war?" Lieutenant Pudovkin warned. He looked to his captain and back to the executive officer. "That *is* what you suggest."

"They are in our territorial waters and must be challenged," Konev insisted.

"The Americans love their cable television, rock and roll, and fast food," Pudovkin countered. "They'll not risk war."

Konev rose to his feet and pounded the table. "You would dismiss their trespass? You would point at hamburgers and televisions as proof of their benevolence?"

A hush descended on the wardroom of K-389. Captain Borodin assembled them at the end of their third day of war games, the beginning of their second night tracking an American submarine as it shadowed the fleet above. The *USS Tautog*, they surmised, had spent days monitoring the exercises and gathering intelligence on tactics employed by the Red Fleet.

"Warmongers," Dimitriev declared. "We must challenge the American incursion or invite more of the same."

"Are we prepared to do this?" Doctor Anatoli asked. "Are we prepared to send a submarine only recently overhauled back the Komsomolsk for repairs?"

"Will we communicate with the fleet first?" Lieutenant Dovzhenko asked. "They'll go n-n-nuts if we deviate from our orders."

Boreyev shot a glance at Mikhail and nodded. "If we do, and Lieutenant Koryavin's theory proves true, we can confirm it by contacting the fleet with our intentions."

"Unless they refuse to tip their hand for so small confrontation," Captain Borodin said. He poured himself a fresh cup of tea. "We need something threatening but not dangerous, something defensible in a court martial and effective in communicating our displeasure at their trespass."

"What about a training accident?" Mikhail wondered aloud. "Zhora . . . Lieutenant Ivankov used to tell me how submarine tactics revolve around deception and misdirection. We might be able to execute our orders and still threaten the invaders."

"Ready tubes two and four," Captain Borodin ordered from the periscope station.

"Captain, wait," Ayatollah shouted. The short, grizzled petty officer trotted to his captain. "The Tactics Coordinator's figures are-

"Enough!" Dimitriev screamed. "Lieutenant Koryavin is an educated and decorated officer and Captain Borodin is your commanding officer. Obey your orders or see yourself in chains in the bilge."

"Tactical Coordinator," Captain Borodin said loud enough to command silence, "set torpedo enabling at one-six-hundred meters."

Mikhail nodded and brought the microphone to his lips and spoke in a low tone. "Torpedo room, set torpedo enabling at one-six-thousand meters."

"Captain," Ayatollah said, "we've three minutes before the start of today's exercises. I wouldn't want us to-"

Dimitriev glared. "Petty Officer . . . Yudin, shut up and mind your sonar panel!"

Ayatollah tugged at his beard. "Aye, Comrade Zampolit."

"Fire Two!"

Deep within the ship a thump and hiss signified the first torpedo's launch.

"Helm, ahead flank-flank," Borodin ordered. "Left full rudder, come to course zero one five."

The engineer's bells rang on the helm panel and the ship lurched. The engines thrummed in response and deck vibrated.

"Fire Four!"

Another launch shuddered through the deck and sent a shiver down Mikhail's spine. He watched the torpedo tracks lengthen across the tactical chart. Two red lines closed on the squadron a mere two kilometers away. Ayatollah watched his sonar screens go green-white with noise as the ship picked up speed. He threw up his hands but didn't mention a word to the Captain.

"First torpedo," Mikhail reported, "running on course and closing. Second torpedo, same. One-four-hundred meters to target."

Pipes in the overhead rattled. Ventilation ducts rumbled. K-389 broke her previous speed record by two kilometers per hour.

Minutes seemed to stretch into hours. Mikhail reported the closing distance to target. Captain Borodin ordered an all engines stopped. Gorelov, the helmsman, and duty electrician waited for the simulated hit. Mikhail tracked the torpedoes through the fleet's center and beyond.

"What happened?" Captain Borodin asked. "Why haven't they engaged?"

"I'm looking into it, Captain," Mikhail replied.

"New sonar contact, Captain," Ayatollah reported. "It's the American submarine, *Tautog*. They've sped up and turned to run. It seems our torpedoes have passed beneath the fleet and are bearing toward the American submarine."

Captain Borodin turned to Mikhail, grinned, and stepped off the periscope station. He strolled to the tactical chart. He cleared his throat and donned a mask of concern. "Oh no, will our torpedoes hit the foreign submarine?"

"Captain, I've made a horrible mistake," Mikhail explained. "I ordered the torpedoes to engage at sixteen thousand meters instead of sixteen hundred. That's why our torpedoes missed the fleet."

"Two new contacts, Comrade Captain," Ayatollah reported. "Helicopters, distant, skimming the surface near the *Tautog*." He pressed his headphones tighter. "They're dropping sonar buoys." He laughed. "The fleet's mistaken the American submarine for us."

"How?" Borodin wondered aloud. "They're not even in our operating box."

"Captain, the fleet has launched a salvo of training depth charges." Ayatollah's jaw hung agape.

Captain Borodin looked again to Mikhail. "Lieutenant Koryavin, get us up to periscope depth so we can clear up this matter. I'll be with Lieutenant Dovzhenko in the Radio Room to speak with the fleet about this horrible accident."

A familiar voice rippled through the deep and echoed from the sonar panel. "Teg Vy yemu."

All the crew in the Command Center laughed at the fleet's parting message to the *USS Tautog*: *Tag, you're it.*

I'm Old, But I'm Not Dead

THIRTY-THREE

Aboard the K-389 at Petropavlovsk-Kamchatsky-50, a submarine base in the Soviet Far East

Before the hull first kissed the pier, the captain insisted the officers and crew give all their equipment a thorough shakedown. Seconds after the tugs finished mooring the ship, he'd boarded an awaiting limousine adorned with the admiralty's insignia.

"We only noticed the leak when we shut it down after we pulled in," Kipchak said over his shoulder. He led Mikhail to 'the bomb', an oxygen generator that took purified water and used electrolysis to separate the oxygen from hydrogen. Most submariners called it the bomb out of respect for the dangers it posed: electricity, hydrogen, and oxygen, all kept under pressure within a series of tall metal cylinders.

The two marched through Missile Compartments Forward and Aft. There, Mikhail locked eyes with a weary Boreyev. Not since Komsomolsk had the two shared a word or a meal. The missile officer kept busy readying his tubes to receive sixteen ballistic missiles. Once aboard, either of these compartments would carry enough rocket fuel to melt the entire ship in half and more firepower than most nations on Earth. Without a word, Lieutenant Boreyev returned to his work. His petty officers huddled around him while he outlined their evening's plan.

A veil of filth still remained in the Auxiliaries

Compartment, an odorous mixture of human waste, mildewed insulation, and oily smoke. Mikhail's throat tightened and dried when he entered and remembered.

"You've not yet isolated the leak?" he asked.

Kipchak pointed to a bottle of soapy water atop the generator. "I've found it with that. It bubbled up nicely. But I'll need replacement gaskets, nitrogen to purge with, and permission to begin such dangerous work. I know what to do, but protocols require a qualified generator expert at least oversee my work.

Mikhail glared at the tangle of pipe and wires that comprised the oxygen generator's control system. A cold dinner sat in his stomach like he'd swallowed a stone. According to his watch, sunset passed by outside an hour ago. This last new problem cropped up with him only a few ladder rungs from freedom. *Nika's only a kilometer away. Her, a real shower and real food, all just a short stroll from here.* He'd stared up the ladder well at the cool blue twilight sky and sighed.

"We'll work it together," Mikhail said. "It'll go quicker."

Kipchak nodded and smiled. "I'll get the tools together, Comrade Lieutenant, if you want to get the nitrogen and gaskets."

Within an hour, the two sat amidst a dismantled manifold, both filthy.

"Tell me again," Mikhail began. "How is it a farmer's son knows so much about machines?"

The young man had shown an aptitude for machinery and Mikhail recruited him from the galley as a mechanic's apprentice.

"My grandfather worked in the army motor pool," Kipchak answered. "During the Great Patriotic War," he added proudly. "Back home afterwards, he used to earn things in trade fixing the tractors and combines."

"He taught you?"

"He went blind. I was a horrible farmer. My father finally let me be my grandfather's eyes. We'd travel for days and come back with more to eat than my father put on the table."

Up on deck, the crisp air refreshed Mikhail after hours in the Auxiliaries Compartment. The sentries huddled over the mid-ships hatch and reveled in the warm draft wafting up from within the vessel. The submarine town bustled nearly as much at midnight as it had when they arrived near noon.

Komsomolsk and Petropavlovsk–Kamchatsky–50 showed Mikhail the glaring disparity between the nation's poverty and these hidden oases reserved for military forces and Party apparatus. He remembered Nika's reaction when he'd offered to buy her new bedding when he puked on hers. He'd not known such wont since his childhood days on the farm. The memory plucked a chord in his heart. Surely Nika took his offer. Certainly she awaited his arrival in the town's apartments set aside for naval officers. Hopefully, he'd have a few weeks to get her settled in before they deployed again.

"Don't look so glum, son, there'll be other nights to see what this town has to offer."

Captain Borodin's encouraging words startled Mikhail. He looked at the old captain. Fatigue of another kind weighed heavy in the man's eyes. He looked tired and forlorn. Mikhail felt guilty for his personal desires.

"It's not that," he said.

"Really?" Borodin grinned and slapped Mikhail in shoulder. "I'm old, but I'm not dead. I remember those days."

"Looks like you had a rough day too, Comrade Captain."

Borodin's pleasant features faded and his gaze fell to the flotsam bobbing in the water between the hull and the pier. "We may be headed for trouble."

"Us, Comrade Captain?"

He lifted his face and met Mikhail's gaze. With arms outstretched he spoke. "We, all of us, the whole world." His hands fell to his sides and he looked beyond Mikhail, to the two sailors standing sentry. Engrossed in their own sea stories, the two alternated between laughs and scans of their post's perimeter.

"Forget what I said," Borodin muttered. A short tense laugh escaped. "That's ludicrous, I know, but no one else needs to know what worries me now, not just yet."

Captain Borodin left Mikhail to go and commiserate with the sentries before he descended into the ship.

"You didn't miss much," Doctor Anatoli said from the pier. His words spilled out like an overturned bowl of gravy. He leaned against a pallet full of crates, his eyes half shut.

"Shut up," Mikhail shot back. "Why aren't you restricted to the ship?"

"The vodka's better but the women . . ." He winced. "The women are too respectable, too domestic. They're no Nika, that's for sure." After two blinks, each long and deliberate, he replied to Mikhail's question. "My section's all shipshape. I've only got to count my pills and enemas until someone gets sick or hurt."

"You're drunk. Let me help you down the ladder."

Anatoli wobbled over to the ship's brow and crossed it like a deckhand in a typhoon. Hunched over and shuffling half a step at a time, he pulled himself across by the guardrail, hand over hand. By the time he'd gotten halfway across Mikhail raced to his aid, held him upright, and escorted him aboard.

"You miss her, don't you?" Anatoli asked. "Nika?"

Mikhail stopped and looked the doctor in the eyes. "I do."

"Don't. It's not worth it. Life's too short and too harsh to hold onto such things."

"I found a friend."

"I'm your friend."

"She was my first lover in years."

"Whoa," Anatoli said, backpedaling. "I'm not that kind of friend." His eyes widened. "Years? Really? A young man like you?"

Mikhail nodded.

Anatoli lunged forward and jabbed Mikhail in the chest with a boney finger. "You're too damned sullen. Life's too short to put on a sour face." He chuckled and shook his head. "It's too short to go that long without a woman."

Mikhail laughed. "You've never gone alone so long?"

The doctor frowned. "Goodness no! I'd lower my standards before I risked another maddening drought. Fat, short, hideous, at some point I don't care."

"Even married?"

Anatoli burst out laughing and slapped Mikhail on the shoulder. "Married? Those are at the top of my list, not the bottom."

"Why?"

The doctor put a finger to his nose. "Life's too short to have a wife, unless it someone else's. They don't cause a fuss or hang around long enough to rearrange your furniture to suit their tastes."

With help from the sentries, Mikhail lowered Doctor Anatoli into the ship. The man muttered more of his wisdom while three sober men helped him descend. Once done, Mikhail returned his attention to the wisp of nothing swirling in the corner of his mind.

Wife, the word conjured memories of the papers he'd given Nika and the offer he'd made. A reasonable woman would've jumped at the chance. Her indignant response had shocked him. Her lack of reason baffled him. He snickered to himself. Nika hardly seemed reasonable. But then again, he felt she'd been moved too, in love too, eager for a friend too.

Mrs. Koryavin

THIRTY-FOUR

Compared to Komsomolsk, the streets of Petropavlovsk-Kamchatsky were spacious and clean. Shop fronts displayed items for sale instead of empty shelves. More cars, more bicycles, more everything adorned the city with no name. Known only by a generic designation, Petropavlovsk-Kamchatsky-50, served the military and no one else. Encircled by fences, guards, and thick hedges beyond, the closed city included every convenience of a city with all the security of a fortress.

He stood on the curb and stared at the building labeled: Naval Officer's Housing. The walk from the ship had accentuated his isolation from the world over the past weeks. Fresh air, car exhaust, and pools of stagnant rainwater all assailed a nose accustomed to diesel, ozone, and amine. He even relished the stench of a nearby dumpster. The sky's blue, the concrete's porous grey, and little green shocks of weeds delighted him. *Three weeks beneath the sea, only three weeks; will I go mad after three months?*

Mikhail's heart beat beneath his tunic like a hummingbird's while his stomach clenched up like a fist. With a bottle of vodka and a can of caviar under one arm he entered the lobby. Wide, with a low ceiling, it still seemed expansive compared to his weeks aboard K-389. Walls of yellow, trimmed in white, looked new. Nautical paintings hung on every wall except behind the counter. Pictures of the admiralty and Soviet leaders stood in a row behind the two uniformed clerks, a young woman and an older man. They greeted him cordially and listened to his story before issuing him a key.

Carpeted floors muffled his footfalls as he ascended the stairs. Yellowed bulbs cast the hallway in a jaundiced light. He stared at the brass number nailed to the door. He glanced at the door's knocker and the knob's lock.

Worst case, you get to sleep in a real bed.

He unlocked the door, entered, and his jaw dropped. An elfish woman stood in the kitchen to his right. She stood barely five feet tall with short blond hair combed by a tornado and skin tanned by the moon.

"Who the fuck are you?" he asked.

"I'm Mrs. Koryavin, who're you?" Her smile faltered.

"I'm Lieutenant Koryavin," Mikhail managed. Sweat cascaded from every pore and his grip on the vodka bottle tightened. "I'm not sure we've met."

"Let me explain," she said in a child's voice.

Mikhail marched to the small table between them and set his gifts down. "You're not Nika. I don't know you. There's nothing to explain. Get out."

"Wait, wait, wait," she pleaded. "Nika couldn't come. She wouldn't. She offered me a chance to escape. We share the same problems, she said. We could overcome them together, she said."

"But I love Nika. I don't even know you," he snapped. He walked to the door and flung it open. "Get out."

"I'll die without your help."

"A girl crafty enough to steal Nika's ticket out will find a way to survive, always."

He grabbed her upper arm and marched her to the door. She clawed at his fingers and planted her feet. Tugging and grunting, her efforts only slowed her exit. Mikhail put a hand against her slender ribcage, shoved her out and slammed the door.

"Please," she cried through the thick door. "Please don't do this."

"Shut up or I'll call the front desk."

He looked to the kitchen table and spied the packet he'd given Nika a month ago. Crumpled and split, a charred corner caught his eye. He lunged for it, snatched it up and emptied the envelope's contents. Every page that touched the corner bore the scar of fire and smelled of smoke. Within, the letter he'd written, though crushed and rumpled, it remained sealed and otherwise unscathed.

Mikhail raced to the door and flung it open. The startled waif stared up at him. He grabbed her by the arms and picked her up off her feet until her face hovered inches from his.

"How did you come by this packet?" he growled. "Where is Nika? What happened to her?"

"I didn't want to upset you," she cried.

"Answer me."

"The whole building was in flames." Her last word choked in her throat. The girl collapsed in his arms and sank until Mikhail set her down.

"Nika and I were alone upstairs when it began. The bar was full. People were running everywhere."

Phantom smoke curled in Mikhail's nostrils. His own fiery experience played with his senses as she continued.

"She calmed me down when I watched the fire spread up the stairs." She drew her arms in and hugged herself. She sank to the floor and wrapped her arms around her knees. "We didn't panic until it began to burn the floor from the rooms below. We saw the flames between the boards and smoke."

Mikhail heard footfalls shuffling and looked to see another young officer and his wife stop a few feet into the hallway from the stairwell. He reached down and tugged at her shoulder.

"Come in for a minute," he muttered. "We'll figure this out."

She looked up, her soft green eyes peering through shocks of golden hair. Fatigue cast her features in a washed out light.

She'd not slept well, nor ate much in days.

When he grasped her outstretched hand a smile touched the edge of her mouth and brought her eyebrows up.

"You still aren't staying with me," he warned, "but we'll figure something out."

Dead. Burned in a fire and broken by a leap from her second story window, Nika died a week after Mikhail handed her a ticket out. She'd struggled with drugs and worried about her life alone if it didn't work out. In her dying breath she'd handed her opportunity to someone who might use it. She'd confided in this little woman all Mikhail's faults and fears. She'd broken his trust with a trusted friend, then sought to do them both justice with his parting gift.

Nemetskiy Devushka, the boys at the bar had called her, 'German Girl.' At least that's what she'd told him last night. Blonde, pale, and boney, she'd fit the description as far as any Soviet sailor might guess. Her demure demeanor contrasted with what he'd expected from a girl so named.

She moaned beside him and his breath halted in his tightening throat. He marveled at her naked back. Small, gentle and sweet, she'd been so many things Nika hadn't. According to her, Nika had figured out that all three of them shared a common tortured past. She'd also discerned how differently she'd coped. Nika had stared lust in the face and defied it to hurt her. With a warrior's mind she'd turned affection into a weapon to survive. German Girl had surrendered time after time, conceded a piece of herself each time to remain alive. In the end, Nika's strength became her strength too. Now she's dead.

The alarm clock buzzed beside him and he jumped before he slapped it silent. German Girl turned over and reached out for him. Her cool hand caressed his jaw line and she smiled.

"You'll need to shave," she murmured.

He slid away and stood. He examined the room and sighed, *no vomit this time. Maybe Nika knew something after all.*

"We'll sort this out," he said. "We've got to, soon, before I deploy."

She offered a pouting frown. "Am I that bad?" She shut her eyes, grinned and stretched. "I thought we were a good fit."

After a silence that hummed with tension in Mikhail's head, he hurried to get ready. Just before he ran out the door, he looked back.

"Look, I can't keep calling you Nemetskiy Devushka. It's not even a proper name. What shall I call you?"

She hugged the doorframe and ran her hand along its curved molding. Her eyes widened as she spoke.

"Vladlena."

The Wolf and the Rat

THIRTY-FIVE

Outside the Petropavlovsk-Kamchatsky-50 submarine base

Snow-blanketed mountain peaks ran in a jagged line across the western horizon. The sun's afterglow illuminated the sky and painted the thick clouds above mauve. Rocky outcroppings and forested hills had watched over them as they had slept. Zhora crawled out from the shallow grave he'd dug the night before. Sevastyan stood waiting. Zhora brushed clumps of black earth and grass from his clothes. Without a word, they marched to the hillcrest and peered down at their objective.

"You betrayed Vasili," Sevastyan said.

Zhora looked to Sevastyan. The century-old monster crouched a dozen feet from him, poised to fight. He held his arms out, claws twitching, shifting on the balls of his feet. His fractured golden irises caught the meager night light and flickered like candle-lit lanterns. He bared his fangs and hissed.

"Will you betray me too?"

Zhora turned his attention again to the closed city of Petropavlovsk-Kamchatsky. It occupied a swollen patch of land that stretched out from the hilly woodlands into Avacha Bay. Like the ships it harbored, the base remained attached to the mainland by a thin isthmus, a crossing well guarded, fenced with barbed wire, and well lit.

"I betrayed a fool," Zhora answered. "Are you a fool?"

Winfield H. Strock III

"I have been. I think that ends today."

Before Zhora uttered a reply, Sevastyan closed the distance and clamped a hand on his throat. Despite every effort to break free, Sevastyan picked him up and shook him. Fingers like a vice dug into his neck. He heard his bones grind and sinew squish. He felt his own black blood ooze from his wounds.

"You do not fear me," Sevastyan hissed. "That seems foolish. I am more vampire than you'll be in the next fifty years. Your transformation has only begun. You cannot match my strength or speed; nor ferocity learned from the best predators of the wild."

"The grave holds no fear for me," Zhora managed in a gasp.

"You lie," Sevastyan said with a snort. "I should kill you."

"Let us go our separate ways," Zhora suggested.

Sevastyan brought him closer and growled. "You made no such offer to Vasili."

"You mourn a simpleton human and threaten your own creation?"

Sevastyan lowered Zhora until his toes touched the ground . . .

. . . then hurled him.

"Yes."

The night sky flew by in a blur before he impacted a rock outcropping with a crunch. His shoulders bent backwards and his spine felt stuffed with broken glass.

"Vampires are hard to slay." Sevastyan conceded while he strolled to stand over Zhora. "And seldom stay dead."

The creature's eerie golden eyes dimmed and his focus fell backward through time. "And they hold a vendetta forever."

He walked beyond Zhora, deeper into the woods. Every attempt to move brought lightning bolts of pain. His neck ached and burned. His eyes burned with tears that refused to come. Between blinks he realized the night sky had vanished. Dawn approached. Above him Sevastyan

186

loomed, a boulder in his hand.

"This will pin you down until the sun burns you away."

He dropped the stone into Zhora's crumpled lap. An explosion of anguish shoved his consciousness aside. Disjointed sensations kept him aware while shock insulated him from drowning in agony. The world wobbled in and out of focus. Sevastyan descended from above and hovered over him, his grey face centimeters from his own.

"You're so clever," the revenant said with a toothy grin. "You may yet escape." He drove a finger into one of Zhora's open wounds. It felt like a hot sliver of steel.

"Know this," Sevastyan clutched Zhora by the jaw, "we are enemies."

Clawed fingers dragged across Zhora's cheeks.

"I despise how you treat others, how you abuse your talents. I am a wolf, a proud predator."

He stood and wiped his hands on his tattered tunic, examining them with a sick grimace.

"You, you are a scavenging rat. Should you live, do not cross my path again."

Unable to lift the boulder, Zhora sought to sink out from under it. He'd grown accustomed to the gristly grind of flesh and bone as he dug. The morning's birds startled him and hastened his pace.

With bare fingers, fingernails scraped off hours ago, he burrowed beneath his right hip. Deeper and deeper his flank sank. The stone budged by millimeters until he beheld his left leg. The midnight sky gave way to brighter blue.

With a branch worn smooth from all his attempts he tried again to dislodge the boulder atop him. The branch dug into his pelvic flesh when he worked it between himself and the stone. He tensed his muscles in an attempt to create a firm fulcrum to press against.

With an agonized and angry howl he pushed, careful not to surge and snap his only tool in half. The horizon warmed to a pinkish hue. Grit and bone crumbled with his effort. The boulder budged. Hope fed his strength. He drew in a deep breath and pushed again. Pain spread out from the stick's tip. He held his grip with one hand and frantically dug with the other. He spied his right foot and laughed.

Above, the sun's rays grazed the treetops. From the guard-towers far below, soldiers cried out. His screams had drawn attention. He gritted his teeth and prepared for one final shove. The stone moved and moved. A wet ripping sound accompanied a new pain. He growled and moaned. His hipbone now served as his prying point. His lower abdominal flesh had given way. Black blood, thick and sticky seeped into his trousers and shirttail opposite his appendectomy scar. With his left leg free, he pushed against the ground and the boulder rolled off. Forgotten parts now felt numb:, groin, thighs, knees, calves, and feet. Soldiers trudged nearer. Numbness gave way to a hive of bees stinging every millimeter.

On his stomach he crawled and panted.

"You there, stop." The selector switch of an AK-47 punctuated the stranger's order.

"*Bozhe moi*, what's happened? There's blood everywhere."

"My captors left me for dead," Zhora answered with a cough. "Come, help me up."

"Let me get a medic up here."

"No, I'll be fine. Just help me get up, quickly."

"Is that a naval uniform? It's filthy. How'd you end up here?"

"Yes, I'm Lieutenant Ivankov. I've been kidnapped for weeks now. I have urgent classified information to give to the admiralty. Now hurry and help me up."

The soldier grabbed his shoulder and turned him over. White-hot pain licked up his arm to the base of his skull. As soon as the man saw Zhora's face he froze. Other searching guards shouted, nearer than before. Zhora clutched the man's tunic and pulled him close. He sunk his teeth into his screaming throat and silenced him.

Fishing with Father . . . chasing after a dog . . . watching Father go to sea on a trawler . . . Mother drinking, crying, tucking him in bed . . .

Zhora floated like a barge through the soldier's youth while he drank. As bone and muscle reacted to fresh blood, the pain of his body's regeneration snaked through every injured part. Agony rose from newly rejuvenated nerves.

The soldier shriveled in his hands and grew lighter. When nothing flowed from his torn throat Zhora cast the drained corpse aside and rose.

Though sore, his crippling injuries lessened in severity as seconds ticked by and he felt the hot blood flowing within. The warmth in fingers and toes, the human feeling he'd normally felt after a good feed failed to blossom. It coalesced in those broken parts and felt hot as welding torches searing each cracked bone back together. Fractured bits felt soft, not wholly bone just yet. He ran a hand across his neck. The holes left by Sevastyan's stabbing claws had vanished. And like that, hunger twisted in his stomach and urged him to hunt.

Ravenous and searching, he felt the dawn's indirect light stab his eyes. The sunlit trees chilled him with fear. Only the hillcrest saved him from a fiery death. A robin-egg blue sky and golden rays across the bay below sent him scrambling to dig a new grave, to sleep through this day angry, aching, and starved.

Love and War

THIRTY-SIX

Naval Officer Housing at the Petropavlovsk-Kamchatsky-50 submarine base

Atop the apartment's roof, Vladlena greeted Zhora. She wore a long coat, a scarf, and held her arms tight around her, shivering. Zhora hardly felt the cold. He wore the uniform he'd stolen from his quarters aboard K-389 a month ago and kept clean in a canvas bag along with the identity papers that got him past the base's gate. He'd only asked her to wait for him on the rooftop out of concern for their secrecy. It struck him how comfortable the brisk night air felt. She looked at him with wide eyes aglow with adoration. It took her a moment to realize something amiss.

"Where's the other?" she asked. "Where's Sevastyan?"

"He's abandoned us. My plans scared him."

Vladlena's animated features revealed her concern before she spoke. "Will you manage without him? Is there any way I can help?"

So eager to belong, so hungry to please. As he approached her at the roof access door he stopped, cupped her face in his hand and smiled.

"You've already done so much," he said.

"I would do anything for you," she whispered. "I love you."

So pretty, not his type, but pretty. Petite, with an impression of innocence so perfectly played, she'd likely broken many a man's heart in her whoring days. Her guise of a proper, sweet, hometown girlfriend had kept her alive and off the streets for months. Zhora had seen her desire to serve him, her anxious urgency to fall under someone's protection. His plans included nothing of her beyond the next few days. He'd not seriously considered his promise to her until now. *She might be a better partner in this after all.* He put an arm around her and walked her into the stairwell leading down into the officers' apartment building.

"If you're brave enough and strong enough, I might need you to accompany me aboard our submarine."

Her eyes lit up and she bounced on the balls of her feet.

Once inside the apartment, Zhora got to work. Vladlena brought him a grocery bag of cosmetics and followed him to the bathroom.

Zhora looked in the mirror and fought the urge to scream. Seeing himself, merged with something else, something monstrous gradually taking over his features, it set his two halves, human and creature at odds with each other. Horrified at his slow slip from humanity, another part of him crept out from the shadows of his mind to admire it. His fingers curled into a fist and rose to shatter the twisted image.

"Why do this, master?" Vladlena asked. "You look beautiful as you are."

"That's the power of the vampire talking." He grabbed his own hand to bring it closer, to apply the foundation for his disguise. "My powers will not hold the attention of more than one or two people at a time."

"What do you really look like?" she wondered.

"You'll see soon enough. I've got to walk around with my crewmates, possibly for weeks before we'll control the ship."

"And how will I get aboard?"

"Leave that to me." He looked over his shoulder, leaned back and checked the apartment hallway. "You're certain Mikhail won't come home tonight?"

She nodded. "He'll be aboard until tomorrow night at

the earliest. He's on duty tonight."

"And he doesn't suspect you?"

"He's as naïve as they come. He was sad to hear about Nika's death, but that didn't stop him from sleeping with me the first night."

She frowned. "He wasn't much in bed though, kind of timid."

"Don't judge him harshly," Zhora snapped. "He's a good man who's led a rough life."

Vladlena sidled up beside Zhora and caressed his shoulders. "But he's nothing like I imagine you'd be. You seem wonderfully passionate yet tender, like a storybook hero. He behaved like a cowardly clumsy boy."

Zhora whirled about and had her neck in his hand before he realized. He held her up against the wall, her face reddening, not a noise from her lips. Her wide eyes bulged. Tears welled up and trickled down her cheeks. He set her down gently and she gasped to regain her breath.

"He is the closest friend I've ever known," Zhora said. He sat and resumed donning his makeup mask. "He's clever, only he doesn't have the confidence to act."

"Sorry," she gasped. "Sorry I-

He dismissed her apology with a wave of his hand. "You're not to prey upon him once I've made you a vampire, understood?"

"Yes, sorry." She crept closer and ventured to rest her hands on his shoulders. "When will that night come?"

"This is when your mortal self is most important, while you learn from Mikhail when the ship departs. We'll need to time my arrival for the night before. That's when I welcome you into eternity."

Zhora leapt from rooftop to rooftop, careful to slip into the shadows when the guards looked up. Each leap thrilled him more. Though immortal by most standards, the fear of falling pitted against his need to go exhilarated him to the point of feeling his pulse again. In those weightless moments between leap and landing, he felt free, alive, powerful. His landings lacked his mentor's grace.

Sevastyan had always made it look so easy.

The soldiers acted more nervous than normal. They scanned their areas with purpose. Conversations between the men remained hushed and short.

They must've discovered the man I consumed in the woods. Clumsy of me but unavoidable.

Nearer the docks he beheld two great cranes. They loomed over K-389, each holding an encapsulated missile, each partially inserted into the ship's missile tubes. On deck, between the two teams guiding the ordnance stood Lieutenant Boreyev to supervise.

They shouldn't even be handling missiles in the middle of the night, let alone with two teams and two cranes.

Naval infantry cordoned off the pier and kept an alert vigil over their charge. Just outside their perimeter Zhora spied a shining black limousine adorned with the admiralty's insignia. Captain Borodin stood with the Admiral and two men who wore suits of deep blue and grim expressions. Their eyes scanned those nearby whenever Borodin and the Admiral spoke.

With a curt salute, Captain Borodin dismissed himself and marched aboard his ship. The ship's visitors entered their vehicle and sped off.

From the corner of his vision Zhora noticed the other ships docked nearby, their crews also scurried on deck. Knots of men worked to weld, paint, and repair their ship. Another ship had formed a line out to supply trucks on the pier and passed cases of food hand over hand into the mid-ships hatch. The fleet prepared to head out to sea en masse.

A typhoon? An exercise? His outermost extremities tingled while he imagined the only other possibility. *War?*

When Two Liars Agree

THIRTY-SEVEN

Aboard K-389, at the Petropavlovsk-Kamchatsky submarine base

"The KGB and GRU have done the impossible," Captain Borodin told Mikhail and his other officers gathered in the wardroom, "they've found something they can agree upon."

Borodin chuckled alone at his snide aside. Mikhail knew what everyone else knew, their hastened pace to get underway bode ill for all. They'd all seen the other submarines hurrying alongside them. Lieutenant Boreyev's division had worked through the night loading missiles. Whatever provoked a fleet to action and the admiralty to visit also stole any humor from their captain's message. After seeing it in their faces, the captain relented and continued.

"The Americans and their allies are mobilizing for an exercise dubbed Able Archer," he began.

Only Dovzhenko looked relieved. Captain Borodin met the man's gaze.

"Able Archer is an annual exercise," Dovzhenko explained. "They practice coordinating command and control elements. It's nothing to worry about."

"This time it is," the captain warned. "Able Archer '83 differs in ways that suggest the exercise is a ruse, a disguise for real war. Communications have been excessive this year and real forces are participating on an unprecedented scale. For this reason, Strategic Rocket Command has placed all nuclear forces on Alert Status Two and ready to implement Status Three within twenty-four hours' notice."

"B-b-but it's just an exercise," Dovzhenko insisted.

Zampolit Dimitriev stiffened. "Just last year President Reagan promised to, 'leave Marxism and Leninism on the ash heap of history'."

"The Americans have been probing our defenses and goading our forces for years," Borodin said.

"Their Pacific fleet mobilizes even now under the guise of a separate effort," Captain Konev added. "They've assembled the largest armada in recorded history."

"Pieces of a puzzle are coming together," Captain Borodin explained. "We must demonstrate to our enemies, we are not fooled nor will we be bullied."

"We will deter that, won't we, Comrade Captain?" Pudovkin asked. "We will avert nuclear war, right?"

Captain Borodin nodded. "That *is* our purpose. And by deploying all forces now, we show our enemy that we know what they're doing and will answer their violence with violence should they test our resolve."

"What now Captain?" Doctor Anatoli asked.

Captain Borodin leaned forward and let his shoulders sag. His head hung low enough for his forehead to rest on his interlaced fingers. After a deep breath, he sat up and answered.

"Liberty for all hands must be revoked and shift work preparations to get underway will continue until we put to sea."

"But we're undermanned," Dovzhenko countered.

"There's no time to wait for our roster to fill," Konev replied.

The captain looked to Doctor Anatoli. "Go to the hospital and see if there are any sailors fit to go with us."

He turned to Dovzhenko. "Talk with Michman Gorelov and see if he might scrounge up some lost souls at the barracks or the brig. I'd be willing to speak favorably on behalf of any sailor willing to pull his weight aboard K-389."

"Aye Comrade Captain," Lieutenant Dovzhenko replied.

The captain looked to his officers. "Lieutenant Boreyev will need assistance loading the missiles. He's but one man, and though his men are good, they'll need an officer's supervision around the clock."

"I'll be fine," Boreyev insisted. "My men and I will be ready."

"I could lend a hand," Mikhail added.

"No," Borodin answered. "The oxygen generators need your attention if we're to remain submerged during our patrol."

"Once I've verified our charts are ready," Lieutenant Pudovkin said, "I can step in."

"Very good, Comrade Lieutenant," Captain Borodin said. He looked around the table and stood. "Dismissed."

Mikhail waited for the others to file out after the captain brought their meeting to a close. Borodin rubbed his eyes, stood and poured himself a cup of tea. He motioned for Mikhail to join him as he poured a second cup.

"Comrade Captain," Mikhail began nervously, "I have an awkward situation."

"Tell me plainly, we've no time for delicacy."

"I have a wife. I hardly know her. I need to let her know I'm leaving."

Borodin stared, mouth agape. "You? How . . ." His voice trailed off before he shook his head. "Never mind, it's done." He inhaled the tea vapors, let out a sigh, and continued. "All married men will be allowed a phone call home. Keep in mind, these calls will be monitored to ensure we leak no secrets."

Mikhail nodded. "Thank you Captain."

The two sipped their tea in silence.

"My wife and I were suddenly married," Borodin murmured into his cup. "We'd snuck behind our parents' backs enough to learn where babies come from. And we learned the price of a parent's love. As angry as they were, they helped us in those early years."

"I didn't realize you were married."

"Often I think we feel the same way." He gazed into his cup, his eyes darker, his posture hunched over as though burdened. "One more deployment and I hoped it would all change. I wonder if we'll even recognize each other."

"Captain, you seem convinced this time of war," Mikhail ventured. "I'd never known you to be pessimistic or alarmist. I'd always considered you wise enough to see through Party paranoia."

Borodin looked to Mikhail. In the old captain's eyes he saw a stranger, a scared and frail man.

"Military and civilian intelligence," Borodin began, "they've never been on the same page. Their politics prevent it. When two liars tell the same lie, it must be true."

Mikhail and Seaman Kipchak looked at their handiwork. Both oxygen generators hissed and hummed while the gauges and indicator lights all affirmed their success. The two men were unrecognizable from each other. Covered in soot and sweat, stripped down to undershirts and blackened workpants, they looked more like coal miners than sailors. The rest of the machinery division applauded their efforts and offered each a taste of the boat's first batch of 'bilge vodka'.

In the few weeks crossing the Sea of Okhotsk the seasoned veterans showed their new crewmates how to make the harsh concoction. The men gathered and brought their cups together, a wild assortment of canisters, lids, and hollowed out filter housings. They clunked together like a junkyard wind-chime before the chortling band threw back their brew in unison.

Mikhail felt a nerve running from his chin along his jaw up to his ear sing with the tartness of his drink. He looked forward, to the clock. In fifteen minutes he'd be eligible to call Vladlena. He downed his cup, bid his men adieu, and raced up the ladder. Up on deck the early spring breeze cooled his sweaty, exposed upper body. He ran across the brow and stopped to stand in line with the other husbands.

Not until now had he bothered to admire the surrounding countryside. Great mountains swept across the horizon like statues of the seas he'd seen, great waves of stone capped with snow. In their troughs verdant valleys beckoned. Avacha Bay dazzled with the evening's amber rays.

In front of him, Chief Antonev cradled the phone with both hands, his eyes red with mounting tears and his lip tightened to hold back a blossoming sob.

"You listen to your momma, Kristina" the chief ordered with a sniffle. "And you help her without her having to ask. Some day you might be a chief's wife with children of your own. If you don't behave now, it'll all come back on your head when you get married."

When the pudgy Antonev realized Mikhail stood nearby he straightened his posture and drew in a deep breath.

"I love you too."

Gingerly, slowly, he hung the phone up and retreated from the booth.

With a stone face he looked to Mikhail and nodded. "It's all yours, Comrade Lieutenant."

The phone rang and rang. He hung up and tried again. This time, as he thought to hang up, she answered. She sounded groggy and confused.

"Vladlena, I'm sorry to do this to you so soon, but I won't be home for a while."

"How long?" He heard her whine as she stretched.

"Weeks, that's all I'm allowed to say. The dormitory staff will get with you later and fill you in on what you're allowed to know."

"Um, okay."

"So long as I'm gone, the navy will look after you. The dorm staff can answer any questions you have. The only thing you cannot do is leave town."

"Why would I want to do that?" She sounded awake, shocked.

"I don't know, just in case you didn't want to stay

together."

"Do you not want to?"

"I'm not sure. You aren't who I was expecting. You aren't who I invited. I don't know, but we can figure this out when I return. Maybe Nika was right about us. Maybe we'll be good for each other."

"I hope so," Vladlena said with girlish poutiness. "I enjoyed our one evening together."

"Me too." He wondered how true his words were. They came out so easily yet dragged across his heart as they did.

He looked at his watch, wondered if he'd forgotten anything, and looked over his shoulder at the line of men waiting to make their calls.

"I've got to go, Vladlena. I'll see you later."

Crackling static filled the silence until she replied.

"*Proshchay lyubov.*"

He hung up the phone and stumbled back to the submarine. *Goodbye, love? How can she say, 'goodbye love' when we hardly know each other?* He laughed at himself. *How could I sleep with her so easily after what she told me about Nika?*

He descended the ladder and meandered forward. As he passed between the missile tubes he thought of their purpose, of what they spent day and night loading inside each. Nearly thirty thousand kilos apiece and loaded with enough nuclear firepower to raze dozens of cities an ocean away, deterrent weapons endangered the crew more than the world.

Overshadowed by two nations bristling with weapons, hatred, and more courage than sense, Vladlena's farewell convicted his heart. *I should've given her a better goodbye.*

Your Love Will Die

THIRTY-EIGHT

Naval Officer Housing at the Petropavlovsk-Kamchatsky-50 submarine base

In the apartment's bedroom, the two admired their handiwork in the bureau's mirror. Vladlena's hair had changed color again, the third color in as many months. She'd voiced concern about crewmen recognizing her from the Komsomolsk bar. That had been her excuse. Zhora suspected she merely enjoyed the attention he'd given her and the added fascination her new color might bring.

"Red," Zhora said with a chuckle, "you had to choose bright red."

She offered her cutest, most innocent smile and nodded. "I thought it appropriate. Don't you?"

Zhora spun her from admiring the mirror and pulled her close. Her body felt white hot against his. Her droning heartbeat brought maddening hunger upon him. So close, so delicious, she stood ready and eager for his bite. In that moment a twinge of regret darkened his thoughts.

"Tonight, your love for me will die," Zhora murmured.

"No, no, master," Vladlena insisted. "I love you more than anyone in my whole life. Why would you say such a thing?"

"When I drank of your blood that night of the fire, I knew you. I knew your thoughts, dreams, and nightmares. To make you a vampire, you will drink my blood and know me. I doubt you'll relish the experience."

Vladlena recoiled a millimeter. Pressing against his strong grasp, she fidgeted in a panic before he drew her attention back into his eyes.

"Would you rather I leave you as you are? Or would you rather I consume you entirely?"

She fell back into his arms and leaned her head back, exposing her pale pulsing throat.

"Do it, make me immortal. Take me into your family."

Her sudden surrender drove his aching thirst over the edge. Like a stampede against a now open gate, he sunk his teeth into her offered flesh and fed. Her love for him swelled in his frozen heart while her steaming blood thawed it. In his warming hands her body felt delicate and soft. She collapsed in his grasp and let out a moaning sigh.

Not again, don't die, don't let my wild hunger kill you like it did Nika.

He set her on the bed and cut his wrist open with a knife. Dark ichor, thick with clumps, oozed out like molasses. With her head in hand, he pressed his bleeding arm into her open mouth.

Vladlena grimaced and squirmed. Zhora recalled his first reaction to Sevastyan's blood. Tar and fetid carcass, that's what it smelled like. It tasted even worse. It'd taken all his courage and waning strength to draw in his first drink.

"Drink, Vladlena, drink and live forever," he whispered. "If you don't drink you'll die tonight."

He felt the sting of her bite and the ache of her sucking his wound. She swallowed a gob of the thick substance and coughed. Her eyes rolled back in her head and her limbs went limp. He pushed her mouth against his wrist.

"Drink!" he shouted.

Her eyes widened, her pupils darkened. She clutched his arm and drew in a deep quaff. A spider web of pain quivered through his blood vessels as she drew in her second gulp. A puddle of fire spilled in his brain and ran in all directions. As it did, Vladlena's expression changed with each trickling tickle of agony. Excited and delighted at first, she shed tears and growled with anger before he pulled his arm away and stumbled backward into the apartment's living room where he fell with a crash.

He licked his wound and watched the bleeding stop. He stood and looked into the bedroom. With dark blood smeared across her lips and cheeks, she lay on the bed, her eyes open with a blank stare, no longer breathing.

"Get up," he whispered. "Get up."

Nothing.

Half an hour later, in the bathroom Zhora finished applying his makeup. He stood and started packing his things. A knock at the door startled him and he dropped his bag.

"Open up," a muffled voice commanded. "We've heard reports of a disturbance."

Zhora strode to the door and peered through the peephole. Outside stood the night watchman; an old man with a uniform, a badge, and a flashlight.

Zhora opened the door and smiled. "How can I help you?"

The watchman blinked several times and tried to shrug off the vampire's camouflage. Zhora had seen this reaction before in only a few. This man was no simpleton, no mind of clay to be molded so easily.

"Turn on some lights," the watchman insisted. "I'm to make a quick inspection and report to the front desk what I've found."

To Zhora's surprise the man produced a pistol and aimed it at his heart.

"Keep your distance and lead me through the apartment," the guard said.

Zhora escorted him through the living room to the kitchen. He opened the refrigerator and offered it for inspection.

"Funny, Comrade Lieutenant. I've my duty, same as anyone else." He motioned with his pistol. "Show me the rest."

When they entered the bedroom and Zhora flipped on the light, the watchman gasped at Vladlena's corpse.

"She's dead?"

Zhora turned to face the man. "It seems so."

"You're coming with me. You're under arrest." The watchmen now held his pistol in both hands. He retreated slowly.

Vladlena gasped. She coughed. She spat blood and rolled off the bed.

"Are you alright Mrs. Koryavin?"

She rose slowly, wheezing, her back to the watchman.

"Mrs. Koryavin," the watchman asked, "what's this man done to you?"

"He saved me."

She turned and smiled, Zhora's maroon blood still stained her teeth, her lengthening fangs. Her eyes, no longer vacant, burned with the hunger of a new vampire, a yearning Zhora remembered all too well.

The watchman shifted his aim to Vladlena and the color drained from his face.

In that instant Zhora lunged at the man, crushing his wrist until the pistol fell to the floor. He clamped his other hand over the man's mouth as he drove him against the wall.

Vladlena ran over and clawed the man from Zhora's grasp. She sunk her freshly spawned fangs into his throat and drove him to the floor. He flailed in her clutches, each struggle weaker than the last until he lay perfectly still. Wet lapping noises accompanied growls and satiated moans from the girl as she fed.

When she finished Zhora stepped back and waited. She stood slowly and turned to face him. Bright red blood stained her from her nose and cheek bones down her neck and blouse. She blinked and blinked again.

"I've seen so much," Vladlena murmured. She looked back at her first victim and back to him. She frowned. Love no longer shined in her eyes.

"Vasili?" she asked between pants. "You . . ."

"Yes."

"And Nika?"

"I'm sorry, but yes."

"Sevastyan hated you."

"And now," Zhora ventured, "do you?"

"Hate? No. I saw your purpose with Vasili's death, your pain with Nika. But your jealousy, I wonder if it made you kill her."

"I wonder the same thing."

Vladlena wiped her mouth and embraced Zhora. She got on her tiptoes and kissed his cheek. "I'll never hate you. You're my savior."

Back From the Dead

Aboard K-389

Mikhail stood with Lieutenant Pudovkin on deck, who had supervised the final missile load while Boreyev rested below. Mikhail had come up for fresh air and joined his new friend to watch another submarine head out to sea. Slipping out in the dark, aided by tugs, the shining steel shadow glided through the shallow waves of Avacha Bay. Only the *K-389* remained.

The intercom crackled to life and from it, Captain Konev spoke.

"All officers report to the wardroom immediately."

Mikhail marveled at the changes in the submarine over the past few days while he picked his way through the passageways. Onions, turnips, and carrots hung from the ceiling in Level One. The men worked together better, sang as they toiled and joked while they packed their bunks. The exercise with the fleet had forged them into crew and impending war galvanized their efforts to remain cheerfully ignorant of the dangers ahead. Seaman Kipchak now wore petty officer's stripes for his masterful work on the oxygen generator. Boreyev had regained his earlier bravado and swagger. Whatever fever forced his earlier confession he'd left behind in Komsomolsk. Scents from the galley, fresh black bread, fish chowder and cabbage, mingled with the ship's industrial odors of diesel, amine, and hydraulic oil.

The mixture of mechanical and organic aromas comforted Mikhail in his submarine home.

Mikhail entered the wardroom and found his seat. A glass of vodka sat before him. Captain Borodin entered through his door and all the officers stood to greet him. He brought his vodka glass up and waited for the others to do likewise.

"We head into the deep, to guard against Armageddon beneath the waves. The only way anyone back home knows we've succeeded is by the recurring dawn. If we fail in our primary mission of deterrence, they will only know when their lives become ashes, a shadow burned into the rubble of civilization." He hoisted his glass higher. "To peaceful anonymity."

As one they tipped back their glasses and drank.

"If anyone feels they cannot pull the doomsday trigger, should it come to that, let me know now."

The room fell silent.

He smiled. "That's good to know, because I can't afford to shoot any of you. We're undermanned as it is."

Nervous laughter rippled through the wardroom.

The phone behind the captain's chair buzzed. He picked it up and spoke in low tones while Konev spoke with the officers about their assignments. Mikhail watched as his captain's jaw slackened and his eyes widened.

"Lieutenant Koryavin," the captain said. "Come with me, I've a special assignment for you."

Mikhail followed his captain out into the passageway and up to the Command Center. He stepped up to the periscope and peered into its optics. Slowly he rotated it aft and fidgeted with the focusing knobs. He stepped back and invited Mikhail to look.

"Tell me what you see."

Mikhail nodded and grabbed the periscope's handles. Two men stood on the brow, the sentry, Petty Officer Vetrov and . . .

"Zhora?"

"Is that Lieutenant Ivankov?" the captain asked. "Is that

even possible?"

Mikhail watched Zhora explain to Vetrov who he was, why his name bore a line through it in the deck log roster.

Captain Borodin smiled. "Why don't you go up there and make sure. Wait until later to catch up though, we've got to get underway within the hour."

Mikhail scrambled up the Command Center ladder. He looked up and watched Pudovkin's men getting the bridge ready. Halfway there, he turned left and pushed open the hatch built into the side of the ship's shark-fin sail. Beneath the sailplanes he emerged on deck and resumed his race to the mid-ship's brow.

Zhora stood with Vetrov, talking and laughing, a full duffle bag over his shoulder. Halfway across the missile deck Mikhail slowed his pace. Scars across his friend's face reminded him of the horrific nature of his disappearance. Paler than he'd remembered, the blood vessels in Zhora's face stood out, a faded roadmap on washed out parchment. He looked sick- jovial and energetic- but definitely ill.

The man turned and threw his duffle down. He ran to Mikhail and wrapped his arms around him. He pulled back to hold Mikhail by the shoulders and examine him. In that moment all his imperfections faded and Mikhail beheld the handsome academy friend who'd misjudged his brotherly love. Bright eyes and a flash of his smile brought Mikhail to tears.

"I thought you were dead," he began. "We held a service. I mourned the loss of my best friend. How are you here? Who can I thank for this miracle?"

Mikhail leaned in and kissed him on both cheeks.

"Misha, it's so good to see a familiar, friendly face."

"Comrade Lieutenant," the sentry shouted from the brow.

Mikhail and Zhora looked to Vetrov. The young sonar operator held a phone in one hand.

"The captain sends his respects and requests that you two get your asses to work."

Zhora jogged back to the sentry's post. The petty officer

tried to hand Zhora his duffle and grunted. The bag moved not a millimeter.

Zhora grabbed the bag and hoisted it over his shoulder.

"*Bozhe moi*," Vetrov exclaimed. "What've you got in here, an anchor?"

"I had to get a whole new kit. I couldn't know that you didn't dump all my stuff for another officer to take my place."

Mikhail led Zhora across the missile deck and helped heft his friend's duffle down the ladder. He struggled to handle the bulky bag which he estimated to weigh at least fifty kilos.

"Nothing of yours has been disturbed," Mikhail replied. "We're undermanned and we've been too busy to ship your things home."

Zhora looked to Mikhail and smiled. "And who's served as Tactical Coordinator in my absence? Will I be stuck on Damage Control instead now?"

"I served in your place," Mikhail answered. "Now I'll go back to Damage Control."

Zhora winced. "Oh, sorry, I'm sure you'll do well there."

"Shut up," Mikhail countered with a chuckle. "I really enjoyed my time at Tactical but you're the best choice."

"Nonsense, you're just as good as me." Zhora shook his head. "Who am I kidding, you're right. I am the best."

Mikhail stepped back from the ladder into the Command Center and helped guide the duffle bag to the deck.

"You smug bastard."

"Good to know you two are back on friendly terms," Captain Borodin bellowed from the Periscope Station. Laughter rippled throughout the Command Center behind him.

Mikhail turned to see the entire Command Center manned to get underway. When Zhora dropped in behind him, everyone applauded. But when their comrade turned to face his crew, a hush slowly overtook the room.

"Let me set my things down on my bunk and I'll be back to take my station," Zhora said. Some jumped as he broke the silence.

"Lieutenant Ivankov . . . go and see Doctor Anatoli first," Captain Borodin muttered. "I, uh, want to be sure you're fully fit for duty before . . . before we shove you back into action."

"Aye, Comrade Captain," Zhora answered.

Zhora marched through the corridor of *K-389* and greeted new crewmates curtly while acknowledging familiar faces. Only now did the audacity and lunacy of his plan sink in. He faced over one hundred men, most in peak physical condition. They'd already be on their guard around him based on rumors surrounding his death. With men at every watch-station around the clock, Zhora understood Sevastyan's fear and cursed at his own ego.

"I heard you'd survived," Doctor Anatoli said as Zhora stood in the doorway of Sick Bay. "I had to see it for myself."

Zhora entered the cramped room. "Oh Doctor, you've no idea what I've been through."

He pulled the door shut before he began his story.

Flushing a Stalker

Mikhail examined the tactical chart once more before he grabbed the microphone.

"Captain, radar shows the fleet at nine thousand meters and closing at twenty KPH, sonar reports ample sea beneath us, six hundred meters."

In the Command Center's red lighting his chart looked blood-soaked. To his left he watched Captain Konev at the periscope scanning the horizon. With his height, Konev bent at nearly a right angle to peer into the scope. In the blackness of midnight he'd had nothing to report since leaving the navigational lights of Avacha Bay.

On the chart a spider web of tracks converged ahead. Despite nothing in sight as far as the horizon, radar showed a fleet bearing dead ahead.

"Very well," the captain replied from the Bridge. "Communications Officer," the captain continued, "send coded message to fleet as follows: Diving within fifteen minutes.

"Aye, Comrade Captain," Dovzhenko nervously replied from the Radio Room.

"Want to see something impressive?" Konev asked Mikhail. He nodded and the executive officer invited him to the periscope.

"Keep your eyes on the bearing I've set."

The slightest difference in shades of black separated the sky from the sea through the scope's lens. With the ship's roll the dark demarcation pitched back and forth. Then it happened.

A constellation of lights flickered on, starboard greens, port reds, and blinking whites; the fleet shed the shadows. From the radar operator's station Mikhail heard a dozen different electronic tunes play, a symphony of radar systems probed outward from a fleet no longer hidden. From the sonar operator's headphones every manner of active sonar chirped, squealed, and bellowed from half a dozen ships ahead. The fleet that hounded them across the Sea of Okhotsk now pounded the depths and scanned the skies.

Through the scope Mikhail watched helicopters rise and spread out. If any Americans hid beneath the waves to follow the *K-389*, their pursuit wouldn't be easy or go unnoticed.

Mikhail pulled away from the scope and looked to Konev. "Thank you, Comrade Captain."

Konev's grin glinted with the scarlet light. He leaned forward and looked Mikhail straight in the eye. "You did well when it mattered earlier. The *Tautog*'s crew will think twice about invading another training exercise."

Dropping his gaze, Mikhail explained. "Lieutenant Ivankov taught me much when we were in the academy together."

Konev stood straighter and looked down his nose, his eyes half closed. "Don't be so quick to give others credit." He slapped Mikhail on the shoulder. "I see potential if you can just find the courage to be your own man."

Captain Borodin slid down the ladder from the bridge with Petty Officer Kipchak behind him. He pulled the hatch shut and spun the locking mechanism.

"Dive the ship," Captain Borodin ordered Gorelov.

The Michman sounded the diving klaxon and threw the ballast vent switches. The ballast tanks around them rumbled while the air geysered out. Gradually the ship tilted downward.

"Depth, twenty meters," Gorelov called out.

214

"Down scope," Konev said as he folded the periscope's handles in, turned the valve overhead, and watched the shining steel cylinder descend.

"Thirty meters."

The hull creaked and the decks popped. The fleet's sonar cacophony rang through the ship's hull.

"Tactical, lights," Konev said.

Mikhail flipped a bank of switches from red, through off, to white. Everyone winced and blinked as the room flashed white with florescent light.

"Forty meters."

Quiet tension drew tight across the room.

"Fifty meters."

For minutes the sonar rattled the hull while inside only the ventilation and ticking clocks uttered a sound.

"One hundred meters."

The clash of sonars stopped, all of them but one. It transmitted a coded message for their submersible friend. Mikhail noticed Ayatollah concentrated on this final signal with a pencil in hand, scribbling furiously.

Konev glared at the clock above the helmsman and gripped the Periscope Station's guardrail. Captain Borodin strolled over to the Tactical Station beside Mikhail and examined the chart.

"Ayatollah, what do we know?"

The sonar expert stroked his beard while he referred to his notes.

"The fleet reports clear sailing ahead."

"Helm, come starboard five degrees to course one-one-zero," Konev commanded, his eyes still glued to the clock. "Ballast Officer, bring the ship to two hundred meters."

Borodin looked to Ayatollah and his protégé, Vetrov.

"Keep an ear focused on the starboard side," the captain cautioned, "especially directly abeam."

"They're looking for an American submarine?" Mikhail asked in a whisper.

Captain Borodin shook his head. "A blanket of silence, a ghost, it'll be as big as a submarine, but not American."

215

Mikhail held his gaze and waited for his captain to explain.

"*K-314*," Borodin added, "one of our newest submarines. He will challenge any intruders."

"Two hundred meters, Bridge Officer," the Ballast Officer bellowed.

Ayatollah pressed his headphones to his ears and rotated the directional knob next to his screen. He glanced at Vetrov and scowled.

"You keep running the standard search," he said through clenched teeth. "I'll look for our escort."

From the Command Center's opposite side, Gorelov shouted. "Aft planes not responding!"

Mikhail watched the Michman pull upward on the Helm's control stick. Gorelov switched circuits and tried again. He looked to Konev and shook his head. The ship continued its downward tilt and descent. Big as airplane wings, the aft planes near the twin propellers could force the sinking ship to the surface or, if jammed downward, drive it to the bottom.

"Compensate with ballast," Konev ordered.

"We need less speed," Gorelov countered, an urgent keen to his voice. "We're two-ten and falling."

"Helm, maintain speed," Konev insisted. He grabbed the intercom and punched the button marked, 'Engine Control.'

"Engineer, seize control of the aft planes. Establish a zero bubble."

"Aye, Bridge Officer."

Captain Borodin held his breath a moment. "Where's our escort?"

"I can't find them anywhere, Captain," Ayatollah replied.

The captain bit his lip. "They're supposed to come in off our starboard beam, turn down a reciprocal course right beneath us, and chase away anyone in our wake. Speed, course," he swallowed hard, "and depth must be maintained. If not, either the tactic fails or . . ."

"Two-two-zero meters," Gorelov reported. He kept an

eye on the ship's depth while his hands worked the ballast console to pump variable ballast from the bow to sea. The pump's meter clicked, its liters per second gauge pushed against the red band. The ship's angle remained downward.

"Submerged contact, forward the starboard beam," Ayatollah bellowed. His eyes widened. "He's close."

"All hands, brace for collision!" Gorelov shouted into his intercom.

K-314's active ping shook Mikhail out of his skin. Close and shrill, it ripped down the ship's hull. *K-314* had begun to sweep *K-389's* blind spot in the baffles.

Mikhail watched a bright swath cut across the sonar screen. As the contact peeled off the screen, everyone held their breath and looked to the bulkheads. A dull *whush-whush-whush* echoed through the ship's steel skin. When it faded the hushed Command Center breathed a collective sigh.

The ship's downward angle tapered off. The Engineer reported they'd isolated the problem. Gorelov reported an end to the ship's decent with a grin. Gradually, the meters ticked off the depth gauge and *K-389* was under the crew's control again.

Ayatollah wiped the sweat from his brow. "Who's got a cigarette?"

"Helm, hard to port, come to course zero-seven-seven," Konev commanded. "Ballast Officer, set ship's depth to three hundred meters. Once we're on course, Gorelov, accelerate to ahead full, both engines."

"Wait!" Petty Officer Vetrov said.

Mikhail watched Captain Konev's face flush and his upper lip curl in.

"What is it, Petty Officer Vetrov?" Konev asked. He leaned back and cast his gaze down. "Why have you countermanded my order?"

"The *K-314* has flushed a stalker, Comrade Captain," he answered sheepishly. "I thought we might hold still and identify our foe."

Captain Konev stepped down from his station to stand

beside Vetrov. He straightened his slouched back and stretched his neck. When he'd worked the kinks out, he glared at Ayatollah while he spoke. "Vetrov, you have three minutes."

Captain Borodin gave his executive officer a nod before he left the Command Center.

"Good idea, Vetrov," Konev conceded. He patted Vetrov on the head. "But don't be so quick to countermand me again or I'll take back that new stripe you earned."

Chef's Surprise

FORTY-ONE

The diving klaxon sounded and Chief Cook Antonev nodded his approval. A rumble from the ballast tanks set his nerves at ease. The waves upset his stomach and the deep left all that rocking and swaying behind. He wasn't cut out for being tossed atop the waves. That's why he'd jumped at the chance to cook aboard a submarine. He loved to cook almost as much as he liked to eat, and he'd always heard the navy ate the best. So before the army managed to conscript him, he found his way into the navy.

He watched his galley team serve the crew. Each smile in the cramped quarters warmed his heart. Almost as much as he loved to eat, he loved to satisfy the crew's appetites too.

Gradually the ship tilted downward. As *K-389* slipped beneath the sea, the hull creaked and the decks popped. Antonev flinched at the symphony of sonar that rang through the ship's hull. It sounded like a concert of poorly tuned instruments.

He shut his eyes and smiled. Boiling cabbage in the kettle and an oven stuffed with black bread baking transported him from the cramped galley aboard *K-389* to his boyhood home in the Urals. Mountains guarded the back door to his parents' home. From the front he loved to look down at distant towns, little jewels of light at night and clustered coal clouds by day. He'd helped his mother cook and clean as a boy. Not until he reached his teens did his career in the mines begin. Only after the coal choked his throat for the hundredth time did he consider a naval career in cooking. More than anything, the scents of a home cooked dinner gave him peace among a crew of thugs, idiots, and slobs. He rubbed his ample belly and his mouth watered.

The sonar bombardment subsided and Antonev made his move.

"I'm going below to check on the stores," the chief bellowed to his men. "The crew probably dumped everything in a pile in the bilge. Our luck the eggs will be on the bottom and they'll blame us for it."

On his way out he tucked a fresh loaf under his arm. He waddled to his bunk and withdrew a bottle of vodka before he headed aft. He squeezed through his first watertight door with a grunt. The passageway between missile tubes remained empty. With everyone at their stations for the big dive, Antonev tromped down the ladder humming. No one would crash his private party.

Where's that case of caviar?

The chief bent over, wheezing as he did. He grabbed the deck-plate handle and hauled it up. Beneath the deck, the bilge lay swallowed in the dark.

I should've marked it on my clipboard. I'll die before I manage to search each of these bilges.

"All hands, brace for collision!"

Michman Gorelov's voice jolted the chief upright. Muscles in his back snapped like a towline tied to a boulder and his knees buckled. He fell. His shins struck an edge of steel. It felt like a guillotine across the bones. His nose smacked against the deck plate he'd propped up and exploded with blinding pain. He tumbled into the bilge and fell unconscious.

Antonev had owned a cat as a child and recognized the first sensation he felt as he awoke. A tiny rough tongue lapped at his face. No, not tiny, the tongue belonged to a cat bigger than any he'd seen. He blinked and blinked until his eyes found their focus and he groaned a gasp. Only light from the level above seeped into the bilge. Angle irons, pipes, and the ship's ribs reflected the meager fluorescent light in a blue-grey hue. Just beneath the bridge of his nose, bright red hair bobbed before him.

"Whasss habbening?" he managed through cracked and swollen lips.

He blinked again and beheld an angel's face above his own. Her soft green eyes glistened like a night-lit swimming pool. Shocks of hair red as the enamel star on his uniform practically glowed. Elfin features on a petite face revealed a knowing gaze and a carnal smile.

"Shhh," she whispered with a grin.

He shut his eyes hard. His blurred vision made her deep red lipstick look smeared all across her chin. Icicles of pain pierced his knees, neck and nose.

"You're hurting, I know," she added. "I'm going to help you forget that. We're going to have some fun before you go back to work."

The ache in his throat became fire and his limbs faded away. The submarine's sounds receded. His whole body sank into a dream.

He looked out the front door of his childhood home. Beautiful as ever, he watched his angel walk up the gravel road to greet him. She stood a head and a half shorter than he. She wore a sheer black gossamer dress.

"Ew," she whined, "you look fat and gross."

He examined himself. Except for his attire, his full dress uniform, he looked unchanged from a moment ago in the bilge.

"It's alright," the angel offered, "I can fix that. Let's find something a little more my style."

Darkness leapt across the sky and vertigo swept him off his feet.

"Who's that handsome man?" she asked.

In the dim light, Antonev struggled to see. Oily odors,

grit-filled air, he realized where they stood and immediately noticed the man who held her attention.

"That's me fifteen years ago in the coal mines."

The angel giggled. "I know, silly. I know the answers as you think them, sometimes sooner. I'm an angel, remember?"

Antonev watched his former self shovel debris from the cavern floor. The boy wiped sweat from his brow and left a streak of coal dust. He recalled endless hours in the mountainside. He watched his father trudge by and shoot him a disapproving glance. He'd never worked hard enough for his father. And when he did, he never worked smart enough.

Slender hands took his and planted them on firmly curved hips. He jumped at the sudden contact and looked down at his angel.

"That's right, I can be your angel," she said with a nod. Her lips remained parted when she finished. He caught a glimpse of her tongue within and felt a surge of heat.

He realized he wore his own youthful body now. But he didn't merely wear a younger form, he felt his young strength humming through thin wiry sinews. He felt hormones course through lean muscle.

"We can have all sorts of fun down here."

She brought a finger to his lips. "So long as it remains our secret."

"You live in the bilge of a submarine? That's insane. I must've hit my head pretty bad."

She cupped her hand around the back of his neck and pulled him closer. She stood on her toes to meet her lips to his. The warmth of her wet kiss sank into his body. He grabbed her by the back of her head and around her waist and guided her to the tunnel floor.

Before he managed to undress her, he felt the touch of her velvet skin against his. A drum began to beat, fast at first but it slowed with every couple of beats. The drumbeat shook the cavern walls.

The angel pushed him away effortlessly. He hovered on all fours above her. Panic distorted her sweet features.

222

"Uh, oh," *she murmured. The drumbeat swallowed her voice. He read her lips and expression.*

"I've got to go."

She brushed him aside to stand, and as he joined her, she whispered in his ear.

"We'll do this again sometime, if you like, if you can keep a secret."

"And if I can't?

Her soft eyes hardened. "Then I won't be an angel anymore."

Her tone chilled him and he shuddered. Shouts, muffled and faint, eroded his dream. The coal mine shadows faded in a white light that pervaded the scene from all around.

He heard his own moans echo against the bilge. A crewman peered down through the open bilge hatch at him. The boy's concern and shock struck him as odd, until he tried to move. Every injury he suffered before his dream screamed for him to halt.

"Chief," the petty officer said. "Hold on. The doctor's on his way."

A Midwatch Revelation

FORTY-TWO

Mikhail trudged forward through the reactor tunnel, barely aware of his surroundings. He'd once been enthralled by the concept at work beneath him. The core of uranium below generated heat hot enough to burn through the Earth, able to mutate flesh. And yet science leapt to harness its potential with coolant, the pressure vessel, and the control rods.

What enthralled him now lay a hundred meters ahead, his bunk. He dragged his feet through Auxiliaries Compartment, with only a nod to Petty Officer Kipchak as he passed. Inside Missile Compartment Aft he stopped. Doctor Anatoli stood in his Sick Bay, streaks of blood all across his examination table/bunk. He looked up from the gore, a cigarette pinched between his lips.

"Chief Antonev," Anatoli said in answer to the unspoken question. Ash from the cigarette dusted the bloody streaks as he spoke. "The man took a tumble during the excitement."

"A tumble? It looks like he was murdered."

The doctor chuckled. "The average body contains five and a half liters of blood. That lard-ass likely holds seven."

"How'd it happen?"

"He was checking the inventory." Anatoli snickered. "With a bottle of vodka and a fresh loaf of black-bread." His laughter faded until only a thin smile remained. "The unexpected dive tipped the bilge hatch onto his head, knocked him unconscious and he dropped to the bottom."

"I thought a chief knew better than to leave a hatch unlatched," Mikhail wondered aloud.

Anatoli nodded and tugged at his chin. "He seemed anemic. That might've explained his oversight."

"Anemic?"

"Yes, you might recall an illness sweeping through the shipyard?"

"Yes."

"Well, it looks like we brought it with us. Chief Antonev seems infected, him and half a dozen others."

"*Bozhe moi*," Mikhail muttered.

Anatoli reached out and grasped Mikhail's shoulder. "Don't worry. It's not fatal and after it's run its course, we'll all be fine."

Mikhail looked to the doctor's blood splashed glove on his tunic. Anatoli withdrew his hand and apologized. He took a long drag before he flicked his ash into the trashcan.

"What about Zhora?" Mikhail asked. "Has he recovered from his assault?"

Anatoli shook his head and shook his cigarette at Mikhail. "He's got no broken bones and very little scarring."

"Does he seem calmer, quieter?" Mikhail asked.

"Wouldn't a nearly fatal beating change you?"

"I guess," Mikhail bit his upper lip. "Where's he been all this time?"

The doctor turned back to the gory mess and resumed scrubbing the blood away. "Ask him yourself. I've got a lot to clean if I'm to get any sleep."

"I could help you," Mikhail countered.

"No, no, you look beat as it is. What happened?"

"The aft planes failed and leaked hydraulic fluid everywhere."

"Get some sleep, Mikhail," the doctor said with a weary grin. "You've got more work tomorrow. I'll be free to sleep in so long as the crew can stop falling in the bilges."

The walk through Missile Compartment Aft felt like a dream. Boots marching toward him shook him from his sleepwalk. Boreyev and Dovzhenko, iron-faced and bleary-eyed, stopped short of the watertight door between Missile Compartments Aft and Forward. Boreyev entered the security code and escorted the Communications Officer into Launch Control. Their lockstep march through that armored door only meant one thing, missile targeting orders from Moscow.

Mikhail's stomach grew cold and drove a chill along his spine. He picked his way through the steel door and looked at the combination lock on the Launch Control door as he passed.

"Sorry to disturb you, Comrade Captain."

Zhora's whispered words startled Mikhail again. He'd made it into Operations Compartment Forward, unaware of his past progress through the ship. To his left, Zhora crept out of Captain Konev's stateroom. Mikhail noticed the darkness beyond his academy friend.

With a wink and a nod, Zhora explained. "I had to wake him up. He needed to approve the new torpedo settings and search patterns." He held up a clipboard with three folders attached. "The search plan and roster needed a revision too."

Mikhail marveled at how good his friend looked. Glossy hair, unblemished skin, his strong Russian features would've made the sculptors of Yuri Gagarin's Monument proud.

"Are you alright?" Zhora asked.

Zhora's smile had an odd effect on him. Certain he was no *pidor*, Mikhail still found himself drawn closer. A thin wave of fear, unexpected and unexplainable, rippled across his thoughts and woke him again.

"I'm fine," he managed, "just really tired. I practically sleepwalked here."

"Get some rest then," Zhora said. "You want me to tuck you in?"

"Don't do that, please. It's not funny and if others hear you-"

"If others hear, I hope they've sense enough to mind

227

their own business."

In the span of his words, Zhora's countenance transformed. The handsome lieutenant's brow furrowed and seemed to jut out. His hypnotically peaceful eyes burned black.

"I saw murder in your eyes."

Captain Borodin's words echoed in Zhora's flash of fury. The shipyard superintendent, Chendev, had looked into such a gaze with a knife at his throat. He must've been pleased to see *K-389* leave. As much as Mikhail denied it then, he witnessed it for himself and shivered. A cool hand on his cheek shook him out of his waking nightmare.

"Calm down, Misha, I'm just angry at those who can't understand me. They judge one minute and dive into their own dark desires the next."

"What happened to you, Zov? Where've you been? How'd you survive?"

"Slow down," Zhora whispered. He stepped closer and put his other hand on Mikhail's other shoulder. "Sailors from this very ship beat me and my lover."

"That's insane, your own crewmates?"

Zhora nodded. "Ivan died and those men left me for dead. An old man found me and nursed me back to health in his own home. Stricken with amnesia, neither of us knew where I belonged for weeks."

"Who, who did this?" Mikhail found himself shaking, his fists balled tightly.

"Let's not bother with that now," Zhora answered, shaking his head. "Just know why I burn with anger. Please understand how I've only ever sought to live my life, different from others but no more a criminal than those who hate me. I wanted a life left alone with my kind of love."

Mikhail unclenched his fists, reached up, and grasped Zhora's shoulders.

"I know about your tortured past," Zhora blurted, desperately. "I know it's made love difficult for you."

Zhora grabbed Mikhail's face and lunged in for a kiss.

His lips felt cold and his breath smelled metallic, like the smell in your nostrils after a bloody nose. He held tight and pressed his lips tighter. Mikhail held still and waited for his friend to release him. When he did, Zhora's captivating, beautiful gaze had returned.

"I'd like you to consider *us* once more before you close that door."

"Stop it. Stop thinking I'm going to become something I'm not. Isn't that what you accused your parents of doing? I love you, Zhora, as a brother. Please, be satisfied with that."

That's what Mikhail meant to say. That's what he wanted to say. But Zhora's gaze kept his mouth clamped shut.

Deterrence

FORTY-THREE

"The control cable," Senior Lieutenant Kirkov, the Ship's Engineer, said. He tossed an oil-soaked cable beside the wardroom tea set. A dark stain spotted the blue felt tablecloth. The insulation bore cracks. Frayed wires splayed out near the end attached to the aft plane control solenoid.

"Well, don't think we want it on our dining table," Dimitriev said. He recoiled from the evidence and waved his hand at it as if to shoo away a spider.

"This is unacceptable," Konev growled. "This should've been discarded in Komsomolsk. Were you not Ship's Engineer during the overhaul?"

"Yes, Comrade Captain," Kirkov answered with a shallow nod.

"Two submarines were endangered by your negligence." Konev tilted his head back and glared at the Engineer. "I will inspect your compartment for other oversights once this meeting finishes."

Kirkov's face reddened. His eyes darted to Mikhail.

"If we hadn't followed Lieutenant Koryavin's *bold* plan," Kirkov shouted, "*my* men would've seen that cable to the scrap pile."

"Careful, Kirkov," Doctor Anatoli murmured.

"Another sixteen missiles stand ready to defend the Motherland because of so bold a plan," Zhora said.

Mikhail noticed Zhora's fists balled tight, pressed into

the table. The man's anger crackled in the air around him. Mikhail thanked the cooks for not having set the silverware out.

Kirkov stood, picked up the scrap cable, and threw it at Mikhail.

"If he's good enough to pin another star on, let him wear this too."

Captain Borodin stood and looked to Kirkov. He stared into the Engineer's eyes until the man took his seat and examined the oil stains he'd put on the wardroom's blue velvet tablecloth.

"Lieutenants Koryavin, Ivankov, and Boreyev were instrumental in the plan you slander," Borodin said in a low-level tone. "A plan I put into motion."

"I meant no disrespect, Comrade Captain," Kirkov replied.

Zhora laughed. "You meant exactly that."

Captain Borodin drove his fist into the table. In the silence, he spoke.

"We are at war. It's not official, it's not come to blows yet, but the battle lines are being drawn. Last night, the Americans flew a single bomber straight for Moscow. Interceptors met them at the border of international airspace as it turned away."

Dimitriev gasped. "Reconnaissance. They test our vigilance, record our responses. Deception. They prepare for a full scale attack after they've created a false pretense to justify their actions."

"Why, why would they d-d-do that?" Dovzhenko asked.

Pudovkin shook his head. "The Americans won't jeopardize their lavish lifestyle."

"The Germans used their own troops in Polish uniforms to begin their invasion," Zhora answered. "Our own aircraft along the border were mostly destroyed on the ground by their sudden assault."

Boreyev leaned forward and looked to his comrades. "Lieutenant Dovzhenko and I input new missile targeting data from last night's message. Launch Control stands ready to burn the Americans off the map."

"I hope we get that chance, Lieutenant Boreyev," Konev replied. "Be ready to launch at a moment's notice."

"No!" Borodin shouted. "That's not our purpose out here."

Mikhail watched everyone turn to their captain and gaze in disbelief. The drone of ventilation, the whine of electric lights, only these filled the chasm of silence. Konev's posture waivered and Mikhail noticed the man's pallor. Paler, less energetic, the Executive Officer looked as tired as Mikhail felt last night. Zhora looked like a steel trap, ready to spring on the next officer to speak. Dovzhenko's eyes darted to each man at the table. He looked ready to hide underneath the table at the next harsh word. Dimitriev examined Captain Borodin as if he were a rare specimen, a mutant.

Captain Borodin sat down and withdrew a cigar from his pocket. He rolled it between his fingers, his gaze fixed on it. He put it under his nose, rested it on his thick mustache and inhaled.

"These were a gift from the Admiralty from our poor communist cousins in Cuba."

He stood, turned, and went back into his stateroom. Mikhail heard the man rummage through his locker and cabinets.

Dimitriev and Konev looked to each other. Captain Borodin returned with a humidor under his left arm and a pistol in his right hand. Again the room fell silent. He tossed the humidor onto the table.

"If you're like me," he began, "you enjoy a good cigar. The world is full of such marvelous riches."

He aimed the pistol at Dimitriev and slowly swept the room, careful to meet each officer's gaze from across the Makarov's iron sights.

"The Americans hold their gun to the world and dictate terms."

He lifted one leg onto his chair and hiked up his pants leg. From a small leather holster attached to his calf he

233

withdrew a second pistol. He tossed it to Zhora while his aim held at the man's face.

"Pick it up." Borodin said. His countenance darkened. "Pick it up and aim it back at me."

Without hesitation, Zhora drew the weapon. He aimed the pistol on his captain and smiled.

Borodin smiled back. "Lieutenant Ivankov either wishes me dead, or . . ."

The men looked from pistol to pistol, officer to officer. Mikhail spoke up.

"Or he knows what you're doing. He understands your intent."

"Very good, Lieutenant Koryavin," the captain replied. "Tell the others, Lieutenant Ivankov, what I'm trying to say."

"So long as we aim at each other, everyone can enjoy a cigar," Zhora answered. "So long as the captain and I believe in the other's resolve to shoot, the concept of nuclear weapons maintains peace."

Captain Borodin's grin widened and he set down his pistol. But when he reached for the humidor, Zhora stood, clutched the box of cigars, and kept his aim.

"And when one of us does something foolish or unpredictable," Zhora said in a low tone, "the whole system falls apart."

Borodin glared down the gun barrel at Zhora.

"And that's what the devious, duplicitous Americans seek to do with this Able Archer '83 exercise," Borodin growled. "We must prove our courage and demonstrate our foreknowledge of their trap to keep them from ever springing it."

Zhora let go the cigars, set the pistol on the table, and sat.

Captain Borodin opened the box and passed it around. When he got to Zhora, he held the box just out of reach.

"A bold demonstration, comrade," Borodin said.

"I thought it a meaningful addition to your lesson," Zhora answered.

Borodin extended the cigars, served the entire wardroom, and sat.

"We hope to see another humidor like this in the future," he began, "but if we don't, if we fail in our mission of deterrence, no one will have another cigar again."

An Angel's Fury

FORTY-FOUR

"We need a brave, strong man like you," the angel told Antonev. "I could make you an angel, like me."

In their dreamland rendezvous, he lay beside her in the mine he'd worked as a teen. Men worked along the opposite wall. They sang *Dark Eyes* while they hammered and shoveled. He looked to his naked angel and smiled. She fit the song in so many ways. He yearned for her and feared her. He'd crawled out of his bunk and hobbled down to the bilge just to get another taste of her passion, another glimpse of her beauty. In the wild throes of lovemaking, he'd felt a sharp pain and his strength wane. Even now he felt himself fade from his own dream.

"I've not been brave or strong in a long time," he murmured.

"We'll see about that," she answered. She snuggled closer and wrapped her arm around his neck and her leg over his hip. Another sharp pain preceded another interlude of passion.

A distant rumble tumbled overhead while she straddled him. He fought to ignore it, but when dust trickled onto his face, his concentration fell and he opened his eyes. Panicked shouts and agonized screams ricocheted off the tunnel walls and he threw her off. Thunder deep in the mineshaft brought him to his feet. He watched his younger self and father race toward him, toward the exit over his shoulder. His father stumbled. Men stepped over him, trampled him, all while Antonev past and present watched, frozen. A plume of dust gushed out from deeper in the mine and the younger Antonev turned from his father's plea and ran into the daylight.

The pain he'd thrilled in, the stab in his shoulder that invited every lustful moment between Antonev and his companion, bit hard and deep. New pains, fingernails into his arms and a network of agony across his whole body, brought him to his knees. The mine darkened until blackness hung over his eyes like an executioner's hood.

"You!" the angel screamed. "You let your father die."

"I couldn't help him," Antonev whimpered.

"You abandoned him. You had your father and left him to die."

"I'd have been trampled too," he sobbed. He felt his fingers burn down to the knuckles and fall off like a cigarette's ash. His feet too felt consumed by fire.

"You'll be no angel like me. You'll die, die right now."

"B-but why?" His chest felt cold, wooden.

"You threw away what I never had, a father who loved you."

The dream peeled away and he saw his angel once more in the bilge's dim grey light. Blood covered her lips and chin. Her eyes gleamed with hate. Her bloodstained teeth looked too long and too sharp. She hissed and dove into his flabby neck one last time.

We've Got a Madman Aboard

FORTY-FIVE

Mikhail and Petty Officer Kipchak sat amidst a sea of parts, tools, and blueprints. Oxygen Generator Two, what remained of it, stood nearby, impotent and incomplete. On the workbench sat the charred remains of a solenoid and a cracked gasket. What should've been a simple repair ballooned into a nightmare when inspection of similar fittings revealed a common fatal flaw. Every gasket bore signs of dry rot. Wherever they'd been or whatever decade they'd been crafted in, they were in no shape to fulfill their purpose.

"*Bozhe moi,*" Mikhail murmured.

"It's pretty well fucked isn't it?" Kipchak observed. "And there's not enough replacement gaskets aboard to put it back together. We'll operate with one generator until we get home or operate this one with gaskets ready to fall apart."

The ship's stores had been stripped bare. Mikhail examined the last reject and let his face fall into his hands. No replacements, no sleep, and if Generator One suffered the same fate, no oxygen.

A scream woke him. He hadn't realized he slept until the scream startled him awake. Kipchak too awoke with a start. Both stumbled to their feet and sought the source. Forward they ran, through the watertight door into Missile Compartment Aft, between the missile tubes. Doctor Anatoli poked his head out from Sick Bay.

"Was that . . .?" Anatoli began.

"Come, doctor," Mikhail yelled over his shoulder as he passed, "I think someone's hurt."

Once at the ladder Mikhail slid down. He heard a thick gurgling sound behind him and turned. The Fire and Security Watch, one of Boreyev's men, lay on the deck. He thrashed about clutching his swollen throat. Mikhail knelt beside the man.

"Calm down, comrade," he whispered.

Wild reddened eyes rolled back in the man's head. His hands fell to his sides and he died. His Adam's apple looked misshapen, like he'd swallowed a child's building block.

"Comrade Lieutenant, look," Kipchak gasped.

The petty officer had opened the bilge hatch that had injured Chief Antonev days ago. In the bilge, the chief lay, dead. His eyes hung half-open. Swaths of blood streaked across his neck and collar. Beside him, rolling lazily, the watchman's lit flashlight lay.

Captain Borodin collapsed into his chair at the wardroom table. "I wanted a small meeting to get our facts straight before the rest of the crew's involved."

"Chief Antonev's second trip to the bilge defies logic," Anatoli told Captain Borodin. In the wardroom, the doctor, Mikhail, and Boreyev sat across the table from three captains, Borodin, Konev, and Dimitriev. Like whitewashed posters of their former selves, with dark circles around their eyes, Mikhail realized how they looked like a council of dead men. No doubt nightmares and tough decisions plagued what time they might steal to sleep. But they seemed more than tired, less than alive.

"The man was in no shape to descend that ladder, but he did," Anatoli explained. "Whatever his business down there, and with who, we only have a few facts."

"One, he already suffered injuries falling into that bilge days ago."

"Two, he'd suffered from the same disease that many shipyard workers did, a form of anemia."

"Three, shortly before a cardiac arrest, he ejaculated in his uniform."

At the last fact, Mikhail watched the captains exchange uncomfortable glances.

"Is that what killed him, a heart attack?"

The doctor nodded.

"What about the blood on his collar and throat?"

"A small wound on his throat suggests he'd snagged it on something in the bilge or his sexual encounter might've included some physical abuse."

"Sex?" Dimitriev asked as he recoiled. "On a submarine full of men, preposterous."

Boreyev shook his head and his nose wrinkled. "There are those who prey on men."

Captain Borodin leaned forward. "And the watchman, what happened to him?"

"Bludgeoned in the throat."

". . . possibly by his own weapon," Mikhail interjected. "His truncheon's not been found."

Anatoli continued. "The injury and swelling closed off his airway. Only an emergency tracheotomy, performed immediately, could've saved him."

"We are looking for a sexual pervert and a murderer." Boreyev said. His nostrils flared and he pounded the table. "We've a murdering *pidor* on board."

"Possibly," Anatoli answered. "It's not the only explanation."

"But you said," Dimitriev sputtered. "Discharge. You said . . . the, uh, discharge."

"But in his uniform," Mikhail replied. "Who has sex with their pants still on?"

Doctor Anatoli frowned and pulled at his chin. "Corpses have been known to urinate, defecate, and even ejaculate."

Dimitriev squirmed in his seat. "How do you even . . ."

Anatoli shrugged. "How's it happen? Chemical breakdown, blood pooling, a dozen factors come together in the end."

The zampolit shook his head. "No, how do you even know this kind of morbid detail?"

"Doctoring's not all penicillin and bandages," he answered.

Mikhail watched a chill ripple through the eyes of his comrades.

"But there is a person missing from this scene," Boreyev said, "my man's murderer."

"One thing's for certain," Captain Borodin said, "he can't have gone far."

"I've heard enough to be convinced," Konev said. He looked to Borodin. "I'll alert the crew, we've got a madman aboard."

You've Got the Wrong Guy

FORTY-SIX

Zhora hovered over the sonar display, headphones on, scribbling notes. With a grease pencil he connected a thin line of dots on the screen, a wisp of a trail. Ayatollah looked up from his display and squinted at his lieutenant's work. He returned to his own controls and directed his attention to the bearing Zhora pointed out. With his headphones pressed against his ears, he strained until he merely shook his head.

"How can you make a submarine out of that?" he wondered.

"My ears aren't as old," Zhora answered with a grin. *And I've supernatural hearing.*

"Not even the young pup hears that well." Ayatollah nodded to Vetrov.

"Inexperience then."

"Is it the *Tautog* or *K-314*?" Ayatollah asked.

"Not sure." Zhora shrugged. "I'm only so good. That's where your expertise comes in."

After another hour with his sonar crew, Zhora made his way to his stateroom. Not entirely tired, but mentally fatigued, he slipped into his bunk. Sleep wasn't what he'd call it. No dreams came. It always panicked him a bit to begin. He closed his eyes and felt a trap door open beneath him. His stomach lurched and his limbs drifted away. Falling and falling, fear upon fear, each time he hoped to wake before his descent ended.

A slap across Zhora's face woke him, not the sting of it, for he felt none. That the blow jerked his head to one side, that did the trick.

"Somebody's a heavy sleeper," Lieutenant Boreyev said.

Zhora blinked until his eyes adjusted to the bright florescent lights. Launch Control, known for its bright lighting, and code locked door. Bound to a chair at the arms and ankles, his mouth taped shut, he let out a muffled chuckle. *Not a good time. Not the way I expected things to go, but this might be fun.*

Boreyev loomed over him and yanked the tape off. Two missile division petty officers flanked the stocky lieutenant. Arms crossed, each held a wooden truncheon and their most menacing glares. He sensed two more behind him.

"Are you going for a second time to try and kill me?" Zhora asked.

"We went to dispense justice," Boreyev replied. "You happened to be on the wrong side of it. I hadn't meant to kill you until I realized what you were and what you might say if we both returned to the ship."

"So why aren't I dead yet this time?"

"I want to know why you killed Chief Antonev."

"I didn't."

Boreyev slapped him again, harder. "They've already said, a *pidor* rendezvoused with him in the bilge and killed him. You're a *pidor*. Antonev's dead. I want to know why."

"You think I'm the only one aboard? You're dumber than I thought."

With a growl, Boreyev drew his own truncheon and drove it into Zhora's stomach. He felt it, a nudge against his innards. They squished in and rebounded. A dull ache spread out slowly.

"Who," Boreyev demanded. "I want names."

"It's not a club you imbecile, there aren't meetings and membership cards."

Boreyev roared before he slapped Zhora again. Over and over he struck, each time spitting his hatred out like a prison labor chant.

"You're a *pidor.*"

"You deserve to die."

Boreyev closed his hand and continued, punching with his fist.

"I'm only . . ."

"Seeking . . ."

"Justice."

Panting, slobbering, Boreyev stepped back and scowled.

Zhora examined the man, wild-eyed, red-faced, and full of disgust. *Boreyev would've made a perfect admiral's son.* That's when it hit him, harder than any blow from his tormentor.

"Yanukovich," Zhora whispered, "you killed Yanukovich."

"I did," Boreyev answered flatly.

Bruising, Zhora felt it blossom beneath his deadened senses. Blood oozed from within his nose and lip.

"You'll have to kill me . . . again," Zhora said.

"Maybe." Boreyev frowned.

"Probably." he winced.

"Yes." he flashed a smile.

Boreyev drew in a deep breath and his eyes gleamed. "Or we might have one more pervert to interrogate before this is all over."

"No."

"Your bunk buddy from the academy," Boreyev said with a grin, "Koryavin."

Zhora strained against his bonds. "Don't you dare."

"He'll crack, I'll wager," Boreyev laughed. "I might have to hurt him extra, just for all the trouble he's caused."

One petty officer gasped. With his club he pointed at Zhora. "What is that?"

"What happened to his face?" the other asked.

Zhora realized what Boreyev hadn't. *The makeup, they've smeared it.*

"It's a bruise," Boreyev scoffed. He turned to smack

each man. "It's blood. What's wrong with you two? You didn't get squeamish out at Black Warf, why now?"

The two men stammered for an answer and Boreyev refused to hear it. "Go and fetch Lieutenant Koryavin. We'll get to the bottom of this or at least have two less *pidors* to worry about."

"You'll not get away with this," Zhora pleaded. "Please don't go further down this path."

Boreyev chuckled. "If Yanukovich's death taught me anything, it's that a big enough conspiracy can keep any secret."

Zhora surged against his bonds. The ropes burned as they dug into his skin. He hoped the tearing sound wasn't his flesh but he couldn't be sure. His captors watched, stunned, before they charged.

Blow upon blow bludgeoned him to the floor even as his ropes fell slack around him. He reached out and found a wrist . . . broke it. One truncheon fell to the deck. One petty officer screamed and backpedaled from the fight.

A boot struck his nose. He flew into the bulkhead. The room wobbled out of sync with his vision. Blood, black and sour, his own, filled his mouth. More steel-toed strikes found his ribs. A club cracked across his collarbone. Shock stripped him of control while pain sank in and caught fire.

A hundred men aboard, and I can't handle five. Sevastyan, you coward, I hope to meet you in hell and strangle you for eternity.

He heard the armored door burst open. Shouts rose in his muffled ears. More men raced in to join the fight. Boreyev fell from sight. Men shouted and screamed, clubbed and fell. Then silence.

Michman Gorelov stood over an unconscious Boreyev. Petty Officer Kipchak crouched over Zhora and scooped him up in his arms.

"I'm getting you to the doctor," Kipchak whispered as he stood.

Zhora looked up at the young man's face as they bobbed along through the passageways to Sick Bay. Aquiline features, his lips in a permanent smirk, and playful eyes, Zhora's heart felt lighter even as it ached.

"You're adorable," Zhora murmured through swollen lips.

Kipchak shot him a shocked look. "I dreamt you said that when we thought you dead."

"Kiss me," Zhora whispered.

Kipchak grinned and shook his head. "Not now, not here. I'm not nearly as bold as you."

Duty

FORTY-SEVEN

"My fault, Comrade Captain."

Michman Gorelov stood at attention in the wardroom. Two bruised lieutenants sat opposite each other. Zhora's left arm hung in a sling. Bandages covered his nose. Boreyev's head was wrapped in a bandage and his right hand sat on a splint. At the table's head sat Captain Borodin flanked by the zampolit and Mikhail. Borodin looked better than he had two days ago. Though still pale and painted with a hue of fatigue, he looked more himself, ready to step into the sunlight one day instead of a coffin.

"Lieutenant Koryavin, you investigated Yanukovich's murder," Borodin said. He glared at Mikhail. "Are you a part of this cover-up?"

"We had no solid evidence," Mikhail answered.

"More of my mess," the Michman interjected. "Yanukovich's murder was an accident, a blanket party gone wrong. I didn't want a witch hunt, not for a *pidor*'s killer, not without a scapegoat. I warned Lieutenant Koryavin to stop."

"And this 'party', you've said you're to blame for that too?" Dimitriev asked.

Gorelov nodded. "Lieutenant Boreyev and his men heard my stories. I told about the old days." His gaze grew distant and he shook his head. "I miss the earlier days. If we were out of line, we were punished. We feared our leaders. We feared failure."

"You sought to teach the men through your stories?" Borodin asked.

Again Gorelov nodded. "My duty."

He cleared his throat. "Mention of *pidors* came up. I told how we handled them."

He clenched his fists. His prominent brow furrowed. "But we didn't kill crewmates. We kept 'em in line. We drew the boundaries. I've served with *pidors* before. Never liked it, but we made 'em part of our crew. We taught 'em what we wouldn't stand for."

"But," Dimitriev said. The rest of his words hung in his gaping mouth.

"Lieutenant Boreyev took your advice too far," Captain Borodin said. "Lieutenant Koryavin took your advice despite his own best judgment. For that, Lieutenant Ivankov nearly died, Seaman Yanukovich did."

"Murderer. Lieutenant Boreyev is a murderer," Dimitriev said quietly. "And you . . ." He looked at Zhora, and quickly looked away.

The captain's phone buzzed on the bulkhead behind him.

"Captain . . . yes . . . Are we clear? Bridge Officer, ascend and capture the latest radio broadcast."

Captain Borodin looked to each man in the room and ended with his gaze on Michman Gorelov.

"What I say now must never be uttered again. The crew's discipline relies on men like you, on trials such as Yanukovich's. But these things must be delicately handled or good men must face the firing squad."

The room pitched upward. Deck plates creaked and popped as the ship headed toward the surface. The communications panel buzzed with chatter between the stations responsible for periscope depth safety.

Captain Borodin stood and clasped his hands together. "If you teach your students how to swim by throwing them in the water, it may work. But if they drown, you're a murderer. They need a dedicated lifeguard."

He stepped around the table until he stood beside

Gorelov. The Michman towered over him. Borodin reached up and put a hand on his shoulder and shook Gorelov as he spoke again.

"You encouraged good discipline without taking an active role in seeing it through. Michman, you will explain this pyramid of misjudgment to the crew. You will explain to them that when vigilante justice leads to the death of crewmen, no matter what their crime, they push me to action."

Dimitriev raised a hand to his chin before he spoke. "And the crimes we've uncovered today, what will become of them?"

The captain's shoulders drooped a millimeter and he sighed. "That depends on how everyone conducts themselves in the coming weeks. We stand on the edge of war. We need every man. Should these men distinguish themselves, I'll consider dropping their matters entirely."

"Wait. Wait a minute," Dimitriev insisted.

Everyone turned to face him.

"We're still no closer to knowing who murdered Chief Antonev."

"No," Borodin answered. A nervous chuckle escaped. "But at this rate, we'll solve the murder or all be dead before long."

Mikhail walked back to the Auxiliaries Compartment. He and Kipchak had fashioned new gaskets from rubber and canvas suits the crew had for chemical spills. He found Petty Officer Kipchak at a workbench, hammering out gaskets with a punch kit and carving them into shape with tin snips. Half a cup of bilge-vodka and an ashtray already full sat beside him. The young man hummed a tune Mikhail had never heard before.

"What's got you so chipper?" Mikhail asked.

"Borscht," he answered without looking up from his

work.

"They're having it for dinner?"

Kipchak laughed. "No. Never mind."

He held his latest creation up to examine in the light. He turned his head and rotated the gasket in his hands. With a nod he tossed it in a pile beside the oxygen generator blueprints. At the end of the workbench sat a trashcan with half a chem-suit's worth of poorly cut gaskets.

Mikhail's mind wandered while he pondered Kipchak's cryptic answer.

"You got Lieutenant Ivankov to Sick Bay?" Mikhail asked.

"Yeah."

"I heard he was pretty bad off. I heard you feared he might die."

"Yeah," Kipchak answered. "Looks like I overreacted."

It hit him, sort of. "Wait . . . borscht, you hate it. We talked about this, didn't we?"

Kipchak met Mikhail's gaze. He held his tongue a minute before he answered. "Yeah, we talked about *it*."

His tone, his eyes. *Ohhh.*

Kipchak nodded. "Yeah. Turns out I've always liked borscht. I've just been afraid to admit it."

Angel in the Dark

Petty Officer Adaksin stared into the dark corner and sighed. Of all the compartments, Missile Compartment Forward burned out light bulbs quicker than any other. Other electricians said it was the ghost of Chief Antonev trying to get some sleep.

Kirkov will have my ass if I don't keep these lights lit.

He marched aft to fetch a replacement. He noticed another patch of darkness and stopped to annotate its location. Adaksin hastened his pace only to stop, shocked, on the other side of the next watertight door. Shadowed corners also dotted Missile Compartment Aft. He ran his fingers through his hair, grabbed a tuft and held tight while he pondered.

It's spreading. How's that possible?

Back by his workbench, in Engine Room Forward, he examined schematics. The lights in question were powered by separate circuits. He clutched his hair again and thought. Their locations struck him as odd, always at a corner or a dead end passageway, always along the ship's hull.

"Adaksin."

Lieutenant Kirkov's voice, like a violin out of tune, shocked a shudder out of him.

"Adaksin," Kirkov said again, "wake up and tell me what you're doing with *my* prints."

Adaksin stood and turned to face Lieutenant Kirkov.

Anger flushed the thin man's typically jaundiced complexion. The circles of sleepless nights bracketed indignant hazel eyes. As much as the captain pressured the Ship's Engineer to keep everything running, the man had no concept of delegation. He ran himself ragged minding the business of petty officers while the Engine Room languished. Everyone knew his scores in the academy and engineer's school. Everyone knew because Kirkov never shut up about them. Adaksin hadn't attended either school, but ten years as a submariner had taught him how to keep a ship running.

"Sorry, Comrade Engineer, I noticed several lights out in both Missile Compartments and thought I might find a common problem."

Kirkov sneered. "Oh did you? Let me see what you've got."

Adaksin explained to Kirkov his research path and showed him the electrical distribution panels in the affected compartments. He watched Kirkov's face grimace and scowl at the mystery just as he imagined his own did moments ago, only less ugly, less smug.

"Well, there's nothing connecting any of this," Kirkov exclaimed. He gasped. "The light bulbs." He turned to Adaksin. "Tell me you've already replaced these light bulbs."

"No, Comrade Engineer."

"*Bozhe moi*, Adaksin, you'll get us both before the blue table. Get out there and light the place up. We're not some gulag or slum. Konev will have us both in the wardroom staring at papers for dismissal by patrol's end."

"But it seems-

"Go, now. We can play with your theories once the lights are on and I'm not up to my armpits in the mess the shipyard left me."

Kirkov yanked the prints from the workbench and began to fold them. The papers crumpled and clumped but failed to fold. Kirkov growled and tried harder. Adaksin watched, careful to clamp down his laughter.

"Go, go, go," Kirkov screamed without looking up from

his paper puzzle. "What are you, deaf *and* stupid?"

With an armful of boxed bulbs, Adaksin marched from darkness to darkness. At his last stop in the Missile Compartment Aft, he nearly stumbled over a man passed out on the deck. He moaned and rolled from his stomach onto his back. Adaksin hurried to plug in the bulb.

A new petty officer, a man brought aboard at the last minute lay at his feet. Adaksin knelt beside him.

"You, are you alright?"

"Don't leave me," he whispered, eyes still closed.

On the deck beside the man, a single drop of blood glistened in the flickering florescent light. Cool to the touch and pale as a ghost, Doctor Anatoli's warning rose from recent memory. *The disease, acute anemia he'd called it.*

"I won't leave you, comrade," he answered.

The man's eyes widened. He clutched Adaksin's arm.

"No, not you, my girlfriend, she was just here."

Back to replacing light bulbs, Adaksin mulled over Doctor Anatoli's explanation.

"A hallucination; in the middle of the Pacific, underwater with a hundred men; there are no girlfriends here."

That's what the doctor had said when he got the man to Sick Bay. The doctor hadn't looked much better himself. If it wasn't contagious, how had new cases popped up, Adaksin had asked. Anatoli had shrugged.

One last light bulb and I can grab some sleep.

"Don't, please," a soft, feminine voice pleaded. "I like the dark. It's where dreams come true."

In the depths of the dead end, from between the ribs of the ship, crawl spaces where only pipes, ducts, and conduit existed, a woman's face emerged. A halo of shining red hair encircled a wan petite face with glistening eyes, pale green as the Caribbean surf, and lips red as blood on a fresh wound. She wriggled up and clambered closer. Lithe as a snake, she slid out from among the ship's arteries of electricity, water, and air.

"Who are you?" Adaksin asked.

"I'm an angel," she whispered. "Come, stay with me awhile."

His brain itched; something felt wrong all along the top of it. But his desires sang a lullaby to logic and he stepped into the dim corner.

So short and slender, she held her arms up and pulled him into her embrace. So soft, her cool caress made him feel weightless. Something pinched the crook of his neck. He winced and wrestled to escape, half a breath before his knees buckled.

He sank into a sea of time. Hand in hand he strolled through his past with the crimson haired waif. They stood beside a wood stove and watched young Vadim Adaksin studying. In the meager light the boy strained to read. He scribbled notes as he progressed.

"You were a clever boy," the shadow angel observed. "Why aren't you an officer?"

"You've seen ahead, haven't you?" he asked. "I hear in your voice, you know why."

As if on cue, his father stumbled into the kitchen and glowered. He leaned over the table and snatched the book.

"No son of mine will ever be more than another steel mill worker. It's what you were born to do."

The boy clambered for the book, his father held it higher. The boy jumped up on his chair. When he leapt upon the table, his father limped to the stove, opened it and threw the book in.

"You think you're special?" his father asked angrily. "You think you're smarter than me? Get your head out of the clouds. Quit looking down at your own family."

The woman's name came to him, Vladlena. She shook

256

her head. "He didn't have any faith in you," she said.

Within a few steps they moved from his childhood kitchen to his first assignment in the navy, a tugboat. Two sailors doubled over with laughter. He'd just explained how he expected to apply for the academy. When they'd calmed down and dried their eyes, they explained the impossibility of his dream.

"No one's given you proper credit for your wits, have they?"

He drew in a deep breath. Somehow, in this museum of his failures, her words hit harder than any hard-knuckled foe. Tears welled up in his eyes, fury burned in his chest.

Vladlena tugged at his chin and leaned in for a kiss. "You'll make a perfect addition to our family of misjudged orphans."

It's Only Murder

FORTY-NINE

Michman Gorelov examined the men assembled in the mess hall.

They looked exhausted but determined. A self-ignited fire still burned in their eyes. They muttered and chuckled among themselves while he peered in from the passageway. Chiefs sat among petty officers and even seamen. Not every chief had been invited nor every petty officer.

He checked his uniform and reviewed his notes. *Notes, I barely know my letters, can't hardly spell. This paper looks just as bad as my homework in school.* He drew in a deep breath and marched in.

"You lot ready for the good news?" He offered a big smile, as false as his two front teeth.

The men stood from their benches as one and remained silent.

He motioned for them to sit. "This isn't that kind of meeting. I'm not here to tell you how fucked up you are or how our patrol's been extended."

Hushed laughter rose and fell.

"I called this group of men together first." He watched them all, to a man, lean into his words and focus. "The reason must remain our secret."

"First secret: you men *are* the leaders of *K-389*." He waited and watched his words sink in. The humble looked amazed and the proud sat straighter in their chairs.

"You each command respect and have earned the trust

of your comrades. Rank doesn't give you this, you were born with it."

He leaned closer and narrowed his gaze. He scanned the room and met each man's eyes before he spoke again.

"We're in a rough business. We rely on each other. Our nation relies on us. Not everyone who joins the Red Fleet is cut out for what we do."

Quiet, heavy as a lead vest, pressed each man a little lower into his seat.

"You know what I mean. We make our own justice, to protect ship and crew."

The men looked to each other, some to him, and nodded.

"Seaman Yanukovich died for two reasons. The first, he didn't fit. Second, I fucked up."

Jaws dropped, a wave of gasps crossed the room.

"I told stories of how we handled Yanukoviches in the past. I shared good advice for a problem that won't go away . . . ever. As long as there are armies and navies, there'll be outcasts who must be made to fit."

"But, Comrade Michman," Ayatollah said, his hand raised, "you only did what any good michman would."

"Ayatollah's half right. Nobody puts a swim instructor in jail, unless one of his students drowns."

Many frowned, but a few widened their eyes.

"Officers have books of law, stacks of regulations to follow," Gorelov said. "We have the unwritten law of warriors."

Most nodded. He crossed his arms and scanned the room. "Questions?"

Michman Ovechin raised his hand. Ovechin had arrived with Konev and Pudovkin. Short, trim, with a fiery glare, Ovechin had whipped the Engine Room crew into shape. He'd taught them to take pride in their work and their workplace.

"How does the death of a *pidor* weaken us?" Ovechin asked. "Won't we just get a replacement?"

"Who would you rather trust in a life boat while you slept, a murderer or a *pidor*?"

Ovechin scowled. "That's not a fair question."

"Who would you rather trust in a life boat, Lieutenant Ivankov or Lieutenant Boreyev?"

"Ivankov," a voice from the back of the room shouted. Gorelov and others craned their necks to see. Petty Officer Kipchak stood to remove any doubt. "Lieutenant Ivankov."

Ayatollah stood and frowned. "Are you saying . . .?"

Gorelov pointed to Ayatollah and let his furrowed brow silence the sonar operator. "I'm saying, how a sailor conducts himself as a sailor matters. How he gets his kicks, long as he's not barking up my tree, is his own business."

"But it's just a *pidor*," Ovechin said.

"And it's only murder," Gorelov answered angrily. "Once murder's out of the bag, it spreads. Soon everybody's on somebody's shit-list. We don't kill our own. Leave that to the courts."

"So, it's okay to . . ." Petty Officer Kipchak swallowed hard before he continued. He sounded hoarse and his voice cracked. "It's okay to administer blanket parties and such to our crewmates?"

"With proper oversight," Gorelov explained. "Used sparingly. As the ship's leaders, I expect you to keep the rest in line. If any problem seems too big come see me."

"What about the sickness that's spreading?" Ayatollah asked.

"What about the woman?" Ovechin asked. "Some of my men share the same dreams. A red-haired woman visits them."

"Strange things happen when a bunch of sailors get crammed together," Gorelov said. A nervous chuckle escaped. He didn't know what he meant. "Stranger things have happened than a bunch of men dreaming about the same whore in their last port." Many took his lie for what it was. It didn't help him and, as he scanned the room, it hadn't settled the concerns of his men either.

The second group trickled in, grumbling and moaning as they packed in. A third and fourth group would pile in later today, just like this one. These were the sheep and the bullies, the slow witted and the slovenly. Every crew needed sailors to man the watch but not every man deserved the title.

Those not shambling like zombies picked and poked at each other. A brutish petty officer, one of Boreyev's men, roared above the crowd. "Sit down and shut up."

"You lot ready for the good news?" Gorelov began again.

A couple of men collapsed onto the tables in front of them. Others moaned.

Boreyev's brutes stood and scowled at their comrades. Others from the Missile Division stood. One cradled a broken wrist, Ivankov's work. Another bore two black eyes. Gorelov smiled at his own handiwork. The scowling missile-men, those not disfigured, offered their most imposing countenance to silence dissent. The grumbling subsided.

Gorelov motioned for the men to sit. "We're in a rough business. We rely on each other. Our nation relies on us. Not everyone who joins the Red Fleet is cut out for what we do."

Dumbfounded looks and glazed-over eyes stared back at him.

"You know what I mean. We make our own justice, to protect ship and crew."

The men looked to each other, some to him, and nodded.

"Seaman Yanukovich died for two reasons. The first, he didn't fit. The second reason: some of you took it too far."

Jaws dropped, a wave of gasps crossed the room.

"Trust your chain of command to handle issues you bring to us. And if you don't trust them, trust me. The Fleet doesn't kill its own."

Only a handful shut their gaping mouths and nodded.

"Questions?"

The room erupted with the panicked cries. They spoke of listless nights, of nightmares and unnatural fatigue. More mentioned the red-haired woman in their dreams.

Many had seen her themselves.

None in the first group had.

Pale men made the majority of these ranks.

Few in the first group had.

Gorelov noticed a handful sat quietly and watched the chaos. Their sinister smugness chilled Michman Gorelov more than Arctic ice.

They know something, something dark.

He'd been adrift at sea once, thrown overboard by a rogue wave on the mid-watch. Though his ship tried to find him, he watched their search in the moonless night take them further and further away. They disappeared over the horizon. Daylight came and he contemplated his own death. They found him, but in those hours he felt his first fear since childhood. Right now, he felt as he had when his ship first slipped out of sight.

Sure hope a bright day follows.

A Game of Chess

"Do you think he'll be alright?" Lieutenant Pudovkin asked.

In the wardroom, Mikhail watched his new friend play chess with the Communications Officer, Dovzhenko, while he waited to hear about Doctor Anatoli from the doctor's assistant. The sallow scarecrow had never looked so near death. The medical aide thought it'd been contracted from Antonev's corpse or any of the other couple of dozen men who looked pale and shuffled about in a tired stupor.

"He looked dead," Mikhail said. "I thought he died right there in Sick Bay."

"And it was right after he bandaged up Zhora?"

Mikhail nodded. His chair felt harder, wobblier.

"Zhora looked fine," Pudovkin observed. "He hardly had a scratch on him from the beating he'd taken only an hour before."

"What happened to Antonev's c-c-corpse?" Dovzhenko asked.

"Freezer," Pudovkin answered with a shiver. "He's in a giant plastic bag in the back of the freezer."

"He's the only one who's died from that disease," Dovzhenko said while he moved his rook out into the open.

Pudovkin slid his bishop over and toppled the rook.

Dovzhenko's eyes twinkled and he smiled while he brought his own bishop deep in Pudovkin's territory and claimed his queen.

"You're not thinking clearly, Pudovkin," Mikhail noticed. "What's on your mind?"

The Ship's Navigator scanned the room, empty save for the three.

"You don't really think we'll go to war, do you?" Pudovkin asked.

"Hard to tell," Mikhail answered. "It sounds like the Americans are goading us, hoping we'll fire first so they can claim to defend themselves."

Pudovkin examined the board and frowned. He moved his pawn to block the bishop's retreat.

"Judging by Konev's words," he murmured, "he'll need no goading to push the button."

"True enough," Dovzhenko admitted. He rocked side to side in his seat, then swung his knight around to put his friend in check.

Mikhail leaned in and whispered. "He doesn't really understand what that would mean, I think."

"Exactly," Pudovkin replied. He grimaced. "He's ready to burn the world for a flag."

"You don't think the Americans are prepared to do the same?" Dovzhenko wondered.

"It's not how they think," Pudovkin answered. "I know. I've seen them, in Egypt." He tried to shift his king and found only one legitimate move.

"You saw sailors doing what sailors do," Mikhail said with a shrug.

Dovzhenko brought his other knight to bear, checkmate. "Ronald Reagan called us an evil empire."

Pudovkin tipped his king over. "And we call them an evil empire, harmless rhetoric."

"The zampolit showed us a movie from America recently," Dovzhenko said, "*Wars in the Stars*, or something."

"So?"

Dovzhenko's eyes widened. "In it, an evil empire is lured to a rebel base where they're annihilated."

"It's a movie," Pudovkin said.

"Dimitriev calls it conditioning."

Pudovkin offered a wry grin. "Dimitriev is a moron. He serves the Party because he qualifies for nothing else."

At the Navigator's last comment Dovzhenko cringed. His eyes darted to the wardroom door and the captain's door. When nothing happened, he straightened up, stood, and poured the three each a cup of tea. All the while the youngest officer looked pensive. When Dovzhenko sat, he stared into his cup as if searching for the answer to a riddle. Soberly he looked up at Pudovkin and spoke.

"America goaded Japan into attacking Pearl Harbor, only to discover they'd missed every aircraft carrier based there. The Anglo alliance cared more about their imperialist holdings in the Pacific than Russian blood spilt defending our homes."

Mikhail watched the two men study each other. Dovzhenko's sea green gaze gleamed with faith in his words. Pudovkin sighed and his frame sank a little lower. The tanned, fit Black Sea officer looked weary, no longer eager to argue his point. When he met Dovzhenko's eyes he winced as though wounded. He turned to Mikhail, desperation in his eyes.

"What about you, Mikhail?" he asked. "What do you think?"

Mikhail swallowed hard. He picked up his cup of tea and tilted it back until it emptied. When he pulled it away from his lips he found both men looking at him, awaiting his answer.

A knock at the wardroom door startled the men to their feet. The medical aide peered in and gave Mikhail a nod.

"The doctor will survive, Comrade Lieutenant. He's very weak right now but improving slowly."

Mikhail stood and picked his way around the table to the exit. Once the medical aide left Mikhail offered his answer. "I think both sides try to bend the minds of their people to their agendas."

Dovzhenko frowned and recoiled. "How can our people be conditioned with facts?"

"Who tells you they *are* facts?" Mikhail retorted before he stepped out.

Anatoli lay on his own examination table. A thick layer of blankets covered him. The jaundiced face Mikhail had come to know looked the color of old papers and just as fragile. Tiny bruises dotted his forehead and cheeks. His breathing dragged through his nostrils and mouth and rattled in his lungs. The doctor had been the first to truly welcome him to Komsomolsk and the *K-389*. He'd understood Mikhail's quiet solitary nature. Although always quick to cheer him up with a change of subject or a brisk walk into town, Anatoli also remained a mystery.

Afraid to wake him, but needing to connect somehow, Mikhail said a silent prayer. He didn't even know to whom or what he prayed, but it helped him to voice his concerns and best wishes.

Please get well. Don't die. Help us fight this anemia you've spoken of. Help me find another way to block out my past and embrace a future with Vladlena, or whoever I can find that'll be able to stomach me.

Zhora, Nika, and now Vladlena, Mikhail had been through a whirlwind of relationships after a lifetime of nothing. Now it looked like nothing loomed ahead, nothing except the friendship of an old doctor who kept his past a secret.

Hunger and Hate

Two oxygen generators fought Mikhail and Kipchak's efforts to keep at least one running. Another sleepless night yielded more questionable parts. Generator Two would need to be shut down and number One would need parts borrowed from the leaking unit until they found a cause. The speaker above the two dozing men crackled to life.

"Security team, report to Engine Room Forward!"

Mikhail looked up from his work met and Kipchak's gaze. The petty officer tightened his grip on his pipe wrench and Mikhail nodded. He grabbed a crowbar.

"Let's go," he said.

The two raced up the ladder and through the reactor tunnel. Through the oval doorway ahead they heard panicked screams and a devil's roar. From the hatch leading to the lower level, a man clambered up. Wide eyes and a fear-twisted face greeted them when he rose to his feet. His coveralls bore splashes of deep crimson. He tore past Mikhail, and continued his exodus.

Below, wails and howls continued. Mikhail examined the space around them. Engine Room Forward held all major electrical distribution for the ship. Motor generators, rectifiers, and transformers divided the steam generators' output into all the various voltages and frequencies needed to energize everything from light-bulbs to the sonar systems. From the sounds below, a madman threatened to plunge the ship into darkness.

Mikhail nodded to the port crawl space while he jerked a thumb over his shoulder to starboard. Kipchak swallowed hard and nodded. The two men spread out and picked their way between the ship's ribs. With one more glance, they descended.

Blood. Mikhail noticed the deck-plate beneath him puddled with it. Streaks of thick red shined on the nearby guardrails. He shimmied down and spied the ship's Engineer, Lieutenant Kirkov. From a gash in his throat, blood pulsed lazily.

"What's wrong with you, Adaksin?" a man cried. "Let me out. Leave me be."

"None of you listened to me," Adaksin growled hoarsely. "I warned you something was wrong." He pointed to Kirkov. "I tried to convince this bag of bones. I tried to make sense of the lights going out."

Mikhail squeezed between a bundle of cables and a ventilation pipe to see one man, the crier, Panarin. Pudgy, sweating, and speckled with blood, the petty officer held a shorting probe in one hand. He cowered behind the narrow length of copper. The electrician's teary eyes darted to Mikhail and back. He drew a deep breath and found his courage.

"Tell me," he managed, "tell me about the lights."

Adaksin's hands went to his hair. He clutched it, tugged on greasy fistfuls. "They weren't on the same circuits, none of it made sense, except for where they were."

Mikhail heard Adaksin sniff the air. He heard the silence of a suspicion.

Feet shuffled closer to Mikhail. He looked down at his weapon. Crammed in the crawl space, with no room to swing, it might as well be welded to the ship's hull. Panting rose above the compartment noise. The panting grew nearer. He watched Panarin's gaze follow Adaksin. The plump electrician's mouth hung open, ready to scream. He glanced at Mikhail and shook off his fear.

"What about 'her'?" Panarin shouted. "You mentioned a woman earlier, didn't you?"

The madman's footfalls turned back, toward Panarin. "So beautiful," Adaksin murmured, "so deadly."

Mikhail fought to keep quiet while he untangled himself and tiptoed onto the deck. Adaksin, a narrow shouldered, raven of a man, leaned into each step as if towing a barrel of concrete. From behind, Mikhail noticed swaths of blood painted the man's uniform. Adaksin halted and dropped his gaze.

"She knew me," Adaksin whispered. "She knew so much about me."

"Why are you covered in blood?" Panarin asked. "Why did you kill Comrade Kirkov?"

"So very hungry." The low guttural sound grew into a chuckle, then outright laughter. "Why not feed on a fool? Kill two birds with one . . ." Silence.

"I hear your heartbeat," he hissed as he turned. His forehead and high cheekbones looked white in contrast to a blood-soaked mouth and chin. His eyes caught Mikhail's attention. The world slowed and his reflexes thickened like mud. Adaksin's mouth widened, an ever-expanding fanged grin.

"You're heartbeat pounds in my head like a drum." His eyes glazed over.

"Don't," Panarin cried.

"I'll deal with you later, fatty," Adaksin said with a snarl. "This man looks like he means business." He glanced at the crowbar. Mikhail's reflexes returned.

It's the eyes.

Mikhail swung upward, wildly. The crowbar caught Adaksin in the chin and ripped open his flesh. The blow threw the madman's head back with a snap. Adaksin stumbled backward, but still stood. He leveled his gaze on Mikhail and roared. Agony contorted his expression while murder glowed in his eyes. Panarin ran and tackled Adaksin around the waist. He hung on the monster and pulled him to the deck.

Adaksin turned on his tackler. They tumbled on the deck. A wet noise, like a bite into an over-ripe tomato,

271

startled Mikhail. Panarin shrieked. Blood gushed onto the deck beside the two tangled men. The portly electrician's cry rang in the metal cabinets surrounding them and drowned out the electric hum. Another bite, fleshy wet with a crunch and a crack, and two of Panarin's fingers fell to the deck. He stood, stumbled backwards, and fell like a sack of cement. He squirmed and whimpered. Adaksin turned again to Mikhail.

He charged. Mikhail thrust his crowbar into the man's stomach. He halted, wide-eyed, his mouth in a silent 'o'. He grasped the length of iron and pulled it in deeper. He pulled Mikhail closer. Mikhail jerked his weapon from side to side. By centimeters, hand over hand, Adaksin drew nearer. Each attempt to wrest free and evade only urged the man to shove closer and pull faster. Mikhail found himself pinned against the bulkhead, the wriggling crowbar screeching across the steel beside him. A fanged grimace crept closer. In his throaty growl Mikhail heard an animal. In his wretched breath he smelled death.

"You officers, all alike," Adaksin hissed.

Whistles blew above. The security team had entered the compartment. Adaksin pulled another hand's width closer. His next handful would be Mikhail's flesh.

Metal clattered behind Adaksin. Kipchak came into view. He'd clamped his wrench down on the bloody crowbar and leaned on it to drive Mikhail's foe away. Adaksin twisted and growled.

The security team slid down the ladder one by one, each armed with a short club, each aghast at what they found. The two men stared at the struggling rabid man, covered in blood, howling like an animal.

"He's killed Kirkov," Mikhail shouted. "He's likely killed Panarin. Kill him."

They charged into action, clubs held high. They pummeled and bludgeoned the man until he lay on the deck, moaning. Bones cracked, flesh tore, blood pooled. The smell struck Mikhail as odd, like rotted meat.

They Come in Your Sleep

FIFTY-TWO

Captain Borodin stood before a handful of his officers. Mikhail scanned around the wardroom table: Dimitriev, Zhora, Boreyev, and Doctor Anatoli, an eclectic gathering.

"Four brave sons have died," Captain Borodin began. "They're not my sons but I mourn them all the same. I didn't kill them, but I bear the guilt all the same."

Mikhail watched his captain. He'd lost weight in this first week underway, at least five kilos. Sleeplessness had set his eyes within darker sockets, ashen craters. His bright eyes looked clouded.

"Madness. Surely you cannot blame yourself," Dimitriev insisted. "Madness and murder, those are the culprits."

"Zampolit, hold your tongue."

"Captain!"

Borodin leaned into the space between them and glared. Dimitriev cringed deeper into his seat.

"We are teetering on the verge of war," Borodin went on. "We have a mission to protect millions against annihilation. We must be prepared to stare down the barrel of our gun, into the gun of our enemy, and assure them we'll strip their victory of all meaning. Beyond our borders, billions rely on two opposing forces to keep each other in check."

Captain Borodin looked to the zampolit and clapped him on the shoulder. Dimitriev flinched before he met his captain's gaze.

"You will carry this message to the crew," Borodin said.

"Get with Michman Gorelov. The crew respects and loves him."

Dimitriev's features tensed at the unspoken implication. "Aye, Comrade Captain."

"No more deaths," Borodin said. He turned his attention to the other four men. He pointed to Zhora, Mikhail, and Boreyev. "You three worked well enough to get this ship put together on schedule. I'm counting on the three of you to work with Doctor Anatoli. You will find our murderer and isolate this spreading disease."

Boreyev looked to Mikhail. His brow furrowed a millimeter and his lips drew tighter. An iron wall seemed to keep him from turning to face Zhora.

"Doctor," Borodin said, "whatever resources you require, you'll have. Our mission comes first, but we must have a healthy crew to meet that challenge."

He straightened and sat. After a deep breath and long sigh, he eased back in his chair. With both hands raised he invited his officers to speak.

Zhora leaned into the silence. "The doctor and I don't hate each other-"

He leered at Boreyev.

"-and we did manage to find Shulga's killer even if we didn't bring him to justice." He looked to the doctor. "I'd like to work with Anatoli to gain forensic evidence and track the path these illnesses have followed."

Anatoli stuffed a cigarette in his mouth. He produced a lighter, lit his cigarette, and drew in deeply.

"Sure, that'll work," he said with a billowing exhale.

"I suppose Lieutenant Koryavin and I will scour the ship for evidence and a murderer," Boreyev said with a nod to Mikhail.

As Mikhail followed the others out, Captain Borodin motioned for him to remain.

"I need you to step in as Ship's Engineer," Borodin whispered. He shrugged. "At this rate, you'll be in my shoes before we return to port."

Mikhail peered through the torpedo room door. Ayatollah and Vetrov sat between the inner torpedo stowage racks. The redheaded boy stared back at Mikhail and muttered to his comrade. Ayatollah held the ship's boat hook, a ten-foot-long wooden pole with a brass dull-headed hook on one end. He scraped at it with his knife, whittling its round base to a sharp point.

"What's your business?" Ayatollah asked as Mikhail bent to pass through the portal into the torpedo room.

"Petty Officer Judin, where are you manners?"

He didn't look up from his work. "Sorry, Comrade Lieutenant, I've lost myself these past days."

"What're you two doing here?"

"Sleep," Vetrov said, "they come in your sleep."

"Who?"

"The vampires."

Ayatollah raised his newly crafted weapon, a wooden spear, and pressed into Mikhail's chest with it. "We'll need our sleep and we'll need the right weapons to kill them when they're discovered."

Mikhail pushed the point aside. "Are you threatening me?"

"No, Comrade Lieutenant, just making sure demons know what to expect when they come looking for our blood."

"Explain, please."

Vetrov stood, eyes wide. "You were there. You saw the blood and fangs."

"The doctor assured me what I saw was exaggerated by fear and shock," Mikhail said, his voice wavering. Another voice, from the primal shadows of his mind, responded otherwise. *Fangs, blood, yes, Adaksin's gone, changed, replaced with a demonic double.*

"We'll sleep in shifts," Ayatollah explained. "Vetrov and I will watch over each other."

"With this pole, we'll slay them before they're in arm's

reach," Vetrov said with a nervous laugh.

"Vampires? Old folk tales; you believe this?"

Ayatollah nodded, a grim scowl on his face. Vetrov looked to his mentor before he too grimaced and nodded.

"What do you believe, Comrade Lieutenant?"

"I-I'm not sure. I was there-"

From the cracks in his mind's civil sanctuary, the voice whispered again. *But you are sure. You refuse to believe the terrifying truth.*

"That's why we sleep here," Ayatollah said. "They come in your dreams. Some say they've seen the same woman Adaksin spoke of. They look in her eyes and get lost."

The eyes . . . remember Adaksin's? You nearly drowned in them.

FIFTY-THREE

The crawl space, aptly named and dreaded by all. Mikhail squirmed between the ship's frame and bundled electrical conduits. He shined the flashlight ahead and above. He and Boreyev had begun their search for the watchman's missing weapon, a short, thick wooden club. Doctor Anatoli had warned them to keep an eye out for a different kind of danger, rats.

"This disease might be the result of rabid wharf rats," he'd said. "Don't go down there without a knife."

He'd also asked him to bring back any rat turds he ran across. And though Mikhail hadn't found any droppings, it smelled like one waited for him around the next pipe or wire-bundle.

The ship's frames, like giant titanium ribs, acted as a shallow wall between Mikhail and Boreyev. The stout missile officer's curses poured over the barrier and kept Mikhail silent. Boreyev's displeasure helped ease his own misgivings and chuckle occasionally.

Skittering, scratching sounds further up the hull caught his attention.

"Hey, Boreyev, did you hear that?"

"I've heard you giggling like a little girl, that's all."

Mikhail shimmied faster and pulled himself along the hull by the handholds above him. "I think it's one of those rats."

His skin crawled with chills and he remembered to draw

his knife. Almost vertical, now, Mikhail heard it again. When he looked up, whatever made the noise shifted out of sight. Dust flittered down like snow. One fleck stung in his eye. He flinched and shook his head. The corner of a pipe bracket caught the edge of his brow and tore a stripe of agony.

"*Yebat!*"

Several meters below and one frame-bay over, he heard a throaty chortle.

He shone the flashlight up again. Only flakes of dust and a minefield of more angle iron greeted his weakening beam. Blood oozed into his eye. He flinched again and brought his hand to wipe it away. His hand scraped across another sharp bit. The flashlight fell from his hand. Through clenched teeth he growled. With a quick sweep of his leg, he caught the light before it dropped out of sight.

A whisper from above caught him in the middle of recovering his torch.

"Mikhail?"

He looked into the darkness and saw nothing. He widened his eyes until they ached to see. He bent down and stretched his hand out for the flashlight. Fingers felt for the slick cylinder. Nothing. He heard something slither down the crawl space, sliding closer. He turned his gaze from the darkness above to seek the torch and found it. Sour, rotting-meat stench, sank into his nostrils and his stomach quivered. Once he wrapped his fingers around the flashlight, he peered above him. Shadows upon shadows, nothing more. He brought it up; light swept about and wobbled until he steadied it to shine above him.

A face stared back. He gasped and cringed before the features came fully into focus.

"Vladlena?"

Neon red hair hung down from around her pale features. Mikhail swore he'd seen a demon at first, a grey skinned, white fanged demonic version of his surprise wife.

She grinned at her name and slid down a little closer. "Mikhail, I hadn't expected to see you here."

He laughed until a dusty cough stopped him. "I'm supposed to say that."

She offered a pouty frown, her eyes not fixed on his. She reached out and touched the cut on his brow.

"Ooh, you've been hurt. Let me kiss it and make it better."

Fear rippled through him before her rejoined gaze comforted him like a warm blanket on a cold winter night.

She shouldn't be here.

But she is.

She can't be here.

Aren't you glad?

Of course, but . . .

She loves you, surely you can see it.

She's not . . . she's . . . impossible

Her lips upon his wound felt cool, her tongue coarse. He felt like he hung in a hammock, perfectly fitted to his body, snug enough to immobilize him in comfort. She descended closer and unbuttoned her shirt. She nestled in-between his chin and collarbone and kissed him. He wanted to kiss her but couldn't move. Her hands ran down the front of his shirt, her nails dragging with sharp steady pressure down his torso.

The ghost of his stepfather crept in. The way she clutched at him, controlled him, caressed him while he remained immobile and helpless. His stomach churned. His throat went dry. Without another warning, it came, vomit erupted.

She shrieked. He fell. She clawed at him as he slid down the hull's side. Her nails felt sharper than before. They dug and tore at his uniform and flesh underneath.

Angle iron and cable brackets struck and scraped his shins and shoulders. He found his limbs again and put his hands out to halt his fall. As soon as he did, he reconsidered, hastened his descent, and screamed.

"What the hell's wrong with you?"

Mikhail looked up and shook the fog from his mind. He'd hit his head on the way down. Boreyev stood over him, staring down from the bilge hatch. The pungent odor of vomit and the slick soggy spots on his uniform reminded him of what just happened.

"Seal this compartment," he ordered. "There's a stowaway in the crawl space. She may be the key to everything."

"Did you not hear the announcement? We're to man our stations. We're to ready missile tubes for launch."

"Fine, do that, only seal this compartment. Post guards on the doors, don't let her out, and seal the compartment."

Minutes later, from Launch Control, Mikhail spoke to Captain Borodin over the phone.

"We've armed the men in the compartment from the Launch Control armory. We'll need armed teams from Damage Control to enter and begin their search."

"You said, 'she'," Boreyev said. "You saw a woman?"

"Yes, a woman with red hair."

Boreyev's disapproving frown fell. Shocked, his words came out in a whisper. "You saw *her?*"

"I'm not sure what you mean?"

"A dozen men, maybe more, have all seen a red-haired woman in their dreams. She always seduces them."

"These men tell you this?"

"I've seen it myself."

"We've got to capture her," Mikhail said.

"But if she's real and in our dreams... How's that possible?"

"Lieutenant Boreyev, let me go direct the search teams while you ready the missiles."

Boreyev nodded and turned to his men. As he began a litany of orders and received a swarm of reports, he focused on readying the missiles.

Makarov pistol in one hand and flashlight in the other, Mikhail raced to meet the security teams. Two four-man teams, one forward and the other aft awaited his instructions. From outside Launch Control, he motioned for the forward team to join him. They trotted to the aft team and he outlined his plan.

"Two men in middle level, two men in lower level," he began, "don't let your crewmate out of your sight."

He pointed to the men from the engine room. "You four will follow me. We'll begin the search aft and work our way forward."

Frame-bay by frame-bay, they lowered their slimmest man into the crawlspace. He grunted and cursed. He emerged dustier and dustier.

The intercom crackled to life.

"Comrades, we'll be at battle-stations for several hours." Captain Borodin's words sounded glum, tired. "We'll have Damage Control bring rations to you at your posts."

Somewhere below, a man screamed. Gunfire, muted and distant, *crack-crack-cracked.* More shouts, more gunfire. Mikhail ran to the nearest ladder and slid down the rails. A scream and a feral growl rose from the lowest level. Mikhail motioned for the mid-level team to join him before he dropped down the nearby hatch.

"You hurt me," Vladlena whined. She cradled her forearm while she inched closer to a lone petty officer. His partner lay on the edge of an open bilge hatch. His arms convulsed in rhythm with the blood pulsing from his throat.

"Your friend and I were having some fun and you ruined it," she said with a pouting frown.

"Vladlena!" Mikhail shouted.

She looked to him. "Misha!"

In that split second, before she captured his thoughts, he shouted to the petty officer. "Shoot her. Shoot her now."

His jaw dropped before determination set in and furrowed his brow. Time moved at glacial speed. Her eyes widened, shock and fury contorted her soft features. She lunged and clubbed the Makarov free with a weapon of her own. It was the missing truncheon. The pistol skittered into the bilge. She wasted no time turning to run.

Mikhail kneeled and spoke to the men now climbing down the ladder behind him.

"Fire!"

Two pistols rang out behind him. Sparks flew from the missile tubes beside her. He took careful aim, exhaled, and squeezed the trigger. She fell to the deck. He motioned for his men to go after her. Once they trotted past, he rose and ran to the two men who'd discovered her. The disarmed man sat on the deck, shaking.

"She's real," he murmured. "She tried to kill Sergei."

His comrade had stopped moving, blood spattered into the bilge beneath him.

"He's dead, comrade," Mikhail said. "She'd have killed you next."

Gunfire erupted again. Mikhail watched two men step back and unload their pistols into Vladlena. At first she seemed to endure it, like a hard rain. She rose to her knees, on all fours before the final shot, to the back of her head, felled her.

Mikhail ran to see her and knelt down. His heart jumped into his throat at her appearance.

"Bozhe moi," one petty officer cried, "what *is* she?"

Her skin now looked translucent and grey with a network of black blood vessels. The bullet wounds oozed with the darkest blood he'd seen. White spots of puss rose to the surface and dissipated. Mikhail recalled a calf caught in a barbed wire fence. It'd been there, dead, for days in the Russian summer. Vladlena's corpse issued a similar odor. Amidst a cluster of bullet wounds in her face he noticed her teeth. Long, thin and white, they were the cleanest part of her corpse.

"Bind her," Mikhail muttered. He stood, looked the men in the eyes and spoke again, louder. "Bind her tightly."

"What?" One man asked while the other simply nodded

and ran off.

"Don't ask, just do it." Mikhail examined his former lover. "Get chem-suits on before you touch her." He leveled his pistol on her. "Go, go and get dressed. Notify Doctor Anatoli too. Whatever this contagion is, it creates madness, ferocity, and a resilience we can't ignore."

I Make Do!

FIFTY-FOUR

Mikhail and Zhora carried the body to the uppermost level of the Missile Compartment Forward. Wrapped in a body bag, still bound, Vladlena's corpse felt astonishingly light. He'd known her, felt her in his arms for one night in his apartment, she'd never felt so fragile and small.

He swallowed hard, yet the fresh film of vomit remained. The putrefied sludge that had slid out of Vladlena seemed like blood from something dead a week at least. Her contorted features amidst the bullet wounds bore only a passing resemblance of the woman he'd known and looked more like a museum waxwork creature.

"We had to line them up in upper level," Zhora explained. "We wanted to re-examine wounds, causes of death, and signs of commonality."

Once she was hoisted up, Mikhail followed. As his head rose above middle level's ceiling and his eyes beheld the upper level deck, a mélange of odors hit him. Disinfectant offered a protective acidic ring around a blossoming rot. His stomach, already empty and sore, clenched tight.

A row of corpses lay head to foot down the narrow passageway between the missile tubes and the hull. Doctor Anatoli looked up from one mottled frame and nodded.

"A few more tests and I'll have this mess back in the freezer."

"This woman doesn't even look human," Mikhail offered with a shudder.

Zhora unzipped the bag at those words and examined her. Curiosity quickly turned to revulsion and then Zhora's reaction stepped outside Mikhail's expectations. He shrugged as though he'd not just looked into the face of evil.

"Did you know her?" Mikhail asked.

"No." A wry smile emerged before he spoke. "I heard she called you by name and you her."

"She . . ." Mikhail stumbled for an answer, fumbled for a lie. He stepped away from his friend and walked alongside the assembled corpses. "I knew her, a little. I slept with her once."

"Seems Nika really reversed your fortune with women," Zhora said sardonically.

"Zhora! What's wrong with you?"

"What?" He shrugged.

"A woman's dead. Her corpse looks like a demon. Is there anything left that touches your heart?"

"One or two." Zhora eyed Mikhail playfully.

"Every day you seem colder, stranger. What's wrong?"

Zhora doubled over with laughter. "Look around you." He straightened between chuckles. Mikhail noticed how his laughter never touched his eyes.

"My world *started* upside down," Zhora explained. "I made do."

He clenched his fists. "My father exiled me. I made do."

"I held false hope in you and fell," he moaned.

"People are dying." His voice rose and rose. "The world's at war." Screaming now. "No one loves me! BUT I MAKE DO!"

Soviet Resolve

FIFTY-FIVE

Mikhail watched Captain Borodin and Lieutenant Dovzhenko enter the Command Center from the Radio Room. Borodin's eyes stayed fixed on a single sheet of teletype paper while he ascended the Periscope Station. Dovzhenko followed with the eagerness of a shamed puppy.

The Tactical Station felt awkward, unfamiliar, after his encounter in the crawlspace. Doctor Anatoli's last words still rang in his ear. *We've enough to fight without fighting each other.*

"All nuclear forces shall prepare a demonstration of Soviet resolve," Captain Borodin read into the microphone. "At noon, Moscow time, *K-389* will approach launch depth, pressurize and unlock tubes for launch."

Dovzhenko, nibbled at his fingernails while the Captain read.

"We will stand ready to launch for the duration of the American exercise, 'Able Archer.' Everyone must stay alert and steady. To threaten annihilation and hope never to unleash it, that's our purpose."

With a nod to the Ballast Control Station, Michman Gorelov lined his panels up and tapped the helmsman on the shoulder. The ship pitched upward. Each pop and creak of the hull and decks seemed louder, more dangerous.

Captain Borodin switched the selector on his intercom and spoke. "Launch Control, make tubes one and sixteen ready for launch."

"Aye, Comrade Captain." Boreyev's stern reply gave Mikhail a shiver.

He shrugged it off and examined the dials at Gorelov's station, the gauges and dials for hydraulics and pressurized gas systems. Launch Control taxed Mikhail's systems the most. Miles of hydraulic pipes, pistons and actuators served the sixteen missile tubes amidships. Hydraulic fluid heated to near boiling with all that work. Each launch canister would need to be equalized with the sea pressure outside. Ice formed on the reducer valves under such a demand.

Ayatollah startled Mikhail as he stood, headphones pressed against his ears. He nodded to his protégé, Vetrov and turned to the captain.

"Submerged contact, bearing three, zero, zero," he whispered.

"*K-314?*"

Ayatollah turned to peer at his screen. The green screen gradually filled with new data on their latest find.

Fear widened the sonar operator's eyes and he turned back to Borodin.

"No, Comrade Captain. It's the *Tautog*."

Borodin stiffened in his stance and drew in a deep breath. "I suppose they'll be the first Americans to know how serious we are."

Pipes in the crawlspace sang while they pressurized missile tubes. Mikhail looked at Ayatollah. The man looked like a thief caught in a spot light. Both men knew the systems were telegraphing the ship's position and intent. No other operation sounded like launch preparations.

As if to confirm, the USS *Tautog*'s sonar offered its own song. Like a blacksmith's hammer it pounded against *K-389*'s hull with a steady maddening rhythm. Mikhail fought to ignore it while he compiled data from Ayatollah and Vetrov's stations. Slide rule in one hand, pencil scribbling in the other, his jaw dropped at what the numbers told him.

"Range, five kilometers and closing," Mikhail reported.

"*Tautog*'s speed, twenty-four KPH."

Others in the Command Center, Dovzhenko, Gorelov, Vetrov, each looked back at him, shocked. Gorelov looked to the captain.

"You have your orders, Ballast Officer," Captain Borodin said. "Nothing they do will deter us short of a torpedo."

Mikhail traced the American submarine on his chart. Closer and closer, louder and louder, the *Tautog* remained on a collision course.

At a depth of ninety meters, *K-389* slowed to three KPH. The ship dangled kilometers above the Pacific's bottom like a helpless right whale for the *Tautog* to strike.

"Captain," Boreyev's voice bellowed from the Periscope Station's speaker, "Tubes one and sixteen ready."

"Two kilometers and closing," Mikhail reported. "Speed unchanged."

"They're g-g-going to hit us," Dovzhenko screamed. He clutched the Periscope Station's railing.

Captain Borodin glared at the panicked Communicator. His gaze fell upon the man's grip at the rail. "Lieutenant Dovzhenko, prepare a distress buoy. You have two minutes."

"Aye, Comrade Captain."

Ayatollah stood up from his console again. "Another contact, Captain!"

From the hull, a new sound emerged. The bird chirping sonar of *K-314* collided with the *Tautog*'s ringing ping. Mikhail scrambled to plot it on the chart. A smile emerged.

"*K-314*, bearing two, two, zero," Mikhail began, "range three kilometers, closing on the *Tautog* with a speed of forty KPH."

Mikhail watched Ayatollah and Vetrov tracking on their screens, jotting down notes. He noticed a jagged patch of bright green on the young sonar-operator's display. Before Mikhail pointed it out, Vetrov announced it.

"*Tautog*, changing course and speed."

Mikhail heard a collective sigh while he worked his slide rule. Mikhail plotted the ships with the new data. His chest tightened. He looked up from his figures and looked to Captain Borodin.

"Collision course," he murmured. He cleared his newly dry throat and spoke louder.

"The *Tautog*'s turned away from us, but is on a collision course with *K-314*."

Silence. Only the ship's machinery droned on, that, and the incessant sonar pings of two submarines as they closed.

Seconds rolled into a minute.

Over two hundred men between the two ships held fast and charged on. How many knew? Three nuclear reactors, tons upon tons of steel, the collision's enormity ballooned in *K-389*'s silence.

One minute grew into two.

Mikhail cringed inside. *K-314*, he knew, would not flinch any more than Captain Borodin.

Ayatollah's mouth hung open while he listened to his headphones. He kept his unblinking gaze on the sonar display.

They heard the impact through their own hull. The sharp squeal of metal on metal and the thunder of two steel behemoths resounded through *K-389* like a distant storm. A handful of hushed gasps rippled through the Command Center.

"Alarms from both ships," Ayatollah muttered, his hands pressing his headphones tight.

"*Tautog*'s blowing to the surface," Vetrov added. He squinted at his screen and cocked his head while he listened. "One of the ballast tanks is leaking air."

Borodin looked to Ayatollah, a glint of hope in his eye. The senior sonar expert shook his head. "*K-314* is sinking. He'll be below the layer before we hear him implode, but . . ."

"Let's hope their deaths aren't the first in a new global war," Captain Borodin said.

No More Fear

FIFTY-SIX

Dovzhenko poured over the teletype. Nothing. He went to the radio consoles where his two radio operators worked to train their equipment on the next broadcast from Vladivostok. Whatever new fears the Americans' exercise evoked, Soviet military commands were poised for war. No sign of an end in sight, no hint at a misunderstanding to silence the rattling sabers on both sides. If the Americans didn't bring it about, his own nation might out of a paranoid overreaction. Monitors sprang to life as the broadcast came in. The operators fine-tuned their gear and set the recorders and teletype to print. Encrypted signals were entered and the printer click-clacked a legible message.

"Doing alright Comrade Lieutenant?"

Dovzhenko jumped at the greeting and spun around.

"Ivankov, Lieutenant Ivankov," he muttered. "You aren't s-s-supposed to be in here."

"Boreyev comes in here," Zhora countered. "Why not me?"

Dovzhenko looked to the operators. "Why don't you men go grab some tea."

They nodded, rose, and left without a word.

Once the cypher-locked door shut, Dovzhenko collapsed into an operator's chair. "What are you doing Ivankov? You know this room's restricted."

"And yet I'm still here." Zhora stepped closer. He slipped by Dovzhenko and sat in the other chair. He offered the man a cigarette.

"I don't smoke, cancer."

Zhora laughed and took it for himself. Once lit, he drew in a deep drag. "I only recently picked up the habit. My near-murder left me less afraid of death."

"Really?" The nervous Communications Officer fidgeted with the torn edge of his seat.

"I've only told a few comrades what happened. It's a horrid tale really. Beaten nearly to death by my own crewmates."

Dovzhenko's mouth gaped open and his gaze met Zhora's. He jumped up and rushed to the door, disabled the cypher keypad, and scurried back to his seat.

Zhora grinned. Dovzhenko sat, transfixed. As he began the story, he decided to include Mikhail at the academy, his love for men, his father's exile. He told about his mother's cold conversation over the phone. Emotional pains he'd forgotten resurfaced. Sorrow rose within him but stopped short of tears. His body seemed incapable. When he told of Ivan, the whore whom Boreyev had bludgeoned to death beside him, tears threatened again.

"And that's when I fell out of the window onto the street. Boreyev and his comrades left me for dead."

"And he's not been arrested?"

"Justice for a *pidor*? They'd rather promote the real monsters to admiral, like my father."

"It doesn't matter. It's still not right."

Zhora reached out and patted Dovzhenko on the cheek. "That's sweet of you to think that, pleasantly naïve."

Dovzhenko recoiled from his touch and averted his eyes. "I'm not . . . um . . . I like women, Ivankov."

Zhora chuckled. "Not every touch is a prelude to sex. Besides, you're not my type, too effeminate."

"I'm not effeminate," Dovzhenko said with a frown.

"Youthful, then, perhaps that's it. You've not a scrap of beard hair, have you?"

"No." His voice trailed off and he stood slowly. "Why did you come here?"

"I'm forming a group of comrades of my own, to counter

the bullies and judgmental clods of the world. I thought you might be interested."

Zhora stood and inched closer. Dovzhenko backed up until he hit the radio cabinet. His eyes darted toward the locked door.

"Don't be afraid. I won't ask you to do anything you won't want to do yourself."

"I'm n-n-not afraid."

"Of course you are," Zhora countered with a piteous smile. "You've been afraid of your crewmates, afraid of your inadequacies, afraid of your past I suspect."

"W-w-what . . . makes you think all that?"

"I have powerful hunches these days."

A whimper escaped the officer but he remained in place, paralyzed.

"I must show what I didn't tell you about my miraculous survival. I must better know you, to gauge whether or not you'll fit in the new world better than the old."

Zhora leaned closer and bared his teeth. Dovzhenko failed to notice anything beyond his eyes. He felt suffocated by a dreamy fog.

"D-d-don't . . . n-n-no."

"It's nothing like what you fear. There'll be a sharp pain followed by a pleasure that burns, like when you crawl out of the sea on a summer day. You're shivering and lay down on the hot sand. It burns but it soothes the chills away."

Before Dovzhenko protested again, Zhora sank his teeth into him. Sharp pain gave way to the kind of pleasure that comes from scratching an itch raw. The crook of his neck felt warm and wet. His limbs convulsed and felt afire before they slipped beneath a sleepy fog. His mind sank into a blissful oblivion.

"Shuddering, stuttering Leonid, where's your brother now?"

Two boys cornered young Leonid Dovzhenko outside the schoolhouse. They'd poked fun at him as much as they dared. Leonid's older brother had protected him from much. He'd dealt his share of painful justice. He'd been a bully like these boys. He'd recently shipped off for the army and left little Leonid to learn how to handle himself.

"H-h-he's in the army," Leonid replied. "He'll be back in a couple of months."

"No he won't," the rusty haired leader proclaimed. "He just said that to keep you from crying."

"Besides," his pudgy minion added, "there won't be much left of you by then except a piddling idiot."

"I'm n-n-no idiot." Leonid knew this. He'd always scored well on tests. Only his clumsy mouth overshadowed his intellect. But it seemed stuttering had branded him an imbecile by his peers.

"If you aren't an idiot now," Rusty-Hair said with a sadistic laugh, "you will be by the time we're done bashing your brains in."

"D-d-don't."

The two closed, fists held up for him to see without losing sight of their vicious grins. Dovzhenko brought his own fists up only to sink to the ground and cover his head.

The first blow thumped like a melon. Though Leonid flinched, he gradually realized, the blow hadn't struck him. He looked up as the pudgy boy screamed. Zhora stood over him and drove a fist through his open mouth. Teeth and bone cracked and caved in. Leonid looked at the other boy. He lay on the ground, the back of his head bloodied and sunken in.

"You're too brilliant to treat like this. But the world is ruled by boys like these," Zhora said. He offered Leonid a hand. "I mean to change that. You'll have justice at your fingertips and vengeance in your grasp."

Dovzhenko awoke briefly and muttered. The schoolyard smells gave way to the submarine's ozone and metal odors. Zhora lifted his face up to meet Leonid Dovzhenko's wide eyes. Blood gleamed across his lips.

"But, but, I don't want to die," Dovzhenko whispered.

Zhora hovered over the man's hot pulsing throat and offered a throaty chortle. "Accept my offer and never fear anything ever again."

Disarray

"Get back there and get the engine room under control," Captain Borodin had whispered. "I don't like what I'm hearing, and if Konev or Dimitriev gets back there, we'll have men lined up for court martials for the next week."

Mikhail stepped out of his stateroom, into Operations Compartment Forward's middle level passageway. Before heading aft he looked forward, into the torpedo room. Vetrov stared back, his red hair gleamed in the light. *It's brighter than usual.* He looked around. *Or is it darker everywhere else?*

A pair of crewmen sat outside the ship's freezer, eyes glued to the thick insulated door. Unshaven, with sunken tired eyes, they looked like labor camp prisoners. Mikhail knew what vexed them and almost understood why. Antonev, Adaksin, Kirkov, Panarin, Sergei, and Vladlena; the bodies stacked in the back of the freezer left little room for food. Padlocked against thieves, these men held no faith in steel against whatever they feared. One brandished a knife and the other fondled a truncheon absentmindedly. Mikhail noticed the wooden club's handle, whittled down to a sharp point.

Through the watertight door he entered the Missile Compartment Forward. The central passage reminded him of a nightly walk. A chain of light ran along the center, flanked by shadows. Above, the pipes sang and valves hissed, two missile tubes demanded constant attention to keep them pressurized equal to the ship's depth. Moscow needed them ready to respond should their deepest fears prove true. He continued his march aft. With each step he noticed how far-gone the crew had let the ship slip into chaos. Bits of trash lay strewn about, wisps of dust collected in the corners. Light fixtures winked or remained dark. With everyone at their action stations, the passageway seemed like a ghost town. In Missile Compartment Aft things looked the same. His own Auxiliaries Compartment looked only slightly better.

Through the Reactor Tunnel and into the Engine Room Forward, Mikhail felt like he'd entered a museum. The lighting remained bright but he'd yet to see a soul. He edged around the desalination plant and found his newly inherited department. Huddled together near Engineering Control, they looked weary, with distant stares, like men on the battle-lines.

Michman Ovechin noticed Mikhail and stood. "Comrade Lieutenant, I hadn't expected you."

"Someone had to take over as Ship's Engineer eventually."

Ovechin invited Mikhail to walk with him. Mikhail noticed a long piece of pipe tucked into the Michman's belt. One end had been wrapped in electrical tape. Alternating layers of washers and nuts made the other end heavy and knobby, like a medieval mace. In the midst of his comparison, Mikhail realized . . . that's exactly what it's meant to be. He looked to the other men. Each wore or brandished their own archaic weapon fashioned from their surroundings.

Ovechin watched Mikhail. "It got out of hand for a bit after Adaksin," he admitted. "We've got a few minor injuries. Folks thought they saw rabid crewmates around every corner for a bit."

"I see. And the rest of the Engine Room?"

Ovechin nodded. "We watch each other closely at Engineering Control. From here we can monitor most functions. When necessary, a pair of men inspects the engine room." He snickered. "It practically runs itself."

"Nuclear power and submarines have no room for 'practically' or 'most' in their vocabulary. We're one slip from the ocean floor or radiation sickness for the whole crew."

"Agreed, Comrade Lieutenant, but the men fear each other. They fear being alone and attacked. I've made this compromise to keep the engine crew from bludgeoning each other whenever they round a corner."

The two continued through the Engine Room. Mikhail pointed out details amiss, dribbling leaks pooling up, and unsafe conditions set up to avoid manual operations.

"Too many systems bypassed or cross-connected Michman. We just witnessed the sinking of our escort. The next threat we'll face alone. This Engine Room isn't ready for such a crisis."

"Of course, Comrade Lieutenant, but how do we address their fears? Many men won't go forward to their bunks. They fear anything forward."

"Then we'll bring everything aft," Mikhail ventured. "We'll search these spaces until we're confident they're safe. We'll have mattresses and food scavenged from forward, or meals brought to the Reactor Tunnel door. We'll take our lessons of radiation contamination and apply them to whatever's claimed some of our crew."

Four hours later, Mikhail exited the Reactor Tunnel with Michman Ovechin and watched it shut and lock behind him. Through the thick glass porthole he waved at the petty officer standing watch, guarding the security of twenty-two men.

They'd scoured the compartments for stowaways and rats, any contributor to contagion. They'd send a foraging party forward to confiscate mattresses from their own bunks and dry food rations stored in the missile compartments.

Mikhail had opened the aft armory and emptied it into the hands of his men. All on watch now wore a Makarov on one hip and their crude cudgels on the other.

"You think the captain will approve of your plan?" Ovechin asked.

"It is already in place," Mikhail answered. "I've solved his problem of an inefficient Engine Room. I'll face him with those facts and we'll see what comes of it."

Ovechin nodded.

Mikhail marched forward while Ovechin returned through the tunnel door. Outside Launch Control, the lights were brightest in the compartment. He turned to examine the door. Locked shut with a sign scrawled in large letters: For Entry Step Back and Be Examined.

Mikhail went to knock on the door and felt tension against his shin. A thin wire tightened to his right and a handful of metal refuse, tea tins and washers, jangled.

"Stand back," a voice bellowed through the armored door. "What do you want?"

"I'd like to speak to Lieutenant Boreyev. Is he there?"

After a pause, the door's slot opened, where Mikhail had once slid in his identity papers. A pair of glassy eyes peered through.

"What is it, Mikhail?" Boreyev's voice held tension and fear.

"I'm taking similar measures in the engineering spaces. How are you doing for food and bedding?"

"We'll manage. What else? Why stop here?"

"I wanted to be sure it was you who commanded here. I wanted to be sure our missile systems were under control."

"The dreams have stopped," Boreyev said with a nervous sigh. "Those of us who were sick have begun to recover in only a day's time. I'm not coming out of here without good reason."

Mikhail took a step closer. He watched Boreyev's face flinch from the peephole.

"How many men are in there, Boreyev? It must be cramped."

"Ten, plus myself."

"But you've a division of sixteen. What happened?"

"I chose my best ten. The others must make their own way."

"Once I'm sure the Engine Room is safe, in twenty-four hours, send your outcasts aft."

"I had to choose," Boreyev insisted. "To survive, to fulfill our mission, I had to choose."

Mikhail stepped back and faced forward. Before he took his first step, Boreyev spoke once more. It sounded like a plea, a repentance.

"I had to choose, I had to."

Riot at the Mausoleum

Mikhail heard shouts ahead in Operations Compartment Aft before he passed through the narrow, oval, watertight door. He bent, tucked his head through and watched a man fall on the deck in front of his boot. One catatonic watchman over the freezer looked up, his nose bloodied, a fist sized red patch covered his upper lip, cheek, and bent nose.

At the man's fall, the mob gathered outside the freezer door fell into a full melee. Mikhail stared, stunned, before he rushed in to pull men from the pile. Fists flew, arms swung, Mikhail wrestled one, two and three men loose.

"Stop this!" The high-pitched scream slowed the brawl. Mikhail stood and stepped back. He looked across the scrum to the zampolit.

"Captain Dimitriev is right. What's the meaning of this?" Mikhail asked.

The men untangled themselves and came to attention. Last to stand, Ayatollah, explained.

"They must be jettisoned."

"What, who?" Mikhail asked. Already an answer curled up under a crack in the back of his mind like poison gas.

"The creatures our comrades have become," Ayatollah shouted, his voice hoarse, "they must go before they kill us."

"Creatures?" Dimitriev snorted. "And you, a grown man."

The zampolit looked around and picked Mikhail out. "What're you doing here, hmm?"

"I just came back from the Engine Room. I'm the new Ship's Engineer, or haven't you heard?"

Dimitriev glared. Mikhail read the look on his face plainly enough. *Don't show your contempt for me in front of the crew.*

"Sorry, Comrade Zampolit, I've been so busy, I forgot my place."

"We must honor our dead, not cast them out like rubbish."

"No."

The voice, loud and commanding, came from beyond the chaos, from behind Mikhail. He turned to see the face of a man ready to defy tradition and the Party. Michman Gorelov marched by as Mikhail turned to see.

"They go out the torpedo tubes."

"Michman Gorelov," Dimitriev said. His voice trailed off and his countenance changed. His condescension lost steam at Gorelov's gaze.

Mikhail observed the somber resolve in the man's face. The words he'd spoken to a superior were non-negotiable.

"There is a disease-

"Corpses. They're dead," Dimitriev sputtered. "They're isolated."

Gorelov scanned the faces around him. "Leave us."

He grabbed Mikhail by his arm while the others dispersed, muttering. Mikhail noticed for the first time, Gorelov had armed himself with a pistol. Once others left, Gorelov explained.

"Fear and panic, that's the disease. Can't be sealed off in a freezer."

"Come, you two," Dimitriev said, his voice quivering, "Come with me."

Before Gorelov left with the zampolit, he peered into the cafeteria and assigned two men to keep watch on the freezer.

Mikhail followed Dimitriev into the wardroom where the

zampolit grabbed the captain's microphone and addressed the entire submarine.

"All officers meet in the Wardroom at once."

Mikhail looked at the men assembled. Captains Borodin, Konev, and Dimitriev looked late for their own funeral. Lieutenant Pudovkin's tan had faded until his skin looked bluish. His eyes remained half shut and he smacked his lips as if constantly parched. Doctor Anatoli, Gorelov, Zhora, Dovzhenko, Boreyev, all these appeared as healthy as the day they'd reported aboard. Throughout the ship he'd seen others drained of color and vigor while others remained spry and full of energy.

"What've you men done?" Konev asked. His voice came out like a breathless sigh.

"Mutiny. We've the makings of a mutiny." Dimitriev said while he pointed to Gorelov.

"Fear'll pull the crew apart, Comrade Captain," Gorelov said. "I'm doing my best."

"He wants to disgrace the families of our fallen and jettison their bodies to become food for the gulls and crabs."

Captain Borodin raised a hand and the room fell silent. He pointed to Zhora and Doctor Anatoli.

"Tell us you've found something," Borodin said.

"Our problem involves three separate events," Zhora replied. He turned to Anatoli.

"A rare form of anemia struck the shipyard and crew," the doctor began. "It still lingers with some of us. No cure has been found yet."

"Bullshit!" Boreyev growled.

Borodin shot a stern glance at the Missile Officer before he beckoned for the doctor to continue.

"We suffered casualties from a rabid stowaway. She infected one crewman. Now that they're dead, that'll end. I recommend we subject the crew to a quick examination to be sure."

"And the monster I saw in place of that woman?" Mikhail asked. "What explains that?"

"Hallucinations brought on by a refrigeration leak," Zhora explained. He waited for his words to sink in before he continued.

"All *monster* sightings have occurred in the lowest levels. Likewise, Chief Antonev saw a seductive hallucination over the rabid woman where you saw a monster. Your *fang* sighting in the Forward Engine Room occurred in Lower Level. The refrigerant, heavier than air, has settled in the lowest levels."

Mikhail stared at Zhora who offered a gradual smile. "Sorry, Misha, I know it's hard to realize, but your eyes have deceived you."

"No, I know what I saw," Mikhail replied.

"Evidence says otherwise," the doctor said.

"You saw her yourself," Mikhail bolted from his chair. "Pull that woman out of the freezer and see how wrong I am!"

Zhora looked to Anatoli before he offered Mikhail a piteous shrug. "Neither of us saw anything more than a bullet-riddled woman."

Anatoli looked at him. "I'm afraid reviewing her corpse won't help. The post mortem test for rabies requires brain tissue. In my hurry to solve this mystery, I didn't preserve the skull or face."

Boreyev stood and pointed a stubby finger at Zhora and the doctor. "You two, you're in on it. You're in league with the demons."

"Both of you sit." Captain Borodin said in a level tone.

"This ship stands on the verge of chaos and our nation on the brink of war. As soon as the nation's danger passes, I'll surface and radio our situation."

"But the crew," Gorelov began.

"Jettison the bodies if it'll help," the captain answered.

"It won't," Anatoli replied, "not scientifically speaking."

Gorelov nodded to the captain then shot a glance at the

doctor. "It'll ease their spirits."

"See to it, Michman," Borodin ordered. "I want Lieutenant Boreyev's brutes to help keep the process orderly."

"Aye, Comrade Captain," Boreyev replied.

"Also, bring the ship to periscope depth long enough to ventilate the ship, twenty minutes should do the trick."

Captain Borodin dismissed his men, crossed his arms and rested his head on the table. Mikhail watched everyone leave. When the door clicked shut behind the last man, Borodin moaned.

"You've been my father," Mikhail said. "You've guided me where my father failed. You've shown truer love for me than the stepfather that took his place. I hate to see you like this."

The captain rolled his head until he met Mikhail's gaze. "That's kind of you to say. But it makes things harder now."

"Why?" he asked.

"I envy those already dead. I wish I were going out that torpedo tube with them."

Mikhail leaned across the Wardroom table. "You can't say that. These are the moments you spoke of months ago. This crew needs your leadership to face what's happening."

Borodin looked up. His lips parted but his words came late. "War on the horizon, I'm prepared for." He shook his head slowly. "But hatred and murder, I've killed those men as surely as if I'd put a bullet in their head."

"No, Captain, no."

"The evil and madness, I invited it when I turned a blind eye to Yanukovich and Shulga's murders. I denied those boys justice. I brought this curse upon *K-389*."

Love's Desperation

FIFTY-NINE

Zhora raced through the ship and ran to Auxiliaries Compartment. From the watertight door he peered in. Petty Officer Kipchak sat at his workbench, a pair of tinsnips in his hand. Muttering and growling, he cut more gaskets from chem-suit material.

"Kipchak, we don't have much time."

The man looked up, surprised. "For what?"

"Do you love me? Do you think you *could* love me?"

Kipchak's eyes darted to the ladder above and below before he answered. "What? Now? You have to ask this now?"

"Yes." Zhora entered the room and glided to Kipchak and took him in his arms. "Soon, what this crew thinks won't matter. Nothing anyone thinks will matter. But before that time comes I need to know if I've found a soul mate or not."

Kipchak flashed a blushing smile. "You're handsome, courageous, and bold, a good start for sure."

"I've saved you for this moment." He grabbed Kipchak's face by the jaw and tilted it back. "I'd hoped you felt like me."

Kipchak relaxed in his arms and let out a shuddering sigh as Zhora drove fangs into his throat. He moaned and whimpered, clutching Zhora tighter. As he drank in Kipchak's blood, the man's memories flooded in and washed the present away.

"Why, Grandfather, why don't they appreciate what we

bring them?"

From the back of an American Studebaker truck Zhora watched Kipchak, a boy of twelve, drive his grandfather through the dusty brown of the summer countryside.

"Pride," the old man said. He scanned the horizon as he spoke, his eyes white with cataracts. "No one wants to owe their life to another, especially when it's their son."

"But I love them. I can't stand to see them hungry."

"I know."

"I didn't start this because of that though."

"I know that too. You're not a farmer like your father. You're a tinkerer like your grandpa."

"I'm not like the other boys in school, Grandfather."

"I know."

"It's not just tinkering that makes me different."

"I know that too. You'll never find a wife to suit you. You lack the fire in your blood for women."

"I love."

"Don't."

"Don't love?"

"Don't share your love with anyone. Express your love for everyone instead."

"What does that mean? It doesn't make sense."

"I know what you mean and you know it's forbidden. Redirect your love elsewhere. Have compassion on the world. Focus your heart on that. That way you'll survive hatred and earn the trust and respect of others."

"But that's no kind of life."

"It is a Soviet life. Bury your tragedy in your service to others. Who knows, maybe one day you'll find happiness like your father did."

Zhora sobbed. It wasn't supposed to be this. He was supposed to find hate or hurt and offer justice. This old man spoiled the moment. But still, Kipchak would be a good companion, a lovely, handsome companion.

"I've ached for this moment all my life," Zhora whispered.

"But the others," Kipchak said, his voice weak and breathless. "They'll . . ."

"They'll do nothing."

"What?" Shock colored his reply, revulsion made him flinch.

Gently, Zhora set Kipchak down on the deck. He rolled up his sleeve and pierced his arm with a razor sharp fingernail. Blood, thick, black, with strings of puss, oozed from the wound and hung like sap from his pale flesh. Kipchak's eyes widened and his mouth opened as if to scream.

"Drink and become my eternal love."

"No," he whispered. "God, no."

Zhora cupped the man's skull and brought it up while he lowered his bleeding arm.

"Don't deny me this. Don't throw away a love you know exists."

Kipchak tried to turn away. Zhora forced his mouth upon the wound.

"Drink, drink or die."

He felt a tug in his vein, a creeping pain. Kipchak drank but too weak, too little.

"Drink, damn you!"

One last draw pulled a line of fire through Zhora's arm before the boy sagged in his embrace.

In for a Penny, in for a Pound

The lead cook supervised the exhumation from the freezer. He swore anyone contaminating the food would have it deducted from his rations tenfold. He hadn't counted on deducting rations from dead men.

"*Yóbanny v rot!*" he shouted.

Two body bags filled with potatoes lay on the deck amidst a stunned huddle.

"Who the . . ." Vetrov whispered.

"Maybe they've been gotten rid of already," one observer offered.

"Don't be stupid," Ayatollah grumbled. "You can't fire a torpedo tube without everyone knowing."

"Why steal a pair of corpses?" Captain Konev asked.

"Wait," Ayatollah said. "Which ones are missing?"

"Adaksin and the woman."

Ayatollah's mouth drooped open. "The same ones Lieutenant Koryavin said had fangs."

"Ridiculous," Konev sneered.

Gorelov said nothing before he trotted up the nearby stairs to the Command Center and grabbed the microphone.

"All hands to quarters, set security condition one. Isolate all compartments, arm all security teams."

Konev ran in behind him. "What are you doing?"

"Something's wrong," Gorelov answered. "Gotta find those corpses before things really go to shit."

From under the port main engine, Mikhail heard nothing. Steam-powered, loud, and fire-hot, his inspection demanded he climb where no designer expected a man to go. From the steam manifold above to the condensers below, Mikhail had already inspected the starboard engine and had the burns and stains on his coveralls to prove it. Careful to avoid the same flesh-searing handholds, he crawled out. Michman Ovechin greeted him, a concerned expression on his face.

"They've called for security condition one. All compartments are to seal themselves."

Mikhail wiped the sweat from his brow with his sleeve and regretted it. Grease slid and mixed with his perspiration and hung above his brow. "Good thing we've already done that." And then it hit him, *Kipchak and the rest of his former division.*

"Take our men and advance on Auxiliaries Compartment. I want to ensure my men there are alright."

"Yes Comrade Engineer." Ovechin scrambled up the nearby ladder.

The title struck Mikhail as odd. He'd been a fresh junior lieutenant half a year ago. A senior lieutenant now, without the new epaulets sewed on yet, responsible for one third of the ship now. None of that mattered in the gory mayhem or threatening nuclear thunderheads. He raced up the ladder and picked his way through the steamy spaces to Engine Control.

An armored box, like Launch Control, it housed a series of panels to answer the ship's bells, regulate the two reactors, and trim the electrical power plant. Cool air blew in from ventilation ducts and made it the most comfortable, coveted place within the engineering compartments.

Mikhail sat in a corner chair with a commanding view of each station. Beside him, he picked up the sound-powered phone set and listened. His men looked over their shoulders, each anxious to hear the news.

"The murderers are at large," Mikhail relayed. "Michman Gorelov will take a team compartment by compartment to search."

What Mikhail heard next took his breath away. He tore the headset off and dropped it to the deck. He slid from his seat and shuffled out the armored door. The humid heat smothered him now, like a bath towel shoved down his throat. Tears blurred his vision. The reactor tunnel door seemed a kilometer away. He wiped his eyes only to have stinging, stinking grease smudge his view. Mikhail fumbled to clear his vision. He ran through the watertight door. He pressed on through three more. He met Ovechin beside the workbench and saw Kipchak. The young man's face looked burned-black with dried blood. Mikhail fell on him and pulled him close while he choked back a sob. Close to him now, he smelled the sour stench of spoiled meat.

"Get me a damp cloth," Mikhail ordered.

"I think we should-

"A damp cloth, now!"

Ovechin stepped back.

Through his despondent fog, Mikhail realized someone else drew near.

"Mikhail, let go of Petty Officer Kipchak," Doctor Anatoli said softly. He knelt beside Mikhail and took hold of the young petty officer. "Let me examine him."

"He shouldn't have died," Mikhail whispered. "Not him."

"We all die someday, Mikhail. I know it's tragic but don't stop me from doing my duty."

Anatoli tugged at Kipchak's body.

"Help me get him to Sick Bay."

"Certainly, sorry."

With Ovechin's help, they got him into Sick Bay.

Gorelov lead a team of three others into the lower level of

Missile Compartment Aft. The bilge they'd found Antonev in was right beneath their feet. The four men, armed with flashlights and pistols, inched their way through the compartment. The men kept steady aim but fear quivered the corners of their eyes as their gazes darted from shadow to shadow. Lieutenant Ivankov had called him down here. The Lieutenant had assembled his own team and started his search in the Missile Compartments. Zhora Ivankov emerged from between the missile tubes ten meters ahead.

"What'd you find?" Gorelov asked.

"I've found the corpses and I think I know who's behind all this."

"Good. Where's your team?"

Ivankov offered a deep throaty laugh. "Behind you."

Gorelov spun around in time to see each of his men snatched off their feet and pulled up to the ceiling. There, two familiar faces wore horrid masks, Adaksin and Dovzhenko. The crew's nightmare woman hung from a perch beside them. Each bore sharp white fangs before they sank them into each sailor's throat. The wet crunch chilled Gorelov. He aimed his pistol, only to have Ivankov sweep in behind him and crush his wrist. The gun clattered into the bilge below.

"I'm sorry, Michman Gorelov," Zhora began, "I respect you too much to relish what must happen."

He spun Gorelov around until they stood face to face. The broken bones throbbed with shock-muted pain. The creatures behind him drank in his crewmates noisily. Gorelov offered a snarling smile.

"When you lured me down here, I figured it weren't for caviar and vodka."

"I can't use my usual tricks," Zhora explained with a pouting frown. "You're too strong."

"I'm nearly fifty," Gorelov said with a chuckle. "I'm hardly strong."

"It's your will, your resolve. Others set their spiritual houses on sand and the slightest nudge topples them. Yours sits upon some hidden rock. I cannot pry your mind open with fear or entice you with fantastic promises. You've a very concrete concept of the world around you."

Gorelov nodded. "And it only took twenty years and a dozen beatings in the navy for me to figure that out."

Zhora Ivankov chuckled. "I only had to suffer one."

"About that, I'm sorry. I feel partly to blame."

"What is it the British say? In for a penny, in for a pound." Zhora shrugged. "But truthfully, I bear you no ill will. I respect you, as I've said. You speak from your gut. From your own words I understand that you don't condone murder but you encourage motivational training to get everyone on the same sheet of music."

Blood splattered to the deck behind him. One creature grunted like a pig rooting around in the slop. He heard a boot drop, and then another.

Gorelov's jaw tightened and he came to attention.

"I know my duty. You should've known yours. You shouldn't to have ever sunk so low."

"Your comrades killed me! I only came back because a vampire took pity on me. He gave me a chance to set things right, to offer justice to those who cannot defend themselves."

Corpses fell to the deck, one, two, three, behind him. Zhora pointed to his horrific crew.

"The lonely whore, the abused underling, and the brilliant stutterer, these I've rescued from your kind. We will begin a new revolution to abolish the judgments of generations of brutes like you."

And when the madman's pointing finger fell, the feast began anew. Each creature fell upon Gorelov and drove their white knife-teeth deep.

Doctor Anatoli's Secret

SIXTY-ONE

Mikhail watched Anatoli examine Kipchak's body. With rubber gloved hands and shining clean instruments he prodded at the only wound on the young Petty Officer.

"Fascinating," Anatoli whispered.

"What?" Mikhail gasped.

"The wound's begun to heal."

"Kipchak's dead, his killer's loose. What's wrong with you?"

The doctor pulled away from the table. "Sorry, I wished I'd seen this before." He squeezed by Mikhail and out the Sick Bay door. "I'll give you a moment alone with him before I continue my examination."

"No, that's not what I want."

The doctor shut the door . . .

. . . and locked it.

Mikhail flipped the lock off and pulled it open a centimeter before it stopped. Anatoli's metal probe blocked the door. The thin ribbon of steel bounced and flexed when he pulled, but failed to yield.

The doctor's voice seeped through the narrow opening, like poisonous smoke.

"Kipchak will be hungry when he wakes."

"What? He's dead." He screamed. A primal fear, carried within human DNA through the centuries, warned otherwise. *Run.*

Anatoli leaned against the door and Mikhail heard him

flick open his lighter. A snake of cigarette smoke slithered in.

"You asked before, what my last name was and why no one knew it." His introspective tone intensified Mikhail's panic.

Mikhail froze a moment. "What are you talking about?"

"It's a secret I expected to take to my grave. Not even that will matter now."

A noise to Mikhail's right startled him. Kipchak's arm had fallen from the examination table.

"Do you remember reading about the defense of Leningrad during the war?"

"Yes, why?" He pulled and pushed on the door. "Why'd you lock me in here? What's this all about?"

"I lived there as a boy. I was eight when the Germans cut off the last road into the city. Bombs and gunfire, screams, fire, and death. My father was on the front. I lived with my uncle, a doctor. Uncle kept me from digging graves and trenches by insisting to the army he needed my help to heal the injured."

Kipchak's body let out a rattling, gurgling sigh.

"As the siege went on, things grew desperate. The schools don't go into that kind of detail. People starved, and when they starved they ate everything, horses, pets, vermin, bugs, and eventually each other."

Mikhail searched the closet-sized room. He pulled out drawers, emptied shelves, and turned to items crammed between ducts and piping along the outer bulkhead.

"Uncle and I never starved. The army made sure we had bread when there was bread. We had meat more often that many. So many wounded, so many amputations . . ." The doctor's voice trailed off. "A special squad began to crack down on flesh-eaters. Ghouls they called us."

The unzipped body bag crumpled open, wider and wider. The body inside writhed to life.

"Let me out," Mikhail shouted.

"The boy will be very hungry at first," Anatoli said. "He won't even recognize you until after his first feed. Zhora was very clear about that. I'm to know what that's like someday in exchange for helping to cover up the real reason for the deaths aboard."

Kipchak sat up, his eyes still shut, and pivoted until his feet fell from the table's edge. Except for the smears of blood and cadaver's complexion, he looked like a man struggling to awake for the day's labors.

"Uncle and I were found out, but our contribution to the war effort protected us . . . for a while."

Mikhail's scrambling search uncovered a collapsible gurney, army green canvas with hinged wooden supports. *Wood.* He tugged and cursed until he pulled it out and stopped to look at his crewmate, his undead crewmate. Kipchak's eyes opened and he turned his head slowly to meet Mikhail's gaze. Bloodshot eyes reflected no recognition.

Anatoli's casual confession continued.

"But when our usefulness ended and charges were leveled, we ran. We ran and ran, serving communities and criminals. Many of those criminals were corrupt officials. Eventually, our services earned me my medical credentials, forged to relieve a young lieutenant from transfer to Vladivostok."

Kipchak hissed. Slumped posture straightened and his sluggish movements grew fluid. In the moment Mikhail admired his crewmate's grace, the monster lunged.

"I almost wish I saw what you're seeing," Anatoli said. "I'd like to see this miracle firsthand, to see the future Zhora promised me."

Mikhail brought his wood and canvas shield between them. Fingers, cold and strong, clawed at his exposed hands. With a shift and a shove, Mikhail allowed the creature ground but also shunted him toward the door. The creature bashed him against the outer bulkhead. He felt Kipchak's cold body press against him through the canvas with unreal strength. Between each pulsing push, Mikhail retreated away from the Sick Bay door until nothing stood between his vampire comrade and the room's exit.

"I can't let you out, Mikhail, I'm sorry," the doctor said.

"Of all my companions, you've been my favorite."

Kipchak's attention shifted from Mikhail's fight to the unchallenged door. He pounded and scraped, growled and moaned. With the gurney still between them, Mikhail lowered his shoulder, planted his feet, and charged.

The doctor's thin metal probe jamming the door shut snapped. Anatoli let out a startled yelp, then a scream, then nothing. Mikhail peered around the door. Kipchak hunkered over Anatoli and had only allowed a few squirts of blood to escape. He alternated between wet gnawing and slurping, grunting and moaning as he fed.

Mikhail opened the door wider, until it bumped against the doctor's twitching foot. Mikhail froze, unsure whether to retreat or run. His lungs clung to his next breath. Mikhail pushed and pushed until the shifting knee caught Kipchak's attention. Kipchak jerked his head to observe the limb. Mikhail held still.

I'll have to shut the door if he sees me.

Kipchak's hunger won out and he went back to his feast. Mikhail allowed himself a shuddering breath. In millimeters he pushed the door wider, shoving the doctor's leg further and further. Like a dog guarding his bowl, Kipchak tightened his grip on the corpse and pulled it away from the door in sharp tugs. Mikhail looked back into Sick Bay at the gurney that saved his life. Its wooden sides and Ayatollah's boathook whittled into a spear, he made the connection.

It's a stake, call it what it is . . . and get one yourself.

He couldn't imagine salvaging the gurney over the feeding creature's head. He barely found courage enough to squeeze out of Sick Bay. He longed now for its safety, that closet with a door. He eyed the lock as the door slipped from his fingers and shut under the pressure of Anatoli's stubborn foot.

Then it hit him. In all the electric fear he'd missed Anatoli's most startling admission.

Zhora, Zhora's behind this. Zhora's a . . .

Vampire.

Evil with a Capital 'E'

SIXTY-TWO

From his sonar panel, Ayatollah surveyed the Command Center, paying attention to the features of each crewmate. Teeth, eyes, pallor - Ayatollah found no evidence of a monster among them. But if Lieutenant Koryavin's accusations were true, his division officer was chief among those creatures. Koryavin had called from the bowels of Auxiliaries Compartment, beside the trim pump. He'd recounted Kipchak's death and Doctor Anatoli's betrayal.

The story left Ayatollah disoriented, as though his faith were a spindly rope bridge swaying in the breeze. Though he'd holed up in the torpedo room to steal sleep, and armed himself against an impossible foe, this confirmation of ancient fears still shocked him.

Grandmother had taught him the old ways, the old wisdoms. She'd known the tribulations of her Jewish heritage from the Tsar through the Revolution and the Great Patriotic War. Allowed to retain their faith in private, she educated all her grandchildren despite protests from their parents. She told of a world full of miracles to save the faithful and curses to humble the proud. She spoke of demons and angels that walked the Earth.

These stories from childhood kept him wary and alert. He'd guarded his faith and his person as a precious treasure constantly under siege. But to face evil with a capital 'E' felt surreal, felt like a fairytale.

In the hours since the freezer mutiny, three separate

murders occurred. Each claimed their victims had shown signs of the maddening disease. The doctor's examinations had proven otherwise.

"Command Center, this is Lieutenant Ivankov. I'm in Missile Compartment Forward, Level Three."

The voice from the speaker hardly sounded like a demon, yet he found himself clutching his chest, where his Star of David pendant hung beneath his uniform.

From the Periscope Station, Lieutenant Pudovkin grabbed his microphone. " Report, Ivankov."

"Michman Gorelov never made it," Zhora replied. "Our murderer remains in one of the forward compartments."

Pudovkin looked to the Tactical Station where Captain Borodin stood flanked by Captain Konev and Zampolit Dimitriev.

Borodin looked to his comrades. Dimitriev offered a blank stare and a shrug. Konev pursed his lips before he spoke.

"Lieutenant Koryavin has secured the engineering compartments. Lieutenant Boreyev retains control of Missile Compartment Forward. We need Koryavin's men to push forward to secure the rest of the ship."

Captain Borodin unbuttoned his shirt and withdrew a long golden chain. A pair of keys and a tiny cross hung from it. He handed it to Captain Konev.

Ayatollah stared at the iconic crucifix. It seemed to catch the lifeless florescent light and magnify it, animate it.

"Take these, my missile key and secure locker key," Borodin said. "You and Captain Dimitriev will go aft, take charge of Lieutenant Koryavin's men, and reclaim the ship from aft forward."

Konev looked at the chain and back to his captain. He grasped the cross and started to unhook it from the chain. Borodin stopped him with a gesture.

"I want God to go with you," Borodin said. "I'm too old for the fight ahead. I'll command the ship from here."

"Religious? You?" Dimitriev gasped. He drew in a deep breath.

Dimitriev's eyes gleamed and his grim features failed to hide his glee. "It explains your weak leadership, this vessel's quick dive into chaos."

He clapped a hand on Konev's shoulder. "With you in command and me at your side, we'll whip this ship and crew into proper shape."

"Shut up, Zampolit," Konev said. He scowled at the man's hand, as though a seagull had just shit on his uniform. Dimitriev withdrew his hand and offered an apologetic nod.

Konev turned and shook his captain's hand. He marched to the doorway heading aft and looked back.

"Come along Zampolit." Konev said.

Dimitriev pulled his Makarov pistol from its holster and examined the weapon. He swallowed hard, holstered it, and nodded. "Let's go then, if we must."

Borodin looked to Ayatollah. Eyes weary and alight with a flicker of resolve told Ayatollah what he didn't want to hear.

We in this room are dead men. We will buy time for Konev's victory, but our end is already in sight.

Ayatollah offered a reassuring smile but it faltered under the weight of his captain's gaze. Borodin walked over to him and patted him on the shoulder.

"One last patrol for me," Borodin said. "I knew that before we left but I hadn't expected so final an end to my career."

Pudovkin joined them. "Captain," he began, "we've not heard of an end to the American exercise. In fact we've heard nothing at all."

Borodin frowned. A single eyebrow arched. He and Ayatollah looked to the Ballast Panel. The depth gauge read twenty meters.

"We are still at periscope depth," Borodin observed.

Others in the Command Center followed the captain's eye to the Periscope Station. Behind Pudovkin the display for raised masts and antennas showed two blue lights, the periscope and . . .

"We still have our radio antenna raised."

"Have you spoken with Lieutenant Dovzhenko?" Borodin asked Lieutenant Pudovkin.

"I tried but there's no response. He mentioned yesterday they had problems with their intercom."

Only the ship's sounds occupied the following silence. One by one, crewmen looked forward, to the Operations Compartment Forward watertight and beyond to the Radio Room.

Borodin took a step forward and stopped. He drew his pistol and looked to Pudovkin. "Let me go look."

Ayatollah watched Borodin as he took slow deliberate steps toward the door. A sound shocked him, it was his own voice.

"Captain, wait," Ayatollah said. "Let me come with you."

He pulled a makeshift weapon from his shirt, a wooden paintbrush sharpened into a stake. He held it up for Vetrov to see. The boy's mouth gaped open while he dug out his own. Borodin walked to the watertight door and grasped the handle before he looked back. With a weak smile he motioned for Ayatollah to join him.

Through the watertight door, behind his captain, Ayatollah crept. The radios' hum gave him hope until he sniffed the warm ozone-laden air. Carrion, ripe and strong, clung to his nostrils.

"They're dead," Borodin said as he surveyed the room. "Dovzhenko's gone and his two operators are dead."

The radio operators still sat in their seats, one white as a sheet except for his bloodied throat. In the other chair the corpse's face remained obscured, smeared with black blood. The stench hung in Ayatollah's lungs. In the far corner, Captain Borodin crouched over teletype papers poured out onto the deck.

"The corpses," Ayatollah said. "We've got to jettison them."

"Captain?" Ayatollah whispered. He gripped his stake tighter.

Borodin turned to meet his curious gaze. Less weary

than before, the captain grinned and pointed to the deck.

"It's here," he said, "the message came after these two died. The threat of war has ended. Our orders to stand down and return to port should come within the next twenty-four hours."

Ayatollah relaxed and allowed a sigh. Behind him, the other operator's chair creaked. Vetrov's low frightened whimper turned his attention. The black, bloodstained body writhed and slid until it fell to the deck. Like a snake with its first experience with arms and legs, the corpse twitched and flinched in uncoordinated spasms until it managed to sit upright. Its eyes opened and shut but its mouth only opened wider and wider as it moaned.

Three men stared at it, struck dumb and paralyzed by its unnaturalness. And then it clambered to its feet and flung itself at Vetrov.

The boy screamed. Ayatollah lunged. He met the creature mere centimeters from its prey and pinned its head with his forearm against the port radio cabinets. In his sudden move he'd lost his wooden weapon. Ayatollah's pendant felt warm against his chest. The demon hissed.

"Kill it," Ayatollah said, breathlessly. He inhaled and shouted, "KILL IT!"

Vetrov fumbled for his own stake. The monster's strength grew with each desperate moment. With each increase, Ayatollah fought to reclaim his grip on the creature. He shut his eyes and muttered one of his grandmother's prayers. When he opened them a pistol loomed into view and exploded. Captain Borodin fired every round from his pistol into the monster's face until it fell limp in Ayatollah's grasp.

"The madness has spread," Captain Borodin said, wheezing. "We must contain it."

"No, that's not the end," Vetrov insisted.

The boy plucked up his stake and drove it into their foe's heart. It screamed. Tar-like blood oozed from the wound while the flesh crumpled and curled in on itself.

"Good work, lad," Ayatollah gasped.

Captain Borodin examined the now desiccated vampire, using his gun barrel to open and inspect the mouth. Needle teeth caught the room's light and gleamed. A malformed mouth and mottled skin revealed a thing between man and monster.

"We need to alert the crew," Ayatollah said.

"What *is* this?" Borodin asked, his eyes still fixed on the creature. "It seems more than a disease, evil, insidious."

Ayatollah grabbed his captain. "I need to tell you about Kipchak, Ivankov, and the doctor."

Anarchy

Locked in Launch Control with a dozen frightened men, Captain Konev's stomach chilled.

Hardly a bold move to reclaim the ship.

Just as he'd won the Missile Officer's confidence, Grandpa Borodin made everything worse with his story of vampires, wooden stakes, and crewmen not truly dead.

"Lieutenants Ivankov and Dovzhenko are not what they appear," he'd said. "They walk among us as crewmates but feed on our blood while we sleep."

Borodin elaborated his dark fairytale and shoehorned every odd occurrence into his story. Had he been a movie producer for the State, he'd be among the best. As a ship's captain, he'd crumbled under the pressure and threw every shred of credibility into the trash heap.

Inside the small fortress, a dozen men now stared at each other, waiting, wondering how they'll ever return to their status as a crew again. Konev smelled cabbage and caviar, stolen from the stores below. Body odor, urine and shit hovered beneath the pleasant aromas.

"Now," Lieutenant Boreyev began, "now you know why we stay holed up in here."

Dimitriev nodded. Konev gave the zampolit a narrow sideways glance.

"Ramblings of an old man," Konev countered.

"You don't understand," Boreyev said.

He stepped within centimeters. The stocky lieutenant

grabbed him by his tunic and pulled him closer. Konev looked down at the man, unshaven and filthy, he hardly looked like the officer he'd been months ago.

"I killed Ivankov once already."

Konev frowned. "Impossible. And why tell me only now?"

"For the same reason you question our captain, I'd have been mistaken for a madman." Boreyev looked to his men. "I didn't witness this alone. Some of this lot were with me when we raided the apartments on Black Wharf."

The men surrounding them nodded, their features solemn, their eyes dark.

"So you sit here and wait," Konev spat back, "for what? You're *plan* has no end game. No matter what you think is out there will only grow in strength while you wither away. Join me. Help me. If not, shoot yourself now and save yourself a long boring wait for a painful end."

Darkness. Light vanished from the world. In a capsule of titanium and steel, a hundred meters beneath the sea, nothing remained when the electricity failed. Ventilation fans purred to a standstill and every odor hung like a dirty sock across Konev's nose, humid and thick.

A chuckle reverberated through the steel walls of Launch Control.

"I'd rather save you all for later. We'll need you men later if we're to keep our strength."

Zhora's voice sounded smooth, syrupy, almost drunk.

"Lieutenant Ivankov," Konev shouted. "Stop this at once."

"Stop what? Is it the taunting that bothers you?"

A screeching of steel peeled through the room. Thumps, bumps, and scratches came from every corner.

"Stop it!" Dimitriev shrieked. "Maybe I can salvage your career if you just stop. We've been through a lot. I understand how pressures drive a man to horrible things."

"Do you? Do you really understand?"

"Of course I do," Dimitriev whimpered. "Stop this, please. We can straighten this out, I assure you."

"Don't lie to me, Zampolit. You forget, I've seen you from

the inside out. I tortured you with nightmares and you tortured me with memories of you prior evils."

Something heavy and metal struck the door. Afterward it scraped and shifted for a moment.

"You're not getting in here," Boreyev growled. "And if you do, we're a dozen armed men."

From the outside, a crackling sound sputtered and spat at the door. White sparks flickered and flashed from the door's seam. A snake of smoke curled between door and frame. Konev smelled melting metal and ozone. Where the two met, door and frame, the metal glowed like an ember.

They were being welded in.

Zhora's laughter held Konev's breath.

"I'm not interested in getting in, moron," Zhora said. "You're being saved, rationed, for when this ship fully belongs to us. We'll need a regular blood supply between raids."

"No," Dimitriev cried.

The zampolit stumbled to the door and pounded on it, screaming 'No' with every blow.

"Somebody shut him up," Boreyev growled.

"No," Dimitriev begged, "wait, don't."

Blam.

In the gun-flash Konev beheld Dimitriev's panicked pitiful face.

Dimitriev fell to the deck, sobbing. "Why? It's not supposed to be like this." He moaned. "Somebody get the doctor, I'm hurt pretty bad."

Blam.

The gunfire resounded in the cramped room. Somewhere in the dark, one of Boreyev's men snickered. "I've wanted to do that for months."

Nervous laughter rippled through the dank room.

Konev held his breath. Slowly he drew his pistol and backed along the bulkhead. He thought about the butchers outside Launch Control and the anarchy within. He pressed the Makarov's barrel against the roof of his mouth.

Blam.

Zhora is the Key

SIXTY-FOUR

Mikhail slipped through the watertight door into the Reactor Compartment. *Where are the guards? Why haven't they-*

Hands grabbed him and threw him to the deck. After hitting hard, a thick piece of steel pinned him down. He heard the door slam shut.

"It's Koryavin," one voice cried out.

"Don't matter," another growled, "we're all that's left of the crew."

"Poslenski?" Mikhail ventured. "Petty Officer Poslenski?"

"That's how they get you," Poslenski said. "They trick you into thinking they're sane, then they eat you."

"Ew, he's got that stinkin' black blood all over him," said the other sailor.

"That's it, then. Nothing for him but one clean shot through the skull."

"Listen," Mikhail shouted. "Just wait a damned minute. This blood came from Kipchak. I found him dead, his face covered with it."

"It's contagious," Poslenski said. "You'll turn rabid soon enough. Don't try whining out of it."

"I've not been bitten, you idiot," Mikhail explained, "and it's not rabies. Lieutenant Ivankov and Doctor Anatoli have been covering up the true culprit, themselves."

"The doctor? That old bag?"

"He's dead now, killed by Kipchak."

"But you said he was dead. Who killed him?"

"Ivankov."

"But he's not got rabies."

"NO ONE HAS RABIES."

"What's killing everyone then?"

"Vampires. Lieutenant Ivankov, and Petty Officers Adaksin and Kipchak are vampires. So's the mysterious woman everyone's seen in their dreams."

"Oh, yeah, the woman," the quiet sailor said, his voice trailing off. He snickered.

The opposite door to the reactor tunnel opened. Through it stepped a man in a gas mask and radiation suit. He carried a box of crackers and pan of water.

"You three, stay here. Don't kill the Lieutenant, just yet."

"What?" Poslenski cried. "What are you doing? You can't quarantine us."

"Ovechin chose the most expendable men to guard this post," the man behind the mask admitted. "He chose the dumbest, laziest bastards in the Engine Room. Sit tight and you might live to see another sunrise."

Poslenski ran for the door. Mikhail rolled over and sprang to his feet. The thick door slammed in the brutish mechanic's face. He swung his weapon, a giant pipe-wrench. It rang as it careened off a door thick enough to withstand a kilometer of sea pressure.

On his feet and facing his captors, Mikhail remembered Poslenski and the man known only as Laska. Machinists, malcontents, Michman Ovechin had already warned him of their best traits.

Laska wielded a cheater bar nearly a meter long and six centimeters thick. He held it high, like an American baseball player. Anger flared in his dim features.

"You're going to get us killed," Laska hissed.

Mikhail looked to Poslenski. He checked the grip on his weapon and glared.

"If I have," Mikhail explained, "it's already happened. Killing me won't solve anything."

"Course it will," Poslenski said as he closed. "We get a bigger ration of those crackers and smell one less pile of shit while we wait."

Mikhail backed up until his probing hands found the bulkhead behind him. After a quick scan of the room, he crept aft, along the bulkhead. The simpletons closed slowly. Each stole sideways glances, waiting for the other to strike. Mikhail lunged for the light switch and dropped the small room into darkness.

In each compartment flashlights hung from prominent racks for emergencies. Mikhail hoped these men forgot such details amidst their anger. He stole one and rolled away. Two heavy impacts against the bulkhead he'd been leaning against gave him hope.

He crawled along the deck, careful to listen for their breathing, stumbles, and muttered curses.

"Wait," Poslenski whispered. "Let me get a flashlight."

Shit. Mikhail brought himself to a crouch.

"Laska, step back a bit. When I turn this on, he'll probably aim for the light and hit me with whatever he's found. Keep ready to hit him when I turn on this light."

Shit, shit, shit. He rose and crept to where he expected to find Laska. When the light flickered on, he found himself staring at the scrawny, frightened man. He lunged, lightning quick, and punched him square in the nose. The man's weapon clattered to the deck from a hand gone limp. Mikhail clambered for the steel cheater-bar just in time for an explosion of pain to release his grip just as quick. The room rolled and pitched until the deck jumped up and smacked him in the face.

"Sorry, Comrade, Lieutenant."

The voice sounded like it came to Mikhail in long hollow tube. The Mayday Parade marched to a silent tune within his skull. Tramping, stamping, pounding boots stepped on every nerve inside. No, not an army, just a swollen skull.

"Where are we?"

Michman Ovechin came into focus, hovering above him with a cup of tea held out, a peace offering. "We're just outside Engineering Control. You've been out for about five minutes."

"I need to speak with the Command Center. We need to regain our ship."

Ovechin helped Mikhail to his feet and into a chair. Every discomfort felt magnified, strong tea, a hard chair, lights bright enough to stab his retinas.

Mikhail took the phone offered and tipped back the last drop of tea, swallowed hard, and whispered into the receiver.

"Captain?"

"I'm so glad to know you hadn't been taken," Borodin said. "Did you see Captains Konev and Dimitriev?"

"No, Comrade Captain."

Mikhail felt the despair around him. The submarine's hull and the ocean beyond smothered in on them while monsters lurked within.

Find a bright light, a breath of fresh air, something.

He looked to those gathered around before he spoke again to his captain. "We still control the ship. We can drive home."

"Yes, then we . . . tell the Admiralty we've a deadly outbreak contained in those compartments."

"They have the Oxygen Generator and all the atmosphere conditioning equipment," Mikhail said. "We must retake Auxiliaries Compartment."

"How many vampires are we facing," Borodin wondered aloud.

"Ivankov, Dovzhenko, Adaksin, the woman, and Kipchak."

"But Konev and Dimitriev," the captain added, "and all of Boreyev's men, will they be made vampires too? We've not heard from Gorelov or his security team either. That would raise their numbers to twenty-eight. Ayatollah,

Vetrov and I barely handled one."

"Think of those I mentioned and compare them to those you mentioned. Notice any distinct difference?"

Captain Borodin shook his head. "I don't know the woman and the others seem to have no common bond."

"I knew the woman once. The key is Zhora Ivankov. Everyone I've mention has something in common with him. Dovzhenko's fellow officers regarded him an idiot for his stammer. They jeered at him, snubbed him. Adaksin's haughty behavior to his superiors and his disdain for his fellow enlisted men put him outside everyone. Vladlena and Zhora are reviled for their sexual activities."

"And Kipchak, how does he fit your theory?"

"Like Zhora, he's a *pidor.*"

The men gathered gasped and muttered in shock.

"He's kept it a secret so well," Mikhail explained. "No one knew until recently."

"But everyone else clearly has a darker side to their lives," Borodin countered. "Kipchak seemed like such a good boy."

"I know. That's the one thing that puzzles me most. That and why I've never been touched by the vampires."

"You don't see it, your own theory in play?" Borodin snorted.

Mikhail shook his head and shrugged. "No."

"Ivankov accepted a curse to continue, something he wouldn't wish upon the friend he cherished most. Everyone else he can use, but you he loves too much to manipulate."

Mikhail felt himself sink into the chair. Memories of Zhora, of a friendship misunderstood, pulled him deeper like an anchor tied to a drowning swimmer. He shuddered free.

"We know what we're facing and we know how to kill them," he said. "Perhaps we can surface the ship and, in the sunlight, join forces to purge the missile compartments." He took a deep breath, "We have one final chance to reclaim our ship."

Claustrophobia

Lieutenant Pudovkin shuffled around the periscope and scanned the horizon. Shallow deep blue waves kissed a pale blue sky. Cotton ball clouds hung overhead and loped along with a calm summer breeze. He pitched the lens up and glimpsed the sun, careful not to let it blind him.

A perfect Pacific day a mere twenty meters above.

"All clear, Captain," he reported.

"Very well, surface the ship."

In the next thirty minutes the ship broke the surface and crewmen scurried about the bridge hatch. Eventually, the upper hatch opened and fresh air rushed in. Salty seawater brought with it the aroma of sunshine only a submariner, or perhaps a miner, knows. The damp air teemed with a lively energy. Memories arose in those who caught its scent.

"Get that ladder out and over the side, men," Borodin said. "We've got until sunset to make our move. Anyone still out then will be given to the waves."

A twisted grin rippled across Pudovkin's face. For once, the captain's threat seemed more a reprieve.

Again to the periscope Pudovkin set his eye. Trained aft, he watched Mikhail and some of his men emerge from the Engine Room hatch. So close to the water line, the waves lapped the hatches edges and poured in on those below. One rogue wave and their plan might send them all to the ocean floor.

"I'm ready to relieve you, Comrade Lieutenant."

Pudovkin stepped back from the scope and looked to Captain Borodin.

"Aye, Comrade Captain. The ship is on the surface, speed six KPH, course . . ."

A knot stuck in his throat when he tried to speak. Borodin shook his head and placed a hand on the periscope.

"Go," he said. "Go and save our ship."

Pudovkin nodded and joined Ayatollah in line to ascend. The squat sonar expert handed him a belt with a holstered pistol and a stake carved from a mop handle. After he took and donned the belt, he watched Vetrov and Ayatollah exchange goodbyes.

Along the upward climb Pudovkin's nose caught the less pleasant odors of things gone bad in the narrow ladder-well since they left home. Mildew mixed with the microscopic dead, trickled in during the ship's final moments on the surface a month ago. Up in the bridge, each man took his turn clambering over the edge and scrambling for the ladder. The ship rolled in slow lazy arcs.

Pudovkin descended. Each roll to starboard swept him away from the hull while port rolls slammed him back to it. He grimaced at the chips made in the ship's paint, then laughed. *If that's all we've got to worry about in the future, we'll be lucky.*

Once on deck, he joined the others and marched aft. The rasp and lap of the waves against the ship caught his attention. The sun in the sea laid out to the horizon a blanket of blue velvet showered with diamonds. The water, the peaceful noises of a world unblemished by mankind, beckoned. Pudovkin had seen beaches, surfers, and bikinis, on the television in the American capitol as a child during his father's duties in the embassy. There, his love of the sea began. The submarine had been the navy's perversion of his passion. To see the sunlight now hurt. To climb back into that glorified sewer pipe rippled a chill across his now warm skin. He and the captain's cook stopped twenty meters short, and watched Ayatollah meet the men from the Engine Room.

At the mid-ship's hatch they met Mikhail Koryavin, and two filthy grease monkeys. The mechanics had already opened the outer mid-ship's hatch and now dove into the short airlock between it and the inner hatch. Mikhail looked up from his men and stared at Pudovkin.

That's when courage and cowardice got in step with each other. That's when he turned and ran. Mikhail shouted at him, others shouted too. It could've been an army of angels screaming and he still wouldn't allow himself to comprehend their pleas.

He ran past the sail, until he stood over the torpedo room hatch. He worked to open it and found his fellow conspirators waiting.

"What are you doing?" Mikhail demanded breathlessly.

Pudovkin turned to answer, his pistol drawn. "Don't stop us."

Men climbed up from the torpedo room, men with equipment and provisions.

"We're leaving," he answered. "Come with us or stay, but don't stop us."

The inflatable life raft hissed and un-crumpled beside him. As it took shape, Pudovkin felt its blossoming presence comfort him in his betrayal.

"You would desert your post?" Mikhail wondered. "Abandon your crew?"

Pudovkin winced. "I am surviving. Above all else, I'm a human being."

He watched Mikhail draw his pistol. His aim wavered as Pudovkin stared into the Makarov's barrel. Eyes deep blue, like the sea around them, stared back at Pudovkin as Mikhail lowered his aim.

"Don't," Pudovkin pleaded. "Don't sink our boat. Don't force us adrift in our life jackets. We'll not return to a haunted, doomed ship. I'd rather let death take me in the daylight than face the horrors below."

"Fucking coward!" Poslenski screamed from the sub's deck. He drew his gun and fired. He fired and fired until

Ayatollah clutched the mechanic's arms and wrested the pistol free.

Pudovkin heard the men in the lifeboat scramble, checking themselves for wounds and the boat for holes. But he knew, all but one bullet fell short. And even that one bullet, he accounted for without turning to his men or his boat. Like the whip of his schoolmasters in Moscow, one sharp thump struck his calf. Fire engulfed the wound followed by the cloud of shock. He stood long enough to offer one final salute to his only friend aboard *K-389*. Mikhail forced his gaze from the blood-oozing wound and returned Pudovkin's salute.

"Go," Poslenski screamed. "Go with him if you love each other so damned much."

Ayatollah pistol-whipped the man, and eased him to the deck. Then he too saluted Pudovkin and his lifeboat crew. "Better to weed out those without the nerve than have them fuck it all up."

Pudovkin's calf gave out and he tumbled back on his men. They ripped open his pants leg and got to work. A pair of cooks, an electronics technician, and the administrative assistant, these men began first aid on his bullet wound. He managed a chuckle before the sunlight dimmed and he drifted off.

Last Glimpse of Sunlight

SIXTY-SIX

"The forward hatch is open!" the Ballast Officer shouted.

He pointed to a red circle lit on his panel. Captain Borodin swung his periscope from the mid-ship's hatch to see his administrative assistant and others tugging a lifeboat from the opening. The ship's wake pushed dangerously close to their efforts.

"All stop, rudder five degrees port," he ordered.

Pudovkin came into view, his pistol aimed away from the mutineers, protecting them.

I wish I was with them, Borodin thought. *I wish my duty those still aboard didn't compel me to stay.*

"Quartermaster," he said, "how far are we from shipping lanes or land?"

"We are equidistant from The Aleutian Islands and Hawaiian Islands. Shipping lanes North and South only halve that distance at best."

"Perhaps if the *K-314* hadn't had to sacrifice itself, they'd have a chance," the ballast officer mused.

"Perhaps," Borodin growled. "Perhaps remains a luxury for admirals and politicians. I pray we all find greater grace in the coming days."

Borodin looked to his Command Center team and noticed a conspicuous absence. "Where's Vetrov?"

The others stared back, dumbfounded. They searched quickly. The men shrugged. The Ballast Officer ordered his electrician to search the operation compartments. Borodin turned again to the periscope, fearful of what he expected to find. Other men poured out from the forward hatch. One by one they stood and donned their lifejackets. In a huddle around the hatch, Borodin failed to find the redheaded protégé.

"What do you see?"

The calm voice, Zhora Ivankov's, turned the captain's stomach to ice. He heard scuffling all around and kept his eyes pressed to the periscope, focused on the deserters up in the midday sun.

"I see my last glimpse of sunlight."

"Why have you surfaced? Did you think to trick us, to lure us into the sun?"

"Don't be silly, you're cleverer than that."

"Perhaps, but I must know."

Borodin heard Ivankov's footfalls close, hands cold and hard as iron clamped down on his shoulders.

"I have nothing to say to you, monster," Borodin said.

"Ah, but your blood tells the tale, your blood."

Borodin's nostrils cringed at Ivankov's fetid breath when he leaned closer.

"I've wondered about you," the monster whispered in his ear. "Now I will see for myself what makes a man captain."

"You'll never-

Borodin's angry retort stopped short when Ivankov's teeth sank into his neck. Every muscle seized at first, anxious to resist. But as it dragged the blood out, the creature slithered in, into an emerging dream.

Explosions flashed within coal black clouds. Airplanes droned. Moscow shuddered and erupted from the bombs. Captain Borodin looked over the shoulder of a little boy. Little Lev Borodin, five, stared into a crater. The shattered body within held his attention over the city's destruction.

"Your Aunt?" Zhora asked. He stood next to Captain Borodin. "You found your Aunt like this?"

Borodin nodded.

"This is tragic, but not what I'm looking for."

Borodin sank through the ground with Zhora, through the

fabric of his memory. They stood at the train station now. A pair of men hauled an oblong wooden crate out of the train's freight car on a dolly and dumped it in front of young Lieutenant Borodin. Borodin looked upon the blond-haired, stocky man and smiled. The Lieutenant's tears welled up in his pale blue eyes but never shed.

"Your father?" Zhora asked. "He's in that crate?"

"Yes."

"An unceremonious end. An anonymous box. He died a criminal?"

Captain Borodin shook his head. "The State labeled him so. I and others consider him a hero."

Zhora grinned.

"Your career," he began, "as a young lieutenant, I don't imagine your father's crimes helped you ascend."

"No. It's also why I serve in the Pacific Fleet. I worked long and hard to make captain."

"Where's your mother? She should be here."

"She died while he was in prison."

"None of that makes you angry?" Zhora asked. "None of that makes you want justice?"

"Angry? Yes." Captain Borodin chuckled. "Justice? Justice isn't mine to make."

Zhora frowned and shook his head. "You'll not join me?"

"No."

The dream dimmed. The bombs from earlier returned, only louder. With each explosion pieces of the train station fell away and revealed war-torn Moscow. Captain Borodin felt the air thicken, his chest tighten. The encroaching darkness, thick air, the rhythm of the bombs, he realized what they meant. The heart attack he'd anticipated for years, it flickered the lights and shouted from outside the dream like a bartender . . . closing time. He turned to Zhora and smiled.

"Providence has granted my final prayer."

"No, not this," Ivankov screamed above the din. "You can't die before I've had my answer at least. Why are you on the surface?"

Borodin laughed. The barrage ended. Somewhere in another corner of his mind he knew his limbs had fallen limp. Like a balloon untethered from its anchor, Borodin felt himself soar in his dreamscape. His ethereal sinews hummed with newfound vigor.

"Stay with me, monster," Borodin said. "Stay and experience my death. Stay and die yourself."

"What? NO!"

An argument, Borodin heard a husband and wife arguing around the alley's corner. Borodin embraced Ivankov and walked toward a dim doorway. "My faith gives me strength here I don't have anywhere else."

"No, no, no." Ivankov cried.

The alley turned into a library with dark wooden walls, high ceilings and furnishing fit for a prince. A man in the uniform of a navy captain held a fist high, his belt wrapped within it. A brass buckle, with its anchor adorned with the hammer and sickle bore the red of a young man's blood. The man lay crumpled on the floor, sobbing. Several paces behind the father, Zhora Ivankov's father, stood a woman anyone would've known to be Zhora's mother. Her aquiline features, with sparkling dark eyes and raven hair, Zhora had all this in the body of a man. But none of her bewitching beauty stayed her husband's hand.

"Let me send him to a special school," she cried. "Perhaps they can straighten him out."

"I'm sending him to a special school," Alexi Ivankov growled. "University is a haven for perverse behavior. Intellectuals experiment with everything. No, I've a special school that'll either beat it out of him or teach him to bury it to survive."

Lidiya Ivankov lunged at her husband, clutching his arm she sobbed. "No, not the navy, not a common sailor."

Alexi shrugged her off. She fell to the floor. Young Zhora reached out for her.

"No, not a common sailor," Alexi answered. "That's a death sentence for us both. This boy will become an officer through the academy. This boy will learn to become a proper

man. *This boy will ascend to the admiralty as I will someday. And if he can't, he'll wish he'd never been born."*

Borodin turned to his adult Zhora. The man turned monster held his face in his hands, locked in a silent sob, tears of blood trickling down his cheeks.

"You were mistreated for your crimes against your family. I understand their pain, but I can't understand the hatred poured upon their only son, their beloved child."

Lights flickered in the room. The actors from the past faded away.

"I suppose it's time," Borodin said. "Come with me, Zhora Ivankov. Come to where none of this can torture you anymore."

Zhora clawed from the edge of an ever-expanding abyss and awoke, gasping for air. A sailor barely older than a boy hovered over him. Red hair, pale, freckled skin, and pale green eyes. Vetrov, the genius too young to be taken seriously by his peers, the boy who opened the door for Zhora and his other minions.

"Vetrov, dive the ship," Zhora whispered, still breathless.

With a nod, the boy ran to his task. Every muscle ached. His head felt like it had imploded with the captain's death. He tried to block the images of that moment. They made so little sense to him in those final seconds, fire and ice, pleasure and pain, all shoved through his senses at supersonic speed. And then the expanding blackness, the deepening anguish as his undead body began to die again. *Close, that seemed terribly close, to the real death I slipped from before.*

Dovzhenko leaned over and pulled him to his feet. Even with help, his muscles felt stuffed with broken glass. When he looked at the floor to confirm the captain's death, his eyes scraped within their sockets.

"Comrade Captain," Dovzhenko said with a smile, "the

ship is ours."

"Idiot, no it isn't." Zhora fell forward and let the periscope break his fall. He strained to take control and rotate the periscope for a slow, steady scan. "*Yóbanny v rot!*"

"What is it, master?"

"Dive the ship, dive it now!"

Acting Captain

Mikhail and Poslenski sat within the airlock between outer and inner hatch and stared at each other. The mechanic hadn't been himself since Ayatollah pistol-whipped him. Doctor Anatoli might've said he had a concussion. Judging by the anger in the Ukrainian's eyes, he'd had them before and worked through this one like any other.

"What are we missing, Poslenski?" Mikhail asked. "Why won't it open?"

"Why'd you let those cowards get away?" Poslenski growled.

"This isn't the time."

"When is it?"

"When we get the door open, these vampires killed, and our ship back in order." Mikhail narrowed his gaze. "Trust me, if we get to that point, and the two of us are still alive, we'll pick those bastards up and see they face justice."

The ballast tanks groaned and a hiss aft grew to a roar. Ayatollah dropped into the tight space with Laska close behind. The two pulled the outer hatch down.

"They're diving the fucking ship on us," Ayatollah shouted as he turned the locking mechanism on the hatch.

Poslenski turned his attention to the lower hatch while the sliver of daylight shrank to nothing.

The rush of water across the outer hatch made Mikhail jump at first. He ran his hands along the outer hatch's rim. He took in the dank, nasty air of the cramped space and breathed a sigh of relief.

Ayatollah turned on his flashlight and illuminated Poslenski's efforts.

"Get back," Poslenski warned. "Help me crank this open."

"You were that close to opening it all this time?" Ayatollah whispered angrily.

Poslenki looked up into the shining light and offered a steel-toothed grin. "Officers and technicians, always thinking us dumb grease monkeys don't matter unless the ship don't go or the water don't run."

With the hatch latched open, Mikhail slid down the ladder, careful to land softly. He looked up into the airlock and motioned the others to follow.

"Poslenski, come with me," Mikhail whispered. "Ayatollah, take Laska. We'll sweep the upper level first with each team supporting in a leap-frog maneuver."

In short spurts, they snuck their way around the upper level and ended by the reactor tunnel door. There Mikhail grabbed the phone and dialed Engine Control.

Within half an hour they'd secured the Auxiliaries Compartment, with Ovechin's help, and reconvened at Engine Control where Mikhail addressed the engineering compartments via the intercom.

"I need believers to join me and fight. No one else will do. I need men ready to face the impossibility of our undead comrades. Failure means more than our deaths. It dooms every coastline, every merchant ship that crosses this haunted submarine's path. If you can't fight for me or for your own survival, fight for the men, women, and children of the world who never saw this coming."

Mikhail and Ayatollah waited at the forward watertight door into the Aft Missile Compartment. When Ovechin joined him, he only brought two other men, Poslenski and Laska.

"Either they don't believe or they don't believe they can win," Ovechin said shaking his head.

"Hold these compartments at all costs," Mikhail insisted. "Shut down systems if you must. The front of the ship commands but without an aft to obey, they'll go nowhere."

"I'm not staying behind," Ovechin said with an indignant grimace. "There are plenty back here to mind the panels."

"You are ready to face them, monsters with the faces of our crewmates?"

The Michman nodded and patted his holster.

Mikhail grimaced. "Believe me, please, when I say you'll need more than bullets to slay our enemy."

Ovechin hesitated before he accepted the advice. He whipped a hand behind his back and produced a wooden stake crafted from the aft lifeboat oar. Afterward, Ovechin frowned.

"Why mention the forward compartments, Comrade Lieutenant? We control them."

"The ship's dive," Mikhail answered, "was there any warning? Did you hear the Ballast Officer's announcement?"

Ovechin cocked his head and squinted. "I didn't."

"And neither did we in the airlock. No alarm, no preparations . . . something's amiss."

"So we can't suffocate them." Ovechin said. "They have the forward oxygen tanks to rely on for a week at least."

"We could rob them of power and light, but I think that'd work to their advantage."

"What'll we do?"

"We'll make a cursory search for survivors on our way forward. We might be able to recruit help. The forward and aft sections remain key. With them, we control everything."

"Unless they set fire to the missiles," Laska said.

"If they do that, they serve our purpose," Mikhail replied.

Poslenski's and Laska's eyes bulged.

Mikhail looked to each man. "No one else will become a vampire if they burn the whole ship."

"And if we fail to gain control of the forward section?" Ovechin asked.

"*We* burn the missiles," Mikhail answered. "We save the world."

Though everyone winced at the proposal, no one backed away. Without another word, they stepped through the doorway into the dimly lit passageway of the Missile Compartment Aft, the first level of hell.

A prison abandoned after a riot, that's what the Missile Compartment Aft resembled. Light lenses lay on the deck, shattered and crackling underfoot. Sailors had ransacked Sick Bay. Bandages and broken glass littered the cramped office. Doctor Anatoli's corpse lay just where Kipchak finished him. Some victims lay strewn throughout berthing. And then there were the prisoners, crewmen strapped into their bunks as they woke or hogtied in the bilges where they worked. None they found retained strength or courage enough to join their fight.

And then they reached Launch Control.

"Boreyev," Mikhail shouted, "we're going to open this door. Don't shoot. Don't rush out at us until we know you're unaffected. We are armed and don't want any needless bloodshed."

The door to Launch Control left them puzzled and wary.

With sledgehammers taken from the damage control lockers, Poslenski and Ayatollah bashed at the sealed doorway. Ovechin, Laska, and Mikhail stood back, guns and stakes drawn.

Mikhail's warning to the stout missile officer worried him. The way he'd ended on 'bloodshed' might've driven Boreyev to the wrong and most violent conclusion.

"We're trying to retake the ship from the vampires, Boreyev," he added. "We'll need your help."

The beam cracked free but the door's cypher lock remained sealed. Poslenski crouched beside the large, oblong canvas bag of tools and withdrew a meter-long crowbar. Once wedged into the slim opening, Ayatollah stood ready to hammer it in. He looked to Mikhail and paused.

"Boreyev, as acting captain, I order you to open this door."

"I'm senior officer between us," Boreyev replied. His voice sounded hoarse.

The door flew open. A waft of squalor took Mikhail's breath away. Boreyev and his men recoiled from the light like trolls. Launch Control looked and smelled more like a dungeon cell than the command center for nuclear war. Dark, dank, and foul, Mikhail almost failed to notice the swath of dried blood on the deck. He froze and motioned for his men to hold their position.

"What's happened here, Boreyev?" he asked with a glance at the carpet of carnage.

"Dimitriev and Konev came in, wild-eyed," Boreyev explained. He shook his head and shrugged. "We had to kill them before they got us all killed."

Mikhail examined Boreyev's gaze. Shock and frustration shaped his features and backlit his eyes, but regret never surfaced. Remorse remained absent. Whatever the reason, Boreyev felt justified in his crime.

With a nod to his men, Mikhail relaxed and entered the threshold. The inhabitants tensed as one. Boreyev eyed his every move. Mikhail holstered his weapons and offered Boreyev a hand. Once they shook, Mikhail stood at attention and saluted the stocky missile officer.

"What're your orders, Comrade Captain?"

Assault on the Command Center

SIXTY-EIGHT

Vetrov stared back through the deadlight and grinned. His fangs glistened. He'd barred the watertight door with the pipe wrench in his hand. Built to withstand a kilometer of sea pressure, Vetrov's pipe wrench made this threshold impregnable.

"Damn you, Vetrov," Ayatollah bellowed. "Why?"

Mikhail shut his eyes and envisioned all the ship's systems. Two doors connected the Missile Compartment Forward to the Operations Compartment Aft. Their distinct difference: the hinges. Mikhail allowed a grin.

"Level One," Mikhail said.

Boreyev frowned while he pondered. Gradually, he too smiled.

"Let's go," he said with a nod.

Boreyev ordered a pair of his men to Launch Control, to pressurize missile tubes.

"On my command," he said before dismissing the pair, "you'll vent those tubes inboard."

Each door served an opposite purpose in the event of compartmental pressurization. With Missile Compartment Forward pressurized, the door they faced wouldn't open without a hydraulic ram. But Level One . . . that door would practically fly off the hinges to relieve the differential pressure.

Mikhail followed Boreyev up the ladder, into upper level. Through the deadlight Dovzhenko stared. He held a crowbar to block the door's opening, clinging to it with both hands, hanging there like a weary bus passenger clinging to the safety bar. He looked pitiful, even as a vampire. Unhappy in life as an outcast, he seemed to miss warm-blooded companionship. He seemed dejected by his lot on either side of death.

Boreyev ignored Dovzhenko's plight and tapped at the thick glass with his wooden stake.

"We're coming for you, you bastard," he said. "We'll put you all to rest soon enough."

Mikhail looked back at the men assembled. Each missileman mimicked their leader's glee and brandished their sharpened truncheons. Poslenski followed suit. Ayatollah held a hand to his chest and whispered a prayer.

Gas valves *ker-chunked* and compressed air hissed into the missile tubes behind them. Mikhail listened as the noise rose in pitch and lessened in volume. *Ka-chunk.* Silence.

Boreyev called to Launch Control and ordered the men to vent the tubes and join the battle. Chunk-whoosh. The raspy breeze filled Mikhail's ears. He and his companions fought to unstuff them, to equalize as the extra air crushed in on their eardrums.

"We'll need to be quick," Mikhail said. "They'll figure it out quickly."

"Everyone," Boreyev began, "gather 'round and hold onto something. You'll not want to be launched through the door. Soon as you can, charge. Pistols first to knock them down, then stake 'em."

At Mikhail's command, Poslenski turned the wheel, unlocking the watertight door. Hand over hand, he raced, like a boxer on a speed bag. Escaping pressure squealed in the sliver of unclamped seal. On the door's other side, Dovzhenko looked puzzled. He examined the door. Just as realization settled in his features, Poslenski struck the latch with his wrench.

Air roared. The door thundered open. It catapulted Dovzhenko four meters into the bulkhead with a wet crack. Boreyev's men dove through the doorway, in a dust-fog. Dovzhenko rolled on the deck, slow and moaning. But before he spoke a word or offered any defense, two men descended on him and worked together to drive a stake into the man's back, behind his heart. Dovzhenko thrashed and howled. He threw the men off and rose in a drunken, wavering stance. Blood drenched his face from his scalp which the crash had scraped to the bone.

Ayatollah lunged with his meter-long stake and pinned the man to the wall. He shrieked and quivered. Though he grasped the wooden weapon, Dovzhenko lacked the strength to move it. His legs gave out and his breath expelled a splatter of blood across the first rank of men. All but Ayatollah flinched and faltered. The senior sonar operator held fast, his attention fixed on his foe's face.

From the opening into the Command Center, two sailors emerged, one knelt and the other braced against the passageway frame. Both bore Makarov's. Both unloaded their pistols.

Mikhail and Boreyev and his men returned fire. Within the cramped space of steel, the gunfire deafened and those bullets that missed, gained a second chance. Ricochets bucked and squealed off the walls and pipes. Mikhail blinked and flinched at all the bullets and shrapnel whizzing by. He only noticed he'd run out of ammunition when the pistol no longer kicked in his hands. Ringing ears knew no silence, the deafening blasts had seen to that. Cordite permeated the air with a thin blue film. Moans sank through the ringing. The two assailants lay dead, three of Boreyev's men lay on the deck, one wounded.

Ayatollah and Boreyev looked back at him, shocked. Neither bore any wounds. Poslenski's color had fallen. His face resembled the underbelly of a sea turtle. Three crimson splotches on his tunic spread and thickened until they made one contiguous crimson stain. The bear of a man fell backward onto the deck, mouth agape. Shock faded in his slowly closing eyes.

"He was hardly a good soldier, but I have so few," Zhora

said.

Mikhail looked up from the fresh corpse, into Zhora's eyes. They glowed iridescent around the edges. Resemblances to his academy friend remained, but the undead other within had transformed a handsome man to a caricature of humanity and death. He'd spoken of Dovzhenko's death. He'd called him a soldier. He showed, not remorse, but disappointment, as though he'd lost a chess piece.

It startled Mikhail to see his features move. A genuine and tender smile sat, ill-fitting, upon a demonic face.

"Misha," Zhora said softly. "It's so good to see you, to see you unharmed."

"You, you monster," Mikhail said. His voice came out barely a whisper and he wondered why. He took a step toward Zhora but his left leg melted under his shifting weight. Numbness crept in and the ship seemed to topple until he realized he'd fallen, he'd been shot in his thigh, and any minute now . . .

Restitution

SIXTY-NINE

Zhora laid Mikhail on the tactical chart table. Blood pooled beneath his friend. He growled and fought against the hunger it aroused. He brought his ear to Mikhail's chest. Despite his heightened senses, the man's heartbeat no longer thrummed in his ears. A hushed rhythm, slow and weak, gave him hope.

He bit into his own forearm and pressed the oozing wound to Mikhail's lips.

Vetrov leaned in and watched. "Don't do this," he said.

"And why not?"

"He is our enemy."

"He's no enemy of mine!"

"Tell Dovzhenko! He's dead now because of those men."

"Shut up and step back," Zhora shouted. "Let me handle this."

Vetrov obeyed, but not without protest. "You're just like all the others. Nobody can tell you anything. It's not a revolution you're starting. It's not going to be a new world. It'll be the same old world, with a new elite making the same old mistakes."

"Go! You're so clever, Vetrov, go and capture the Engine Room. Leave me to my one weakness among the crew. Once he's one of us, he'll see things differently. Survival will put him on our side."

Vetrov stormed out, leaving Zhora with only corpses and his dying friend for company.

In the quiet Command Center, Zhora leaned over Mikhail and whispered. "I'm trying to save you. No matter what else I do, in this I'm trying to do good."

His bloody arm slid across Mikhail's lips, the sticky blackened fluid fell from his mouth.

"Come on, I'll not let you die like Kipchak."

Mikhail's lips moved. He muttered something. Zhora pressed his open wound harder. Mikhail coughed and gagged.

"No, no," Zhora pleaded. "You've got to drink it to live."

Mikhail drew a few more coughing swallows before the two plunged into a dream.

As their minds intertwined, Zhora remembered Vladlena's experience and how much of his villainy she'd uncovered. He strained to withhold his secrets and in doing so only caught foggy glimpses of Mikhail's, and shuddered.

Mikhail's stepfather feigned love and fed his perverse desires. His mother's early years were a drunken blur of denial. When Mikhail grew into his teens the cycle of lies and abuse turned darker. Aware of the abuse as such, the young man fought. His mother chastised him for his violent disrespect. His stepfather threatened harm to Mikhail's mother for any future rebellion.

Anger broke the bond between the two. Zhora looked down at his friend and stroked his hair. Peacefully dead, soon to wake, he hoped to undo the villainy of a true monster.

Zhora peered through the deadlight, into the Torpedo Room. Boreyev hung, shackled, between the torpedo tubes. Wrists chaffed red by the manacles remained the only evidence of his captors' tortures. Zhora had been explicit, no blood. He'd not wanted a little fun with his favorite prisoner to become a feast. He unlatched the door, hoisted his burden, and entered. When he slammed it shut, Boreyev awoke with a shudder and a moan.

"I don't have time to have fun with you," Zhora said.

He laid Mikhail on the deck.

Boreyev's head rolled until he found the strength to raise it. With tear-reddened eyes and dust-streaked cheeks, he looked like the chubby, bullied boy Zhora remembered from his blood-drunken trips into the man's mind.

"I'm sorry." Boreyev said in a hoarse voice.

"I'd imagined killing you by millimeters over the coming months."

Zhora bent to tidy Mikhail's uniform and straighten his splayed limbs.

"He's dead," Boreyev said with a sob. "I'm so sorry."

Zhora wiped the black blood from Mikhail's face and stopped to admire the man's handsome features.

He looked up from his task and into Boreyev's gaze. "What would you *do* about it?"

"What?" Boreyev asked.

"If you could fix what you've broken, what would you do to bring back my best friend?"

He squinted and looked to Mikhail's body. Zhora heard his friend's shoe grind across the deck behind him.

"We don't have much time," Zhora said with half a smile.

Boreyev's slack-jawed, newfound horror completed Zhora's grin. But as fast as he felt triumphant, the writhing body behind him reminded him of the costs paid for victory. He felt a forgotten reflexive twinge in the corner of his eye. Tears would've come now, tears and sobbing and pain. Nothing stirred in him except a hunger for blood and the delicious nightmares that came with them. He stood and met Boreyev's gaze one last time.

"With your death, humanity's hope for a bright, peaceful future dies too."

"What? Why?"

"Thieves and assassins rule. Not the ones who honestly ply their trade in the shadows. These hide within false smiles and empty promises. They steal hope and kill freedom. My immortal family won't be so greedy. We'll return evil to the dark and force good to rise in the light of day. In those days, who a man loves will matter less than that he joins your crusade against the night-angels."

Water of Life

SEVENTY

A dark tunnel, Mikhail drifted through a dark tunnel. The din of torture, the cries of the damned, acrid odor of hell's fires greeted his spirit's journey. He felt the soul-tearing pain of death within him, like a farm combine's spinning blades dragging through his flesh like wheat in the fall harvest.

Why hell? Why me?

His lies from his past stood tall in the landscape. He'd helped sweep Yanukovich's murder under the rug. His best friend's beating, he'd ignored.

Other sins bubbled to the cauldron's surface. The whore, Nika. The foul trap he'd fallen into with his stepfather.

Not my fault, none of it my idea. I did what others expected of me. What I did, I did to survive.

Peaceful darkness shattered. Every molecule of his body felt alive with fire. His senses exploded, overloaded by his arrival back into the real world. New smells and sounds called to him. A thirst wrung his insides like a twisted, dripping rag. He felt his skin shrivel and his organs expel their last. Water, sweet and cool beckoned just out of reach.

Relief is near. Drink from the well and live.

He crawled toward the well as it sang to him. Life, peace, and an end to his expanding pain, all these the well promised. Urgency granted him strength to stand and run. Something blocked him in the final moments, vines, gnarled and thorny pulled him from the water's edge. He clawed his way closer until the water touched his lips. Thick and warm, it surprised him how it refreshed him. Each drink took effort and patience. Like a cool salve on burned flesh, the water quenched the fire inside. The song it sang coursed through him. Sensations blossomed, sights and sounds of another time and place. As he sank deeper into his new dream world, the water came easier and his senses sharpened.

A short, fat boy cowered, encircled by taller, leaner boys. They stood a mile from their Moscow school in the dead of winter. The brisk breeze blew through Mikhail. This circle had followed a chubby young Boreyev from the school's perimeter, tightening and thickening as it moved.

"How's it feel to be the runt of the bunch?" a young boy asked.

"Yeah," another chimed in, "how's it feel?"

Fear rippled out from the boy, palpable as Boreyev's earlier hate, and it felt good.. The more the boy feared, the more aroused Mikhail felt. He felt himself retch and heave, but nothing came out. Though he buckled, his eyes remained open.

"Your fat old dad can't protect you anymore," the first boy said. "Your fat old dad pissed off the wrong people. And now he's headed East."

"My father fought in the War. My dad drove tanks," the pudgy boy yelled back.

"Your dad spent his time on his knees, under the general's desk."

"He did not!"

"Sure he did," the first boy said. "Why else would they arrest him in the middle of the night? That's what happens to pidors."

"No, no, no, no," the pudgy boy screamed.

He launched himself at the ring leader, dove on top of him. Before the leaner, taller boy managed to defend himself, Young Boreyev had begun a barrage of blows across the startled boy's face.

Everyone, including their phantom audience, Boreyev

and Mikhail, gasped at the blood. *Blood flew from the boy's face and he screamed. The sunlight flashed in the small knife young Boreyev held. The other children ran.*

"This is what happens to pidors!" little Boreyev shouted.

In that moment the world around shifted again. Half a dozen sailors stood, shocked, and stared at their division officer. He'd screamed those words as a child but in this moment too. Something in those two moments made the same kind of sense to Boreyev and no one else. He stood now, over Yanukovich. In his flashback rage he'd struck the young sailor in the temple. In the lowest level of Missile Compartment Forward Boreyev and his men had hoped to beat sense into the boy. The young sailor's head jerked aside before his body fell limp within his bonds.

A drumbeat reverberated within the dream. It spoke to Mikhail in a way he'd never known before. With each rhythmic beat it warned him.

Get out now, get out now.

It slowed, but as it did, the urgency, the message's volume thundered.

GET

OUT

NOW

Mikhail awoke with a gasp, like a surfacing swimmer. A fever cooled in his veins. The hum of the ship rang sharper in his ears. Each bolt and rivet before him revealed more detail. He marveled at the little imperfections left by the shipyard tools, scars made during the ship's construction. And though eyes and ears felt heightened, he hardly felt his hands, his feet, the movement of air across his face. He didn't even realize what he held in his hands until he looked down.

Boreyev's body, bloodless save for a few droplets around a fresh tear in his throat, that's what Mikhail held tightly. He screamed.

363

New Pantheon

SEVENTY-ONE

"Boreyev killed Yanukovich," Mikhail murmured.

He'd already screamed himself hoarse, locked in the Torpedo Room with only his first victim's corpse for company. His new family knew well enough to allow him time for madness, anger, anguish, and a host of mixed emotions unrecognizable to his former self. He'd broken equipment and tools in that cramped room. He'd lingered by the torpedo tube door and contemplated his own destruction. Tears refused to come for the sobbing he'd endured. He looked at Boreyev's body. He'd stolen the man's life.

"I know," Zhora replied. "I tasted those dark memories too, in Komsomolsk."

"His men killed Dimitriev."

"Yes."

The two spoke in the Command Center, bookended by vampires Vladlena and Vetrov. And though he recognized them, they bore only a passing similarity to the people he'd known. Each stood astride two worlds as two creatures merged within the same body.

"Do you remember anything from the blood we shared?" Zhora asked.

Mikhail strained to remember but only a few fog-veiled images emerged. "Not much. I know your father beat you for your dysfunction."

"Is that what I am to you?"

"Zov, it's what he said. I don't know what you want me to call it. You'd bristle at anything else I might've contrived."

Zhora's appearance shocked him most. Skin that had appeared statuesquely pale, smooth, and firm, now looked wet, translucent, and crawling with black blood vessels just beneath the surface. But these grotesque visages, Mikhail's transformed senses and sensibilities managed to find beautiful in a new way. They felt familiar, kin to the evil within him.

"Welcome to the new pantheon, Mikhail," Vetrov said with a wide plastic smile.

He thought to correct the Petty Officer, to remind him of his rank, but then Mikhail just laughed.

He looked to Vladlena. She smiled and waved. Her demure features from their night together had vanished. She looked like the redcaps he'd heard of as a child; beautiful but soulless, petite and lethal. These small elves stained their caps with their victims' blood.

"We will be the new gods," she said.

"Hush, Vladlena," Zhora said. "Mikhail's induction wasn't like most. He needs time to adjust. Let's concentrate on making our home safe."

Zhora drew everyone's attention to the blood-puddled chart table, where he'd laid a ship's print out like a battle map. Mikhail examined the blood, his blood.

"In my panic to save you," Zhora began, "Ayatollah escaped back into Missile Compartment Forward."

"Wait," Mikhail said. "When you . . . saved me, you mentioned Kipchak."

"Yes," Zhora said. He glared at the map before he looked back up to Mikhail. Zhora's lips tightened over his fangs. "He refused to drink. He died in my arms."

"But . . ." Mikhail stopped himself.

Vetrov slapped a hand on the table. "Enough about him. Where's Adaksin? What about Laska's plan? When will we gain the Engine Room?"

Zhora glared at the boy-vampire, scowled, and bared just the tips of his teeth.

"Sorry, master," Vetrov said with a sigh. "But we've got to take control, right?"

Ignoring the boy, Zhora turned again to Mikhail. "Laska has adopted your ploy of pressurizing compartments to gain entry. Adaksin led a charge into engineering."

"Laska?"

"Yes. I recruited among the crew, help in exchange for immortality. But they must wait until we've secured a stable food supply before conversion. Otherwise we starve ourselves into defeat."

Mikhail felt dizzy. The hull pressed in all around and the air felt thick. Newly acute senses brought the edges of the submarine closer.

"Zhora, can I speak with you a bit?"

His friend nodded before he looked to Vetrov.

"You're the brilliant protégé," Zhora said with an angry smile, "You figure out our next move while I help Mikhail adjust."

"Easy enough," Vetrov replied. He glared at Mikhail. "Just find and kill all our enemies without regard to what they once meant to us."

Zhora watched the red-haired boy storm out. Vladlena clutched Mikhail's hand and leaned closer to kiss his cheek. He barely felt it through his new skin.

"It's good to have you with us," she said before she left.

Alone with Zhora, in the quiet Mikhail examined the Command Center. Two corpses lay on either side of the portal they'd fired from. A dozen bullets marred their bodies. Blood painted the tactical chart table. At the Periscope Station he stopped and his heart sank. Captain Borodin lay face down between the 'scopes. A ribbon of blood stretched out from his neck. He'd been the man Mikhail wished were his father.

Didn't everyone feel that way? Who murders such a man? What justifies that kind of . . . evil?

"What the fuck is going on and why?" Mikhail's first question led to a long and bizarre answer.

Zhora's story made just enough sense to keep Mikhail on

367

track as he told it. He spoke of the Siberian, the desperate and old-fashioned killer and his eventual betrayal. Vladlena and her sloppy murder of the cook Antonev. And while he told the whole story, Mikhail kept his gaze on his captain. He listened and waited for the moment when this man's death made sense. And as he realized it'd never come, he quivered, fists clenched.

"Why'd you have to come back?" Mikhail screamed. "Why didn't you stay dead to me, to us?"

Zhora stopped, his mouth agape in mid-sentence, and winced. "What else would you have me do? Wander the wilderness like that old fool, Sevastyan?"

Mikhail crouched beside Borodin's body and pulled the man's hair from his face. He revealed a peaceful expression. The captain looked as though he might awaken and share with Mikhail dreams of home and family.

"He'd still be alive." He looked up from Borodin to glare at Zhora. "I'd still be alive."

"In the grand scheme," Zhora began, "his death will be a small price paid for justice and freedom for all."

Mikhail stood and marched to Zhora. He clutched his collar and pulled him closer. "No," he shouted. "You can't do that. You can't speak about justice in the same breath that you justify his death."

"It'll take a while before you see the world with your new perspective," Zhora said.

"Madness, your new perspective is inhuman madness."

Zhora pushed him back and unrumpled his uniform. He held his head higher, chin jutting out. "We'll offer freedom to all those like us, the bullied, downtrodden, misunderstood outcasts. In the new world we'll become all the evil they'll need to unite and love each other unconditionally."

He took his place beside Borodin's body, drew in a deep breath and stood taller. "We know we've become monsters. We understand, we must become the new world's villains in order to save others like us. We are ready to shoulder that burden."

Mikhail's knees gave way and he fell to the floor. The

world wobbled in his head. Nervous laughter bubbled up. He laughed his lungs empty before Zhora ventured to ask.

"What's so damned funny?"

"You," he chuckled. "You're ready to 'shoulder the burden'?" He sighed, stood, and leveled his gaze at Zhora. "You're comfortable living a heartless, selfish, vengeful life?

Zhora glared back, his lips pressed thin. In the silence swelling between them the sounds of the ship crept into Mikhail's thoughts. His concerns and fears became infinitesimal in the shadow of a newly realized evil. He noticed Zhora stare and realized his mouth hung open.

"Where are the missile keys?" Mikhail asked.

"Safely tucked away."

"Vetrov and Vladlena mentioned godhood. Will nuclear war be your genesis? Will you reform the world in your own image, dead and defiled, imitating life?"

"Misha," Zhora said softly. "What happened to the quiet farm-boy I knew?"

"I grew up. And then you killed me."

Zhora shook his head and let his shoulders droop when he cast his gaze to the deck. "I hadn't wanted this for you. I wanted to keep one last thing pure about my past life. You were to be a haven of my humanity."

Mikhail recoiled. "A pet to keep on a short leash?"

"A confidant and conscience."

Mikhail stepped closer and held out his hand. "Give me the missile keys and I'll be whatever you need me to be."

Zhora's set jaw relaxed and his steely eyes softened. He looked at Mikhail's palm and then met Mikhail's gaze. Love warmed Zhora's dark eyes and he blushed. Mikhail wondered whose blood reddened Zhora's cheeks.

"I'd love to accept your offer," Zhora said. His posture sank a centimeter. His eyes dropped to the hand offered. A reluctant smile emerged. "But-

"Confidant, conscience, and . . ." Mikhail stepped closer and put his outstretched hand on Zhora's shoulder. "Friend."

The glimmer in Zhora's eyes dimmed.

"Let my life mean something to me," Mikhail said. "Let our friendship save humanity."

Zhora stepped back, unbuttoned his tunic, and withdrew a steel chain with two keys and a small cross.

Mikhail turned to see Captain Borodin.

"His strong faith nearly killed me," Zhora admitted. "He tried to hold onto me as he died, to drag me into that abyss."

From above Borodin's body a voice startled Mikhail.

"Kipchak's not dead!" Vladlena's voice crackled from the intercom.

Zhora leapt to the Periscope Station's mike. "Where is he?"

"He's in the compartment beyond the missiles." Her tone changed from her first elated report. "He seems angry. He's ignoring me and working really hard on some machine. It hisses and clicks."

Mikhail's new supernatural ears heard the machine she described and his stomach clenched.

Doomed Ship, Damned Crew

SEVENTY-TWO

Blood-splattered bulkheads blurred by. Like his mentor, Sevastyan, Zhora leapt and ran, barely scraping the deck and missile tubes. He flung open the door to Auxiliaries Compartment. Vladlena still stood by the intercom, the microphone in her hand. In the center of the room Kipchak stood between the Oxygen Generators.

"Stop where you are," Kipchak shouted.

"I'm so glad you're alive," Zhora said. "I thought I'd lost you."

"Alive?" Kipchak screamed. "I hope to die. I never wanted this."

The young man focused on the Oxygen Generator, his hands blurred from valves to switches and back again. The pipes whined with pressure. An alarm horn sounded. Kipchak only grimaced and hastened his supernatural pace.

"What're you doing?" Zhora asked. A glance from Kipchak explained it all. The young, lion-hearted petty officer's bright green eyes, once afire with life and the love of living bore the burden of murder and monstrosities too much to endure.

"This ship's doomed. You and your ghoulish friends may love this *gift*," Kipchak growled, "but I want this nightmare to end."

"But," Zhora began. "I thought we loved each other. I thought my soul found its mate."

Harsh laughter erupted. "I loved you as a man, a warm-blooded, living man. Had I known your heart then we'd have been . . . but now we're monsters, murdering demons."

The Generator hissed with building pressure. A dozen old gaskets crumpled out of place. Amber lights flashed to red across the board. Zhora looked for a way to shut it down. Nothing. No way to save Kipchak except to-

The room tipped over and he flew out the watertight door. He crashed into a missile tube before he realized, he'd not been blown back. No explosion expelled him. He'd been thrown. He looked up and met Mikhail's gaze just before he sealed himself in the compartment with Kipchak.

Seconds after the hatch latched shut, just as a stunned Zhora reached the door's deadlight to peer inside, the sabotaged machine exploded. A fireball pressed against the thick glass. The shockwave reverberated through centimeters of steel. Only flame-licked smoke remained.

After the final flames died, Zhora dove into the Auxiliaries Compartment and into the piles of rubble. The room resembled a cave with its black walls warped and deck misshapen. Power had been shut off and ventilation secured to starve the flames. While he searched, Zhora felt a presence enter the room. It stood a meter behind him with no heartbeat and the stillness of a supernatural creature.

"We can't bother to look for them." Vetrov insisted. "We've got a ship to command and a crew to overtake."

Zhora picked through the flesh-singeing debris. Each flash of pain spurred him on. He tossed twisted bits of metal and wire aside. Each unidentifiable charred chunk he examined, fearful of what they might reveal. Alone, he felt utterly alone without those two men.

"Some of our cattle have gotten free," Vetrov said. "Resistance continues in the Engine Room. We need

The Monster Inside

SEVENTY-THREE

Walrus, the man had been known only as Walrus. Only after Mikhail lunged up from the bilge and drank the fat young sailor's blood, that intimate murder had opened the lad's history.

Walrus suspected vampires early on. With a wild imagination and no friends, he slipped out of berthing early and built a fortified nest beneath the deck-plates in the Auxiliaries Compartment. Though he imagined himself clever and brave, he also found every excuse to hide and wait. His waiting ended when Mikhail's injuries demanded blood.

In the final painful throes of regeneration, Mikhail mulled over his recent blunder. He'd hoped to stop Kipchak. Hope died the instant their eyes met. In those nanoseconds before Kipchak threw the final switch, Mikhail dove behind the thickest piece of machinery within reach. Electricity crackled just before the deafening explosion. The shockwave threw him to the bulkhead. Through eyelids squeezed shut he beheld the blinding fire. Shrapnel peppered his back. Mikhail peered over the motor air purifier he'd hidden behind. Fire-lit smoke cast the room in a hellish light. When he attempted to stand, a distant pain skyrocketed to intimate agony. Under his shoulder blade he felt the hot knife of a steel shard and in the back of his left thigh he examined a length of charred copper pipe protruding from his flesh. He dragged his impaled leg and crawled to the hatch to level three. Along his path he witnessed Vladlena's shapely silhouette through the fiery fog, her hands pawing through the air, searching for an exit. Mikhail hoisted himself over the open hatch's lip and fell through to level three. His body bounced off the steel deck. He crawled to the bilge's edge and slithered into the soupy mixture of water, grime, and oil. Cool and soothing, he hardly noticed as consciousness evaporated.

Why'd I save Zhora from the explosion?

He knew the answer and found himself proud to know his cold heart still clung to compassion.

Those missile keys, Zhora almost offered them to me. Maybe I can save the world from Armageddon.

As much as the explosion hurt, his regeneration hurt more. Broken limbs cracked and stabbed as they unfolded and sinews reclaimed their grasp. The effort left him hungrier. Guilt weighed heavier than the still-warm, fat corpse in his arms, heavier than this nightmare submarine. Captain Borodin's words echoed in the dim bilge.

"By the time you're an old captain like me, you'll need a coffin the size of this submarine for all the secrets you'll keep."

He looked down at half-open, lifeless eyes, drained of blood and dreams forever. He shuddered. Hunger wrung his stomach into knots. The healing left him empty again and the thought of killing once more made him want to scream.

Starvation burned in his stomach and radiated out through his blood vessels like vines of itchy fire. He set his recent kill aside and stood. Portions of his uniform crackled and tugged. Melted to his flesh, these pieces flaked off and revealed half-healed wounds. Newly rejuvenated bone throbbed at his weight and tendons sang with pain. He crept up the ladder and scanned the rubble for anyone. Blackened bulkheads and blown out lights left the room draped in darkness. The watertight door's deadlight provided the only light. Gingerly, he turned the door's latch, pushed it open, and slipped through.

Half the lights still lit Missile Compartment Aft. Shattered lights glittered across the deck between the missile tubes. Forward he tiptoed, from shadow to shadow, until fresh blood caught his attention. A familiar *other,* the monster inside, shoved Mikhail's rational self aside and took control. Senses prickled to life and his breathing grew fast and shallow, mouth open and panting. His pace hastened and he hunkered down into a predator's stance. With preternatural agility he avoided the patches of glass on the deck. All this Mikhail watched, trapped in a dark corner of his own mind, a voyeur. A door caught Mikhail's attention. He whispered to the monster inside his mind: *Sick Bay.*

A body warranted a sniff; dead, drained, useless.

Mikhail whispered again: *Doctor Anatoli's corpse.*

The starving creature growled aloud at the intellectual interruption and tried to brush it away. Sounds and smells painted a picture; labored breathing, blood in the air, a wounded man hid inside Sick Bay. He grasped the doorknob, turned it: locked. With his lips near the doorframe he whispered.

"Is anybody in there?" His own voice sounded strange, pitiful and desperate, deceptively so.

Silence, even the breathing stopped. He pressed his ear to the door and heard a single heartbeat *thrum-tha-thrum.* The drumming drew him to the crack between door and frame.

"Can you let me in? There's no safe place to hide," he whispered.

Mikhail observed how the creature within him sifted through his memories and sought his best options to lure its victim.

"Please," he whined. "I've got to find a place to rest."

His victim shuffled further from the door.

Move on. Find food. Don't fight any more than you have to.

"Lieutenant Koryavin?" Ayatollah's voice halted Mikhail's retreat. Hunger and the chance to feed brought a

377

grin to Mikhail's face. Mikhail shivered at his own actions.

"Yes."

The bolt turned and unlocked with a click. Mikhail fought the urge to charge in. As he entered, a gun muzzle pressed into his cheek.

"Come in, quickly now."

He rushed in and advanced until his foe's back pressed into the forward bulkhead, crammed between examination table and typewriter. Mikhail saw the man's face. Elation and horror turned his world upside down.

Ayatollah.

The monster snorted at the mention of a familiar name for the food. The squat sonar man wore a bandage around his left shoulder. It glistened with fresh blood. The monster grew giddy with both sight and aroma.

"You're a . . . a . . ." Ayatollah muttered.

"Yesss." Mikhail's mouth watered and his fangs felt longer as he spoke. They dragged across his lower lip as he answered. Like a passenger in a car headed for a wreck, he struggled to snatch the steering wheel from the madman driving. He stared, shocked, at the impending disaster and wished with all his heart he were somewhere else. The monster slipped to one side and slapped the pistol from the food's hand.

A bloodied hand came up before him, close enough to bite. But a blinding light, deafening roar, and a typhoon's wind pushed him back. The hand brandished a golden medallion. In that moment the light, sound, and gale burst from within the man who held it, and Mikhail emerged while the monster cowered. In that moment he felt the creature's fear and knew its source. The golden trinkct held no special power. Ayatollah hadn't been given any special power he'd not previously possessed. He'd simply connected perfectly with faith in something that evaporated his fear, filled him with hope and courage, and shut the floodgates of power the monster had drawn from within its victim.

"This wasn't my choice," Mikhail said. "Please, hear me out. Zhora hoped to save me from a fatal wound. I've seen what he plans. I've killed to live. I can't go on like this. I need to feed one more time before I destroy the whole thing. But so long as I'm this hungry I'm dangerous."

"I can't fight them anymore," Ayatollah said. "The gunfire wounded me too. I'd hoped to find drugs here enough to not care what'll become of me, but I can't bring myself to do it. I can't give up so easily."

"I can't fight them like this," Mikhail said. "But I can hardly bring myself to murder more of our crew to heal."

"You nearly did."

"The monster is stronger when I'm starved . . ." His voice trailed off. The aroma of Ayatollah's wound and the rhythm of his thumping heart sank him into murky consciousness.

Ayatollah frowned and examined him. He slapped Mikhail and peered into Mikhail's eyes in search of an answer. When he'd finished his search, he dropped his pendant and held out a hand.

"Murder me then," Ayatollah said. "Help us both. If it will mean the destruction of this condemned ship and its tortured crew, I'll contribute to the fight the only thing I have left to give, my blood."

Mikhail's animal mind leapt at Ayatollah's offer. He'd grabbed the man in his arms, brought him to the floor and bared his neck before he'd known he'd moved.

"Go ahead. I trust you to end this madness properly," Ayatollah said. His voice held a quivering note and his limbs trembled.

"How can you trust me?"

"I have faith that you're Providence's instrument to save the world from another Dark Age."

A nervous laugh escaped Mikhail. "I can't help but find it funny, that your illegal faith might save our Motherland. Perhaps the zampolit can spin a more Soviet tale with your bravery, if anyone ever hears the story of *K-389*."

Ayatollah clutched Mikhail by the arm and glared at him. "Do this now, before my cowardice makes my sacrifice impossible."

Mikhail sank his fangs in and drank. His eyes stung

with tears he'd have shed if he still retained his humanity. A final glimpse of Kipchak emerged and his words rang in Mikhail's mind.

"I want this nightmare to end."

Shared Blood Shared Crimes

SEVENTY-FOUR

The ship's intercom crackled to life.

"Master, we have the engine room," a hoarse voice decreed. Laska, the traitor mechanic had turned Mikhail's ingenuity against their crewmates. By pressurizing compartments one by one as they fought their way aft, the vampire Adaksin and their human minions forced each breach and subdued the last haven for the human crew. Laska sounded proud, and spiteful. "Power will be restored soon."

The lights.

With only emergency lights on, Mikhail had moved freely from Sick Bay forward. A battle for the Engine Room had plunged the ship into near darkness with one tiny bulb lit every ten meters. He hurried through Missile Compartment Forward. He looked back on Ayatollah's sacrifice and managed a smile.

Unlike Boreyev's death, Mikhail hadn't felt like a voyeur hidden in the shadows of Ayatollah's life while he drank it in. Like a welcome guest, he'd been given a tour of the brightest and proudest moments in the senior sonar-man's life. A just father and faithful husband, Ayatollah kept his promises at home and work better than many. He'd been through the usual troubles of youth, the typical tribulations of a young man certain he knew better than most, but his grandmother's wisdom guided him through the harshest times and his father's tough love kept him humble. To Mikhail he'd simply been an old sonar-man. In light of the man's courage and sacrifice he questioned his assessment. As he did, shame chilled him despite Ayatollah's warm lifeblood coursing through him.

Gunfire and angry shouts rang out through the overhead. Brave fools charged across the decks above. Silence followed. Muttering, confusion and frustrated curses rose. An earsplitting wail heralded Vladlena's counterattack. She too had found new flesh through the blood of fresh victims and had regained her strength. Horrified shrieks and agonized cries ended their defiance. The last sound Mikhail heard drove a chill through his spine; a throaty chuckle and rending flesh.

He examined the middle level passageway. A layer of smoke hung chest high. A pair of corpses, broken glass, and spent cartridges littered the deck. He turned and peered forward, through the watertight door, and spied more of the same. He ducked back as fans whirred and the ventilation system thrummed to life. Lights not shot or shattered flickered on.

He darted through the watertight door and bounded forward. In his sock-feet, his footsteps left only hushed thumps as he raced for the Command Center. He rounded the corner, hung onto the ladder rail and pulled himself up the stairs. As he began his final step, a hand, cool and firm, grasped his and helped him up.

"Have you come to your senses Mikhail? Are you prepared to admit what we both know, that you truly love me and no one will ever love you as I do?"

Zhora's question carried the tone one took with a stubborn child. His features, those he gained after his death, Mikhail found beautiful now and he realized, his own internal monster had grown in power and influence. He, Zhora, and the others knew each other from another time and felt a kinship older than man. Before long he knew he'd see the world the same way. He clenched his teeth, pressing his fangs against his gums. *One final lie.*

"Yes, I do love you."

Zhora's smile emerged. "You've come to join me then?"

"Yes." He held out his hand. "Give me the missile keys."

"The world is full of judgmental hypocrites," Zhora spat back. "Maybe a few less will be good in the end."

"You would ignite global war over your own personal vendetta? You used to be my best friend, my hero. What are you now?"

Zhora chuckled and shook his head. "I was more than a friend, admit it."

Mikhail nodded.

"You betrayed me and betrayed yourself," Zhora said. "But I'm prepared to forgive the lies. I want us to be like we were in school."

Mikhail searched his former friend for a hint of his humanity, a glimmer of warmth in his eyes.

"I can still be your hero," Zhora said, "and a hero to the oppressed survivors everywhere. Every kind of freedom for every kind of person; with that axiom I hope to become the next savior of civilization. Those who offer sacrifices shall know the benefit of our blessing and those who don't shall know our hunger. And whoever denies our new world and fights to reclaim the old, will know our wrath."

Mikhail slumped over and clutched his chest. "You embrace this horror because you can't stand the judgment of others?"

"Yes!" Zhora growled.

"And we won't have to hide our love in the apocalypse to come?"

"Exactly!"

Mikhail allowed a weak smile, still clutching his chest. "Then let me offer you my first kiss before we change the world."

Zhora rushed to his arms.

Mikhail met him with a stake into Zhora's heart.

"Forgive me," Mikhail whispered. "I'm sorry, but this must end."

Zhora frowned and drew in half a gasp. Mikhail backed away. He looked over his shoulder and found his prize, the ballast controls. Clutching the stake, tugging at it, Zhora moaned and fell to the floor. He held a hand out to Mikhail.

"When you shared your blood you shared your crimes," Mikhail said. "You killed my love, Nika, and my adopted father, Captain Borodin. You've killed others with no remorse, no thought to the miracles they were. No injury, no hate, no love, is worth the lives you've taken."

Mikhail grabbed the forward ballast vent switches and threw them open. Indicators winked from green to yellow.

He reached for the air valves and kept his eyes on Zhora. The man murdered months ago decayed in seconds, but not before his human features returned. His robust frame shriveled and shrank. His eyes closed slowly, and he seemed to finally be at peace.

"I can't conquer this curse," Mikhail explained. "But it'll never leave this boat."

The lever-operated valves felt huge in his trembling hands. He struggled to wrap his fingers around the release mechanism. Mikhail held his breath and pulled the handles back. Air roared through the pipes and entered the ballast tanks.

Vladlena's wail startled Mikhail. She stood at the back of the room, a swath of blood across her face. Her eyes remained transfixed on her master. Her mouth hung open.

She lunged and drove Mikhail into the ballast console. His lungs seized up, millimeters from Vladlena's face, her breath reeking of soured meat, while she screamed.

"What have you done?"

In her eyes he remembered Nika and the nights they shared. From Zhora, while they shared their blood bond, he'd known what Nika never shared. She loved him. Afraid to say it, afraid to trust anyone with her heart, Mikhail now felt what she never said.

The ship pitched forward. Pots from the galley below clattered and clanged. Debris from the crew's battle slid and crashed.

"I've blown the ballast. But with the forward vents open, we'll shoot straight for the bottom in minutes." Mikhail's voice came out thin and brittle. Streaks of fire shot through his chest with the effort.

"Fix it," Vladlena shrieked.

Mikhail looked at Captain Borodin's face, examined his peaceful features and grinned. Zhora's gift granted him another insight now, as though the man's death released his secrets. Captain Borodin loved Mikhail as the son he'd wished he was.

Zhora's body, a crumpled and desiccated thing, slid by. Charts from the quartermaster's station tumbled from their shelves and alarms sounded as the ship's gyro tripped offline. The depth meter clicked and ticked like a pinwheel in the wind. Mikhail smiled. His heart soared with the love he'd discovered while his ship plummeted to the ocean floor.

Vladlena grabbed his hands and fell to her knees.

"Fix it!" she pleaded.

"That's exactly what I've done. Now I can die."

Steel shuddered and squealed as the sea pressed in. Mikhail burst into laughter. He shut his eyes and welcomed one final pain.

About the Author

Cold War submarine veteran, Winfield H. Strock III, has finally discovered his life's passion in writing. And it only took a brush with death for him to take his calling seriously.

As a hotel night desk clerk Winfield struggled to begin his life anew in the civilian world. Bored by bad television and infomercials, he took to writing as a hobby suited to his solitary job and hyperactive imagination.

Surviving a brain tumor brought his priorities better into focus and his hobby became his obsession. He joined a local writer's workshop (which he now facilitates) and found a series of patient and helpful critique partners.

A fan of thought-provoking science fiction and history, Winfield's first works embraced both in a pair of steampunk novels and a prequel short story. His tales frame familiar and controversial issues within fantastic environments and from challenging perspectives.

Thanks to the Camden Writer's Workshop and the Science Fiction and Fantasy Writers of Jacksonville for helping to separate story from clutter.